THE ELEMENTAL TRILOGY
BOOK ONE

Matthew John Krengel

The Elemental Trilogy Book One: Staff of Elements

Publishing Editor: Mark Vining

Cover painting by Michael Sturgulewski

Interior illustrations by Jonathan Myers

Book design by Michael Sturgulewski

First Printing, 2011

Printed in the United States of America

Odyssey Illustrated Press is a registered trademark

All Scripture quotations in this book are from the King James Version.

ISBN 1463788134

10 9 8 7 6 5 4 3 2 1

THE ELEMENTAL TRILOGY
BOOK ONE

STAFF OF ELEMENTS

MATTHEW JOHN KRENGEL

ODYSSEY ILLUSTRATED PRESS NEW YORK

This book is dedicated first and foremost to God in the hopes that people will read it and then look to the Bible, which inspired more than a few scenes. Also to my wife Julia who has encouraged me throughout the writing process.

TABLE OF CONTENTS

PROLOGUE
The Royal Palace of Juthel

moke billowed from broken windows across the main floor of the castle. The flickering of fires raged in many of the ground floor windows. Thero charged between the open gates and pulled back on the reins of his mount. He leapt from the trembling beast and rushed across the courtyard, his ironwood staff held ready in his hands to battle any invader. Inwardly, his heart fell. The marble steps leading up to the palace flashed past, two at a time as he rushed to the double doors. No soldiers shouted a greeting as he ran and panic filled his mind. He should have known something was wrong, he should have been present to rally the defenders. At the dark portal he slowed, hefting the long rod in his left hand. He eased the door open with the tip of the staff and his heart fell as he took in the sight before him.

Thero stepped carefully through the burned and scarred double doors. Before him on the ground lay six men of the royal guard with their weapons still clutched in their hands. Blood pooled around each soldier, and the royal blue tabards clasped around their chests were rent asunder.

"They died well," he whispered. Scattered around the defenders was a score of roughly dressed thieves and cutthroats all bearing grievous wounds. Most were dead, but two stirred feebly at his passing.

Fires raged in the throne room. Thero glanced inside and then hurried on down the hall. He knew the doors to the royal apartments were in the west wing, and he pressed on towards this goal. The scattered bodies became a second layer of carpeting as he drew closer. Shouts and screams echoed down the broad hallway, and he broke into a jog, forsaking stealth for speed. The heavy oak door that defended the royal quarters lay in splintered ruins, shattered by the thick column of granite still lying by the portal.

Inside, Thero found the crown prince lying on the floor bleeding from a terrible wound in his chest. Rage filled Thero as he knelt beside the youth. The short sword in the prince's right hand was broken, leaving the young man clutching only half a weapon.

"Prophet," he gasped, "I told them you would come. No one believed me, but you promised you would."

"I am here now," Thero said. He gently wiped the blood from the boy's face with the hem of his robe, and brushed his sooty hair back from his face.

"I hid Nathel in the stable," he quietly pleaded, "please save him."

"What of the rest of the family?" Thero asked. He suddenly rocked back on his heels and shook his head as the last breath escaped the young lad.

He carefully brushed the lad's blue eyes closed, and whispered the blessing of Anatari. "Watch his soul oh great guardian, bring it quickly to the Creator's presence."

Thero turned and fled from the hall, making his way past the raging fires and back to the shattered gates. After exiting the castle he turned left, sprinting in the direction of the long stable. As he ran, he whispered a prayer, and then breathed a sigh of relief that the fires had spared the structure so far. Overhead, clouds rolled in mirroring his dark mood, obscuring the sun as he stepped inside. The building was empty, save two men with their backs to him.

"I know I saw the brat come in here," one growled, "Try that pile of hay," He motioned with his sword, "Maybe he is hiding in there."

Suddenly the speaker sensed a presence and spun around. "Well, what have we here? Looks like this poor fool brought a stick to our little sword fight."

Thero's eyes narrowed as now both men faced him. He stepped forward holding his staff ready. Without a word he motioned them forward. The runes of power etched into his staff glowed slightly in the dim light.

"You idiot! That's him," the second thief muttered. "The one they call the Prophet."

"Blah! He's not much of a prophet if he didn't see this coming now, is he?" Both men laughed raucously. Hefting their swords, they stalked towards him.

"Anatari, judge these fools harshly. Forgive me for acting in anger." Thero stepped forward. He launched a lazy strike against the closest of the thieves with his staff. The man skidded to a halt and ducked to avoid the blow, then continued forward. Thero was waiting for the movement. He retracted the staff with lightening speed, and poked the dirty man hard in the ribs. The blow brought a grunt of pain and made the man stumble. In one swift motion, he pulled the staff in again, then bounced the ironwood off the second man's sword, sending it flying. Thero went into a spin as the man scrambled for his weapon; the staff thudded off the thief's head just as he reached for his fallen sword. A moment later the thump of the body falling to the floor echoed throughout the stable.

"You killed my brother!" The first man cried. He rushed forward, swinging his sword wildly. Thero stepped back and then spun his staff hard, the clacking of the ironwood striking iron reverberated off the walls. Moments later, the sword went flying as the staff slammed hard into the fellow's ribs, doubling him over, and forcing the air from his lungs. Two more solid blows from the staff tumbled him to the ground, a small trickle of blood escaping his mouth.

Thero spared the two dead men a single glance and then hurried on into the main part of the stable.

"Nathel, son, where are you?"

From behind a pile of hay a three-year-old boy emerged, covered in clover blossoms. He rushed to Thero.

"Bad men in castle, Thero," Nathel whispered. He buried his face in Thero's robe and wept.

"I know. We must make our escape before more of them come to search the stables."

Thero picked up the young boy and walked down the line of stalls until he found the mount he wanted.

"Sit here, Nathel." He set the boy down near the stall door. A white lightening bolt patterned across the stallion's face and black hair hid his body in the dark recess of the stall. Thero grabbed the saddle and bridle from the stand near the stall. Moments later he emerged, leading the prancing stallion.

"Come Nathel, hold tight to me. We will ride fast and hard tonight." He picked up the young boy, who immediately clung tightly to his robe.

9

Thero swung his long legs over the saddle and placed Nathel in front of him. They leaned forward lying low on the black's strong neck.

"Run fast and run hard, Marhuth. Tonight we need your legs to carry us from danger." He let the black have his head, and a burst of speed sent them through the stable doors. Dozens of men boiled out the castle gate as they emerged from the stable, all eyes turned and watching them. Some men screamed that the Elemental Protectors were come to aid the palace, but most stared in amazement as Thero urged the stallion past.

Thero ignored the shouts and screams. He dug his heels into the stallion's sides, pointing the black towards the fortress gates. Down into the streets of the city they rode, fleeing the carnage of the castle. Overhead the sun broke through the clouds for a moment, and then once again disappeared, the clouds now hiding its feeble light from the world. Urging Marhuth onward, Thero tore through the city gates, sending the few men that tried to block his path tumbling. The road stretched out before them first dipping into a small valley and then climbing up a steep hill at the far end. He stopped on the next hill, turning in the saddle to look again at the city one last time. Over the quiet city a trail of smoke drifted in the sky marking the fires at the palace and telling a horrible story to any citizen that happened to look up.

"Nathel, some day we will return to claim what is yours. Until then we must hide and wait. When the time comes you must have faith that Anatari, master of the elemental protectors, will set right the wrongs done this night."

Thero looked down, only to find the young boy was asleep in his arms. The events of the day had rendered the little boy completely exhausted and drained. He wrapped his arms around his small charge and together they disappeared, leaving the stunned city and nation behind them.

Chapter One
Feast of Spring Rains

even tall wolves stood silently around the steaming carcass of a kylsret. Even the highest-flying bird became easy prey on the ground. The small pack had been patient enough to wait for the right moment. The pack leader stood a few paces away, head cocked, eyes closed. He listened to the faint voice drifting on the winds:

"The prophet has been found. He protects the chosen boy. They are near you in a small village. Find them and kill them. Beware the remaining Elemental Protectors—they are not all bound."

The rains fell mercilessly on the Dunmar Highlands soaking the ground for days without end. Gusts of wind accompanied the rain and threatened to grab anything not weighted down and send it flying. Situated far to the south and west of the lowland kingdoms, the surrounding mountains rarely experienced the heavy spring rains.

Nathel hunched his shoulders against the gusts of wind that threatened to rip his cloak from his throat. He grasped the rough cloth in his left hand and steadied his steps with the staff in his right. The trail he walked beside his grandfather was filled with mud, making the footing treacherous. Between the two, Marhuth struggled to pull one hoof from the mud at a time. The horse carried two oiled leather sacks filled with herbs and spices gathered from the Dunhagmith Mountains. As the rain tapered for but a moment, Nathel glanced at his grandfather. He felt foolish but he wanted to assure himself that he was not alone. Thero walked steadily, holding

Marhuth's reins and using his ironwood staff as a walking stick. With his bushy beard and long legs he made for a comical sight, but there was a strength and solidity that defied any rational ability to explain. His insistence on doing things right no matter what others said made him a solid rock for Nathel.

Nathel sighed and ducked his head as the rains once again strengthened, doing its best to wash the two men from the mountain trail. There were many who had forsaken these upper highlands in favor of the less fertile but safer lands around the village of Comstoll. He involuntarily gripped his staff tighter. With the harsh winter behind them, the wolves would be moving again. Rumors were growing that packs of tall mountain wolves were attacking the numerous flocks more and more over the past few seasons. He shivered at the thought.

Despite the veil of water drawn across the sky, Nathel struggled to watch his side of the trail. Thick stands of pine trees dotted the highlands surrounded on all sides by lush meadows and babbling brooks. A glance to his side told him that Thero, too, kept a close watch on his side of the trail. Looking over the back of the old stallion, Nathel noticed that for the first time he could see his grandfather without standing on his toes.

Last summer had seen his biggest growth spurt. Now he actually looked down at his grandfather's white head. Thero told him once that he looked exactly like his father. Nathel longed to know what had happened to his family those many years ago, but each time he broached the subject, the older man grew sober.

"It is not a good time for such dark subjects," was all that Thero had told him the first time he asked.

Nathel grabbed at his cloak, but the wind tore the hood from his grip and whipped it off his blond hair. He blinked into the storm, when suddenly, before him on the path, stood a mountain wolf of immense size. It snarled at him, lips pulled back into a grin. "Chosen one," It sneered. "We come for you."

Nathel stumbled to a halt, and his eyes went wide at the charging wolf.

"Thero!" Nathel cried. He released his remaining grip on the front of his robe and raised his staff defensively. With a flash of fur and a waft of mist the wolf vanished a step shy of him.

Marhuth plodded on, never missing a step. Nathel blinked, and then stared hard into the steady misting of rain that still fell. The trail ahead of him was empty. He spun around searching the trail behind him for the vanished wolf. In the distance he heard the howl of a lone hunter echo across the mountains.

Thero pulled back on Marhuth's lead rope. "What's wrong, Son?"

"Wolf...on the trail," Nathel sputtered. He wiped the moisture from his face and peered into the surrounding undergrowth.

"Where?" Alarm filled the older man's face as he tried to follow Nathel's searching eyes.

"It was on the trail just ahead of us. It spoke and then charged at me, but it disappeared just before it attacked," Nathel said. He waved his hand down the trail in disbelief. Nothing moved on the trail. Even the surrounding undergrowth and nearby forests remained silent.

"Well, whatever it was seems to be gone now."

"It was there Thero. By the elements, I swear it was there."

"It's not that I doubt you, Son, but whatever it was has vanished." Thero looked back down the trail. The rain clouds overhead were drifting off, carried by a soft wind that flowed up the mountainside.

"A wolf cannot disappear, can it Thero?" Nathel asked the question slowly.

"Come, Nathel. If there was something on the trail it will have left prints. With the rain softening the ground we should easily see if anyone has been on the trail before us." Thero hefted his staff, and dropped Marhuth's reins. The well-trained stallion remained ground hitched where he stood. Flicking his ears at the rivulets of water flowing down his face, he reached over and cropped off a tuft of grass and munched contentedly as he waited.

Nathel followed Thero up the trail, searching the soft mud for any sign of paw prints. Frustrated by the lack of tracks, he drew a sharp breath and stared at the surrounding meadows. How many times had he skipped this path alongside his grandfather? From the numerous trout streams that tumbled down the mountains to the farthest side of Baldtop Mountain, he had camped, fished, and tended sheep across the surrounding hills of the Dunmar Highlands. With only two other villages in the area, friends were hard to find. Thus Nathel learned to be content with his solitary existence.

"Here, Son." Thero pointed. They stood near where Nathel had first spotted the wolf.

Imprinted in the soft mud was the outline of a wolf's paws and tail. Casting about, he found where they exited and entered the underbrush. On a nearby bramble a single tuft of brown fur fluttered in the breeze. Nathel grabbed the hair and turned holding it out for his grandfather to see.

"Well, it seems you were right," Thero said. He took the fur in his wrinkled hand and examined it.

"Would wolves come this close to the village, Grandpa?" Less then half a league away the chimneys of Comstoll reached up to the sky. Twisting puffs of smoke left the stone fireplaces and drifted across a nearby stand of evergreen trees.

"It seems there is at least one that will," Thero chuckled.

He smiled at the joke, comforted by the fact that his grandfather seemed unconcerned.

"Anatari will protect us. The Elemental Pillars still guard the Dark One's prison. If all we must face is a few stray wolves then our worries are for naught. All the same, the air is chilled and I am tired. Let's get to old Stedman's inn."

Nathel nodded. "I could use a sip of his hot cider."

"That's the spirit boy. Come Marhuth." Thero whistled at the stallion. The black horse whinnied once and trotted up the trail to join them, the mud making sucking noises as his hooves dug into the ground.

Nestled against the western side of Baldtop Mountain, the village kept its sleepy existence quiet from the surrounding lands. To the south stretched the Dunhagmith Mountains. Dark and sinister, the peaks reared their heads to lofty heights. To the north stretched a dozen leagues of the Dunmar Highlands, bordered by a branch of the Isies River. Across the roaring waters of the powerful Isies lay the lowland kingdoms. The only contact the hardy folk of Comstoll had with the lowlanders were the scores of wool traders that made the rugged trip each year.

Nathel beamed a smile when they topped the last hill. Before them, lay Comstoll. Nearly a hundred brick and stone homes clustered around the single road leading north. At the end of the dirt road, he glimpsed the outline of the looming two story inn.

Almost as a benediction to their journey, the rain finally broke and the full glory of the sun broke through the cloudy sky, soaking the ground with its life giving warmth. Marhuth shook his thick mane, clearing the remaining water off. Nathel followed Thero down the sloping hill, watching as dozens of children emerged from their homes around the village. The twosome entered the main road, and Nathel listened to the shouts and hails of the townsfolk. Many of the village shepherds thought it odd that he and Thero clung to the outer meadows. Nathel himself often wished they would move closer to town. Normally the loneliness of the distant edge of the western reaches of the Dunmar Highlands didn't bother him, but today he wished they lived closer to the village.

"Grandpa, will we ever live closer to Comstoll?"

Thero glanced over Marhuth's broad back. "Nathel, our livelihood is in the outer meadows. The small flock will never give us enough money to live. We need the income from the herbs we gather and they only grow on the edge of the Dunhagmith Mountains."

"I know." Nathel said, resignedly. He struggled for a moment. "I think it would be nice to have some friends my own age."

Thero frowned, and his reply was interrupted as they arrived at the thick post driven into the ground at the middle of the village square. Despite the early spring rains the thick grass of the square was already turning a dark shade of green.

"Thero, Nathel, welcome back! How has the land closest to the dark mountains faired this spring?" Innkeeper Stedman strode across the grass. Nathel smiled as the tall, thin man shook Thero's hand. He seemed to Nathel to be all arms and legs.

"Things fare as the elemental protectors will them, Stedman." Thero returned the handshake. Nathel wandered about the fountain as the two men stood conversing. On the wide street near the inn, half a score of tables had been laid out.

This year, as in years past, the young women of the village would set out the table placements and long white cloths. Then, as the sun peaked tomorrow, the food would be laid out and the village would gather for the Feast of Spring. For the past five seasons Nathel remembered coming to Comstoll and partaking in the feast. It was a time of celebrating the passing of another winter and the arrival of the spring sun that brought life to the highlands.

"Come lad, let us make our delivery and go to our rooms."

"Yes, Grandfather," Nathel replied. He turned from staring into the fountain and followed Thero down the road to the widow Marith's shop. The village healer paid Thero well for the bags of herbs he brought each year. This year they had bundles of pinkbell and ironwill roots. Thero even had a sack of rare catspaw flowers.

Two hours later Thero and Nathel made their way to the two story inn. Sitting stately at the far southern end of Comstoll, the Shepherd's Crook overlooked the entire town. The inn sat on a slight hill that made it seem even taller than its two stories. A river rock foundation rose to waist height and round timbers cut from the nearby forests made the second story almost as sturdy. The single door leading into the inn was propped open and Innkeeper Stedman stood on the wide porch smiling broadly.

"Welcome, welcome. I had my dear Betsy prepare your normal room Thero. I trust you will join us for supper this night?" Already the succulent smells of fried potatoes and roasting mutton drifted on the air making Nathel's stomach growl in anticipation.

"It would be our pleasure, Stedman." Thero nodded and handed Marhuth's reins to a young lad who stood waiting. "Even more for Nathel by the sounds of his stomach."

Nathel smiled and nodded his head.

"Take good care of Marhuth, son. He was once a mighty warhorse."

The young boy nodded, took the reins carefully and led the big horse away. Nathel looked wistfully around the edge of the inn. A low-roofed stable sat around the far side of the inn. He loved the smell of the dried clover stored in the hay loft.

"Come on, Son. Let's store our gear." Thero's voice faded as the howl of a wolf pierced the mid-afternoon sky.

"They have been crying out for the past few days Thero," Stedman commented. He wiped his big hands on the clean apron around his waist.

"Wolves have been known to hunt close to Comstoll in the past," Thero said. He waved a hand at the nearby mountains but Nathel saw the concern in his eyes.

Stedman grunted and led them into the common room. With the warmth of the afternoon, Nathel breathed a sigh of relief when they entered the door. The room was cool and empty, they passed the long tables and Thero led the way up the stairs leading to the second story. A narrow hall brought them to a room with two beds, and a clean, wool blanket lay neatly folded at the foot of each mattress. Nathel dropped his pack and sank down onto the soft mattress.

"This is the best part of the Feast of Spring, Grandpa."

Thero laughed as he lay his pack next to the bed on the opposite wall, "Soft living son. In my younger days we never slept on feather-filled mattresses."

Nathel laughed as Thero's gruff voice faded off, and glanced over he saw his grandfather laying back on his own soft mattress. Already his eyes were slipping shut as someone fighting sleep but one intent on losing the battle.

Nathel woke with a start some time later. Thero's loud snores filled the room. Outside the wide glass window the sun was slipping behind the Dunhagmith Mountains, staining the sky a brilliant array of red and orange hues. Rising from the bed, Nathel tiptoed to the door and slipped out. The floor boards of the hall creaked under his weight, but the sound went unnoticed. Innkeeper Stedman nodded to him as he crossed the common room and exited the inn. A few dozen steps brought him around the side of the building to the low-roofed stable. The double doors leading into the stable were open and Nathel walked in whistling a cheerful tune. Suddenly he stopped short.

"Marhuth you old coot. How did you manage to get out of your stall?" Nathel laughed. He grabbed the dangling rope and led the crafty stallion back to a nearby empty stall. After double looping the rope to make sure he wouldn't escape again, Nathel climbed the short ladder leading into the low hay loft.

The timbers of the roof brushed his hair when he stood up, and the sweet smell of clover filled his nostrils. Sighing, he sat down in the fodder and closed his eyes. In his mind he pictured a snug house. An older man that looked just like him sat smiling at a wide table. A woman who looked just the way Thero had described his mother moved about the kitchen. Nathel lay back playing out the fantasy in his mind dreaming what it would be like to have known his family.

Arrooooo

The lone wolf's howl broke into his dream and brought his mind back to the dark loft. Nathel clambered to the ladder and slipped down, Marhuth huffed at him and tossed his head. He gave Marhuth a armful of hay and then turned to leave.

"Chosen One."

He skidded to a halt. Near the door a wolf stared at him. Black eyes the size of fists bore into him, and the creature's lips pulled back to reveal even rows of sharp teeth.

Nathel stumbled back, his hand settling against a long-handled fork. The wolf charged, flashing forward as he struggled to raise the fork and defend himself.

"Nathel," Thero called.

Nathel blinked, the wolf was gone. Thero stood in the door of the stable with a single lantern held high looking at him curiously.

"What's wrong, Son?"

"I...I don't know. I thought I saw the same wolf I saw from earlier today on the trail."

Nathel watched as his grandfather raise the lantern high and looked about.

"Let's go inside. The air has an evil taint about it tonight. The wolf pack is close and it's better to have strong walls between us and their snapping jaws."

Nathel nodded and followed his grandfather, pausing at the stable door to secure it tightly.

"Don't worry about Marhuth, Son. He is well able to defend himself against a few wolves."

Nathel nodded and paused one last time at the door to the inn. Overhead a dark cloud covered the bright moon, eerily plunging the world into darkness.

Chapter Two
A New Pack Leader

athel walked the dark hall to their room. He was full and tired. Innkeeper Stedman's wife was an excellent cook and he had eaten far too much. Nathel crossed to the window and looked out across the mountains. High in the sky the moon was visible again. He slipped the window open, enjoying the feel of the cool breeze on his face.

"Hello. What was that?" he whispered to himself. Far out across the mountain meadows, a flash of movement drew his gaze. Behind him the door opened and Nathel heard his grandfather approach.

"Do you see something, Nathel?" Thero asked. He stood next to him at the window looking out across the grass meadows.

"I don't think so. Probably just a mule deer or a fox hunting field mice," Nathel said. He shrugged and turned to his bed, sliding back the thin sheet as he lay down. His eyes drifted shut, just before Nathel drifted off to sleep, he heard the sound of his grandfather latching the window and dropping a heavy bar across the door. Then he drifted off to sleep.

Nathel struggled through the layers of sleep. Then without warning, he found himself atop a wide mountain. All around him clouds raced across the sky and the moon looped overhead. Day and night passed by in the blink of an eye.

"Where am I?" he whispered.

"Welcome to my world, Chosen One," a rasping voice spoke. Nathel spun about, knowing what he would find. The tall mountain wolf sat quietly watching him.

"Why do you keep calling me that?" Nathel asked. He found that he was clutching his staff and he stepped back.

"Are you not the Chosen One?"

"I am a simple shepherd, nothing more. Leave me be."

"Bedbezdal has marked you, Boy. You must be killed. We are coming for you."

The wolf stalked forward, crouching near the ground. Puffs of smoke rose about its paws and Nathel noticed that each step left a blackened paw print.

Nathel held his staff defensively, waiting for the creature to make the first move.

"Anatari will protect me," Nathel said. He tried to sound brave, but his voice cracked with fear.

The wolf pulled back its lips into a grotesque image of a smile, and a croaking laughter ripped from its mouth.

"He cares not for this world any more. The masses have rejected him, and the few remaining Elemental Protectors are falling. Soon they will no longer be of any consequence."

"Water." Nathel shook his head. His mind filled with images of cool mountain pools and tumbling streams. He reeled back as images of mortals wandered across the world, fouling the waters. They went about their lives ignoring the very rivers and streams that were placed in the world to protect them but then there more sinister images of figures in black robes pouring vile mixtures into the waters. Before him the wolf began fading from view as a soft rain fell about him, somehow protecting him from the charging creature.

"One way or another, Boy, we are coming for you."

Nathel's eyes snapped open, Thero stood near the window staring out.

"Grandfather, the wolves!" Nathel's voice faded.

"Yes, I know. The pack is coming. They are moving to their evil master's call. Sleep will be precious this night. Bring your staff. We must rouse the village. Even the walls of this inn will not stop what is coming tonight - only strong arms and some courage and faith will help."

Nathel leaped from his warm bed and pulled his boots on. Thero tossed him the ironwood staff and together they left the safety of the room.

"Stedman!" Thero pounded on the thick door. "Wake up you old fool."

Nathel stood with his back to the wall, waiting. Around Comstoll the mountains echoed with the cries of the wolf pack. He shivered as Thero pounded again.

"What is it?" Stedman pulled open the door. The innkeeper was clad in a night shift and his bleary eyes struggled to focus in the light of the lantern.

"We must rouse the village. The wolves are gathering. I fear they are coming this way."

"What of it? We are inside, they cannot enter."

"Walls will do little to stop this particular pack. If we do not meet them, they will come for us."

The innkeeper's eyes went wide. "I will be right out."

Thero nodded and led Nathel back to the common room.

"We should light more lanterns. It would be best to get a good roaring fire lit in front of the inn."

Nathel nodded and he raced to the front door. "What can we burn, Grandpa?"

"The tables! Pile up all the tables in front of the inn," Thero motioned. He grabbed a nearby table and tipped it over, dragging it close to the front of the inn.

Nathel nodded and hurried across the wide hard packed road, grabbing another table and dragging it back to where Thero stood. He tipped it against the first, then frantically ran and grabbed another. All around the village lanterns began appearing and making their bobbing way towards the square.

"What's going on here," The booming voice called. Del Irchon strode into the circle of light cast by the lanterns. "Why are you moving the feast tables?"

Nathel skidded to a halt as a huge hand closed over his shoulder, the callused palm of the blacksmith digging painfully into his skin.

"The wolves are coming," Stedman said. He stood near the front door of the inn strapping an old sword around his waist.

Del grunted, "It's but a few hunting wolves. There is no cause to destroy the Feast tables. The beasts would never come into the village." A crowd had begun to gather and nearly a score of the village men stood nervously clutching crude weapons. Nathel counted about a dozen short bows among the group, but the rest held swords and staves.

"Leave the tables be! Your foolishness will bring bad luck upon us for the rest of the summer," Del said. His voice rose above the other mutters.

"The pack is coming Del," Thero answered calmly. "Would you care to face them without a decent fire?"

"This is more of your foolishness, Thero. Wolves are wolves and they serve one master, themselves. How many times must you be told to keep your talk of the old god to yourself? They do not exist. The Elemental Protectors are but legends to scare weak minded people!" Del cried. This time the round of agreement was much louder as the crowd swelled to include most of the village.

"Just because you refuse to believe in them does not mean the elemental protectors do not exist, Del," Thero replied. His voice was quiet but it carried easily across the wide road before the inn. "Just as denying the Creator does not change the fact that he sent them to watch over us."

"This is foolishness! There is no creator or elementals, we are all that matters. We control our own fate and there is nothing else that matters," Del growled. His face grew red as he surveyed the stack of six tables, their white tablecloths scattered and ripped.

"I say we drive them both from the village. There is no room here for them!" Del said. He took a step forward.

Nathel suddenly realized that the blacksmith carried his heavy hammer. He grabbed his staff and backed away from the angry crowd until his back touched the front railing of the inn.

His breath came in short gasps and his heart raced as, he clutched his staff defensively. A few steps to his right Thero stood calmly, leaning on his ironwood staff and snorting at the menacing crowd.

"If I am such a fool, Del, turn and look down the road to the south," Thero said. He grabbed the lantern from Stedman's grasp and tossed it high into the air. The impact with the stacked tables broke the small oil container and scattered fire across the stack of wood. The flames blazed high into the air and Nathel felt his blood run cold. Scores of mountain wolves stood silently amid the houses and shops of the village square, the flames dancing in their eyes. Seated near the side of the fountain a creature of immense size opened its mouth and howled into the night sky.

Panic ensued and the snarls of the pack broke out on all sides.

"Get the women and children inside the inn! Drive the creatures back!" Thero's voice boomed. He rushed from the inn and swung his staff in a wide stroke. A charging wolf yelped and rolled away. The sound broke the stunned silence and people began screaming. Nathel leapt forward and angled to the left, skidding to a halt with his back to the fire. A single wolf dove straight at him, snarling and growling as he waited.

It was a black beast. Nathel watched with detached interest; his mind suddenly calm. The wolf charged in, razor-sharp teeth flashing as it leapt into the air, going for Nathel's neck. The beast was going for a fast kill, picking the younger man, the more inexperienced target. Nathel brought his staff up in front of his face to protect against the flashing teeth. The wolf struck the staff, locking its teeth around the end of the staff and bearing its weight down on the gangly youth.

"*It means to bury me under its weight,*" Nathel thought, calmly watching as the wolf started its descent towards him. He stepped forward and ducked his head, bringing the end of his staff down until it rested on the ground. The wolf's weight came down hard, slamming into the unyielding ironwood. Nathel yanked the grounded end of the staff out, letting the creature's weight work against it. Off balance, the wolf released its grip on the staff, but the sudden movements had thrown it too far forward. The wolf came down heavily, impacting its head on a table sticking out from the blazing fire. Nathel stepped back and snapped the staff up. Spinning it once, he brought it down hard on the stunned beast's head. He whispered a plea to Anatari as the cursed beast died. If legend spoke true its tortured spirit would descend to Anatari's brother in the lowest abyss of Hades.

Nathel saw his grandfather engaged against a smaller pair of brown wolves. His staff worked in circles, deflecting the snapping jaws. The creatures lunged and dodged, always moving to keep him from landing a killing blow on either.

Rolling to the left, Nathel struck out with his staff and took one of the wolves facing Thero by surprise. A satisfying crunch sounded as he cracked down on the top of the wolf's snout. The wolf's teeth slammed together and severed part of its tongue. The follow-up blow staved in the creature's skull.

Thero finished his second opponent with a trio of lightning-fast strikes from his staff. He then turned, watching as Nathel once more whispered the plea to Anatari.

"It's always good to offer the spirits of the cursed creatures a chance to be judged for their deeds. Most do not call on the gods when they kill the beasts, and the slain spirits are condemned to wander in darkness until the end of the age."

Nathel caught a glimpse of the snapping jaws of the remainder of the pack. The pack leader was re-arranging his forces. A long line was set in place to surround the villagers. Nathel launched his staff into a blur of activity, constantly battling to keep his back to the fire. His forearms ached from the fight, but he dared not slow. Thero was a circle of death where he fought, his back to the flames across from Nathel. Five wolves lay dead around him and several more appeared as darting flashes working coordinated attacks to break through his defense.

The shouts of the villagers echoed around the clearing as they struggled to arrange a firm defense. Short bows hummed and iron-tipped arrows flew in the night sky, the paths of many ending in a sudden yelp. Single hits did little to slow the tough wolves. It took repeated hits from the arrows to drop them. Half a score villagers stood back, firing as fast as they could pull arrows from their quivers. The remainder fought with their own backs to the fire, battling to stay alive in the storm of flashing teeth.

As he spun a complete circle, he saw the pack leader, standing unmoving in the middle of the melee, always watching the battles on both sides. His howls and barks directed the efforts of the pack to overrun the humans. The battle line was an eerie sight in the half-light of the fading moon. A long line of wolves flashed back and forth as they attacked the desperate villagers. It was a battle that offered the wolves the advantage of numbers alone, but numbers could be enough. More screams ended in frightened cries as four more men were pulled under the flashing teeth and claws of the wolves.

"Fading moon." Nathel said. He spoke the words out loud as he thrust the end of his staff against the snapping jaws of a lunging wolf. A sickening crunch of bone and cartilage sounded in the dim light of dawn. The wolf yelped once and ran. All Nathel saw was a flurry of legs and a waving tail.

Then as Nathel swung his staff in a circle around his body one last time, the sun broke over the rough mountain peaks, bathing the scene in piercing light. A long, mournful howl echoed from the throat of the pack leader and the wolves broke ranks and fled; the sun was never their friend.

Nathel stood unmoving near the gate of the corral. Nearly a score of dead wolves lay in a half circle around him.

Nathel looked long at the remaining villagers around him and then exhaustion took him. He collapsed to the ground, his staff falling with a clatter. Over-head, a single cloud hovered dropping great drops of rain in a rare sun shower.

Matthew John Krengel

CHAPTER THREE
AN UNEXPECTED MEETING

ill he live?"

Nathel heard the question, but his eyelids were so heavy that he could not open them. A voice groaned in the room and it sounded oddly familiar, then blackness once again descended.

Sometime later, he awoke again. This time his eyes snapped open. Thero was bending over the bed staring at him, his bushy beard so close that it tickled his face and drew a quick sneeze. Thero's startled face jerked backwards.

"What happened?" Nathel asked. The voice that spoke was cracked and dry, but it sounded somewhat like his.

"You did well, Boy. You did very well." A smile drifted across Thero's face and he leaned forward in the chair holding out a small cup of water. Nathel nodded his head and sipped slowly, letting the cool liquid flow across his parched tongue and throat. Dark circles stood out under Thero's eyes, the kind that appears when people miss several nights of sleep.

"Are we safe?"

"Yes, Son, everything is safe for now. We have a constant watch posted around Comstoll."

"How long have I been asleep?"

"Two days have passed since the wolves attacked."

Thero reached out a hand, helping him to a sitting position. Nathel quickly realized that all the muscles of his body were tired and sore; it hurt

27

just to move. He leaned back against the wool-stuffed pillow. The blanket was pulled up to his chin and the interior of the inn was dim. Thero rose and bustled about, opening the curtains and pushing the window open letting the bright sunshine into the small room. A knock at the door broke the silence.

Thero moved to the door and opened it wide. "Widow Marith, how nice to see you again." Wispy gray hair stuck out around her green bonnet; her hawkish nose looked ready to leap off her face.

"Someone has to make sure you don't kill that poor boy with your outdated ways." She smiled. The portly widow seemed to enjoy the banter with him. The smile on her round face was replaced with a frown as she pushed into the room. She placed a small iron pot on the narrow table that sat in the center of the room. Nathel held his peace as she felt his forehead, then had him stick out his tongue. Finally after numerous pokes and prodding's she decided he was going to live and promptly moved back to the iron pot.

"I brought something that will take away the soreness and help the boy's body heal itself."

"He just needs some good sleep Marith. You know that as well as I do."

"Nonsense, what he needs is the right mix of herbs. The smell is not good, but they do wonders for helping the body heal."

Thero rolled his eyes from where he was leaning against the wall, watching her move about. Nathel tried to laugh, but his face and stomach hurt too much. He sighed and allowed himself to be fed the foul smelling potion.

He heard Thero mutter something about checking on Marhuth in the stable and the watched him head to the door, leaving him prisoner of the healer and her elixirs.

"Coward. He cut and ran," Nathel muttered to himself so lightly that Widow Marith missed it.

"Nathel, what Thero needs is a loving hand around the cottage. Surly you see that. Some day he will come to his senses and realize what he is missing. Why, I just happen to know a young woman in the village who would be a perfect match for you, too."

He sat staring at her, and a scared look covered his face.

"Go to sleep now, Nathel. We can talk about this later." Marith said. She bustled over to where he struggled to stay up and pushed him down.

"You have been through a rough time. Don't worry, I will be here when you wake."

Nathel rolled his eyes. He wanted friends not a wife. Sadly, he lacked the strength to tell her that fact and so he submitted.

He leaned back in the bed seeking comfort and relief in the thick pillow and warm blankets. A cool breeze filtered in from the window and it felt good. Nathel could see from the sun climbing slowly in the sky that it was still early. Despite the hour, he carefully scooted his body down into the small bed. Just before he fell asleep, he heard Thero enter the door and speak to Marith, but her reply was lost as he slipped off into dreams.

Snowy peaks stood out in the landscape around him. Nathel stood high on the side of a mountain watching a flock of sheep graze contentedly on the lower slopes. The sky was bright blue overhead, but far out in the distance he saw pitch-black clouds. He watched the fast-moving storm as it approached, and he began to move down the mountain, urging the lazy sheep towards the safety of the lower valleys. In the distance he could hear the howls of the wolf pack approaching on the wings of the massive storm.

"We are coming for you, Boy." The voice startled him and Nathel spun, bringing his staff up defensively. Above him on the mountainside, the pack leader watched him, his wolf's head cocked to one side. The beast's eyes glowed red and smoke drifted up from his paws as he moved forward.

"Do you think that puny staff can stop my master from taking you?"

Nathel held his silence as the wolf stalked closer, closing to within a dozen paces, and then stopped. All around him the world faded from sight in a gray fog. Sounds echoed from the gray veil but Nathel saw no one. The bleating of sheep and the barking of herding dogs faded into the distance.

"Do you think that just because the pack ran that you have won? We will never stop pursuing you. Once we start, we never stop. We will guide The Fallen to you wherever you run."

"Why do you want me?" Nathel finally spoke. He stared at the massive wolf pacing before him. Oddly, he felt no fear, just curiosity.

"Because you are the one. The Elemental Pillars have marked you as chosen by my master's sister, and anyone who bears that mark must be killed. It won't do to have one of the chosen moving around. Not when so much is at hand."

He noticed that on the back of each of his hands, a faint symbol shown through the skin. His eyes traced the shield of the Elementals on his left hand and the cross mark of Anatari on his right.

"He will protect me from the likes of you, as will the Elementals." Nathel spoke with conviction. Thero taught him for years that the elemental protectors would defend their own, giving them the strength to withstand the minions of Bedbezdal.

The wolf threw back its head and howled its approximation of a laugh. The sound sent shivers up and down Nathel's spine.

"Do you think the creator cares about you, or this world? He has abandoned it for other works. As for the remaining Elemental Protectors, they are not a threat anymore; we have seen to them." The pack leader crouched low and stalked forward. He pulled his lips back to reveal even rows of wicked, long teeth.

"Did you know, Boy, that if someone is killed here his body also dies in the mortal world?" The words sent another shiver down Nathel's spine, and he crouched into a more balanced stance, holding his staff out defensively. Nathel stepped back, working to keep some distance between himself and the hunter.

"You can't do it, Boy. You lack the faith, the strength of will and the purpose of heart," The pack leader whispered. The words seemed to attack him physically as they curled around him and broke his concentration. A cold sweat dripped down his forehead, stinging his eyes and blurring his vision. Trying desperately to clear his vision, Nathel quickly wiped his face on the back of his sleeve. In that short moment the wolf disappeared from his field of vision. Nathel turned quickly, the faintest of sounds making him spin left then right. He tried to spot the fast-moving creature. There! A shadow passed off to his right, but by the time he faced that direction, it was gone. Slowly Nathel backed up, trying to watch all directions at once. Suddenly, the fearsome beast came with a rush from behind, knocking Nathel's staff from his hands, and bearing him heavily to the ground.

"Now you will die, boy, and the world will be left to The Fallen. The creator will be a dream lost in time, and the Elemental Protectors will be scattered to the winds or destroyed."

The words were whispered in his ear as he rolled and thrashed, in an effort to throw off the pinning weight of the wolf. Wriggling his shoulders, Nathel strained to free his hands but found they were pinned under his chest. He felt hot saliva dripping down his neck as the iron jaws of the pack leader closed on his neck.

"Nathel!"

Nathel screamed as the jaws closed on his neck and began to shake his body.

"Nathel!"

The gray fog began to dissipate.

"We will meet again, boy, and soon. Your friends will abandon you and you'll be alone. Then I will come for you. Welcome to my world, boy."

Matthew John Krengel

CHAPTER FOUR
INVITATION TO LEAVE

athel opened his eyes and screamed, the small room of the inn coming slowly into view. Thero was shaking his shoulders, and Widow Marith stood in the doorway, white-faced with fear. With a trembling hand she made a sign to ward off evil.

"Grandpa?" Nathel's voice croaked. He threw his arms around his grandfather's neck and buried his face into his shoulder. Tears rained down his face.

"It's alright, son. You will be fine now," Thero said. He patted him gently on the back.

Nathel opened his clenched eyes and through the tears saw widow Marith flee from the room, running through the open door as fast as her short legs would carry her. Her footsteps pounded down the stairs and echoed as she crashed through the front door of the inn.

Nathel released his grip on Thero and the older man sat back, his hands resting on Nathel's shoulders.

"Good riddance. That woman has a scream that could wake the dead and everything in between. Of course, she has a face that could send the wakened back to their graves."

Nathel smiled and wiped his face with a corner of his sheet. He struggled to keep his eyes open as Thero fastened the heavy storm shutters closed; but it was a losing battle. Once again, he drifted off to sleep. This time though his sleep was void of dreams, and he rested comfortably, secure in the knowledge that his grandfather was close by and watching over him.

Nathel woke the next morning to loud knocks on the door. The wooden slates shook from the impact of the blows.

Nathel watched Thero shake his head and then turn, leaving the big leather pack where it lay. The door swung wide. "Yes, Mayor Kogsteg? Can I be of service?"

Around the edge of his sheet, Nathel saw the six men of the village counsel standing in a half circle around the broad back of the mayor. Despite the hushed tones, their voices carried well, and he heard every word of the short exchange.

"The boy must leave, Thero!" Kogsteg demanded. Nathel frowned. He had never heard anyone make a demand of Thero before.

I must have really messed something up.

"I know. We are preparing even now. Nathel and I will be gone before the sun has peaked."

The mayor nodded and a round of muttered agreements sounded from the six men packed into the narrow hall. Nathel gaped as he noticed for the first time that the men had come armed. Swords and bows were held awkwardly, partially hidden behind the homespun clothes of the frightened men. Nathel gingerly moved his body into a sitting position expecting to feel the intense pain of the day before. He was surprised to find that his body felt whole and refreshed. The sleep had worked a healing wonder on his sore muscles. The dream of the night before had also faded to a haze in his mind, and all he remembered was the red eyes, the weight of the wolf bearing down on his back, and the feel of the teeth on his neck. Reaching up with his right hand he rubbed his neck, thankful that his hand came away without any blood on it.

More words were spoken but Nathel's mind was busy and he missed the exchange. Thero turned from the door as the men retreated. *Why were they forcing them to leave? Was it something he had done?*

"Ah, good, boy. You're awake. Now then, come along. Let's get you up and dressed. We have a long journey ahead of us." Thero wore a forced smile, and Nathel frowned at the white bearded man, not liking the attempt at deception.

"Am I cursed, Grandfather?" Nathel said. He sat on the edge of the bed, grabbing a nearby cloth and dipping it in a basin of clean water. He wrung the cloth out and began cleaning his face, hands, and feet. Suddenly a thought occurred to him. He turned his hands over, staring at the skin, searching for the symbols from the dream. The skin was clean; no odd marks stood out on the backs of his hands.

"No, boy, you are not cursed," Thero replied. The chuckle from his grandfather was real. The twinkle in his eye told Nathel that things were not as grim as he assumed.

Nathel stood, slowly testing his legs as he did.

He was happy to find that his balance had returned. Happily he moved about the room, pausing to slip his legs into a clean pair of pants and pull a soft wool shirt over his head. At the second bed, he noticed his grandfather was indeed preparing for a journey. Two packs lay on the floor, each half full. A stack of supplies covered the floor next to the bed. His good leather boots were clean and sitting beside the bed. Nathel grabbed the boots and sat back down, the leather soft and supple as it wrapped around his foot perfectly.

"Where are we going, Grandfather?" Nathel asked. He spoke quietly, his eyes fastened on the floor. "Why are they kicking us out of the village?"

"Where we are going will be revealed in time. Even in small towns like this, The Fallen have ears and eyes. We will talk more about it when we are surrounded by nothing but mountains and forests. As for why the village asked us to leave, that is less complicated to understand. They are scared."

Nathel finished pulling his boots on, and he sat on the edge of the bed, waiting for his grandfather to continue.

"The village counsel has decided, based on the ramblings of a scared woman that it is too dangerous for us to remain here. It seems she told them that the wolves were after you, in particular. That, combined with the fact that frightened people make rash decisions without truly searching for the facts, adds up to them telling us to leave. They assume that once we are gone, the pack will leave them in peace.

"Will the pack leave the village?"

"They might but that remains to be seen."

"Why would the wolves be after me?" Nathel asked. He rose and walked to his smaller pack.

Bending over the table, he picked up a thick coil of rope from the floor and slipped it into the leather pack.

"The wolves didn't attack just here, Nathel. They attacked Bowlder's farm on the east side, and Coghother's and Smittlie's. Things went poorly

35

for the Bowlders. The pack managed to slip the latch holding a shutter closed and killed the entire family. The other two were lucky and their homes withstood the attacks."

He thought about the families. The homes were not close to each other. All were shepherds, but the homes were scattered about the small village. Two were on the east side and one on the west.

"They all have boys my age," Nathel blurted. His mind made the connection moments later.

"Yes, Nathel. They attacked all those houses but they gathered here."

Nathel nodded. Nothing made sense but he trusted his grandfather completely. The older man always knew what he was doing.

"What about our flock, Grandpa?"

"I sold them this morning. The mayor paid a good bit more then they were worth when he found out that we would not be leaving until they were sold," Thero said. He grinned and patted the fat purse of coins sitting on the edge of the table.

They worked in silence, Nathel helping his grandfather pack the remaining supplies into the two leather bags. Long straps tied the packs closed and Nathel carried them outside. Marhuth stood tied to the side of the inn waiting for them.

"Tie them on tightly. We don't want them slipping off."

Nathel nodded, pulling hard on the cinch straps. He tied off the straps and pulled on the packs to make sure they were secure.

Thero tossed Nathel his staff. "You did a good job the other night, son. You remembered your training and had faith in Anatari. Those two things saved your life, and most likely mine as well."

Nathel nodded beaming at the compliment. "Thank you, Grandpa."

He waited patiently, rotating his staff in his hands. His muscles relaxed and the sun warmed his body. He enjoyed feeling the coolness of the ironwood beneath his fingers. Conscious of many eyes on them, Nathel watched his grandfather untie Marhuth's reins and together they walked away from the inn.

"There have been many good times here."

Nathel nodded as he followed Thero down the narrow dirt trail leading through the village. A single wide dirt track led them through even rows of houses. He counted the charred homes as he followed Thero, noting that three homes were burned to the ground. The surrounding structures showed signs that the fires had nearly sent the entire village up in flames.

No one walked the streets and the village green remained quiet. He thought he caught a glimpse of a face behind a nearby shutter, but it disappeared quickly. The stone chimneys faded into the dust behind them, and ahead the cool mountain trails opened up wide.

It was called the East Road in the village. Nathel shook his head as he considered the name. It was not really a road but, a narrow trail that wandered south and east. It led them away from Comstoll and into a slow descent out of the highlands. The smoke of cooking fires faded from view and all around them birds chirped and squirrels chattered in the trees. Trips east were a rare occasion and Nathel could not remember the last time he had ventured east of Baldtop.

With a firm grip on the lead rope, Thero led Marhuth. He pointed out the herds of deer and hundreds of wild rams and ewes grazing on the nearby slopes. Marhuth moved steadily, ignoring the huffing of the rams with their curled horns. He glanced when a lazy brown bear rolled out of a spreading willow tree. Nathel hefted his staff, but the bear glanced at them and then dove into the stream in search of fish. Marhuth pulled now and then on the rope as he tried to grab tufts of grass. He rolled his eyes in irritation when Thero pulled up the thick lead rope. Slowly ever so slowly the rough highland hills faded some as they traveled east.

"Where are we headed, Thero?"

"East. There is someone far to the east who can help us."

"Who?"

"You will have to wait and see," Thero replied.

Nathel grunted, not liking the vague answer, but when nothing else followed, he dropped the subject. His grandfather seemed lost in thought, so he returned to watching the passing countryside. The East Road made its way through the stands of trees, sometimes almost disappearing into the thick grass.

The smell of evergreen pines filled the flowered meadows of the foothills, and grassy areas, covered in wild flowers, stretched out for hundreds of paces. Thick stretches of evergreens separated vast meadows and mountain streams from the next stream and meadow. Red, yellow, and purple flowers were home to swarms of bees and myriads of colorful butterflies. The air was alive with insects and birds taking flight as the three travelers plodded steadily through their grassy homes. As the sun neared the tops of the southern mountains, Thero called a halt to the day's journey.

"Let's find a place to rest, Nathel. You are still recovering, and another good night's sleep will work wonders for you."

Nathel nodded, stifling a yawn. He followed Thero as he turned off a hard packed section of the road and led Marhuth through a narrow opening in the thick trees.

"Grandpa, is there a storm coming?"

"The rain is a good thing, Nathel. The water will wash our scent from the land and the pack will have to work hard to follow."

Nathel nodded and he wearily plodded after Marhuth. The trail narrowed until branches clutch at both his arms.

"There it is, Son," Thero pointed.

Nathel looked up but it took him a few moments to spot the dark opening hidden among the boughs. Two hundred paces from the road, the opening was hidden by years of broken branches and fresh growth.

The opening was large enough for Marhuth to slip past the rocks and stand comfortably. Over head a slight break in the trees offered him a narrow view of the approaching storm.

In the evening sky, Nathel could see storm clouds piling up in the distance, ugly black and green. The distant clouds filled the sky until they blocked the evening sun. As they approached the cave mouth, raindrops began to fall steadily; the wind howled in hard from the west. Nathel glanced about. In the distance, the lonesome howl of a hunting wolf cried mournfully.

"Wolves again, Grandfather," Nathel said. He looked about fearfully. He was not ready to face the pack leader again.

"The rain will cleanse our scent from the ground. The pack will have to search long and hard before they pick up our trail again," Thero said.

He sounded confident, and Nathel gripped his staff and stepped into the cave. Stopping just inside the overhanging rocks, he peered into the gloomy darkness. Marhuth stood placidly chewing on a tuft of grass near the opening. Past the outer galley, a second smaller opening led to the inner cavern. Thero motioned him forward, and together they slipped into the darkness. Just inside, Nathel blinked, his eyes struggling to collect enough light for him to see.

A circle of rocks outside the opening sheltered them from the rain and wind. The inner area held a pile of fire blackened wood, showing obvious use in the past as a fire pit. Thero bustled over to the stone circle and stacked small pieces of kindling in the center. He crouched low, using his hunting knife to shave curly, thin pieces of dry wood around the kindling.

Two quick strikes from his knife, and a small shower of sparks rolled onto the shavings, bringing a curl of smoke. The glowing embers ate greedily into the kindling and the surrounding bits of wood. Thero looked up and grinned, "There. Soon we will have a blazing fire."

"Grandfather, I get the feeling that you have been this way before," Nathel said. He looked suspiciously at the older man as he bustled around the cave.

Thero stopped and stared at their packs as Nathel spoke. His head was bowed. "Nathel, I was not always a mere shepherd. Many years ago, I was much more than that. Yes, I have been this way before, but not for many years. Things will have changed, and we must be careful if we are to survive. The world that I knew is gone and the world now is a much more dangerous place."

Nathel stared hard at the older man, feeling slightly betrayed. It was not like his grandfather to hide the truth from him. He opened his mouth to demand an answer but Thero beat him to it.

Thero turned and regarded him, "Try not to worry about it, Nathel. I can offer you my promise that I have never meant any harm to you. I will do all in my power to protect you."

Nathel nodded and went back to spreading out his thick woolen blankets. The floor of the cave was soft and sandy, and the blankets would make it even more comfortable to sleep. The fire blazed away merrily, and the smoke pulled up into a small opening in the roof. Nathel watched Thero produce a small iron skillet. He dropped two thick pieces of mutton into the pan and surrounded it with slices of potatoes. They both crunched on a raw carrot while the meat sizzled and the potatoes fried. Outside the cave the storm raged, dropping torrents of rain and washing all signs of their passing from the face of the grassy trails.

"Eat up, son. We need to eat this mutton in the first day or two. The wrapping will only hold the spoiling at bay for two days at most. After that, it's jerky, bread, cheese, and some carrots. We will only pass through one town the way we are going, because I want to avoid populated places. There are too many prying eyes in the lowlands right now," Thero said. He sounded mysterious when he spoke and Nathel felt a shiver of excitement run down his back. Here he was, finally, on a trip outside of his small village, no sheep to worry about, no more Widow Marith poking her nose into their business.

"Grandpa, why was Widow Marith screaming when you woke me last night?"

Nathel watched his grandfather's face closely as he asked the question and he noted that the older man's face remained carefully neutral.

"She overreacted, Boy. It is nothing to worry about."

"Why, Grandpa?" Nathel persisted. He would not allow the question to be shrugged off that easily.

"You were dreaming weren't you? Do you remember what you were dreaming about?"

Nathel concentrated hard on the few glimpses he remembered from that night: flashes of a massive wolf circling him, and walls of gray mist surrounding him on all sides. "Not much," he finally admitted. "I remember wolves, and sharp teeth closing on my neck."

"While you were dreaming and I was trying to wake you, every wolf for miles around took up the call of the fallen. Imagine hundreds of wolves howling at once, and when you awoke, they all stopped instantly. That was why she was screaming. She considers you one of The Fallen, Boy."

"The Fallen are servants of the Dark One," Nathel avoided saying the name.

"Yes, there are many in the world now who have given themselves fully to the great demon."

Nathel's blank look must have told Thero that he would have to explain. He leaned back against the cave wall and motioned for Nathel to sit down across from him. Outside the cave, the storm broke in all its fury, unleashing a constant roar of lightening and rolling peals of thunder. Thankfully, the ground outside the cave sloped downward and the rain formed small streams flowing away from the cliff.

"Most of what I will tell you has been passed down from generation to generation since the making of the world. It is said that the lost Books of Anatari tell the complete story of how the world was created, but they have been lost since the War of Heaven. Ages ago, the world was formed from nothing, spoken into existence by Elutha the father of the elementals. The work was vast and the will of Elutha held everything together. According to legend, at first there was nothing except him, then he spoke and substance came out of nothing. Then he spoke again and the world formed and the sky was filled with stars. According to long lost legends he made the Elementals to aid in his work. Thousands of elementals each designated to a task, and He assigned powers and skills for them to accomplish their tasks."

"Some were responsible for the trees; others planted carpets of green grass. Thousands wielded huge hammers, making the mountains jagged and the oceans deep. Each had a purpose and each strove to fulfill their task. No one knows how long it took the world to form. Years have little meaning for the One who made time."

"After the world was made, Elutha revealed the five mortal races: humans, dwarves, orkin, dragon, and elf. The most numerous now are humans and orkin. We are also the most short-lived of the mortal races. We count our years in decades, while the rest of the races count their time in centuries, such as the dragon's millennium. When the creator made his will known that the mortal races were to be given rule of the world, Bedbezdal protested. You see, He looked with pride on the world he helped create and wanted dominion over it for himself. He forgot that he was not the one that created the world. Many of the elementals joined him in his battle seeking greater glory for themselves. Half of the elemental host sought to unseat Elutha. In that day battles took place across the entire world, from the heavens above to the deepest pits of hell. The very existence of the universe seemed to hang in the balance. Led by Anatari, the loyal elementals fought bravely to save the world and nearly destroyed all living creatures in the process. Stories etched in caves in the depths of the lands say that the world shook, ocean's dried up, and the heavens rained fire. During the battle the fabric of the universe began to unravel, the elements flowed together and the end of the world was at hand. In order to stop the destruction, Elutha stood and waved his hand. In a moment the battles froze, and the fallen elementals began to see that even their battle had its beginning in the creator. They had been given a choice and they choose poorly. They were sent to the mortal plane to await judgment and given leave to test the mortal races. This gave us free will to choose our path. In the same moment Anatari and her Elemental warriors were sent to protect what had been created and to safe guard our choice."

Nathel listened with rapt attention.

"As the years passed and the mortal races grew in numbers, Bedbezdal, the master of the Fallen, used his power to warp the races, combining them with animals to create five more races: goblin, minotaur, medusa, wraith, and balisk--all dedicated to evil. Although he lacked the power to create beings outright, he was able to tempt mortals. Many gave themselves to his power willingly, and then he was able to create his monstrous forces."

"Most of the fallen elementals were changed when they were cast from the heavens. Bound to the world or to the underworld, they are no longer able to fly to the heavens. Anatari and her Elementals that remained faithful have the strength to hold the Fallen at bay for as long as people who remember the creator remain in the world. Sadly, many have turned and they serve The Fallen. Therefore, they are also considered Fallen, working evil in dark places, waiting for the day when the evil one will be released from his prison far to the north. He will be once again free to physically move across the face of the world, seeking to bring the entire world under his rule."

Nathel sat spellbound as Thero spoke. He imagined winged beings filled with light battling dark smoking demons wreathed in flames.

"How do you know all this, Grandfather?" Nathel asked in a low voice, not wanting to interrupt the quietness of the moment but yearning to know more.

"Most of it is legend, son, Passed down from ages long gone. There are places in the world where the legends of old are still hallowed, not like in the human and orkin kingdoms that span much of the world.

Some still follow the old ways, thankfully not all have forgotten. Had all fallen away, the evil one would be free and all hope would be lost. All that would remain would be to wait for that certain coming judgment at the end of time," Thero said. He shook his head, "Evil will be the day when knowledge of the creator is cast aside. In that day, Bedbezdal's prison will crumble and war will come again to the world."

Nathel nodded.

"Even with all I know, Nathel, I cannot see the future. It is possible that all the world will turn its back on the creator. If that happens, we will all slip away into the grip of the evil one."

Nathel sighed, wishing he could know more, but it was obvious that his grandfather grew tired and silence descended on the cave. Or maybe Nathel thought that was all his grandfather knew, and therefore all he was able to reveal. Both fell into silent contemplation until they drifted off to sleep. The storm continued unabated outside, bringing life-giving water to the meadows and streams outside their shelter.

Chapter Five
The Fallen are Moving

he next morning dawned with a brilliant burst of sunshine, the light came seeping through the cave entrance and woke Nathel with a start. The fire had died during the night and Thero hurriedly prepared a cold breakfast. Marhuth stood hobbled outside the cave entrance munching on the wet thick grass.

"Come on, boy. It's time to get moving," Thero said, as he glanced at Nathel.

Thero grinned at him behind his gray beard and tossed him a piece of bread and a slice of cheese.

Crumbs were stuck in Thero's beard, making him a comical sight, but Nathel only rubbed his eyes, trying to clear the sleep from his head. Thero sighed, knowing that he hag given the boy much to think about the night before. Sadly, he knew there was much more to come.

Nathel grunted. He hated mornings. He stuffed the bread and cheese into his pocket to eat later and rolled his blanket up. Moments later it was stowed into his pack, which he carried outside and tied to Marhuth's broad back. A deep pool of rainwater collected in a rock basin nearby and offered them a clean source of water so they drank deeply before washing. Thero sighed as he slipped his arms into the cold water and cleaned off the travel dust of the day before.

"Come on boy, clean up before we leave," Thero said.

"Clean?" Nathel questioned as he looked down at the now murky water but his grandfather merely smiled and winked at him. With a sigh Nathel plunged his hands into the water and began to scrub vigorously.

The path down from the cave and back to the narrow trail was wet with mud and Nathel clutched at branches to avoid falling. They headed east, walking down the last of the Highland foothills and into the vast wilderness bordering the Dunhagmith Mountains.

The next four days passed quietly, and Nathel and Thero made good time in the lower meadows. Herds of mule deer watched the intruders as they passed through their quiet meadows. Five brown bears paused to inspect them on the third day and two silvertip bears rambled by on the fourth day standing twice as tall as Marhuth and weighing three times as much. Nathel stared at the hulking animals, but the bears simply looked up from their wanderings and then returned to their own business. On the morning of the sixth day, they crested a small hill and looked into the herding town of Rockcreek.

Nathel let out a low whistle. "They even have a wall! What a place." Thero chuckled.

"Well, it's the biggest town I've ever seen," Nathel said defensively. He tapped his staff against the ground in annoyance. Despite his feigned irritation he was excited at the prospect of seeing a real town.

"Rockcreek had maybe a thousand people the last time I passed through. It does look as though it has grown some in the last twelve years," Thero admitted. He stroked his beard as he looked down on the walled town. Nestled safely in the middle of a wide valley, a thick row of wooden poles surrounded the town. Squat log towers offered a slightly higher vantage point for the occasional watchers. Low mountains and foothills surrounded the valley on three sides and vast herds of cattle grazed across the fertile valley floor under the watchful eyes of scores of mounted herdsmen. To the south, Nathel noticed a line of long wooden buildings with a flurry of activity around them.

"What are those, Grandpa?"

"Tanneries, Boy. Rockcreek makes leather, raw leather that is sold across the lowlands. Come son, let's go find a comfortable bed. I would rather not sleep on the ground again tonight," Thero said. "Even more importantly I would like to find a tub of water and a cake of soap." He led Marhuth down the small switchback trail guiding them into the valley.

Nathel's mouth still hung open wide as they approached the wooden palisade that surrounded Rockcreek. The timbers raised to an even height of fifteen paces, and the gatehouse stood a good five paces taller. The wooden gate was banded with thick iron straps and coated with hides.

"Why are there hides on the gate?"

"The locals believe it will help ward off fires and evil spirits. It's all nothing but old wives tales and superstitious nonsense."

The wall timbers were sharpened at the top. Nathel notice half a score of sentries pacing the tops of the inner ramps, keeping a watchful eye at the surrounding mountains. Two men standing near the gatehouse stared idly at the steady stream of people coming and going. The manner of the gate guards seemed lax after seeing the watching archers pace the walls.

"At least we won't have to worry about wolves here," Nathel said. He made the comment to Thero as they entered the gate. He spoke in a low voice, but the reaction he got surprised him. His grandfather silenced him with an angry look and quick gesture with his free hand. Thero glanced over at the town guards, but both of the men seemed more interested in staying out of the bright sunshine than in listening to the conversations of the passing travelers.

"Watch what you say, boy," Thero said, his face red, eyebrows knit in irritation. Thero grabbed his arm and pulled Nathel off to the side of the wide avenue fifty paces inside the gate.

"What did I say?" Nathel asked. The confusion on his face was genuine and his grandfather stared hard at him. Nathel was genuinely confused and the look on his face must have convinced his grandfather.

"I keep forgetting you have never been outside the village. Let's find a spot to talk in private."

Thero led Nathel and Marhuth down the long dirt avenue. Crab apple trees lined the road on either side, covered in pink flowers. The fragrance drifted on the breeze and filled the air. After finding a shaded spot in a small grassy area off the avenue, they leaned up against an old oak tree. Thero studied the surroundings before beginning to explain. The oak was a massive edifice, and Nathel assumed it outdated the city built around it. With its branches reaching high into the sky, it had a body of leaves so thick it could hide a man.

Nathel stood beside Thero as he spoke in a low voice.

"We must not speak of encounters with wolves, or of fleeing from them. Most people consider wolves to be evil, and indeed, in this part of the world, they are right. Many wolves are servants of the Shadow and in league with The Fallen. Once branded as being in league with The Fallen, you will be arrested and in all likelihood disappear forever."

Nathel stared at his grandfather in amazement. "But we had nothing to do with it! It's hardly our fault that the wolves attacked us." Nathel said.

His voice rose alarmingly, drawing the attention of two men as they passed by.

"Too much sunlight today," Thero said. He grinned disarmingly at the men who were staring at them.

"Boy, I don't think you understand. People do not care why. All they care about is that, for some reason, you are connected with them," Thero said his voice so low that Nathel had to lean close to hear him. The two men shrugged, accepting the explanation, and continued on their way down the street.

"Now, let's drop the subject and find some warm food and a soft bed," Thero said. He turned and led Marhuth out from under the towering oak tree and down the street. Nathel stood staring at his grandfather as he retreated. Then he shook his head and broke into a jog down the packed dirt avenue. In the distance, Thero pointed out the sign of an inn hanging out over the street proclaiming rooms for rent.

Behind them in the small grassy lot, a shadow emerged from the leafy recesses of the old oak and dropped to the ground. He was small in stature with dirty, unkempt clothes and greasy hair. Dirt smudges covered his face. Hurriedly the small man glanced around, and then moved to the street. He spotted Nathel and Thero despite the afternoon crowd, and shadowed them down the street. When they stopped to examine an inn's colorful sign he moved closer, standing behind a nearby wagon. He watched as Nathel and his grandfather disappeared into the inn at the end of the avenue. Then he followed them inside.

Far to the north, massive peaks rose to towering heights, piercing the sky. The Mountains were so high they blocked the sun for much of the daytime. Scrub trees and bits of witch grass was all that grew in the rough ground, and the granite peaks were impassible. Separating the Dakretua Mountains from the low lands to the south was a towering cliff, thousands of paces tall. Stretching from one side of the mountain range to the other, the cliff stopped all travelers from entering or leaving the dark mountains.

One pass lead into the Dakretua Mountains, and it remained the only way to access the lands to the north. It consisted of a wide valley piercing the middle of the cliff, running north deep into the mountains. Though unexplored, rumors said it pierced to the very heart of the northlands. Blocking this valley at the edge of the cliff stood a thick-walled castle, the ever-vigilant Fortress of Winds. Controlled by a mysterious group, the fortress guarded the gateway to the mountains, denying entrance to all foolish enough to seek to travel into the dark mountains. The walls reached from granite cliff to granite cliff, controlling the entirety of the valley. Deep inside the fortress, the Chamber of Light guarded the one passage through the fortress, for only one hallway pierced the Fortress of Winds from side to side. All other paths ended in dead ends and lost mazes that ensnared any who tried to penetrate the fortress.

The Chamber of Light was a large room with an arching ceiling that disappeared into the distance. Standing directly in the center of the room was the unmoving figure of a warrior. Filling the room, the wind elemental, Miceali, stood guard. He watched and battled for thousands of years, protecting the chamber, and he would stand until Anatari told him to stop. He faced the entrance that led to the Dakretua Mountains waiting for any of the creatures seeking passage. To pierce the fortress they would be forced to pass him. His hands rested on a gigantic two-handed sword. Plate armor covered every inch of his figure, leaving only his eyes visible behind the helm. A round shield hung at his waist.

Miceali moved his head slightly; a rustling sound drifted from the passage outside the Chamber. Carefully he lifted his sword and moved forward, weapon held ready to strike. It would not be the first time that creatures had tried to enter the Chamber of Light nor would it be the last. It had been many years since the last invader managed to reach this far, but it was not unheard of. Shrinking his size until he more resembled a tall human he waited as the rustling sound increased. Born to fight, he relished defending the chamber, fulfilling his duty to his master.

He stood waiting as the handle turned on the door, and without a sound the door swung wide. Miceali stepped forward, sword held high and his powerful voice rang out his challenge.

He froze, the figure in the door smiled. The challenge on Miceali's lips died, replaced with a scream. A single scream echoed torn from a being that knew no fear.

"No!" The scream of the elemental warrior tore through the room and echoed down the hallways. The warriors of the Wind Protectors that helped maintain the Fortress of Winds stopped where they stood and listened. As one, they rushed towards the walls, weapons drawn. The battle on the walls was short-lived, the defenders were slain to the man. Not one lived through the evening.

Nathel sat down on the rough wooden stool opposite Thero and leaned his staff up against the table. A shabbily-dressed innkeeper motioned for the thin serving girl to take care of them. She tossed her tussled red hair over her shoulder and flounced across the wooden floor. The innkeeper snorted and Nathel saw him retrieve another dirty cup from the counter and began wiping the thick cloudy glass.

"What's your pleasure, gents?"

Nathel nodded to the young girl, smiling shyly at her. Thero snorted.

"What's on the menu for the evening meal, young lady?"

"The cook has a haunch of beef roasting over the fire. It's well-done, but tastes good. The rest of today's menu is beans, potatoes, and warm bread. Two silver pieces each for room and tonight's meal."

"Throw in four slices of fresh bread tomorrow morning for that price," Thero countered. He waited for her to glance at the innkeeper, who listened from the deserted bar. Nathel saw him nod to the unasked question. She turned back and nodded, winking one pale, blue eye at Nathel, "Done, good sirs."

Thero nodded, leaning back in the wooden chair waiting for her to fetch the meals. With a warm smile she bustled to the kitchen at the back of the inn. Nathel caught a glimpse of the large room through a pair of swinging doors at the back of the common room. A large open-face fire pit burned in the corner, sending its heat and smoke up the stone chimney. Over the fire, he saw the over-sized portion of beef rotating slowly, the handle cranked by a young boy.

"Tomorrow we will strike south into the mountains. When we reach the river Rilt, then we will begin the hard part of our journey," Thero said. He fell quiet as the door of the tavern opened, and a small, greasy man slipped through the door. The short man looked long and hard at them, then found himself a seat in the corner of the bar and order a drink. The waitress gave the newcomer a nasty look. Nathel watched as she sloshed his drink down spilling some over the side, the liquid running down the polished surface of the table and dripping to the floor.

"Careful, wench," he snarled. His voice was high-pitched and the young waitress harrumphed as she collected his money and left the table.

Nathel noticed she seemed a bit friendlier when she brought the two steaming platters of food. She deftly set them out on the table.

"Thank you," Nathel said. He offered her a smile and she returned it, taking longer then normal to collect the four silvers. A swing of her long skirt revealed tanned legs almost to the knees then she made her way back to the bar. Thero grinned, shaking his head, and then dug into his platter. He ate with a vigor that Nathel had not seen in a long time. Nathel finished his food a little more slowly and then leaned back in the chair. He watched as the local townsfolk began to drift into the inn. By the time the moon had risen, the common room was full and the noise had risen to a dull rumble. The wide area became a sea of moving bodies and colorful outfits. Traders up from the lowlands clustered around the warm fire, and local tanners and shepherds laughed and sang.

"They come to buy the wool and beef," Thero motioned to the traders. Moments later, music began playing across the crowded room. Two women in colorful outfits both played three-stringed instruments that Nathel had never seen before. Thero sat back and Nathel was glad. He enjoyed the noise and movement.

The moon rode high in the night sky when Thero finally motioned for him to follow him. A wide oaken staircase led to the second floor and the room that they had rented. Thero stopped at the top of the stairs in a dark corner hidden by shadows and motioned Nathel to step out of view.

"There he goes," Thero motioned. Nathel watched the small dirty man as he exited the common room.

"So what," Nathel said. He yawned indifferently, wanting more then anything to go to bed.

"What sort of man comes to a common room, orders one drink, and then leaves without ever drinking it. I think we have drawn the attention of someone already. The walls have ears, Boy. You would do well to remember that."

They walked to the room at the far end of the hall and opened the thick, oaken door. The room was wide and held two beds, one against each wall. A single window looked out over the avenue they had walked earlier that day. Thero closed the door and dropped the heavy bar into place across the door.

"We must be careful, Nathel. You go to sleep. I'll keep watch for a while."

Nathel nodded and dropped his staff to the floor, collapsing into the nearest bed. Sleep came immediately--deep and dreamless.

"Psst, Son. Wake up."

Nathel awoke with a start. Thero placed a hand over his mouth and motioned for him to be quiet. He nodded, watching Thero motioned to the locking bar over the door. Glinting in the light of the moon, a slender knife blade slipped through the crack around the door and began sliding the thick oak piece up slowly. Nathel rose to his feet, moving slowly to avoid making the floor boards creak. He reached to the wall and took up his ironwood staff, a step to the left put him between the wall and the bed. Nathel wanted enough room to fight but not so much that he could be surrounded. Thero took up a defensive position directly in the center of the room his staff held ready. Nathel watched a second blade slip through the crack by the door and held the locking bar from crashing to the floor.

"Here they come, boy. Get ready," Thero whispered. He nodded at the door.

The fight started with a rush, the locking bar flew to the side as the door swung wide. Three men rushed into the room their eyes widening in surprise as they faced Thero's staff. Nathel watched his grandfather explode into action, the staff spinning in circles slapping the arms and legs that came close. Despite the loss of their surprise attack, the attackers were veteran warriors. They pushed forward working to back Thero and Nathel into the corner. Swords flashed amid grunts and the thuds of the staff striking limbs.

It seemed to Nathel the harder they fought the more Thero gained the upper hand. The ironwood lashed out striking hard, leaving bruises and cuts each time it connected. Two of the men fell back into a defensive posture working their attacks together to keep the spinning staff at bay.

Nathel watched from the side, his staff held ready. The man closest to him noticed him after launching an overhand blow at Thero.

"Take the Prophet. I will get Chosen one."

He stepped back from Thero and rushed at Nathel swinging his sword in wide arcs.

The two men threw themselves at Thero in an attempt to bury him under a flurry of blows. Nathel lost sight of his grandfather, his staff ticking off the sword. He faced a seasoned fighter wearing baggy black pants and a brown shirt.

Nathel waited as the man advanced quickly his body balanced, sword and long dagger moved in fast strikes. He struck out with his staff picking off the first strikes and then stepping back, trying to regain the lost space.

His opponent moved forward shifting his weapons lower and attacking again.

Nathel shifted the angle of his staff and once again met the attacks, his staff absorbing the blows. Turning the staff in his hand he jabbed.

Once, twice, a third jab.

The man stepped away two steps, Nathel smiled thinking that he had gained the upper hand. Then his smile faltered as sword and dagger leapt forward, striking hard at his head and stomach in separate slicing routines. Nathel swung his staff desperately, a slapping blow sent the sword wide and he sucked in his stomach and leapt back.

"Not bad boy, most fall for that little trick."

Nathel ignored the raspy voice, focusing his concentration on the weaving sword.

His attacker wielded a short sword and a wicked looking curved dagger. The polished iron of the blades shimmered as the light of the moon broke through the window. The clouds that had hidden it raced off, and the glowing orb filled the small room with a light that made the shadows dance across the walls.

Nathel spun his staff hand over hand, the ironwood deflecting the bladed weapons easily. Catching the top of the staff with his right hand Nathel used his left to snap the bottom of the staff forward striking at his opponent's legs. The short man skittered back; a narrow brimmed hat was pulled low on his face, and his arms protected by hard leather sleeves that fit over his shirt.

"Time to die boy," He said. The words whispered so lightly that Nathel almost missed them, snapping his staff back to the upright guard position Nathel waited for the swordsman to attack.

He came in a rush trying to bury Nathel in the corner of the room, sword and dagger dancing from all sides in an attempt to skewer the young man on their wicked blades. Nathel leapt to the side using his staff to vault onto the nearby bed. Balancing on the soft mattress Nathel retracted his staff and swung hard for his attacker's unprotected head. His staff whistled through the air just missing the roof and came down hard on the upraised sword. The man brought the weapon up to intercept the staff, but he had little idea of the force carried in an ironwood staff. Nathel's hard blow shattered the thick sword, sending shards flying in all directions and drawing lines of blood across the thin man's face.

Nathel carried through the blow as Thero as taught him, using his staff to transfer the entire force of the blow into his attacker. The glancing blow struck the short man's head, and a grunt of pain slipped from the man's mouth as he staggered backwards. He swung his dagger weakly in front of his body. Nathel stepped down off the bed and advanced, his staff held high. One look at the determination in Nathel's eyes and he turned and fled, leaving his two friends to continue the battle one on one.

"Nathel, take the one of the left," Thero said, his voice casual as he deftly deflected the combined attacks from two more short swords. Both men were swinging wildly in an attempt to get past the spinning staff, and both were bleeding from various wounds across the face and hands where Thero had delivered sound blows.

With a feral snarls both men broke from the battle and rushed for the door, fleeing down the hall. Nathel lashed out swiftly as the second of the two attackers passed him, and landed a hard blow to the back of his leg. The audible sound of the breaking bone snapped loudly in the sudden quiet of the moonlit room. A cry of pain broke from the man's mouth as he collapsed to the floor.

"Hold, Nathel," Thero said. He motioned for him to hold his ground.

"They will escape, Grandfather," Nathel said. He moved once again towards the door, determined to make the ruffians pay.

"Nathel!" This time Thero's voice echoed commandingly and brought Nathel up short of the door.

"There maybe more lurking in the halls, and with different weapons." Thero walked slowly, crossing the room to the still-moaning black-clad attacker lying on the wooden floor. Standing well back from the door, Thero reached out, using his staff to slide the door open. As the door moved two crossbow bolts sliced through the air, narrowly missing the staff. A third bolt struck the wounded man on the floor, penetrating his skull and killing him instantly.

Nathel dove for the floor, avoiding the open window and wiggling into the corner of the dimly lit room.

"What do we do?" Nathel whispered. Wide-eyed, he stared at the dead man lying on the floor. The full force of their situation dawned on him with the force of a staff blow. He shuddered, trying not to look at the unmoving form of the man on the floor, the bolt standing up at a weird angle.

Reflecting up from the ground floor in the cloudy glass of the window came a flickering sickly yellow glow. Thero rushed to the window, glanced quickly through the pane, and then leapt back from view. Loud crashes accompanied the whistling sound of two more crossbow bolts. The bolts smashed the glass and stuck in the far wall humming with the force of the impact.

Nathel looked at Thero, his eyes wide with fright. His hands shook as they clutched the ironwood staff.

"Grab your pack. We must move quickly."

Nathel retrieved his pack from the floor near his bed and stood defensively to the side of the door. Thero slipped the straps of his pack over his shoulders and then stopped near the door next to Nathel.

"Follow me, Boy. Whatever you do, stay in my shadow, understand?"

Nathel nodded mutely, his mind struggling with the thought that people were trying to kill him. Thero stared hard at him.

"Stay with me, son. Don't let your mind be your worst enemy. Let your body react to the training we did all winter. Your mind will simply get in the way and slow down your reactions."

Nathel nodded and brought his staff up to the guard position, waiting for Thero to make his move.

"No time like the present, son. Time to trust in the elements to protect us."

Nathel rushed into the hallway behind him. The whistle of crossbow bolts and the snapping of the weapons echoed in the narrow hallway. Nathel ran directly behind Thero. He could see little in the dark hall. Thero's staff spun a blur of motion, his staff striking faster then Nathel could follow. Long strides carried them down the narrow hall and Thero exploded into the knot of men at the end of the hall like a bolt of lightening. Weapons flew into the air and the cries of men joined the thudding of the spinning ironwood staff at the top of the stairs. Then, as suddenly as it had begun, Nathel and Thero were vaulting down the stairs and rushing across the common room. The room remained empty and they crashed through the swinging doors into the kitchen. Thero stood at the backdoor of the kitchen breathing hard, and Nathel heard thumping as the last body rolled down the stairs.

Thero winked at Nathel and grinned. "Nothing like a little exercise to help warm the blood and clear the mind."

The planks of the kitchen door were carved of solid oak and were extremely heavy. Nathel watched as Thero placed an ear to the door and listened. From the front of the inn, cries of "Fire!" began. The alarm bell in the town square rang wildly, calling out the warning.

Thero nodded once again and rushed through the door with Nathel in tow. This time the yard behind the inn remained clear, but Thero did not stop until they were inside the small barn behind the inn. Nathel looked about as they burst through the door of the barn; but the only sight that greeted him was that of the four animals stabled there munching away. Marhuth dozed lightly on his feet as Thero rushed over and slipped the packs on his back.

"Come on, Boy. Give me your pack. We must be gone before anything else happens."

Nathel nodded and slipped his pack over the left side of Marhuth's back. He looped the rope around his belly and fastened it to the harness. The old war horse opened his eyes sleepily and looked at the two hurried humans in irritation. He huffed twice and then took a mouthful of the sweet clover in his manger. He shook his head when Thero grabbed the rope and headed for the side door.

A short time later, Thero led them to the still-open town gate. The sleepy sentry merely glanced at them as they left. Despite the distant fire bell, he must have decided that an old man and his grandson were not a threat as long as they were leaving.

The moon shone brightly and Nathel glanced back twice before the town faded from sight behind a thick stand of fir trees. He saw a bright glow against the night sky as the inn burned. Thero nodded sadly when he pointed out the column of smoke against the moonlight.

"I told you not to mention the wolves. Someone must have heard our conversation. We must be careful. Word will spread among the groups that make up The Fallen. The people of the low lands have turned far in the last decades. Some places have fully given themselves to Bedbezdal, the ruler of the darkness."

"I caused that," Nathel said with a shudder. "My big mouth and careless words might have killed innocent people." Tears rolled down his face as the guilt filled his mind. "Grandfather, I'm sorry," Nathel's voice whispered. He leaned on the bare trunk of a nearby tree, his staff hanging limply in his hand.

Thero stopped. He turned, and walked back to where Nathel stood. "Boy, you did not know any better. These things happen. Whatever happens now we must remember that there are powerful forces at work. We must be careful and watch our words and actions. The Fallen have watchers everywhere. They are constantly seeking a way to release Bedbezdal from his prison to try and bind the last of Elemental Protectors for all time. If they succeed in binding the Elemental Protectors here on the mortal world, they would take possession of the entire world before any could stop them."

Nathel still slumped against the tree as he listened. He jumped when Thero grabbed his shoulders and gave him a gentle shake. "Son, bad things happen sometimes. But Anatari will protect us and those few who still serve the creator, even through the darkest times. What will you do now? Will you allow the Fallen to win? Will you give up here and now or will you continue with me to our appointed meeting, and help me discover why the wolves are pursuing us?"

Nathel straightened slowly and wiped his tear-stained cheeks. He reached down and retrieved his ironwood staff from the ground where it fallen, "I will not give up, Grandfather."

"Good boy. I trained you better then that."

"Grandpa, there is something I am confused about," Nathel started hesitantly. "You said that if the people of the lowlands think we are part of the Fallen we would be in danger. But you just said that the Fallen are everywhere and seem to have grown so powerful that they have people all over the low lands."

"Well boy," Thero started. "What I said was true and odd as it sounds. Many of the people will attack anything that they link to the Fallen. However, given the chance to return to the Creator they turn their backs instead. In that way they have given themselves into the power of the evil one, sometimes refusing to accept truth is the same as actively pursuing evil itself."

"I think I see," Nathel said even though trying to follow the thoughts sent his mind spinning. Finally he just accepted what his grandfather had said and yawned ponderously. Nathel walked beside his grandfather and they continued up the sloping trail. The road took them south towards the rugged wilderness. Moonlight streamed down from the round silver ball hanging high in the sky above their heads. Nathel yawned when they reached the bottom of the hill and started once again up the next hill.

"We will find a place to rest for the remainder of the night, and tomorrow we will enter the most dangerous part of a smaller range of mountains called the Archol Mountains. We must be fully rested for the journey across the Burning Wastes and hope that the water holes have not gone dry."

Nathel nodded, his mind so filled with sleep that he suddenly found they had crested the next hill. Thero pointed to a nearby stand of fir and spruce trees fifty paces off the narrow dirt trail. Rockcreek had disappeared from view; no sound of pursuit could be heard in the stillness of the night.

The fir trees were thick and fully matured, sending their prickly boughs dozens of paces into the air. The trees were fully intertwined along the ground to a height almost taller than Nathel. Pushing aside the thick branches Thero cleared a path for Nathel to pull the reluctant Marhuth through the narrow gap. Once inside the circle of fir trees, three massive hardwoods had grown to towering heights, two oaks and a green spruce. They provided a thick layer of cover. There were signs of other travelers using the encircling trees for shelter. A blackened fire pit was placed in such a way that Nathel decided any smoke would be so dissipated when it cleared the trees that it would be invisible. A thick spongy layer of leaves had built up along the sides of the fire pit and it bounced with each step he took. Nathel spread his blanket over the leaves and found it quite comfortable.

"Go to sleep boy," Thero said. He smiled at him and nodded, "I will hobble Marhuth so he does not feel the need to wander."

Nathel nodded sleepily, his eyes opening and closing as he struggled to remain awake for some odd reason. Then, in an instant, sleep whisked his weary mind away.

Chapter Six
The Burning Wastes

 athel ran as fast as he could, stretching his long legs out in an effort to cover more ground. The streets of Rockcreek flashed past. Behind his fleeing form, men with long black cloaks and steel weapons gave chase. He clutched his staff in his hands tightly. Side streets offered the same glints of shiny metal and flowing robes. The flashing eyes of the wolves mirrored his flight. Nathel's mind raced; fear pulsed in his mind and sweat dripped into his eyes, making it hard to see.

"Help me!" Nathel screamed. He sought desperately for someone to come to his aid, but no sign of life showed in the darkened houses. Loose stones rolled under his feet as he dodged to the side, then careened into a door hanging slightly ajar. The house dominated the block, as it was much larger then the other houses on the street. The bodies of the townsfolk lay dead on the floor, and the bloody tracks of massive paws were scattered about the wooden floor.

"There is no one left alive to help me," Nathel panted. He glimpsed glowing eyes in the door and once again ran.

Nathel went as fast as his long legs would carry him, careening out the back door. He turned down an empty side street, finally breaking out into the town square. All around the square faces and flashing eyes appeared. Every direction he turned was blocked by the Fallen. The shuffling forms of men and woman dressed in black cloaks and carrying bloody weapons appeared in every street. They surrounded him, cutting off all avenue of escape. Nathel stood by the well, turning slowly. The pack leader that had haunted his dream stepped from the shadows and began approaching.

Nathel shook with fear, and despair filled his mind paralyzing his body. Then he heard something that helped calm his mind.

"Nathel." The whisper came in the back of his consciousness. Thero called his name again, helping him to regain his calm and remember who he was.

Nathel's breathing slowed as his mind calmed. One small call had been all it had taken to bring his mind back from the edge of insanity. He brought his staff up to the upright defensive position. He held the top of the staff out above his head, and his hands gripped the cool wood, bringing him a bit of reassurance.

"I do not fear you any more," Nathel said. He proclaimed the words loudly.

"But you should fear me, Boy. I know who you are, and I am coming to kill you." The pack leader appeared in front of him, and the rest of the town faded from view, leaving them standing next to the empty well.

"I am a simple shepherd. Why do you haunt me? I am no hero or warrior."

"Ah, Boy, you do not even know who you are. You will, someday, if I let you survive till that day. But as much as I would enjoy battling you when you have reached your full potential, I have been given my orders: all who bear the mark are to be killed. You were condemned even before that old fool you follow saved you from the fire of your family's castle. You are not as common as he would have you believe."

"What do you know of my family?" Nathel faltered. His voice cracked, betraying his desperation to know more of his mother and father.

"They are with me, Nathel, bound with me in the depths of my icy prison far to the north. My servants dragged them from the fires and I will keep them here forever."

Nathel stumbled against the well, his breath coming in short gasps. On the backs of his hands the elemental symbols pulsed powerfully. Before his eyes the vision of a man and woman bound in chains and burning with eternal fire floated.

"I could set them free, Nathel, if you swore your soul to me. I would set them free in exchange for your life."

"How can a wolf have the power to do this?" Nathel's mind spun in circles.

"I offer you your mother and father in exchange for your eternal soul. Take it or leave it. Know that if you refuse, they will be tortured night and day until you accept."

"Nathel." Once again Nathel could hear the small voice calling him back to consciousness. The pack leader in front of him started to fade.

"You will not escape me that easily, Boy," the creature roared. The massive wolf lunged with lightening speed. He crossed the remaining space of the town square in three tremendous bounds.

Nathel straightened, watching silently as the wolf bore down on him, staff held ready until the last possible moment. The wolf leapt into the air, his flashing jaws aiming for Nathel's unprotected throat. The ironwood staff went into motion as the beast left the ground. Whistling around in a lighting fast strike the hard wood impacted the side of the leaping wolf and sent the creature rolling head over heels.

The impact of the staff woke Nathel from his dream and he stared up into the leafy branches high above him. Thero sat watching him from across the fire,

"The wolves are moving again, Boy, but I think you know that already, don't you?"

"Yes, they are trying to kill me," Nathel leaned forward, propping his body up on his elbows. He looked down his staff and noticed the far end of the staff. A small tuft of fur stuck to the wood.

"The dreams can be very real, Son. You must be careful. If things get too desperate remember that you are in control of the dream, not the wolf. It is your mind, not his. Never pass over into his mind during your battle, if you cross into his mind you will only escape by killing him. He is a powerful foe."

"He told me he was going to kill me, Grandpa. Why, Grandfather?"

"You are special Nathel, your family was special."

"The wolf said he had my mother and father captive, Grandpa," Nathel's voice came out as a whisper.

"That cannot be, son. Your family followed the old gods."

"I SAW THEM, bound in chains and burning," he sobbed. Tears flowed freely down his cheeks.

Thero frowned, "Such a thing is not possible, Nathel. The creature you face is more than just a fallen elemental. Bedbezdal must believe that the

Creator has given up on the world. He must be closer to breaking free of his prison then I thought possible."

"What do you mean, he."

"You saw a vestige of the Dark One, Nathel. The bonds of his prison have all but been set free. The Elemental pillars that guard his fortress must be fading quickly. I hope we are not too late to stop him from taking this world completely, there are so few faithful left."

"Grandpa, when I saw my parents, two symbols glowed on my hands."

"What did they look like Nathel?"

"One was a cross. The other looked round and blue. I saw it before just as the rains began falling."

"The water seal, symbol of the ancient water elementals." Thero fell silent and Nathel could almost see his mind racing.

"We must hurry. The Dark One will be free soon if he is assaulting the seven elemental pillars themselves."

Nathel stared hard across the small fire that crackled in the shallow pit. He wiped his eyes on the back of his hand and took deep breaths to calm himself.

"Go back to sleep Nathel, the wolf will not bother you again tonight. I think you taught him a lesson," Thero motioned to the fur still stuck to the staff.

Nodding, Nathel leaned back into his blanket and was asleep almost immediately - this time his dreams were quiet.

Nathel opened his eyes slowly, squinting at the sun riding high in the sky. "Thero, why didn't you wake me? We could be leagues down the trail by now." He rolled from his blanket and rubbed his hands through his hair. Near the small fire, Thero knelt with a sharp knife in hand.

"You needed the sleep, Son," Thero replied. He turned back to the tiny piece of broken mirror leaning against a rock near the fire. With a steady hand he trimmed the stray hairs from his long beard.

Nathel sighed. He quickly folded his blanket and retrieved two pieces of warm bacon and a slice of bread sitting in a iron pan near the dying fire.

"In two more days we arrive at the edge of the Burning Wastes. Soon you will be thankful for the extra rest. There is little shade in those lands and even less water."

He ate as they packed, carrying the leather sacks to Marhuth and tying them into place. Marhuth huffed at the weight looking up from tuft of grass he cropped right to the ground.

"Let's go, son."

Nathel waited as Thero pulled back the thick branches, allowing him and Marhuth to slip through the narrow opening. The dirt track took them south, ever closer to the mountains in the distance, jagged peaks that pierced the air. Unlike the mountains where Nathel spent his childhood raising sheep, these peaks were barren of vegetation. Hot winds howled down from the peaks, venting an ominous sound across the foothills.

"The winds sweep in from the Burning Wastes to the east. The air is tainted with the desert winds. Water is scarce and most living things avoid these mountains," Thero said when Nathel raised the question.

"At least the smart ones do," Nathel muttered.

Thero chuckled as they walked towards the distant peaks, nodding his head in agreement.

Hours later the foothills climbed suddenly, leading up to a narrow pass. Marhuth struggled to keep his footing on the slippery shale that covered the trail leading between two low peaks. These were the first mountains of the massive range.

The sun beat down with an intensity that made Nathel feel like he stepped on hot coals. Each breath became a struggle and sweat poured from his face. Marhuth panted deeply as he struggled to keep his body moving. The stallion was streaked with sweat and they stopped often to water the laboring horse.

They crossed over the narrow pass between two jagged peaks and started down the far side of the mountain. Nathel could see a stream running down the valley between the arms of the mountains. Sheltered from the sun the air grew cold

"It's like the warmth of the sun was avoiding the areas between the mountains."

"Strange things have been seen in dark places of these peaks."

Nathel shuddered. In the distance, the howl of a hunting wolf punctuated Thero's words.

The water in the small stream was cold to the point of freezing. He shivered as he dipped his hands in the water to take a sip. It smelled odd and left a taste that lingered on his tongue as he filled the water skins.

"How can it go from searing heat on one side of the mountain to freezing on this side?"

"These mountains have always defied nature in a way. Maybe that is why even the animals do not stray into their domain."

Thero led them east, turning to follow the small stream. A game trail cut along the edge of the water, but it showed little sign of use. Brush and thickets threatened to overrun it in many places. At times the water was so narrow Nathel jumped from side to side with little effort.

They made a cold camp that night alongside the water, as no trees were visible in the distance. Twin rocks the size of their cottage provided them with a tiny amount of protection from the howling winds that rose even more powerful as night fell.

Shivering and cold, Nathel wrapped himself in his cloak and his blanket. He huddled with his back to the boulder, trying to avoid the gusts threatening to tear them from the mountainside. Marhuth shifted uneasily; he stayed close, adding his warmth to the sheltered area. Nathel noticed Thero standing near the stream watching the array of colors spreading across the horizon as the hidden sun faded from the sky. In the distance, Nathel thought he could hear the howl of a lone wolf hunting the forgotten trails of the foreboding peaks.

Morning brought a lessening of the wind but held other surprises for the cold, weary travelers.

"Grandfather! The water is gone," Nathel yelled. He stood near the dried stream bed waving his arms.

Thero straightened. The leather straps of his pack forgotten as he furrowed his eye brow at Nathel.

"What are you talking about, Boy," Thero said.

"The stream is completely dried up," Nathel replied. He jogged back to where Thero had set the pack down.

"Show me."

Thero followed him back, moving nimbly around the rocky terrain. A thick stand of brambles blocked the mountain stream from view. After skirting the thorns they stopped.

The gushing water from the night before was gone. No sign of the water remained; the muddy dirt at the bottom of the bed had cracked and turned powdery to the touch.

Thero knelt next to where the stream had been and touched his fingers to the dry ground. Lifting them to his nose, he sniffed the dirt.

"Not even a hint of moisture left in the soil."

Nathel watched as Thero stared long and hard at the dry streambed.

"Come, we must be gone from this place. The protective power from the elementals is fading quickly. The end is coming fast."

He rose to his feet and motioned Nathel to follow him. Nathel's heart raced as they returned to the camp and hastily packed the remaining items. Marhuth shifted irritably. The war horse seemed to sense the unease and his actions mirrored theirs.

Thero led them once again along the narrow trail to the east, moving along the now dry stream bed. Small puffs of dust billowed into the air as their feet rose and fell. The howling winds fell silent and the air grew oppressive as the sun rose and fell in the clear sky. Not a cloud could be seen anywhere. Evening fell quickly and Nathel stopped to stare when the Burning Wastes came into view. He searched for signs of life on the rolling dunes. Endless hills of white sand stretched out of sight to the east, north, and south. No trees or grass grew in the parched desert. The only changes came where jagged outcroppings of bleached stone broke the desert floor.

"How can we cross that?" Nathel said.

He hurried to catch up as Thero led the tired Marhuth down the narrow slope. The air had cooled slightly during the last half of the day, but the approaching desert made the temperature soar again.

"Very carefully, son. Very carefully. Last time I traveled the Burning Wastes there were two pools of water, deep oases in the middle of the desert, protected by the power of the water elementals. They offered hope to weary travelers. Anatari willing, they are still there. The first is two days travel from the end of this streambed, directly east. The second is three days journey east and a bit south."

Nathel stared out across the sands as he listened.

"But it is so hot."

"If we travel at night when it is cooler, we should be across the Wastes in six days," Thero said. He motioned for Nathel to follow him down the slope.

"You want us to start across tonight?" His voice was disbelieving. Nathel stared at the sand once more, a cold sweat breaking across his forehead.

"Safer to start now, then starting during the heat of the day."

"What if the oasis is gone?"

"Then we will all perish and Anatari will be defeated. He and all who serve the creator will be banished to the same icy prison where Bedbezdal has spent thousands of years."

"Are you saying that all hope for the world rests with just us?" Nathel transferred his gaze to his grandfather. The ominous forgotten for the moment.

"Yes."

Nathel fell silent, his mind trying to grasp the enormity of the events going around him.

"Come now, no need for such a long face. I have served Anatari for my entire life. He will not surrender to the Dark One without a fight. Now, we dare not wait until tomorrow. With the stream dried up, we have precious little water. We must complete the first leg of the journey. If either of the oases is dried up, we may not make it across."

Nathel stood where he had stopped. He still balked at the idea of traveling when they could not even know if they would survive the trip.

"Can't we go around the sands? Why risk death?"

Thero sighed; Nathel noticed that the warm winds were already drawing a slight sheen of sweat across both of their foreheads.

"To go around the Wastes would take a score of days. The Burning Wastes are not particularly wide but they extend many hundreds of leagues to the south. To the north the lowlands will bring us in contact with the creatures of the Fallen. Behind us the wolves have caught our scent and are closing in. We must escape them."

Almost on cue a lone howl sounded in the distance to the west, and other voices answered in force from both the south and the north.

"I have never seen a wolf that would dare enter the Wastes. That would be certain death for them. They must travel around and by then we will be safe where they cannot reach us," Thero said. He finished speaking and offered a shrug to Nathel.

"Therefore, we must take the chance that the oases have not dried up. We must hope that the Elemental Protectors have not faded completely from this world. And we must cross quickly," Thero finished. He turned and moved out, leading the reluctant warhorse out onto the drifting sands.

Nathel stared at him until the wolves howled again, this time the sound was much closer. Pushing his confusion to the side, he started forward, hurrying to catch up. The sweat rolled from his brow as he struggled to climb the first dune. The sand rolled easily. Fine and slippery, it slid under their feet, making walking a burden and slowing them to a crawl.

Twenty dunes later Nathel felt exhausted, struggling to place one foot ahead of the next.

"Thero, I don't know if I can make it," Nathel whispered across parched lips. He slumped in the sand with a listless look in his eyes.

"Have another drink, Boy. The sun is setting in the eastern sky, and soon it will be cool," Thero said. He walked over and helped Nathel take a slow sip from the water pouch. The water tasted warm and brackish, but Nathel gulped it greedily.

Nathel glanced at the sun, it drifted low on the eastern horizon. He turned his face towards the wind, drinking in a cool breeze that drifted in from the still-visible mountains. He struggled to his feet and walked after his grandfather, the breeze offering new hope. Nathel felt the sweat drying from his skin.

"We will keep walking for most of the night, at least until the moon peaks. Then we will be within a day's travel of the first oasis."

Nathel nodded. In the distance, the last rays of the sun died, leaving the night sky dominated by the pale moon. The silvery orb rose slowly into the sky, and Nathel stopped to watch for a moment.

Behind them in the distance, the howls of the wolf pack broke across the rolling sands.

"Thero, I thought you said they would not enter the Burning Wastes."

"Seems that times are changing, Boy. The world is changing. The old ways are gone! I do not like it at all." Thero frowned. He stared across the rolling dunes. "The wolf pack is far behind, but if they are running, they will close the distance fast."

Nathel took a small sip of water and together he and Thero plunged down the dune, struggling to stay ahead of the pursuing wolves.

"Morning," Nathel sighed. The sky lightened in the western sky. Nathel's energy was gone, and he stood a moment close to dropping. He gasped for air as he struggled up another of the sandy slopes. His grandfather seemed filled with an unending reservoir of energy, as he led

Marhuth up the rolling dune. During the night, the howls of the wolf pack faded as they lost the scent.

"They are searching for us. The trail grows old quickly in the shifting sands," Thero said.

Marhuth looked horrible. The old warhorse had spent all of his energy trying to move. His eyes rolled about and he stumbled drunkenly from side to side. Nathel saw in the last rays of the moon that his sides were covered in dried sweat despite the cool breeze that had been blowing all night.

"Thero, Marhuth, has had it."

Thero turned and Marhuth stumbled to the side, pulling the thin end of rope from his hand. The noble warrior lay down on the sand panting.

Nathel knelt close by, and Thero walked back to his old friend. He knelt near Nathel and ran his hand over the black hair covering Marhuth's ears. The steed relaxed and his head dropped down into the sand. His labored breath faded with the coming sun.

"He is gone, now. Never was there a more noble creature." Tears rolled down Thero's face as he smoothed the hair on the charger's thick neck.

"Take food and water from the pack and leave the rest. The sands will bury him by tomorrow."

Nathel nodded.

He wiped a stray tear from his own eye and pulled the leather pack from Marhuth's side. Together they worked both packs free of the sand and rummaged through them.

Nathel removed the single remaining pack of dried jerky and his remaining water pouch. A quick shake told him that the pouch bordered on empty. He tied the ends of the two small packages together and dropped them over the back of his neck, settling them so that the straps would not dig into his flesh. Thero dug completely to the bottom of his pack, rummaging around to make sure he had retrieved everything he wanted.

Leaving the faithful steed where he had fallen, Nathel followed Thero. They walked away from the silent dune lost in thought, as behind them, the sun broke in all its fury over the distant mountains. The heat of the day fell on the weary travelers with enough force to make them stumble momentarily.

The sun soared high in the sky, beating down on the trudging pair. Nathel tipped his water skin up. He poured the last drops into his parched mouth.

Running his fingers over his lips, Nathel felt the cracked skin. His tongue had swollen to twice its natural size.

"Grandfather," he whispered. The croaking voice surprised him. Even his heat-soaked body had a hard time recognizing it.

Nathel reached out to his grandfather, his arm trembled with the effort. Suddenly the ground rushed to meet him and the sky went black.

Thero turned just in time to catch Nathel as he toppled face first into the hot sand.

"It's not your time yet, Boy," Thero grunted. He hoisted the limp body of his grandson over his shoulder with strength that belied his thin frame. Placing one foot in front of the last he climbed up the offending dune and stepped out to the crest. In the distance a spot of green broke onto the horizon.

"Thank the Elemental Pillars. The water elementals have not been driven from the world."

Thero smiled to himself. He took a deep breath, and plunged down, attacking the hot sand. The sun had passed its zenith by at least three hours when Thero struggled across the last hill. Before him, spread a small sheltered valley protected by an outcropping of granite. Dozens of trees grew tall and strong, their roots drinking deeply around the edges of the water. Thero stumbled down, moving as fast as he dared. He still felt the ragged, shallow breaths coming from Nathel as he entered the shade of the waving palms. The wind cooled noticeably, and Thero laid the unconscious youth down in the shade by the deep pool of water. Fifty paces at its widest point, the warm winds moving across the surface kept the water in constant movement. Thero moved quickly, refilling his water skin and dripping a small amount ever so slowly into Nathel's parched mouth. Then he attacked the ground, scooping the top layer of sand from the shore. Carefully, he eased Nathel into a small depression. The sandy ground under the top layer was dark, and full of moisture and the effect on

Nathel was almost immediate. He sighed and leaned back on the cool sand, but his skin remained red and puffy.

"Sleep, Son, and dream good dreams. I will stand guard this evening, watching and waiting," Thero whispered in a low voice. Exhaustion deadened his movements and his face showed the worry he felt in his heart.

Had he been too slow, he would not have gotten Nathel here in time.

If Nathel had been in the sun for too long, he would have faded into deep sleep, never to awaken. His body would shut down and his mind would have wandered until it was gathered up by the elementals to the Halls of Anatari. Thero knelt, his staff held tightly in his hands. He bowed his head, touching the ironwood, the runes etched in the surface pulsed and he reached out to the magic of the elementals. It was still strong here and he whispered a call to the power of the water.

Some time later he heard the rumblings deep under the surface of the water. "Thank the Pillars, at least one elemental still lives here," He whispered. The wind died off suddenly, leaving the surface of the oasis a mirror of glass.

As he watched a face appeared and a figure took shape, rising from the surface of the water.

"Why have you wakened me from my slumber?"

Deep and rumbling, the voice reminded Thero of a river roaring, after a long stretch of rapids.

Thero raised his head slowly, "I seek your help, servant of Anatari. I did not wish to wake you from your slumber, O Revered One. Times are desperate."

The water elemental stared at Thero from where he floated above the calm surface of the oasis. "My name is Tymothel. Anatari left my brothers and I to protect the waters of this world many ages ago. But rivers and streams became fouled, attacked by creatures of Bedbezdal. For years uncounted we sought to keep the water clean, and as those that believe in the creator faded, so too did our power. There are few left in the world. Even the warriors of the Mountain kingdom are fading too quickly. They are isolated and they take refuge in their circle of mountains, ignoring the command to spread the words written in the Lost Books."

Thero sat for a long moment. In his absence, things had gotten worse in this part of the world. Next to him, Nathel groaned in his sleep, and in the distance, Thero thought he heard the howl of the pack.

"Tymothel, this boy is near death. Is it within your power to heal his body?" The waters remained perfectly calm as the watery figure slid closer, his feet stepping on the surface of the placid water without so much as a ripple breaking the surface. Without touching the ground, he knelt by Nathel placing his hand on Nathel's forehead and closing his watery eyes.

"He is pursued by Bedbezdal. Even now a pack of the Fallen search through the surrounding deserts. It would be best if you left him to his fate."

"He has been chosen, Tymothel. The Elemental Pillars have given him the power to bring this world back from the brink of destruction. He bears the mark of the Elementals,"

"I am sorry, Prophet. I am forbidden to interfere with the affairs of mortals. Our duty is to stand ready to fight against our brothers who followed Bedbezdal in rebellion against Elutha."

"He has been marked by the Pillars. The cross symbol is on his flesh. If he falls, the world will tremble as Bedbezdal is released from his prison."

"I see." The elemental pondered. "Still, Anatari told us to be vigilant but stand clear of mortals. I will not help directly but I will show you something that will help you. Watch closely," Tymothel said. He waved his hand in a long arc over the water.

Thero watched as a vision leapt up from the water, an arching cavern with a tall pillar of stone rising into the air.

"Hidden deep in the western wall of this pool is a cave. Inside it, on a pedestal, stands a small vial. It is filled with the water of life. The creator blessed it when the world was forming. Many times the water was used to heal those struck down during the War of Heaven. You must dive deep into the pool and retrieve the vial. One drop of it will return the boy's strength and his will to live. Care must be taken though, for just as one drop will heal the body, so much as a second drop will bring death. Use it wisely."

Thero nodded as the water elemental spoke; he began to remove his extra clothing. Standing near the edge of the water he laid his staff beside Nathel on the dry sand.

"I will remain here and protect the lad if the servants of the Fallen should find him. You must hurry. His life is fading fast."

Thero did not answer. He waded into the shallows at the edge of the pool. He took rapid breaths, filling his lungs with air. The water remained pure and clean. He could not help the feeling that he was fouling the entire pool as sand and dirt floated free of his body. When he reached the center of the pool, Thero took one more breath and then dove deep. He kicked his feet and worked his arms as he knifed down into the blue water, crystal clear and deceptively deep. Many long moments went by. Thero's ears popped as the pressure of the water bore down on his body. When he reached thirty paces, he stopped looking around on the nearby walls for any sign of an opening.

There! On the far side! A dark spot in the well-lit pool.

Thero's mind screamed, his lungs crying out for oxygen. Swimming through the water, he closed on the opening. Jagged rocks surrounded a narrow tunnel that led straight out into the bedrock, and darkness closed in as the sun faded behind him. Thero swam even faster, pushing his limbs frantically. The call for air from his lungs grew stronger, and he fought not to take a deep refreshing breath. Lost in the darkness, he slammed hard into the end of the tunnel and lost his control. A fountain of air bubbles escaped from his lungs, as he desperately reached up, searching with his hands for an opening in the rough ceiling.

There it is!

He pushed off hard with his legs, more bubbles escaping his pursed lips. Thero shot up through the narrow opening and broke free of the surface gasping for air. Around him a soft light radiated throughout the cavern where he surfaced. Breathing deeply he fought the blackness that circled his vision. As his pulse slowed, he turned over and floated on his back, resting for a moment as he watched the ceiling high above him. Wide veins of crystal shot across the rocky ceiling letting the light of the bright sun penetrate deep into the wide cavern.

Near where he floated in the shallow pool, a pillar rose out of the dirt. When he felt his body was recovered, he rolled onto his stomach and swam slowly towards the center island. The ground rose to meet him and he sighed in relief when his feet touched the smooth rocks. Thero waded through the last five paces of water, pausing to take in the pillar. Cut from the solid stone, the smooth surface looked to be free of defects.

Scrambling through the knee-deep water Thero reached the stone pillar and looked up. The top of the pillar rose out of sight in the dim light reaching the cave.

"Can't tell if there's anything on top of it," he muttered to himself.

Taking a moment to shake the water from his arms Thero grasped the pillar. He wrapped his arms around the stone and began the hard process of climbing it.

Twice he slid back to the bottom, and the skin of his arms and legs scraped and bruised against the stone, with flagging strength he started up one last time, struggling to hold tightly to the pillar. Working his knees and feet tightly against the stone he finally reached the top. Sweat dripped from his face, stinging his eyes and trickling down his back.

His hand trembled as he reached out, desperate to find the promised vial and return to Nathel. Then he froze. He carefully pulled his hand back.

Something is not right with this

The hair on the back of his neck stood on end and his breath came in ragged gasps. Knots cramped the muscles in his legs and arms, crying out for relief from the continued strain.

Carefully he worked his fingers up until he grasped the lip of the stone, then with a mighty effort he pulled himself up. Scrambling with his feet and straining his neck he looked over the lip of the stone and froze. Sitting in the center of the pillar was a small vial, filled with a blue liquid. It caught the light and released it in blinding sparkles of dancing light. However, between his hand and the vial lay a desert rattlesnake, coiled and poised to strike. The snake sat deathly still, staring at Thero's fingertips that clung to the edge of the pillar. Thero slowed his breathing and then forced his mind to calm. Once again he reached his mind out to the magic of the elements, drawing the calming feelings of a merry stream from the magic and layering it across the snake. When he finished, the snake uncoiled, sensing that the threat had passed.

Then to his surprise the snake looked at him and spoke.

"Had you simply placed your hand on top of the pillar, I would have killed you without a second thought. Once I saw your face, I knew that you were a servant of the creator. Tell Tymothel I have fulfilled my duty and I am going to seek my rest now. I have guarded this vial for three thousand years. Use it wisely."

The snake slithered away. It moved with ease down the vertical surface of the pillar and disappeared from Thero's sight. He reached out with his free hand, grasped the thin crystal vial, and slipped it into the wide belt he wore.

When his feet touched the floor, Thero collapsed on the ground, gasping for air and trying to regain the strength in his arms and legs. Moments later he moved, knowing time remained precious. He slipped into the warm water and dipped below the surface. The return trip went quickly and moments later he surfaced in the middle of the pool.

"I trust all went well in the cavern," Tymothel said. His deep voice echoed from where he stood guarding Nathel's unmoving body.

"You could have warned me that the vial would be guarded." Thero was irritated. He hated when others got the best of him.

"A true warrior would never blindly reach into something." Tymothel answered.

Thero gritted his teeth and swam to the shore with long strokes.

"Does he still live?"

"He does, but his life is fading quickly. Come. Quickly give him the drop now or he will move beyond any help we might offer."

Thero tipped Nathel's head back and opened his mouth, removing the stopper at the top of the vial. He allowed one drop to roll from the narrow top of the vial and drip down onto Nathel's tongue. The effect was immediate, the cracked and chapped skin grew smooth and healthy, and the horrible burns from the withering sun faded from view. Nathel's slow, shallow breath deepened and he settled back into the sand, sleeping soundly.

Exhaustion took Thero where he lay and he slid himself out of the water, leaning against a nearby tree. Sleep took him immediately, leaving the water elemental floating above the pool, a smile on his face. Both of the weary travelers slept the rest of the day away and then most of the night without moving. Tymothel watched them for a while, then sank slowly into the pool of water, returning to his home deep in the pool.

Matthew John Krengel

CHAPTER SEVEN
INTO THE MOUNTAIN KINGDOM

orning brought a brilliant burst of sunshine, and Nathel's eyes snapped open.

"What happened?" he whispered. He remembered the endless sand of the Burning Wastes, but there were no memories of the cool shade around the oasis.

Thero snored loudly, his chin resting on his chest. He leaned against a nearby tree by the water. Near the edge of the water, a small fire burned and a pan filled with eggs and ham sizzled merrily over the fire. Nathel's mouth watered as he scrambled forward, his eyes fixed on the food.

"You passed out yesterday from the heat and almost died.

Nathel jumped at Thero's voice, his grandfather opened his eyes and nodded, "Eat. We will rest here for the day."

He nodded. The fire kept the pan warm but not hot, and Nathel ate his share directly from it. "One of the Elemental Protectors came to our rescue. He has lived in this pool since the creation of the world; it seems he is now trapped and unable to leave unless the flow of water under the pool is restored."

"Well, where do we go from here? The wolves will find us if we stay here too long."

"We will move tomorrow night. Tymothel will point us to the next oasis. Within three days we will be out of the Burning Wastes and then we will enter the Land of Ahtonium."

Nathel's blank look must have told Thero that he would have to explain further.

"It is a mountainous kingdom, ruled by the Sire of the Wyrm warriors. It is one of the most ancient lands, inhabited by a mixture of all the races seldom seen anywhere else. Most avoid the land, believing it is a cursed place, but it is only cursed for those that serve the Fallen. Before we came to live in Comstoll, a rift had grown between the human kingdoms and the Land of Ahtonium. The level of distrust was fueled by the minions of the Fallen. Most humans mistrust the Ahtonians because they are different and, therefore, they label them as evil."

Nathel listened as Thero spoke. He wondered what all Thero knew and where all he had traveled. Nathel remembered little of his past beyond when he had moved into the small cottage with his grandfather.

"Why don't you wash the dirt of the trip away son. The water is warm and clean," Thero said. He nodded to the pool and then leaned back closing his eyes. Immediately light snores proceeded in an orderly fashion from his bearded mouth. Nathel turned and slipped out of his shirt, rolled his pants up to his knees and waded into the water. Finding it surprisingly comfortable, he slipped under the surface, rinsing himself clean. Drifting on his back, Nathel stared up at the sky, the clouds rolling by lulling him into a state of relaxation.

"I hope you are enjoying my home."

Surprised, Nathel dipped his head under the water momentarily. He struggled to clear his face, shaking the water from his eyes and wiping his free hand across his face. Tymothel floated calmly above the surface of the water smiling. The water elemental waited as Nathel struggled to wipe the remaining water from his eyes.

"You must be Tymothel," Nathel said. His mind finally made the connection.

"Yes, I am glad to see you are feeling better." The blue-skinned elemental bent low on the water and examined Nathel, looking him over as if he expected to find a limb out of place.

"Thero told me about you, but I assumed you would not return until tonight. I guess I had kind of drifted off to sleep."

Tymothel did not appear to be listening. Instead he stared at Nathel, appearing to weigh him in his mind.

"You do not seem to be a warrior."

"I am not a warrior. Thero raised me as a shepherd."

This seemed to set the water elemental back on his heels. "The creator works in mysterious ways. The old one said you bore the mark of the elemental protectors. Is this true?"

Nathel held out his hands, the symbols etched in the skin glowing faintly in the bright sun.

"Come, Boy. I have something I want to show you," Tymothel said. He turned and walked slowly to the center of the pool. He watched Nathel swim awkwardly over to where he stood.

"Where are we going?" Nathel asked. He sputtered and floated in the water next to the elemental. Without warning, the water dropped out from under him. Nathel screamed as he fell into a hole forming in the center of the pool, the water whipping in a circle, spinning him around and making his stomach turn. The bottom of the pool approached fast, and he screamed again, covering his eyes as the muddy ground rushed at him.

"You can stop screaming now," Tymothel said. He laughed as the ground rose to meet Nathel's feet gently and lowered him lightly to the ground. Before his feet touched the bottom, the mud dried, offering a hard surface for him to walk across. Before him a door appeared in the water. The elemental walked into the watery door and disappeared through the opening.

"What in the world?" Nathel pushed his hand through the door. It disappeared from sight, then a strong hand grabbed his and pulled him into the watery door after the elemental. He entered a wide room, the sides composed of water and held back to form walls and a ceiling. Doors led off to the sides and the contents of the side rooms were clearly seen through the watery walls.

"Come, Boy," Tymothel walked down into the ground and disappeared.

Nathel hurried to catch up. He found himself in a wide room made of mud. The walls and ceiling were wet and dripped water almost constantly. The dripping water absorbed into the floor as fast as it fell. Standing in the middle of the room was a stand holding a staff. Nathel crossed the room and stared reverently at the ironwood staff. The surface of the ironwood staff rivaled Thero's in smoothness. Unlike Thero's an iron band had been cut into the wood and wrapped around each end. Etched with ancient runes, it lay waiting for someone to wield it.

"This is the first ironwood staff ever created. It is written in the Chronicles of the Last Words, that it will once again be taken up when the world is in dire need. It can only be held by someone bearing the marks of the Elemental Pillars."

Nathel turned his hands over and rubbed the symbols faintly visible under the skin.

"Symbols like those, Son," Tymothel said.

Nathel tentatively reached out and brushed a single finger across the smooth surface. The ironwood seemed warm to the touch, it reminded him of a living creature.

"Someday you will find yourself in desperate need. Call my name and if the elements are with us, I will find a way to you and give you this staff. It will aid you in your coming battles. Until then, I will keep it safe," Tymothel said. He spoke softly as Nathel stared at the powerful staff.

"Why can't I take it now," Nathel asked.

"This staff is not unknown to many who walk the surface. Were it to appear suddenly you would never be able to blend in anywhere and I believe that for a time yet your grandfather will want to try and avoid notice."

Nathel nodded.

"Come. We must return to the surface," Tymothel said. He motioned to Nathel, breaking the reverie that had fallen over him.

Evening had come and the sun had faded in the eastern sky when they surfaced in the center of the pool. Thero waited at the edge of the pool watching for their return. He rose to his feet, arms folded with irritation painted across his face.

"I wondered how long you would stay away."

Nathel nodded to Tymothel who handed him a small pack.

"Fill your water skins and drink your fill before leaving. Walk straight to the east, keeping the moon over your right shoulder. One day of walking will bring you to a second oasis. I can no longer travel there, as the underground rivers have dried. Refill your water skins there and go southeast for two days. This will bring you clear of the Burning Wastes. Two days after that to the east is the Land of Ahtonium."

Thero nodded. He knelt at the pool and filled his water skin. Nathel did the same, and then they rose and walked through the palm trees to the east.

The sun set in the western sky as the oasis disappeared into the distance. The sandy dunes rose and fell under their feet in the half-light of evening, and the moon made its full awakening. Far out in the distance, the mournful cry of the hunting wolves echoed into the night bringing a shiver to Nathel's skin.

The night passed without incident and morning found them walking in a straight line in the middle of a sea of dunes. Nathel found that despite the hostile conditions, life flourished in the dreadfully hot sand. Night brought out all sorts of insects and nocturnal creatures. Scorpions and snakes moved silently, while high flying predators winged across the sky. Thero pointed to the south where towering mounds of sand piled high into the sky.

"What are they, Grandpa?"

"Small creatures akin to ants, but they build towering tunnel systems. The largest I have seen is over fifty paces tall," Thero said. He motioned again to the numerous spires still visible as they plunged down the backside of the dune.

Nathel shook his head, "The world is full of amazing sights, isn't it, Grandfather."

"More than we will ever see in our lives, son," Thero said. He whispered the words so softly that Nathel almost missed them.

Silence descended as they trudged onward, sustained by the food and water from the oasis. Each time Nathel felt his energy begin to flag, he took a small sip of the water skin, his mind reliving the cooling presence of the trees and water.

Night fell, and Nathel cried out as they fell into the remains of the second oasis. He rolled down the hill and came to a halt in the middle of a dried lake. It was much smaller than the shaded pool from the day before.

In the half-light of the moon, he saw dying trees and a dried up hole were all that remained of what had been a lush oasis.

"Grandfather, is this the second oasis?" Nathel asked. His voice conveyed the tiredness he felt in his body.

Thero stood silently, not answering the question for many long minutes. the trees withered even at night denied their life giving water, the sun and heat making short work of the towering palms. Even at night the wind gust in hot blasts.

"Well Nathel, nothing to do but move on. We must make our supplies last for the rest of the trip," Thero said. He walked out onto the dry oasis bed and knelt down feeling the ground with his hand. The sun had baked the ground to a rock hard layer and it there was little they could do. The ground was so hardened that they could not dig through it and see if any moisture survived.

They slept that night in the circle of dying trees, a cool breeze finally rolling in from the east and making the night more bearable.

The next day passed slowly with the sun doing its best to reduce them to dried-out husks. Thero took half the drinks that Nathel did and at the end of the day his water skin remained half full.

"Mine is empty, Grandfather," Nathel said. He tipped his water skin upside down. Thero glanced at the sun which had begun its slow descent again and motioned for Nathel to follow him.

"We will make do with one. If Tymothel was right we should make it out of the Burning Wastes by tomorrow evening."

Far in the distance, Nathel thought he saw a dark line of mountains stretching north and south as far as the eye could see.

"Look, Grandfather! The mountains are close," Nathel smiled. "We can make it before the sun peaks if we hurry!" He danced a small circle around his grandfather.

"Conserve your energy, Boy. Those mountains are far away. Distances are very deceiving in the Wastes," Thero grabbed his arm. He walked along steadily and Nathel fell in beside him again. They had reached a level section of the desert, the long flat plains of hard dirt making travel much easier.

"Doesn't look that far," Nathel muttered.

"Trust me, Nathel. They are a long ways off yet."

Nathel teetered on the edge of exhaustion by the time they cleared the hot sands and entered the cooler air of the mountains. Not only had day passed but the moon had peaked. Their water had run out hours before, and the empty skins lay where they were dropped in the sand.

The mountain air blew in brisk gusts down the rocky slopes, and a line of pine trees greeted them as the moon began to descend. Nathel breathed a sigh of relief when they entered a thick stand of trees. Exhaustion took him immediately and he fell to the ground, his skin a dark shade of red from the constant exposure to the sun. He burrowed inside the thick mat of pine needles and fallen branches and fell asleep almost immediately.

Morning had long gone when Thero shook Nathel awake.

"Huh? What's wrong?"

Nathel sat up banging his head on a low branch. He winced and rubbed a hand across his face.

"The wolves are closing in on us again," Thero said. He pointed out into the mountains to the north.

Nathel listened for a moment and then the mournful cry of the hunting pack echoed through the still mountain air.

"We must cross into the Land of Ahtonium. The wolf pack has never dared enter into that land, as the wyrms defend the land from all intruders," Thero said. He picked up his staff and motioned towards Nathel's fallen weapon.

They headed south, away from the cries of the pursuing wolves. Thero set a punishing pace as they moved higher into the mountains. Nathel shivered the heat of the Burning Wastes all but forgotten as the temperature dropped. Thero led him along a narrow path that cut into the mountains between towering rock cliffs and through high mountain passes. All around him patches of snow held on stubbornly to the desolate landscape.

The howling of the wolf pack grew closer despite the fast pace. Nathel gasped and wheezed, but the sound was all but drowned out by the continuous howls.

Nathel ran along behind Thero they sprinted through a narrow gap leading down the far side of the mountain. Far in the distance Nathel caught a glimpse of green fields and a flowering field of trees.

He glanced back, and the sight added wings to his feet. Across the pass, the wolf pack broke into the clear. Hundreds of mountain wolves pursued. Long bounds took them across the rocky landscape much faster than he could run. At the front of the boiling mass of fur and flashing teeth ran the lean pack leader. Black eyes fastened on him, and Nathel turned back, watching the path as his legs pumped in an effort to find safety.

Nathel gasped for air, and Thero dropped back to run beside him. The older man was running steady and controlling his breathing. Less than twenty paces behind, the pack howled as one. Before them the pass widened, and they entered the far side.

Nathel knew they could not escape. He stared out far into the distance, taking his eyes from the path. In that moment, he missed a rock sticking upright out of the soil. It grabbed his foot and sent him tumbling head over heels. He lay on the ground gasping for air, and Thero skidded to a halt. He raced back, his staff held ready to defend the fallen youth until the end.

The next sound Nathel heard reminded him of the rushing wind, but it was created by the flapping of massive wings. The ground shook, and a pair of huge talons dug into the rocks. He looked up and watched the wolf pack turned as one and flee for the narrow pass leading back to the mountains.

"Old One, you bring strange things each time you come. Never before have you brought a pack of the fallen to our doorstep."

Nathel lay face down in the ground and the voice spoke from directly above his sprawled body. He rolled over stared up at the long neck and fearsome head of one of the dragon kin. Already on edge, he began to scream in fright.

"Oh do stop screaming, Small One. Didn't the Old One teach you any manners?" the wyrm spoke. He stared down at Nathel for a moment, his head cocked to the side. Then his face pulled back from Nathel's field of vision and his hysterical screaming faded to a mere whimper.

"I am truly sorry, Soldier Venthern. He is young and has never been out of the village before now. On top of it all, we were chased all the way from the highlands by a pack of the fallen. Please forgive his hysteria."

A grunting sound came from behind him and Nathel struggled to sit up.

Thero walked around in front of Nathel and offered his hand, pulling him to his feet. "Nathel, please refrain from screaming the next time you turn. Venthern has very sensitive hearing," Thero said. He spoke in a calm voice as he gripped both of Nathel's shoulders. Both of their ironwood staves lay on the ground nearby and Nathel's eyes darted nervously to the weapons.

Soldier Venthern stared on in amusement, pulling his lips back into a fearsome grin. Standing fifty paces long, the wyrm dipped his head down to eye level with Nathel and offered his greeting.

"Do you still serve the creator?"

"May the Pillars bless you and lend strength to your talons, Soldier Venthern," Nathel stammered. Thero nodded from where he stood. Leaping into the air, Venthern spread his wings and flapped furiously, gaining ground slowly. Nathel watched as he rode into the air and swept to the west.

Thero retrieved their equipment, offering Nathel his staff and a reassuring smile. They moved slowly down into the vast valley that encompassed the Land of Ahtonium.

"Look," Thero said. He pointed south towards the staggered mountains with their snowy peaks and tree-lined foothills. Above the tree line Nathel saw the dark spots of immense caverns hollowed into the peaks. Looking closely, the distant tiny forms of armored wyrms came and went from the peak on their assigned patrols.

"Here comes soldier Venthern." Thero motioned into the clear blue sky.

"The fallen are truly interested in this boy." he said. The formidable wyrm swept in from the west and landed lightly on all four legs.

"The wolf pack tried to enter our realm again. This time they were driven back with some loss of life on their part. Their leader is canny, though. He will wait until night when the patrols are unable to fly because of darkness and then they will continue the pursuit."

Thero nodded, "We must enter the capitol with its high walls. We will be as safe there as any other place."

Soldier Venthern nodded, "I will watch your back, Old One. You know the trail to Havening."

Nathel remained silent as he watched the wyrm once again take flight. "Why do they all call you Old One, Grandfather?"

Thero paused as if he knew Nathel would come to this question.

"Once, a long time ago--it seems like another life now--I was someone with whom much was entrusted. I failed, and many people died. Since then, it has been my penance to protect you. Nathel, it hurts me to say this, but you are not really my grandson. Our relation to each other is much more..." Thero paused for a moment before he continued, "...complex."

Nathel stared in shock and his staff once again clattered to the ground as he felt the betrayal flood over him. His mind screamed. Everything he had been taught now crumbled into a web of lies and deceit.

Thero bowed his head in sadness and shame.

Nathel did not see the tears falling from Thero's eyes. Instead, the words still echoed in his mind.

"Not your grandfather."

Nathel turned and fled towards the distant mountains, ignoring the cries of Thero and Venthern. He dodged around boulders and leapt over impossibly long chasms in the mountainous landscape. Before Thero could stop him he had disappeared from sight into the granite cliffs. All that remained was an echoing cry of anguish, torn from the soul of the tortured youth.

Matthew John Krengel

Chapter Eight
The Fallen Gather

hat does the boy know of his past?" Venthern spoke. He broke into Thero's personal reverie.

"Nothing yet. I know beyond a doubt that he is the Chosen One. Marked by the Elemental Pillars. When the wolf pack came at us in the shepherds' village, he fought off half a dozen at a time. I did all I could to hold three at bay. We must find and protect him. If the pack leader is able to corner him we may lose all."

Thero turned his tortured eyes on the armored wyrm. "Follow him. If you can find him, protect him. I will go on to the Ancient Wyrm and ask him to send out the army to find and protect Nathel."

Soldier Venthern leapt into the air. He swept south, flying slowly and searching the ground, watching for the fleeing form of Nathel among the rocks and trees that dotted the mountainous landscape.

Nathel fled in tears. His world had shattered, and he seemed powerless to stop it. Pursued by the fallen, he had trusted in his grandfather to be the solid rock and protect him. Now even that shelter had been torn from him. Overhead, thunderclouds began to boil in from the south, coating the sky and cutting off the sun.

The trail he found himself running along became wide and flat. It led in a direct path between two low mountains. Scrub brush covered the slopes around him, cutting off all chance of running anywhere but straight along the path. All along the trail the slinking forms of the wolf pack circled and watched. They guided him farther from the safety of the Land of Ahtonium. He ran hard along the trail, his breath came in gasps, but he could not stop running. An unseen force drew him on, taking him further and further from the lies and deceit behind him. Tears streamed freely down his face as he ran, mixing with the sweat and making his eyes burn.

"Stop, Boy."

Nathel skidded to a halt. The loose rocks of the path rolled under his feet and he fell heavily, a grunt of pain escaping his lips. He looked up through blurry eyes to see the pack leader sitting before him. Seated calmly on the path, the wolf regarded him with cold eyes. His tail lashed back and forth, reminding Nathel of the house cat he had played with many times in Comstoll.

"Why are you running?" the beast asked.

Nathel struggled to his feet, blood dripping from skinned knees and hands. The pain helped him focus his mind, and he wiped his hands against his trousers. Somehow the spreading red smear made him feel dirty inside.

"Everyone has lied to me."

"That is the way of those who claim they follow the creator sowing distrust and hate unto their own ends. They live to lie and lie to live." The wolf shook its head.

Nathel tried to grasp what the wolf had said but the words kept slipping away. The pain and exhaustion that wracked his body left his mind muddied and confused. The words sounded logical.

"What do you mean, they claim to follow the creator?" Nathel finally found his voice.

"Listen to me, boy. There are many in the world claiming to follow the true powers of heaven. Most do so to exercise power over the weak-minded and simpletons. This man who claimed to be your grandfather is one of those. We of the pack have watched him for a long time, waiting for him to reveal his true nature. Now he has. He is a liar and a thief."

Things were moving so quickly that Nathel felt he was drowning. Thero could not be a liar and a thief. There had to be a reason; he had to be wrong. But Thero *had* admitted that he had lied to him. How much more would it take for Thero to be a thief as well? Nathel slumped down again, as despair overtook him.

"I am without friends," Nathel whispered. His voice was small and quiet, but the sensitive wolf ears caught the remark.

"You are never without friends, boy. Why do you think the pack has traveled across the Burning Wastes and risked entering the kingdom of the fallen themselves to find you. We are your friends. We have always been here for you."

"But I was told that the wolf pack served Bedbezdal, and you tried to kill me. In my dream at least," Nathel finished lamely. His suspicions were once again aroused.

"Who do you think created most of this world, Boy? Yes, we serve Bedbezdal. As for the dream," the wolf sighed, "I regarded you as an enemy then, but now your innocence has been shown and you are no longer an enemy. I would defend you in the face of certain death now, all in the name of the true god of this world."

Nathel watched as the wolf lowered his head and nodded to him. It was a look of respect and a nod of friendship. Nathel rose to his feet and took a step closer to the pack leader.

"That's it. Come a step closer, Boy. I have a friend I would like you to meet."

Nathel's face broke into a big smile, and he started to walk down the trail, following the now-moving pack leader. "Who is it?"

"One of my master's most trusted servants, he would like to talk to you."

Nathel was close to the big wolf when a sudden gust of wind hit him, whipping his hair about. He was forced to lean forward, as he tried to hold onto his precarious balance. Dust and dirt whirled into the air, stirring up a dust cloud and obscuring the trail for many long minutes. The pack leader sat calmly, and unmoving, despite the rushing wind. Nathel noticed with curiosity that the wind failed to stir even the smallest tuft of the wolf's hair.

When the dust settled and Nathel looked up, an armored wyrm sat blocking his path. The scaled creature faced the pack leader and hissed loudly. "Be gone, foul creature. Go back to your master. Tell him your kind is not permitted in the Land of Ahtonium," Soldier Venthern cried. He stood tall in the center of the trail, his head more than triple Nathel's height and his body covered in flexible chain mail. Liquid green eyes flashed with an inner fire as he confronted the wolf. A swipe from a razor sharp right claw sent the lanky wolf dodging.

Nathel blinked suddenly as the dust settled and the haze drifted away from his mind. All around the pack leader hundreds of wolves came into view. The rocky mountain slope seemed alive with tawny mountain wolves.

"You are no longer in your weak kingdom, Wyrm. You have no power here. Go, before the pack removes you from our path."

Nathel fell back on the path as the two enemies faced off. He was caught between the sweet words of the wolf and the feeling deep inside that the noble wyrm was his friend.

Venthern hissed loudly, he flexed his wickedly long claws and pulled back his lips to expose teeth like daggers in his elongated mouth. Slivery chain mail covered the soft flesh that lay unprotected on his belly and neck. The thin membranes of his wings folded protectively and slipped under his armor.

"You think even the numbers of the pack can bring down a soldier of Anatari, a protector of Ahtonium. I have lived for a thousand years and seen hundreds of battles. Come wolf, let us test your resolve," Soldier Venthern challenged. He seemed confident and that assurance made Nathel take another step back.

The pack leader stood, coming to all fours, "Ignore him boy, come to us. We will protect you from the likes of him."

Nathel took a hesitant step forward thinking he would move past the armored wyrm.

"Nathel, do not willingly go to the Fallen. If you go your soul will be lost forever. One cannot return once you have given yourself willing to Bedbezdal. Once in his clutches you are lost forever."

Nathel stopped, staring back and forth between the two forces. His emotions pulled him towards the wily wolf, but a still voice in his mind made him stop and back towards the noble dragon.

"Take the wyrm. Bring me the boy."

The pack leader must have sensed his hold on Nathel weakening; he sent his forces forward with little hesitation. Moving as one, the wolf pack leapt forward encircling the wyrm, razor sharp teeth slashed against the leather straps holding the armor in place weakening the links. Soldier Venthern broke into a fury as the pack moved; snapping jaws caught a wolf in mid leap and severed the creature in two. A slash from the razor sharp claws of his right leg gutted two more and sent them flying into the mists surrounding the path. The whipping motion of his tail worked to protect himself from behind. Venthern fought furiously to keep the hundreds of wolves back. The metal armor held the claws and teeth at bay but the leather straps holding it in place were weakening. Nathel saw a brown wolf bite half through one before Venthern managed to send it flying. Despite the loss of a score of wolves hundreds more flooded forward and even the mighty wyrm could not defend all directions at once.

The pack leader sat on his haunches watching and directing with an occasional howl at the circling pack. The pack swirled around Nathel but never touched him. His staff seemed puny against the forces gathered. He longed to help Venthern but his spirit melted within him. As quickly as the attack started, the pack fell back from the encircled wyrm. Nathel saw the chain armor around Venthern's neck hanging in pieces and the mail covering his belly was missing completely. Ribbons of flesh torn from the wyrm left great drops of blood falling to the ground and red streaks covered his neck.

Nathel watched spell bound, clutching his staff as the wolf pack threw back their heads and howled. The sound was deafening. It echoed back and forth between the snow covered mountain peaks.

"Tell your grandfather, I tried to protect you Nathel," Soldier Venthern spoke in a tired voice. He stood, tall and strong, ready to fight, despite his wounds.

Nathel looked at the wyrm, and felt as though he had awakened from a dream. All around him the eyes of the wolf pack glowed red and their howls took on a sinister sound. Venthern changed some as Nathel watched, the wyrm seemed to become nobler and yet kinder in his eyes.

"Do not weep for me, Nathel. Anatari and the other servants of the creator will bring me home. I will wing across the broad expanses between the worlds."

Nathel wiped the tears from his eyes with a dirty hand. He clutched his staff and moved to stand before the embattled dragon.

"I will, Venthern, I understand now." Those simple words were all that was needed, Nathel looked about realizing for the first time in hours that he still clutched his ironwood staff in his hands. The staff was given to him by his grandfather as a gift. It was a symbol of love and trust in the young shepherd boy.

"If you die today, so will I," Nathel said.

"Nathel do not give up on life yet, there is always hope."

"It's all right, Venthern. Thero may be many things, but to me he is my grandfather and he loves me. The least I can do is stand beside you."

Then in the distance came the answer to the pack. Deep and powerful, it sent shivers down Nathel's spine. The tones shook the very foundations of the surrounding mountains. As the sound faded, snow began to fall from the covering clouds and Nathel saw the worry on Venthern's face.

"They have called their master. A foul creature that has haunted these mountains since time began. He is called, Cruathila, by my fellow soldiers, the name means *One with Ice*. Many times we have sent out patrols to find and kill him. Sometimes, those patrols never returned."

Nathel's spine shivered at the echoing howl; looking down the trail he waited, watching for any sign of movement.

"Here he comes, son."

Nathel stared hard. His eyes were not as strong as the wyrm towering over him. Then, from the mists at the end of the trail stepped a creature that equaled Venthern in size. He gaped, not one but two snapping heads seated on its shoulders. A long thick tail ended in a ball of ice, and massive spikes sprang from the ball as it approached. White fur covered most of its body. The light snow thickened and fell harder as the creature approached.

"What is it?" Nathel asked. He struggled to keep his voice steady. Overhead, a winter storm broke over the mountains. Thick flakes of snow fell and icy winds howled down the slopes.

"He is one of the fallen elementals, a servant of the creator that turned his back on his maker. When the War of Heaven ended, the defeated elementals were banished to the mortal world. Once here, they assumed whatever form they wished. Most have forgotten how to change back into their true forms. Now they are locked forever in the hideous shapes that they chose at the time."

Cruathila closed to within twenty paces of the pair and then slowed to a halt.

"Leave the boy and go, wyrm."

Frost flowed from his mouth as he spoke, icicles formed on Nathel's hair and clothes. The blast of cold air flowed over him, beside him Venthern shivered. The dragon stamped his feet to keep his blood flowing.

"He is under my protection beast, be gone before the army arrives and finishes you once and for all time," Venthern cried loudly. He spoke with power but the chattering of his teeth made the words fall short of the elementals unearthly strength.

"Beware his breath, Nathel, it will freeze you solid. Beware his tail as the slightest scratch is certain death. He has a weak spot in the middle of his chest. It you can strike it hard with your staff you will hurt him and he may retreat," Venthern mumbled. His words came slowly as the frost and cold slowed his blood, slowly sending him into hibernation.

Nathel stood motionless in the center of the trail, the wolf pack withdrew to the upper slopes, watching and waiting. He looked about, sure that the numbers of mountain wolves were still swelling. Thousands of them sat waiting or loped about the perimeter of the area watching for any sign of rescuers.

Cruathila regarded Nathel with grim stare that made his blood run colder then the surrounding snowstorm. Slowly the massive creature rose and padded forward. Each of the ice bound elementals legs were as big around as Nathel's waist. Massive jaws could bite him in two without hesitation. Still he would not run, to flee from the beast would leave Venthern alone and unprotected. He could not leave the wyrm to the mercy of the pack, not after he had shown such valor in coming to his rescue.

Nathel raised his ironwood staff, he offered a salute, and then assumed a defensive stance. He legs trembled as he waited to dodge the strikes of the fallen elemental. Cruathila paused, pulling back his lips and revealing rows of frost covered teeth. At ten paces Cruathila turned, launching the spiked ball on his tail in an overhead strike. Nathel dodged right, throwing his body into a roll and nearly losing his footing as he stood again on the icy trail. Cruathila turned his head as he tracked him and exhaled. Nathel nearly stepped directly into the cone of ice that formed. Scrambling for room, he dodged and squirmed. Each time he desperately avoided the repeated attacks from the mace like tail, and the occasional blasts of ice from the gaping maw.

"You can't keep dodging forever boy," Cruathila said. He stood for a moment facing Nathel head on; the great beast's eyes betrayed its intelligence and pure evil. It was then he realized that the creature was toying with him.

Nathel paused, his breath coming in ragged gasps, "I will not give in."

He whispered this to himself, trying to shore up his faltering courage. One look told him that the creature facing him was not even breathing hard.

In the distance, to the north, the howls of the wolf pack grew louder and more insistent. Something had happened to the north. Nathel prayed that Thero was coming.

Cruathila looked up, the creatures red eyes staring into the swirling snow to the north. A moment later he lifted its massive jaws and howled the terrible sound that made Nathel's blood run cold. A brief flash of light caught Nathel's attention in that moment.

"His chest," Nathel whispered. He stared in fascination; in the center of the beast's chest was a single white gem. Set in the fur, the gem beckoned to him.

"It's his weak point," Nathel muttered. He stepped forward despite the continuing mournful howl.

The tone of the sound shifted lower and the snows strengthened even more, closing in on the trail and cutting off everything. Nathel struggled against the winds and the blinding snow. In the hazy distance he could barely make out the form of the winter wolf. Cold winds tore down the mountains from the south pushing the snow hard against Nathel's face. Venthern sat unmoving, icicles forming from his long tail as the frost sent him completely into hibernation. Nathel squinted against the blinding snow, his eyes fastened on the white stone. Closing his eyes, Nathel leapt forward, he sprinted across the icy slope, unseen by Cruathila. Leaping into the air, he struck hard with the tip of his ironwood staff. He struck the gem and the world went silent. The storm froze as a spider web of small cracks formed around the gem. The impact blew Nathel back twenty paces and left him lying senseless against Venthern's broad chest in the falling snow.

Moments later, Nathel shook his head as he grasped his staff from the ground beside him and struggled back to his feet.

Matthew John Krengel

Chapter Nine
Warriors of the Mountain

 ruathila's howl changed from one of control and power to one of pain and rage. The impact of the staff created a small fracture in the stone binding him to the mortal realm. The pain of the blow loosed his control on the swirling blizzard, allowing the sun to shine through the clouds.

Nathel looked to the north, a patch of red flashed against the fields of white. The familiar figure of his grandfather strode along the rocky path leading hundreds of soldiers. Next to Thero's thin figure strode a dwarf of immense girth. A tall winged helm rode low on his face hiding all but his eyes and a thick beard that fell half-way down his chest.

Around the mountainside the mountain wolves leapt forward flowing down the slopes and into the valley. They broke around their master and attacked the red cloaked soldiers with a fury that rivaled the swirling storm clouds over head.

Nathel heard Thero shouting orders, his voice carrying well along the mountain trail.

"Push the creatures back. Forward!"

Shoulder to shoulder the warriors marched forward, chanting an ancient battle cry. They called for the blessings of the elements and moved into the teeth of the wolves and the roar of the blizzard. Tall winged helms hid their heritage from his view. The only clues were the occasional dwarf warriors who stood half the height of their human and elf counter parts, but twice as wide. Red cloaks and the brilliant symbols of the elemental pillars emblazoned on their shields brought a ray of hope to Nathel. Overlaid on each shield was a large gold cross proclaiming their allegiance to all.

Cruathila fell back a step, his carefully laid plan beginning to crumble.

Nathel looked up in hope. He felt a bit of movement where he had fallen between Venthern's front claws. The heavy snow faded and then stopped falling all together.

Howling again, Cruathila put forth his power strengthening the storm and sending the attacking wolves into a frenzy. They threw themselves at the armored warriors, tearing holes in the tight formation by sheer numbers. Scores of mountain wolves lay dead, staining the snow red with their blood but still more rushed forward. Thero and the red cloaks slowed to a crawl. The snow piled high, making their steps treacherous, and Nathel began to despair that they would make it to him. Already more then a dozen of the soldiers lay unmoving in the white snow, their bodies quickly disappearing, becoming little more then mounds beneath the drifting piles of snow.

Nathel turned back to the fallen elemental; he remembered flying backwards after striking the gem and then darkness had closed on him. His head hurt and blood flowed freely from a cut above his left eye. He scrambled forward, in his hand he still held his ironwood staff, and he struck left and right landing solid blows on the wolves flashing past him. Oddly, none of them would stop to fight him. Then he saw the great white wolf moving, again approaching him.

"Time to die, boy. My master has ordered it."

"Anatari, give me strength," Nathel whispered. He looked up as he prayed. A single ray of sunshine pierced the clouds, lighting the snow around him.

Cruathila limped forward. He seemed bent on finishing the unmoving form of Venthern and killing Nathel.

All about him Nathel heard the shouts and screams of battle. Another break in the wall of snow revealed the long line of red cloaked soldiers still fiercely battling the darting forms drawn from a sea of wolves. As Nathel brought his staff up, he broke into a charge down the slippery trail. Throwing away what he had learned from Thero, he broke into a screaming attack. He rushed headlong towards the angry Cruathila and certain death.

"That's it boy, come to me," the beast smiled. He opened his mouth wide, the frost billowing out. It reached for him, promising a swift death. Nathel threw himself to the side, then he broke the first rule that he had learned from Thero. Never be parted from your weapon, Thero had drilled the lesson into him for weeks on end.

Instead of holding the staff tight, he skidded to a halt. Nathel stretched back his arm and threw the staff as hard as he could; it flew out with the force of a crossbow bolt. Flying like a javelin it hammered home into the already fractured gem binding the great creature to the mortal realm. A deafening thunder clap echoed across the mountain as the gem cracked in half, releasing its power into the air. In a moment, a flash of white light pulsed over the mountains, temporarily blinding the combatants.

The wolf pack cried as one and broke from the fight. They ran hard, fleeing for the jagged southern mountains. The red cloaks stood rubbing the eyes, shaking their heads in an attempt to clear the black spots dancing about before them. The swirling snows of the blizzard vanished as fast as they had come, leaving knee deep snow on the ground. The dark clouds rolled away, and the sun broke through in all its glory.

Nathel stared in amazement as the great wolf fled taking the storm with him. Scores of red cloaked bodies were strewn about the landscape where they had died trying to rescue him. Thero stood silently; he stared at Nathel and waited for him to move.

Nathel walked slowly. He approached the older man with his head bowed and tears forming in the corners of his eyes.

"I am sorry, grandpa."

Those four words brought a sigh of relief and a great bear hug from Thero. Nathel returned the embrace tenfold.

"It's all right, son. I should have told you earlier, but I didn't have the heart. I did know your parents and I failed them. They put their trust in me and I returned to late. You were all I had left and you must be protected, even from the failures of a feeble old man like me. I did my best to make a home for you, but now it seems that even my attempts have fallen short."

Nathel looked up at his grandfather with tears in his eyes.

"You did not fail, Thero. You did everything a real grandfather could ever do for me, in my mind you will always be my grandfather."

"Come, son, let me introduce you to someone."

He followed Thero back to where the red cloaks were binding their wounds and gathering the fallen.

"No one is left behind, now move!" The broad dwarf who had marched next to Thero stood in the midst of a swirl of activity.

"Timoth. This is Nathel," Thero motioned him forward.

"May the elementals watch over you. Good to see you in one piece son," Timoth nodded. He held a huge double bladed battle ax in one hand, a square shield with the gold cross of Ahtonium rest against the ground.

"We need to move quickly. The pack will return soon, the banishing of Cruathila will not hold them back for long."

"What do you mean they will come back?" Nathel stammered.

"Son, the white wolf himself probably did not flee far," said Thero.

Timoth nodded, "You did not think it would be that easy. To get rid of a creature as evil as the white wolf, would take a lot of doing."

Nathel fell silent. He shrugged and waited for Thero to speak.

"Get a detail up to help Venthern," Timoth waved to the struggling dragon.

Nathel marveled at the speed with which the nearby soldier rushed to carry out his orders.

Moments later in the distance, the concerted howls of the wolf pack brought even more of a sense of urgency to the red cloaked warriors. Venthern was beginning to move slowly and he worked his wings in an effort to regain his range of movement. Timoth had the men moving mere minutes after the end of the battle, carrying their wounded and dead. They offered what help they could to Venthern as they trudged back up the long sloping hill. Deep snow layered the ground, slowing them as they marched back toward the Lands of Ahtonium.

Nathel pushed through the snow walking beside Thero at the end of the double line of soldiers. Behind them Timoth brought up the rear, his ax and shield held ready.

"Thero, they are returning," Nathel said. He pointed behind them squinting against the reflected light, the heat of the sun beginning to melt the thick layer of snow. Small pools of water formed on the trail and random streams of muddy water rushed along the deep ravines.

Nathel caught a glimpse in the distance of the pack leader high on an outcropping of rock; he directed the approaching pack back onto the offensive. Moving forward along a broad front they came, leaping the drifts of snow. At first hundreds, then as they struggled on, thousands could be seen. It seemed to Nathel that the entire mountain side was alive with the charging wolves.

"The fallen are truly moving," Thero whispered. He sounded in awe.

"Double time, move you turtles or become a snack for the wolves," Timoth's gravelly voice thundered across the valley.

On they ran, red-cloaked soldiers moving quickly despite the heavy burden of armor and weapons that weighed them down. Timoth shouted encouragement, urging his men forward and upward.

Moments later Nathel ran over the top of a rise in the valley floor and dashed into the narrow confines of steep pass leading across the border. Fifty paces behind them, the wolf pack broiled over the top of the pass in pursuit.

Rocky walls on each side stretched up into the air, blocking any attempt to climb to the safety of narrow ledges. Nathel risked a glance behind them and immediately wished he had not. The pack pressed on, coming closer with each passing moment. He could see the valley walls narrowing slowly but they were still too far apart for the reduced number of warriors to defend.

"Turn, double shield wall," Timoth barked. The pursuing wolves pressed to within twenty paces when Timoth shouted the command. As one the red cloaks turned and rushed to establish a wide front, swords hissed free of sheathes and shields were held chest high.

In the rocky confines of the narrowing valley the screams and shouts echoed loudly. Once again the two forces came together; the wolves leapt and slashed, working in pairs against the well drilled soldiers. Timoth kept the line moving. He continued to give ground, contracting the line as the valley narrowed, each step helping the red cloaks to hold the battle line together. Timoth anchored the center with Thero, Nathel stood behind them. With his staff missing, he was unarmed and unable to join the fight.

"Run boy," Timoth grunted loudly.

"But I can help."

"Run up to the border," Thero cried. His staff became a blur of activity.

Torn but obedient, Nathel finally turned and sprinted up the small rise that separated him from the marked border. A single red flag flapped in the breeze at the top of the hill, marking the border of the kingdom of Ahtonium.

Nathel skidded to a stop when he reached the fluttered pennant, and shouted for joy. Before him in even ranks marched the mustered army of Ahtonium, red cloaks fluttering in the wind and iron shields forming a solid wall, pointing at the border. The soldiers jogged forward, rank upon rank of grim warriors parted and moved around him. Battle cries filled the valley as the men rushed to the aide of their beleaguered comrades. Nathel watched from where he stood as the writhing wolf pack howled and fled. The sight of the cloaked warriors marching down the small rise towards them had broken their will to fight.

In the distance he saw the pack leader rise and nod at him.

"Another time, boy. You will never be free of us," The voice drifted on the wind and faded into the distance. Moments later the pass was empty as the pack disappeared into the rugged mountains. The wolves closest to the holding force pressed the attack instead of fleeing. All along the short line, soldiers were pulled down under the flashing fangs. Nathel grimaced hoping to catch a glimpse of Thero and Timoth but the lines became blurred. The even rank dissolved into a myriad of small fights. His heart leapt in his chest when a flight of arrows lofted into the air. The shafts hung in the air for many long moments and then flashed down.

The wolves without any armor were easy prey to the iron tipped arrows. Hundreds fell dead where they fought and the few remaining wolves broke ranks and fled making for the safety of the southern mountains.

Nathel whispered thanks to the Elemental protectors as he dashed forward searching among the tired warriors for Thero's tall thin form.

"GRANDPA." He called desperately, fearing that his grandfather had been slain in the tumultuous battle.

"Nathel," Timoth gravelly voice interrupted him, "Your grandfather is over here."

He ran down the trail. Moments later he spotted the thin form of his grandfather standing next to the motionless form of a wyrm warrior.

A cry of aguish tore from his heart as he recognized the brown scales and ragged armor of Venthern. The wyrm was lying on the ground, his breath coming in ragged gasps. The teeth and claws of the wolves had torn his wings to tattered ribbons. The skin and scales below the shattered armor was ripped and bleeding in dozens of places. Thero knelt near the dragon's head, he whispered the blessings of the creator under his breath calling Anatari to come and bring the noble warrior to his final rest.

"Venthern," Nathel cried. He threw his arms around the scaly head when he reached the wyrm, tears flowing freely down his face when he saw the terrible wounds that he bore.

"It is alright Nathel, I go to a better place now. I will receive my reward from the creator. Have faith son, and someday you to will receive your reward."

Those words took Venthern's remaining breath and his eyes rolled back, a smile showing on his face. Nathel wiped the tears from his cheek. He looked up and overhead the sun shown down brilliantly on the unmoving wyrm.

Thero sighed. He reached out a hand and gently closed the eyes of the wyrm. Then he stood to his feet and moved back, waiting for Nathel.

Nathel stood. He carefully ran his hand down the cracked scales around the neck of the wyrm.

"Goodbye Venthern. I hardly knew you but you saved my life. May you serve the creator in the next life as faithfully as you served him in this, and may He give your soul peace for all eternity."

Matthew John Krengel

CHAPTER TEN
THE ANCIENT ONE

he return to Kashguth, the capital of Ahtonium was a sober march. Of the initial two hundred soldiers that rushed from the city to rescue Nathel seventy had died, and forty more bore grievous wounds. The priests struggled over the torn bodies of the living, salves of healing were used and prayers ascended constantly asking for guidance and healing. The wounded were tended in great wagons, pulled by teams of shaggy oxen. The priests rode in the wagons or walked quietly beside them, they talked in hushed tones and pushed all but Timoth away when they tried to approach.

Nathel walked in silence wrapped in his own thoughts. The guilt he felt knowing that Venthern and many others had died coming to save him weighed heavily on his mind. The trails back to Kashguth were wide and lined with many trees. Scores of homes dotted the landscape. Built of stone and roofed with clay tiles, they reminded Nathel of Comstoll. The closer they marched to the capitol the more numerous the houses became, some clustered together into small villages. Field after field of sprouting crops marked the fertile lands of the valley nestled into the surrounding mountains.

"There is it, the home of the Ancient One. The city that opens it arms to anyone that believe in the creator," Thero spoke with pride. Still as he looked closer many of the houses sat empty, the windows covered with cobwebs and tall weeds sprouting between the stones.

Through the trees Nathel caught glimpses of the city walls rising into the air, stone watch towers covered in pennants kept a constant vigil on the surrounding lands.

The ancient walled city of Kashguth dominated the landscape two hours march from the southern border. Keeping its distance from the low lands to the north and cut off from Orkin lands by hundreds of leagues of mountains.

Nathel stared open mouthed at the vast collections of walls and buildings. The city wrapped around a towering mountain of rock, Nathel squinted at the towering pillar of stone. Three dark spots near the clouds that shrouded the upper parts of the mountain reminded him of a skull. He opened his mouth to ask Thero but closed it again as his grandfather moved away to speak to Timoth. Instead, he looked closely at the towering walls before themand saw the tiny figures of soldiers as they stood watch on every tower.

"You could put Rockcreek inside those walls twenty times," He said as they viewed the full splendor of the white washed walls and clay tiled rooflines.

"At least if not double that," Thero strode back. He shook his head, "It has grown some over the last one hundred years. At least some still flee from the oppression in the low land kingdoms and find protection and safety in the mountain kingdom."

Nathel remained silent as they approached the city, all around them travelers stepped off the road leaving the hundreds of red cloaks alone on the hard packed ground. The merchants and farmers stood paying quiet homage, their right fists closed and held over their hearts.

"It's a sign of respect for the dead," Thero spoke. He nodded at the silent figures.

"Why the hooded cloak, Grandpa?"

"For now it is best that my face not be seen."

"Why?" Nathel frowned.

"I will explain later Nathel, for now please trust me a bit longer," Thero smiled. He put a long arm around Nathel's shoulders and gave him a brief hug.

The road arced along the bottom of the thick city walls and Nathel looked up, scores of winged helms kept silent watch from above. At one point they passed a massive stone gate, instead of a wide road allowing passage into the city hundreds of stone blocks blocked the access.

"Why a gate that is blocked up grandpa?"

"That is the Palm Gate. It was blocked up thousands of years ago after the War of Heaver. It will remain closed until this world ends. Legend says that when the final battle rages Anatari will come and lead the faithful warriors through the Palm Gate. Anatari and Bedbezdal will meet for the final battle and the fate of this world will be decided. Mind you not all legends are grounded in the books though."

"What books?"

Thero smiled and waved his hand, "A subject best left for later, son."

He stared at Thero blankly not understanding.

"Nathel I have much yet to teach you. I dared not speak of it when we were traveling among the huddled masses of the world. The Fallen are powerful - we would have faced danger on all sides if a wrong word was spoken even once. Even here with some bit of safety there is still a danger of the Fallen attacking us."

"But..."

"I will tell you the story soon, let us get inside the city walls. We must go meet with the Ancient One and seek his wisdom."

Nathel nodded, soon another gate opened up before them, unlike the Palm Gate it sat wide open. Layered wooden planks mounted on iron bars and hinges set in the nearby stone protected the portal to the city. Inside Nathel saw hundreds of people waiting silently.

The presence of the seventy stretchers bearing the dead muted the celebration at the victorious return. The folk bowed their heads fists covering heart in honor for the spirits of the soldiers who had died fighting the minions of the Fallen. The dead were carried on stretchers with their shield and weapon laid respectfully on top of the body, Thero told him in hushed tones that they would be interned in the vaults under the city. Thero explained to him as he walked behind Timoth, there they would lie as their eternal souls sought rest in the great beyond.

A wide, tree lined avenue pierced straight into the city, two and three story houses lined the avenue. The peaked roof tops added a bit of shade from the bright afternoon sun and everywhere Nathel looked trees and flowers greeted his eyes. Clay pots filled with flowers sat in every window and tall trees lined the city streets.

Everywhere he looked his eyes drank in the sights of a bustling city; they passed through wide market squares lined with the stalls of venders. Nathel stared wide-eyed at the stocky dwarves stepping carefully through the crowds, most nearly as wide as they were tall. Not so frequent were the thin forms of elves walking gracefully through the crowds, fair faces and melodic voices marked them from the myriad of humans present. At one corner a tall elvin woman sang a slow dirge. Even from a distance, her voice was clear and strong and brought a tear to Nathel's eye.

"The elves that live here are all that remain," Thero whispered. The voice of the singer faded away as they moved deeper into the city. The buildings drew closer together and the pointed roof tops gave way to clay tiles and ancient stone work.

"Why is that?"

"Their villages once filled the land known now controlled by the Northern Orkin Empire. Nearly one thousand years ago, a ruler arose among the Orkin. He was called Valkin the Mad. He united the scattered tribes of Orkin and molded them into a powerful army. He marched north from where the Southern Orkin Empire sits. They sailed across the Bay of Orn, and slaughtered the peaceful elf villages across the peninsula. It took the combined armies of the low land kingdoms to stop his rampage. Many of the elves were slain without mercy and the remaining members of the race sought refuge here and were welcomed. Even now most Orkin do not know the true story behind their expansion into the northern peninsula. Except for the few that have sought refuge here in Ahtonium, they have been made to believe the land was empty for the taking. The ones that are here are considered rebels in their own country."

Nathel caught glimpses of the hairy forms of the Orkin moving through the crowds, they were equal to humans in size but their hairy bodies and wide pig like snouts made them easy to pick out.

"All of the remaining wyrms also live in the mountain kingdom; they are the only created race able to fly."

"Venthern gave his life for me grandpa. Why?" Nathel finally asked the question.

"That has been bothering you, hasn't it?" Thero glanced at him from below the hood.

"Why would he give his life for a stranger?" Nathel pressed on.

"Sometimes Nathel it is more blessed to give than to receive. Even to give one's life, in the fight against evil."

Nathel shook his head, the thought of dying for a complete stranger made no sense to him.

"I think for now it will remain a mystery," Thero said. "At least for a bit longer," he added as Nathel scowled.

"Venthern was a mighty warrior; he had served the Ancient One for nearly seven hundred years. He will be sorely missed," Timoth said quietly. The gruff dwarf must have been listening to the conversation.

"Enough of this talk, look about you son. This is the greatest city in the world, not the largest but the greatest. This is a melting pot of nations and peoples. Oh we have our problems, but it is one of the few places where a person can walk from wall to wall with no fear of being robbed."

"Feel free to explore. If you lose your way ask any red cloak, they will direct you back to the fortress," Timoth nodded.

"How many different people live here?"

"Almost half of the inhabitants of Ahtonium are human," Thero said. He pointed down the side streets, hundreds of forms teemed back and forth about their work.

"Many have fled the oppression of the believers in the low lands. The worship of the creator is distained in most of the low land kingdoms almost as much as the worship of the Dark One. The residents of the mountain kingdom are considered ignorant savages and if it were not for greed many would cut off all contact with us."

Nathel glanced sharply at Thero, wondering in his mind what Thero's entire story was.

"Yes, Nathel, I once lived here in the capitol. That was many years ago, and it too is a story for another time," Thero fell silent as they walked.

Nathel let the subject go and watched in awe as crowds of people turned to show their respect for the fallen soldiers. Silence blanketed the city except for dozens of lips whispering the blessings of the creator and many calling for Anatari to come soon and bring the faithful home.

The houses nearest the inner wall were made of brick and stone, tall windows set with glass windows to let the light flow freely. The tall panes of glass were a product of trade with the Orkin Empires to the east and north.

Small gardens graced many terraces and balconies of the homes, the flowers giving the city a life that was missing when compared with the small towns. Everywhere he looked hundreds of people crowded the streets. Small shops dotted the alleys, wooden signs painted with bright colors advertised their wares. Nathel stumbled through the pronouncing of the words. One sign proudly boasted 'Finely Crafted Weapons,' another proclaimed 'Fresh Pastries'. Everywhere Nathel looked, colors and sounds filled his ears and eyes.

The avenue they were marching down narrowed even more as it approached the center of the city. Nathel looked up as they entered a break in the line of houses. Before him a second wall separated the outer city from the inner fortress, the inner wall dwarfing the outer. As they approached the gates the long lines of red cloaks turned and marched east. Led by Timoth, they returned their barracks. A ceremonial guard of two hundred somber warriors escorted the dead up to a small ornate gate set into the inner wall; two massive dwarf guards stepped forward from the right and left side of the gate. Wearing full plate armor they were a fierce sight, massive shields held rigidly in front of them and heavy maces hung loosely in their weapon hands.

"Who seeks entrance to the sacred mountain?"

Thero stepped forward leaning slightly on his staff, "The honored dead seek their resting place within the hallowed walls of the catacombs. I and my grandson seek audience with the Ancient Wyrm."

"The dead are granted entrance to go to their final resting place. Who are you that we should grant you audience with the Ancient One?"

Thero remained silent for a moment and Nathel noticed that the thick hands tightened on the mace handles. Then Thero threw back his hood and stood tall. His face grew stern.

"I am The Prophet. I helped found this city and this country. I am the only remaining Prophet who knew the Ancient One when he was in his youth."

Nathel watched in amazement as the guards stepped back. Both released their grips on the heavy maces and flipped up their visors. The two faces filled with shock. Both stepped back to the gate and rushed to work the mechanism. The towering gate swung silently on oiled hinges allowing the procession entrance into the inner fortress.

Nathel walked quietly beside Thero, craning his head to stare upward at the mountain that presented itself to them. A wide courtyard opened up inside the gate and was followed by a second set of gates set into the side of a steep sloped mountain.

"Thero where is the castle?"

"You're looking at it son, the sacred mountain. It's where Anatari stood when the creator banished the Dark One to his icy prison."

"Why not just kill him?" Nathel asked.

"A good question Nathel, why would the creator allow his most trusted servant to rebel? Perhaps it is because elementals, like mortals, were allowed a free will. Other than that bit of speculation, I have no answer," Thero replied

Nathel let the subject drop as he stared with an open mouth at the steep rocky slope of the mountain. Sheer cliffs led to the peak which was clouded in mists.

The inner gate stood closed, guarded by two more heavily armored warriors. This time human and elf swung the double doors open to admit the funeral procession. Once inside the gate the bodies of the dead warriors were taken down a long sloping tunnel that led off to the east deep underground. The long halls were lit brilliantly with glowing balls of glass attached to the walls and they drew Nathel's attention.

"Thero look its amazing, where are the flames?" Nathel walked over to one of the light balls and stared into it. He squinted hard, searching for a flickering flame.

"There are no flames inside the mountain son, flames give off smoke and eventually they lead to death underground. The dwarves value the knowledge of the rocks and the ground. Our people call it alchemy; it is the study of the chemicals and the mixing of things drawn from the depths of the ground. That is how the miners light the tunnel systems and mines that honeycomb the nearby mountains."

"What do the other races do?" Nathel could not contain his curiosity.

"Well the Dwarves are masters of mining, building, and crafting. It is the Elvin that designs and plan the amazing machines, canals, and cities scattered around the realm. The human race is very gifted at farming and herding and it is their bountiful farms that keep our kingdom fed. The members of the Orkin race that live here are experts in trade and they keep the flow of things we cannot make here flowing with their caravans. The wyrm's are the scouts for the army and they keep our borders safe at all times from small bands of thieves and crooks. There are times when the army must be mustered as it was today but those are few and far between, the wyrms are fierce warriors and most turn back when confronted by a trio of wyrm warriors."

"There is a saying passed down from generation to generation. To each is given a gift, let it not be wasted."

Nathel nodded his head as he walked along beside Thero; they entered a wide tunnel that sloped down into the ground. The walk was short and soon Nathel and Thero stood before a third set of guarded gates. Nearly a dozen red cloaks lined the walls, short swords and shields held ready.

"Why so many soldiers, grandfather?"

"The ancient wyrm has many enemies that would like to end his days in the mortal realm, so he is well protected inside the mountains and outside."

The inner gate swung open quietly and they entered a wide room, the ceiling soared up out of sight. Nathel strained his neck looking for the ceiling but it was lost in the shadows. Seated in the center of the room next to a crystal clear pool of water, Nathel saw a dragon of immense size. Standing neck and shoulders taller than Venthern and stretched out twice as long. It was his eyes that drew Nathel forward, eyes filled with wisdom. Deep orbs, they witnessed thousands of years and would continue despite the aged look of the scales protecting his back.

"Welcome old friend," The wyrm said, His voice crystal clear and powerful. Long talons flexed and dug into the floor.

"It is good to see you again Eloha," Thero replied. He bowed his head in honor to the ruler of Ahtonium, Nathel followed suit, bowing his head low.

"Things are spiraling out of control in the low lands again," Eloha said. He immediately spoke to the heart the business.

"Not only in the low lands. Never before have the fallen challenged our borders so aggressively," Thero responded. He walked up the wyrm and looked intently at the scene that floated in the crystal water. Nathel stood on his toes but the surface of the pool remained misty and hard to see.

"The Pool of Time is clouded. It will not be of use to us. Bedbezdal's minions are moving across the face of the world, he seeks the hearts of mortals. Many have answered his call and many more will. A time of darkness is coming. Anatari may not be able to rescue mortals; the creator may allow us to sink in the mire of our own making."

"But there must be something that can be done?" Nathel blurted. He spoke without thinking; the words drew a sharp glance from Thero but no response.

"There is always a path to salvation," The wyrm spoke. He turned his massive head and looked to Nathel who stepped forward, a pleading look in his eyes.

"Sometimes is not enough to have a path. There must be those with the courage and faith to obey. Are you one who would do that young mortal?" The wyrm's eye bore down on Nathel.

"I am just a shepherd," Nathel muttered as he bowed his head. Inwardly he wanted to say yes but his mouth would not form the words, he wanted to scream yes and be as brave as Venthern, but something kept him from speaking.

"There is a way to thwart Bedbezdal yet. However, it is a dark path, narrow, hard to follow, and difficult to see the end."

Nathel raised his head but the words still failed to come out, doubt gnawed at his soul.

"Do you know what must be done to stop Bedbezdal from ruling the mortal world?" Thero asked. He stepped forward.

"The Pool is quiet on all but one thing. The army must march to the Fortress of Winds if we are to weather the coming storm. I dispatched a messenger to the Fortress of Winds over two months ago to seek the knowledge of the Wind Guardians. We have received no reply from the guardians. It is my fear that something has happened. If the fortress falls, Bedbezdal will bury the low lands with his armies. Combined with the growing power of the Fallen in the low land cities, the scattered kingdoms could be swept away before we even have time to muster our defenses."

"Have you tried to warn the lowlanders?" Thero asked. He seated himself on a low stone bench near the edge of the pool.

Nathel stood listening to the conversation still struggling in his mind. One part of him said that he would be the one to obey; he could follow the straight narrow path. The rest of his mind kept telling him he was a simple shepherd nothing more.

"What can a skinny shepherd from the Highlands do for such a desperate cause? The creator must want someone who is taller and stronger. How can they use someone like me?" he whispered the words so lightly that neither Thero nor the Ancient Wyrm heard.

Nathel turned; he wandered about the throne room. He stood for many moments examining the tapestries that hung from the walls, soaring murals of ancient battles decorated around the room. Finally he stopped in front of a large glass mirror and stared at the reflection.

"I am just a boy, the creator would never send Anatari to call me," he repeated.

Turning away Nathel dropped into a chair and leaned back. He yawned tiredly. The fight on the border had taken much of his energy. The battle inside him sapped the last of his strength and he quickly slipped into sleep.

Matthew John Krengel

Chapter Eleven
A Choice Offered

elcome back to my world boy," the wolf stared at him. "Stay away from me!" Nathel cried. His voice rang out strong this time. In his mind the image of Venthern dying on the mountain slope gave him courage.

"Is that any way to greet an old friend? You misunderstood what happened before. We were simply forced to defend ourselves against the aggressive soldiers of the king of the wyrms."

"You killed Venthern. All he wanted was to help me."

"You misunderstand boy…"

"STOP!" Nathel's voice thundered out. "I will not let you haunt my dreams any longer. You are the enemy of Anatari, and that makes you my enemy."

The wolf exploded into action, throwing himself forward with his teeth bared. Deep throated growls echoed from the black creature, and fire flared from his eyes.

Nathel rolled left, bringing his staff up in front of him to protect his head and throat. Spinning the ironwood in a rapid circle in front of his body he crouched, waiting for the attack that never came. The wolf stared up at the gray sky ignoring him.

"What are you waiting for?" Nathel screamed. He used his left hand to slap the staff to a halt and strike at the wolf.

It dodged and leapt away, whirling to face the unseen enemy in the gray mists.

"Another time, boy. My master has plans for you."

Nathel looked up as the gray mists thinned and a brilliant light shone in the distance. Then in a flash of silver, the image of Soldier Venthern soared over head. The wyrm soldier wheeled in the sky and dove, his body rocketing like a spear for the crouching pack leader. The wolf took one more look and then he fled disappearing in moments. Venthern flashed by and wheeled about again, this time winging to Nathel and dropping something to the ground at his feet.

"Nathel you must awake, you are in great danger."

"But I saw you die Venthern," Nathel stammered ignoring the warnings of the noble wyrm.

"You must awake now Nathel. If you do not all is lost," Venthern cried. The urgency in his voice finally sank into Nathel and he nodded his head. He wished he could speak with the wyrm but knowing he must wake his body.

Nathel jumped up from the soft chair his mind racing, the throne room was quiet. Over by the pool he saw Thero and the Ancient Wyrm deep in conversation, Thero gestured as he spoke, pointing to the pool.

Nathel rose to his feet, he leaned on his staff and looked about.

"My staff!"

Nathel held the weapon up; he stared in disbelief at the ironwood rod. He trotted over to the double doors, pondering the appearance of the weapon. The doors guarding the entrance to the throne room of the fortress swung open quietly when he pushed on them.

The red cloaks guarding the gate nodded to him as he stepped into the tunnel.

He looked down the tunnel, in the distance a ball of light winked out, leaving the far side of the corridor in absolute darkness.

"Do the lights ever fail?"

The guard on the left looked down the tunnel and watched as a second light failed bringing the darkness five paces closer to the door.

"Sound the alarm someone is in the fortress," the red-cloaked guard said. His voice was unnaturally calm; reaching up the guards closed the visors on their plate helms and drew their swords.

Nathel stepped back to the door, he watched the red cloaks raise their shields and step forward. Down the corridor a third globe of light failed, allowing the wall of darkness to come to within ten paces. Nathel retreated back into the throne room running to where Thero and the Ancient One were still deep in conversation.

"Thero, something is happening outside,"

"What do you mean, boy?" Thero said. He looked up sharply.

"The lights in the tunnel are failing. The red cloak said someone is in the fortress."

Thero leapt to his feet grabbing his staff, the Ancient one turned to face the double doors. The sounds of fighting echoed through the doors as the heavily armed guards engaged the unknown foe in the tunnel.

Nathel dove behind the stone edge of the pool as the double doors exploded inward, tearing them off their hinges. The battered and torn body of one of the guards hurled across the throne room, coming to rest at the Ancient one's feet. Nathel gasped in horror as a living wave of darkness entered the throne room. The darkness crept forward, filling the throne room until Nathel and Thero were back against the cold stone of the Pool of Time.

"Time to die old one," The voice that spoke sent shivers up and down Nathel's spine and left his arms weak.

"So Cruathila, you have returned to your original form. The boy's blow hurt you much more then you let on out on the border," Eloha said. He drew himself up matching the darkness with the power in his voice.

Nathel watched as the darkness thinned, slowly revealing the blackened and smoking creature - a vaguely humanoid creature with curled horns of a ram, a fiery whip and smoking flail clenched in clawed fingers.

Nathel dove for cover as Cruathila struck out with the flail smashing it into the edge of the pool. The stone surrounding the serene water crumbled and the throne room shook. The water began spilling, lost forever from the device.

"You are no match for me old one, this will be your last day in this world. This is the end of Elutha's last bastion of believers on this world."

Cruathila stepped forward towards them, leaving burn marks etched into the marble floors with each step.

Thero grabbed Nathel and pulled him to the side, "We cannot interfere in this fight. He is a foe beyond our skill. Come, we must raise the alarm in the city."

Nathel turned and looked at the Ancient One but the wyrm simply nodded his head and motioned for them to leave. Drawing himself up to his full height, the wyrm stepped forward and the battle was joined.

Nathel and Thero fled along the dark tunnel, behind them the fortress shook as the two immense beings traded blows in the expanse of the throne room. The Ancient Wyrm calling on the Elements to strengthen him and guide him, while Cruathila hurled curses and mocked at him.

Thero and Nathel burst through the outermost door of the fortress and skidded to a halt. The carnage in the courtyard shocked them, and packs of wolves prowled the walls. The battered bodies of at least a score of red cloaks lay scattered about the ground under their posts.

As soon as they exited the gates the chase was on. Nathel and Thero charged for the gate. Immediately the gate swung closed and they cut to the left, aiming for the stairway to the wall. The stairs flew by under their feet, and Nathel followed Thero as they raced to reach the top of the thick wall. Two wolves leapt out at them and this time it was Nathel who swept his staff right and left. The blows cleared the stairs and on they charged.

When they arrived at the top of the stairs Thero lunged to the left and raced along the top of the wall. Behind them a dozen wolves boiled along the wall in pursuit. Glancing back, Nathel could see the dark forms of the Fallen mixed in with the wolf pack.

"The Fallen," Nathel shouted. His voice carried over the howls and shouts of the pursuers.

"I know, son, keep running! We must reach the tower at the end of the wall, there is an alarm bell there. The army barracks are close, but we must gain their attention!" Thero yelled. He glanced over his shoulder as they charged headlong around the corner of the wall.

A wolf and two humans dressed in black cloaks rushed to meet them as they ran towards the tower guarding the corner of the wall. The humans wielded knives and short swords. They attacked with abandon, while the wolf hung back. Nathel brought his staff up and lunged forward using the superior reach of his staff to attack.

Right and left Nathel blocked the blades and then struck hard with the ironwood staff. His blow sent the knife from the first human's hand spinning out over the dark courtyard. A second snapping blow left the hand hanging uselessly, the bones crushed. Grunting, the man turned sideways working his remaining sword in a series of thrusts and slashes that were nowhere close to hitting him.

Nathel suddenly cried out in surprise when a bolt of fur and teeth leapt past the human and drove him back against the hard stones of the parapet.

"THERO!"

Thero saw the charging wolf and struck hard at his human opponent knocking him off balance. With a cry Thero's opponent tumbled over the wall screaming until he landed on hard pavement sixty paces below.

Pivoting on his right foot Thero turned and struck hard, his blow catching the charging wolf in the side. The force of the strike took the wolf in mid jump and combined with his momentum sent the howling wolf over the outer edge of the wall as well. Nathel breathed a sigh of relief as the dark form crashed into the street near the army barracks.

The remaining man clutched his crushed hand to his body as he fought, feral snarls dropping from his lips.

"You will all die," his hood fell back as he spoke.

Nathel gasped as he stepped back, his staff sagging towards the ground. Pale and drawn, the man's face was twisted with evil.

"Die creature, you chose your fate long ago."

Thero strode forward his staff suddenly glowing softly in the darkness that filled the walkway atop the wall. The ironwood met the black sword and the edged weapon shattered into a thousand pieces.

"Not this time Prophet," he turned and leaped off the wall. The only sound was the thump of the body landing on the stones below.

"Go sound the alarm," Thero cried. They crashed into the main floor of the tower, "I will hold them here. The alarm bell is atop the tower."

Nathel nodded, he raced to the ladder and went up three rungs at a time. Throwing open the trap door on top he burst into the bright light of the full moon.

"There is it," he muttered. Held up by a wooden post was a large bronze bell, he grabbed the rope attached to it and pulled hard. The ringing of the alarm bell sounded clear and loud echoing across the nearby rooftops. Nathel raced back to the front of the tower and looked over the city, and still silence reigned.

"Come on, someone must be out there," he whispered.

Then, with a shout a thousand soldiers burst from their barracks, gathering into squads as they ran. Hundreds streamed for the fortress. Nathel watched as groups of the Fallen leapt from alleys and chaos erupted.

The red cloaks fought with courage and soon hundreds more fanned out across the city as the resistance near the castle was destroyed. On the horizon Nathel watched thick columns of black smoke rise against the moonlit sky across the city as bands of Fallen set fires and battled with the mustering soldiers.

Racing back to the ladder, Nathel went down in a controlled slide, dropping on the balls of his feet. In the confines of the room Thero battled two more black cloaked fighters and Nathel leapt forward with a savage cry and swung his staff wildly. The ploy worked as the wild swing forced the men to pull back fearing to pit their swords against a hard blow from the ironwood.

Nathel smiled as Thero took advantage of the lull to roll to the left and launch a strike against the leg of one fighter, a loud crack sounded and he collapsed clutching at his broken limb. Nathel struck the second man three times. His staff crushing the black weapon and then snapping the black-cloaked figure's head about and then sent him flying backwards.

Nathel stared at the limp figure in front of him on the floor. His stomach turned uncontrollably, it was first time he had been confronted with the body of someone trying to kill him. Battling wolves was one thing but killing a human left a sad feeling in the pit of his stomach.

"Boy, he was trying to kill you, he left you little choice," Thero puffed. He placed an arm around Nathel's shoulder.

"He will be judged, but for the Fallen they have already made their choice. There is always room for them to repent while they remain on the mortal world but once on that wide road to destruction it is most hard to turn back."

Nathel nodded, he wiped a sweaty hand across his eyes, "It sounds like the army is in the courtyard."

Moving to the door they cracked it open, through the opening they saw hundreds of red-cloaked soldiers swarming across the courtyard. The fight was vicious but the end came quickly, the Fallen lacked the numbers to fend off the well trained soldiers.

Thero and Nathel rushed down the wall and took the stairs down in leaps and bounds rushing to where Timoth was standing by the gate.

"We must get into the fortress," Thero said. He motioned for the nearby troops to follow him, they charged to where they found the fortress gates closed tightly and barred from the inside.

"Tear some timbers from the barracks and get them in here. We need to get through these gates," Timoth bellowed. He sent teams of soldiers scurrying for heavy timbers to be used as battering rams. Other groups of soldiers combed the outer castle flushing out any remaining wolves and black hooded humans.

"Sir, we are still meeting resistance in the city, and the fires are making it hard," a panting red cloak skidded to a halt near Timoth.

"Take ten more squads and get the fires under control. Roust the city militia if you must, but I want Kashguth cleared."

"Yes sir!"

"And search the sewers, I want to know how they managed to get hundreds of the pack and Fallen into my city," Timoth bellowed at the retreating messenger.

Moments later the teams dragged three heavy timbers into the courtyard. Two ropes were used to loop the timbers together and then a dozen more ropes were used hold up the timbers while six dwarves pulled back and let the makeshift ram slam forward.

"How long will this take," Thero asked. He stood back watching as the red cloaked warriors worked feverishly to break into their own fortress.

Timoth turned to Thero, "Might take hours to break through those gates, we never thought we would breaking into our own fortress."

Nathel and Thero watched as they continued to slam the ram home into the iron bound oaken gate. They paced and waited, even taking turns helping to swing the massive ram. Finally the first cracks appeared two hours after they started.

Morning was breaking over the walls and the sun was peeking out in the mountain sky when a cheer erupted from the assembled soldiers.

Five hundred fully armed and rested guards stood, they waited to rush the corridors of the fortress. Nathel could not help noticing how their red cloaks were almost black in the half light of morning.

CRASH!

A tremendous roar echoed through the courtyard as the ram slammed one of the gates free of its hinges, the thick oaken planks finally splintering. A second blow tore the planks away and bent iron bands. The red cloaks pulled their weapons and started into the dark tunnels, dozens of torches held high. At each intersection more than a score of the soldiers veered off and moved down the side tunnels. Sounds of fighting echoed through the quiet halls and Nathel heard Timoth bellow for more troops into the side tunnels. At each turn, small pockets of wolves and Fallen lurked round the corners, and hid in store rooms. They fought furiously and to the death when discovered.

Nathel and Thero moved along the main tunnel holding torches high, Timoth followed at a run motioning for remaining soldiers to follow. They had to reach the throne room as quickly as possible. Nathel glanced back as they approached the doors. More than a hundred red cloaks were still with them when they ran down the sloping tunnel to the gilded double doors.

A lone figure waited for them, a long black cowl hid his face and Nathel skidded to a halt behind Thero, his staff held ready.

"You're too late Prophet. Once again you have failed to see the rising power of the Fallen. Eloha, eldest of the dragons and father of his race is dead, succumbed to the power of Bedbezdal. Your strongest ruler is dead before the war has even started."

The shadowy creature spoke with a hiss, his hands folded inside his sleeves and even his feet shrouded in black cloth.

"Be gone foul creature," Thero growled. He advanced with his staff held ready. Nathel and the red cloaks advanced with vengeance in their eyes.

"Ha! Puny mortals, what has an elemental have to fear from your weapons?" Throwing the cowl and the cloak from its back the creature leapt into the air. Bat like wings shot out on each side of its vaguely human form, long fangs hung from its mouth. Flapping its wings in long strokes the monster shot down the tunnel so fast that Nathel barely had time to duck.

Thero turned and pulled open the door. The scene before them stunned Nathel into complete silence, his words died on his tongue. Eloha lay across the floor, gaping wounds showed across his body. Clenched in his massive jaws lay was the body of Cruathila, the creature covered in an equal number of wounds. As Thero, Nathel, and Timoth approached, the Ancient Wyrm gave one last burst of strength and threw the lifeless body of his killer across the room. It crashed into the wall and lay still for a moment. Then Nathel watched as it dissolved into a black oily substance that faded into the ground leaving behind only a black stain forever etched across the floor.

"I have finished my course old one," The words were weak as the life blood flowed from the Ancient Wyrm.

Thero walked closer patting his side, tears flowing down his face as he prayed quietly asking Anatari to guide the soul of the dying ruler of Ahtonium quickly to the arms of the creator.

The Ancient Wyrm nodded to Thero and then turned to Nathel, "Son, you have been offered a great task. If you reject it, the mortal world will fall to the shadow of Bedbezdal. No, don't speak just listen, you must find the Chamber of Life."

Motioning to the wall the Ancient Wyrm nodded to a shimmering door that appeared in the wall, "Through that door is a small gold bell. Take it and ring the bell inside the room where Elutha stood when he formed the world and ring it once. If Bedbezdal is loose in the world, he will come to the call; he will not be able to resist taking something so precious for his own. Once he is inside the chamber of life, ring the bell a second time. He will be bound again."

"Above all, believe son. He would not abandon the world. Even when it seems most of the world has abandoned him."

Nathel nodded, "I will try do as you ask Ancient One, kneeling down he bowed his head before the wyrm."

The Ancient Wyrm nodded his head once accepting the answer and then quietly laid his head down on the cold stones of the floor. His eyes closed and the movement of his sides stopped as the breath left his body. Nathel watched in awe as a shimmering light surrounded the massive body of the Ancient wyrm. Rising up into the air, the wyrm twinkled brightly then disappeared in a burst of light.

"Anatari has taken a faithful servant home," Thero said. He bowed his head in sorrow, the surrounding red cloaks all bowed their heads as silence descended across the throne room.

Chapter Twelve
The Bell of Creation

 week of hurried activity followed. Nathiel waondered about in a daze as the funeral preparations were made for the Ancient Wyrm. To his amazement, Thero took charge and ordered people about like he was the next in line for the throne. The respect shown to Thero amazed Nathel even more. No one dared to argue with or even question his orders. Indeed, there was more to the old man then met the eyes.

Three days after the assassination, the funeral occurred in the cavernous throne room. The bare granite blossomed overnight, covered with a layer of flowers. The chanting prayers of a score of priests echoed off the walls. Dressed in a new doublet and a silken shirt, Nathel stood in the far side of the room while the ceremony of remembrance was conducted. After the ceremony Nathel slipped down the main tunnel and walked slowly out of the mountain fortress. Overhead the sun shone brightly and he squinted at the blinding reflections as he walked across the stone paved courtyard.

"It seems like the whole world knows Thero except me," Nathel muttered. He kicked a small stone and immediately regretted the action; the soft boots did little to protect his foot. Even the small stone stung his foot bringing a momentary mist to his eyes.

He could not shake feeling betrayed some at the sudden changes in his grandfather. Trudging slowly deeper into the city, he stopped to examine the varying structures intertwined down the street and he was soon lost in the maze of streets and shops. Thankfully his doublet was cool and a fresh breeze was blowing down from the east. Squads of soldiers moved about discreetly checking and rechecking every corner of the city. Nathel rested on his staff as a patrol crossed the street in front of him. The sergeant leading the patrol nodded to him. Nathel thought he recognized the dwarf from the battle in the courtyard but it was hard to tell.

Not knowing why he stopped, he turned and slipped into a nearby inn. The sweet smell of scented candles filled the air, and a small fire crackled merrily in the stone fireplace. Only three other people were present and Nathel sat down at a table pressed to the side of the room. He carefully leaned his staff against the wall and rested back in the leather padded chair.

"Good day sir, can I help you with anything?" asked a serving girl. Her smile was infectious and Nathel found himself grinning like a fool. A flip of her wrist tucked long locks of blond hair behind her right ear. Deep blue eyes fastened on him as he spoke.

"Can I get a mug of spiced cider," Nathel continued to smile. She was pretty and his heart beat a bit faster.

The maid nodded and winked at him, she turned and walked across the front room of the inn with a graceful sway. Nathel never paid any attention to the girls of the shepherd's village but for some reason this girl seemed different. Nathel continued to smile the entire time as she delivered his hot-spiced cider.

"How much do I owe you?"

"For you its free," she waved her hand in the air.

Nathel stared at her trying to decide whether she was joking or serious.

"Why is that," he finally decided that she must be serious.

"Anyone traveling with the Prophet must be important."

"The prophet? You mean grandpa?" Nathel stared at her, and then he motioned to the chair across from him. "Can you sit down for a minute?" Nathel asked. All thoughts of her beauty had been forgotten as the troubling feeling that there was much about his grandfather that he did not know.

She glanced at the other patrons but shrugged finally and slid into the seat. "What is it?" she asked as she leaned forward on her elbows. With her chin supported on her folded hands she waited, apparently missing the sudden change in Nathel's expression.

"Everyone keeps treating my grandfather with so much respect and reverence," Nathel began pausing as he ended the sentence.

"Of course, how else would we treat one of the greatest prophets to ever walk the mortal world?"

"Prophet? What do you mean prophet?"

The girl gave him an odd look. She leaned back in her own chair and stared intently at him. She seemed to be trying to decide whether he was joking or serious."

"Thero the Prophet and the Ancient Wyrm founded this city thousands of years ago. It was the two of them that built this country and defended it from attacks while Ahtonium was struggling to survive its first winters in the mountains."

"But that would make grandpa thousands of years old!" Nathel's voice raised an octave in disbelief.

The blond girl nodded as if it was most normal thing in the world and that just irritated Nathel even more.

Once again she nodded, after a moment she must have decided that Nathel was not going to ask her name so she rose and left the table offering a sympathetic smile to him. Nathel sat silently sipping on the warm spice cider and rolling the whole situation over in his mind. "I wish we could go back to being simple shepherds in the Highlands," he muttered quietly. With a sigh he rose to his feet and made for the exit. He left a small silver coin from the pouch that Thero had given him as a way of saying thanks to the blond girl.

Troubled thoughts filled Nathel as he walked slowly down a side street. With his mind completely occupied, he spent the rest of the afternoon just wandering from shop to shop. He stared through the windows and ignored most of the shopkeepers, and indeed most seemed to know he was not buying. Sunset found him walking the streets near the fortress. The shops around him showed signs of age, the mortar peeling loose and cracking in many places. Nathel paused in front of an old chapel. Weeds grew in the corners of the building and cracks laced the stained glass windows. A stone cross sat by the door with a small sign etched in gold proudly proclaiming.

'Chapel of Hope. First chapel constructed in Kashguth.'

Nathel felt a pull on his heart as he looked at the old building and he found his feet carrying him into the small chapel. Ten stone benches ran down the center of the room and a stone lectern sat at the front of the room facing the benches. At the front of the chapel a large window faced the setting sun; two figures graced the surface of the stained glass. Above an image of Elutha floating over the world, hands stretched out. Etched in the base of the pillar was the simple phrase.

Matthew John Krengel

He gave his own to save the world.

A tear crept out of Nathel's eye as he stared at the window with the last rays of sun shining brightly across the chapel.

He slipped into the nearest bench, and buried his face in his hands and wept.

"I don't know what all of this means but I know one thing. I will not let others continue to sacrifice their lives for me. I can be the one to do what must be done," he whispered. The anguish and torment of the past days fell away with those words and peace filled him. "Faith and courage," Nathel whispered where he sat.

Nathel rose and walked resolutely out the door, heading back to the gates leading to the fortress. The phalanx of red cloaks at the portal to the castle nodded to him as he entered. After a short journey down the tunnel, he soon stood in front of the golden door in the throne room.

His hands trembled as he opened the golden door, before him opened a small room. On a stand in the middle of the room sat a tiny golden bell suspended from a finely woven chain. Nathel reached out and removed the bell and chain from the stand turning the artifact over in his hands, the craftsmanship was flawless. Despite its age the chain and bell gleamed brightly, shining with an inner power. Inscribed in flowing script on the bell was a sentence and it took Nathel a few minutes to work through the carved script.

"He who rings this bell at the seat of the world will bring salvation or damnation to the world."

Nathel furrowed his brow, rolling the phrase over in his mind. It seemed plain to him but he shrugged and pulled the chain over his head, slipping the bell down under his shirt. The rest of the small room was bare and so he went in search of Thero. It took some doing but after asking half a dozen soldiers and servants in the recesses of the mountain fortress he finally found his way to the lower galleys.

"What's wrong son?"

He found Thero in the armory with Timoth, they were deep in conversation. He felt a wave of suspicion again when the conversation cut off suddenly as he approached.

"I have decided to accept the Ancient Wyrm's task."

A smile blossomed on Thero's and Timoth's faces, they turned from the forge. Timoth dropped the piece of armor he held in his thick hands and clapped Nathel on the back.

Nathel reached inside his shirt and brought out the bell, "I found this in the small room off the throne room."

Thero glanced about and Timoth reached up slapping Nathel's hand and shoving the bell back inside his shirt.

"You must never show that to anyone. It is the reason, the Fallen test us constantly. If the Fallen know that the bell of creation is moving they will spare no expense to take it from you. You will wade through rivers of enemies; the Fallen will throw everything at you that they can muster."

The confused look on Nathel's face must have been evident to both because they stopped berating him. Thero pulled him over into the corner of the armory whispering quietly in his ear.

"The bell was used by Elutha when he made this world, no one knows why he used the bell but he did. In the Lost Books it is written, if the bell is rung in the seat of the world by a faithful person, Bedbezdal will be bound for another thousand years. Sent away from the mortal world to a prison of the ringer's choice, this would bring a time of peace and prosperity for the world."

"That sounds great," he started, but Thero held up a hand.

"There is a second passage to the same prophesy. It states that if a person dedicated to evil rings the bell in the seat of the world things will go much differently. Anatari will be bound for the same amount of time. This would give the world over to Bedbezdal and we will be plunged into darkness. A time of pain and suffering that would spell doom for mortals," Thero said. His voice was quiet, hardly above a whisper.

"Why has no one taken the bell before now?" he asked. Nathel's hands shook, the importance of what he held, beginning to sink into his mind.

"There is only one person in the world that can touch the bell son, and you are him. Come, there is something else you should see."

Thero nodded to Timoth and the three of them left the armory, Thero lead the way deep into the maze of tunnels and warrens. The catacombs spread out below the fortress seemed to move in random directions. They walked in silence for a long time. Finally, they arrived at a wooden door mounted to the stone of the tunnel walls.

Thero motioned to Timoth who removed a large iron key from his belt and unlocked the door, the three of the entered the room and Timoth closed the door behind them. The room was empty except for a wooden table and a single book resting in the center of the wooden surface. Six chairs circled the table and Thero motioned for them to sit. Taking one of the chairs at the head of the table, he looked at Nathel and took a deep breath.

"Nathel your parents were not simple shepherds, your heritage is much more then you have been told."

Nathel sat rigidly waiting as Thero unfolded his past.

"Your parents were the king and queen of the Kingdom of Juthel. Of all the low land kingdoms Juthel is the most populous and most powerful. Other then the Orkin Empires they have the largest army and control the most territory. Twenty years ago your uncle lured your parents out into the countryside and ambushed them, killing them both, and then he seized the throne. He and the Fallen now control the kingdom of Juthel. Sadly, I arrived in the capitol too late to warn them of impending coup. I took you from the capitol and went to live with you in Comstol hoping to keep you safe until such time as we could return to the low lands. Somehow the Fallen have discovered that you have a part in this. They do not realize that you are the rightful king of Juthel but they know you have been marked by the Pillars as special. Only a member of one of the royal families of the kingdoms can touch the bell. Even more, only a person touched by Elemental Pillars can remove the bell from its resting place. You are that person touched by the Pillars, and you are the one who can carry the bell to the seat of the world. You must protect it as you would protect your very life."

Thero voice was quiet as he finished speaking, Timoth stood by the door keeping an ear to the timbers to listen for any intruder who might try and over hear the conversation.

"This book," Thero touched the leather bound book lying in the center of the table with a reverent hand, "Is the last remaining genealogy of the kingdom of Juthel and is the only remaining proof of you heritage. Your uncle removed all other traces of your parents and their rule from the kingdom. With each year that passes, more of the common folk forget their heritage and fall under the sway of your uncle and the minions of the Fallen."

Nathel leaned back as his mind struggled to grasp his grandfather's words. Things had moved so quickly lately it seemed that each time he thought he had a grasp on what was going on, everything changed again. He reached forward, opened the leather bound book, and paged through dozens of genealogies. On the last filled page of the book was a partial line of names, the last name in the list was Nathel Terod of Juthel, son of Maria and Tero of Juthel.

A tear slid down his face as he slowly read the names, he could not remember anything about his parents but just being able to read their names touched his heart. Silence descended on the room as Thero and Timoth seemed to be lost in thought, finally Nathel looked up and broke the silence.

"We must travel to Juthel and search for clues left behind. They will lead us where we must go," His voice was determined, "We will not let down the sacrifice of so many people."

Nathel sat waiting while a broad grin spread across Thero face, "We may yet be able to beat the Fallen and Bedbezdal."

"Thero, why?" Nathel interrupted.

"Why what?"

"Why wouldn't Elutha make his victory assured on the mortal world?"

Thero's smile faded as he sat down beside Nathel and put his hand on his shoulder.

"Nathel, Elutha had no wish to be followed by mindless zombies. I must tell you I have asked myself the same question from time to time. As the creator of the world it was in his power to remove the Dark One from the world any time he wished. Instead he gave the Dark One the freedom to tempt the hearts of mortals but by that same token Nathel, the creator shows us his power each and every day. His victory is assured Nathel. The question is who will stand with him?" Thero said.

"I think I understand but what will ringing the bell do?"

"It will remind the creator of his promise to save those who still stand with him."

Nathel frowned, "Remind him?"

"Not for his sake, son, but for ours." Thero explained. "To give us time to reach to the mass of people who have never heard and by their ignorance are bound in Bedbezdal's clutches."

Nathel nodded.

"Nathel you must protect the bell. The world is slipping fast. There are precious few who still believe outside our mountain walls. Even here things are not good, never have the fallen been able to enter our borders. You now carry the most precious treasure in the world and the fate of the world is now in your hands."

Matthew John Krengel

Chapter Thirteen
Into the Lowlands

 athel and Thero rode out of Kashguth two weeks later. Each rode a brown gelding chosen from the royal stable for their steady temperaments. Nathel struggled to find his balance on the smaller of the horses. Staying in the hard leather saddle took all his concentration, and when he added holding his ironwood staff he found it difficult to hold his balance. The staff rapped against his head, hands, and every other part of his body, it was almost more than he could handle. The road north was wide and packed hard with rocks and gravel. A shallow pair of wagon ruts cut through each side as dozens of wagons pulled by shaggy oxen rumbled down the road, their cargo covered with heavy tarps. They road itself followed the lay of the landscape dipping into low valleys and skirting the edges of steep hills. Thero rode first much of the time and he rode slowly giving Nathel time to relax and enjoy the bright sunshine. Away from the ring of mountains the weather grew warmer in the center of the great valley that encompassed the Kingdom of Ahtonium. As they rode, Nathel watched the terraced landscape. Each hill was covered with sprouting fields of corn and wheat. Many orchards in full bloom filled the spaces between grain fields.

Quaint villages tucked into the spaces between hills came and went along the road, many with a babbling creeks tumbling from the higher hills. White washed walls and thatched roofs filled the villages and smiling farmers and craftsmen worked in the fields and in rustic shops along the main streets of the farming villages. Over the next three days they rode steadily, traveling through the most heavily farmed lands of the kingdom. The morning of the forth day they entered the center of the great valley and saw the edge of the great salt marsh for the first time.

"It's huge," Nathel stood near his gelding staring at the vast bogs of water and great shaggy trees. Tangled roots erupted from odd angles making the trees appear to be climbing right out of the ground.

The road swept out and around the humid marsh dancing along the edges of stagnant pools of water, stretches of thick reeds, and stands of juniper trees. Long vines laced the trees and stretched up into the air cutting off any view of the inner areas of the swamp from the road.

"Why this swamp, in the middle of such a lush valley grandpa?" Nathel stared out across the stretches of standing fetid water and thick swamps.

"There are hot springs throughout the area, combined with thousands of lava vents in the middle of the swamps which makes the surrounding land warm year around. And all the water soaks into the ground making the land in the middle of the swamp spongy and the vegetation thick. The bugs are also thick." Thero noted in irritation as he slapped a persistent gnat.

Turning their horses back to the north they rode on, moving quickly in an effort to avoid the armies of insects that rose to greet them. It was late in the evening on the fifth day when they left the swamps behind, Nathel sighed in relief as he began riding uphill into a rocky landscape covered in forests and hardwood trees.

Thero kept up a running conversation filling in the silences that fell as they rode, offering tiny bits of information that led Nathel to ask questions, and offered Thero even more chances to share his vast knowledge.

"The dwarves work many rich mines in the northern reaches of the kingdom."

"What do they mine?"

"Iron, gold, silver, you name the mineral and it's found in these hills somewhere."

Two days later they came into view of an imposing fortress, built across the top of a broad hill the walls rose to towering heights. Perched at its commanding location, it defended the pass leading into the kingdom. In the distance Nathel could see the snow-capped mountains that encircled the Kingdom of Ahtonium protecting and isolating it from the outside world.

"Few passes exist that allow access to the mountain kingdom, and only this pass is large enough to allow movement of armies and large trade caravans."

"Is that why the fortress is here?"

"Yes, it is our first line of defense against any invaders."

Nathel gawked at the imposing structure as they rode past the iron bound gates of the castle; thick-limbed dwarven sentries stared down with grim faces at all who passed. Red lacquered helms hid their faces and weapons were held ready at all times. Stone towers soared over one hundred paces into the sky and Nathel counted hundreds of archer's slits covering every approach to the castle.

"Jechiro is the ancestral home of the dwarven race; the castle is almost as old as the fortress in Kashguth. Maintained by the dwarven race, the castle has never fallen to an invading army. While it stands, the kingdom stands. If it falls there is little between destruction and us."

They skirted the edge of the villages that hugged the walls of Jechiro at about midmorning and Nathel found it hard not to gape at the mingling of people around the walls. Although dwarves were the most numerous, there was a sprinkling of each race there just as in Kashguth.

"Are we stopping grandpa?" Nathel asked.

"No," Thero responded. "The fewer contacts we make the better."

The commanding fortress faded from view as the ground sloped down leading into the low lands and the fertile plains and vast forest dominated by the human kingdoms.

Evening approached three days later when they reached the city of Aptush straddling the Riesce river, the capitol of the small human kingdom of Aptu.

"This city has struggled to survive for decades. They earn most of their money taxing the caravans going to the mountain kingdom or selling foodstuffs to those making the long trip down river towards the Southern Orkin Empire."

"It's so dirty grandpa," Nathel observed. The air was rank with the smell of dead fish and the river ran thick with waste.

"Yes it is."

"Not like the streets of Kashguth at all." The edges of the sprawling city were filled with beggars and sod hovels. Dirty children played along the sides of muddy streets and dashed around the hooves of the horses begging for coins from those passing by. Mangy curs barked constantly, adding to the symphony of noises that assaulted Nathel's ears. A wide ditch on the side of the road funneled the sewer and garbage away from the main part of the city and directly into the fast moving river. The further into the city they rode the cleaner the dwellings became and the less filth was visible.

"It's still there son, it's just funneled underground instead of above." Thero pointed to a hole in the nearby street that was covered with a rough iron grate, "All the water funnels below ground inside the city instead of above ground like outside."

Riding slowly to avoid the gathering crush of people they finally arrived at the inner city gate and fell in behind a long line of wagons and merchants. Nathel fiddled impatiently as sunset arrived, he was glad when they finally made their way to the gate. A bored looking guard in a dull steel breastplate motioned then forward eyeing the traveling pair with interest. Despite the unkempt condition of his armor a wicked looking pike rested in the crook of his arm. The weapon was clean and appeared sharpened, Nathel noticed, and they stopped where the guard stood blocking the street.

"What's your business in the city?"

"We are simply weary travelers seeking shelter."

"You will have to do better than that, if you expect me to allow you entry to the city," the guard motioned to his hand expectantly. A look of irritation crossed his face as he made his demand for a bribe more obvious.

Thero grinned and tossed a gold coin into the air at the surprised soldier who yelped as he struggled to catch the flying gold piece. The pike clattered to the ground and the gold piece fell just beyond the man's dirty outstretched hand. Thero motioned Nathel forward and they rode past the now angry guard, entering the city despite his feeble protests.

The dirty streets outside were not seen inside the city, the streets were paved with hardened clay bricks and stone. Clay and timber houses lined the roads.

"They separate the business and housing just like they do with poor and the rich, the lines are never crossed. If you are born poor you will die poor unless you leave the city and go somewhere else. But then, leaving the city takes money for supplies and the poor cannot afford it so they live and die in the same squalor year after year."

Nathel nodded as he rode beside Thero. Gilded carriages pulled by teams of horses moved swiftly along the streets. Pedestrians and shoppers leaped to the sides to avoid being run down.

They stayed that night in a small inn, a quick meal in the common room and Nathel immediately returned to the room. He fell asleep the instant his head touched the pillow.

Two weeks later they were travelling across forested lands when they crossed the river into Juthel. Nathel noted the difference in the soldiers that greeted them at a small outpost manned by a score of professional soldiers watching over the narrow bridge. Steel breastplates shined brightly in the morning sun and made Nathel squint against the blinding light. Swords were strapped to each belt and thick wooden shields hung ready around each waist. The river below the bridge raged and roared as it tore across the rocks and thundered away to the east.

The small bridge looked sturdy; it was narrow enough to allow one wagon at a time to pass over. A thick squat tower overlooked the river crossing and Nathel caught a glimpse of two more border guards standing at the top of the tower with heavy crossbows in hand.

"Your business in Juthel?" The tone of the question offered no room for argument.

"We are from the city of Hasefrum, we are going to visit the royal library," Thero answered respectfully. There was none of the smiling and laughing as he had done when bribing the guards in Aptush.

Nathel watched Thero dismount and walk to the small tower. A weathered wood lectern sat near the tower and a heavy bound book rested on it, the slight breeze riffling the pages. Thero took the quill and ink and signed his name on the ledger. When this was complete, the soldiers stood aside and motioned for them to continue on down the wide road.

When they were more than a league down the road Nathel turned to Thero, "What was that about? I thought that since the Fallen controlled the kingdom this would not be so orderly."

"Your uncle may be one of the Fallen, but he is a very controlling man. Juthel is a model of orderliness and prosperity. Most of the people living in Juthel have no idea that the Fallen control the country. The common folk assume that since the kingdom is so prosperous that they are doing the will of the creator. All the while your uncle is leading them down the wide path to destruction. The temples are empty and the priests who support the old ways have been expelled from the kingdom."

"But," Nathel started, "How can evil work good?"

"You must remember, Bedbezdal is Anatari's bother. He witnessed Elutha's work to make this world. He helped with much of the creation of the world, just because something seems good on the outside does not mean it is good. Take the Cathil plant that grows in the Highlands. On the outside it appears good and wholesome. However, when you approach too closely, the most beautiful plant can kill you."

Nathel nodded, "I think I understand, the Dark One is a master of deceit."

"He is the father of lies, never forget that Nathel. It may well save your life someday."

Thero voice was soft and Nathel barely heard the last words.

Both fell silent as they rode, Nathel kept turning over in his mind what his grandfather had said and hoped that someday he would completely understand.

The countryside was green and full of life, hundreds of cottages dotted the landscape and log fences divided the fields. For the most part they rode in silence, Nathel lost in the thoughts that this vast and rich kingdom was his by right.

"Thero, will I ever be king?"

"Put those thoughts out of your mind boy," Thero said. "We must carry through our duty to the world. It may be that we can worry about avenging your parents and the lost throne of Juthel after we have fulfilled our task." Thero's voice was stern and it left no room for argument.

Nathel opened his mouth once thinking to protest that it was unfair, but a stern look from his grandfather silenced him.

Almost one week after they crossed the river into Juthel they rode into view of the capitol, nestled in the middle of a wide plain.

"It's even bigger then Kashguth."

"Yes, it is one of the largest cities in the world. Only the Orkin capitols surpass Juthel in size."

They sat for a long moment looking at the imposing city. Thick stone walls soared into the air and sturdy towers interrupted the block of the wall at regular intervals. The plain around the city was alive with orchard blossoms and waving fields of grain, a wide canal cut into the plain brought water from the nearby river. Nathel traced the hundreds of irrigation ditches weaving out into an intricate web around the city.

The city itself was bigger than Kashguth, and the castle at the center was much more imposing.

"They carted those granite blocks in from the mountains to the west. It took years to haul them across the plains. It was a sight to behold."

Nathel kept quiet. Nearby, a merchant wagon rocked and swayed as it plodded down the road. Two men dressed in leather were carrying bows and gave Nathel and Thero hostile stares as they rode escort behind the merchant.

Nathel ignored their stares; instead he turned back to the soaring towers that watched over the city. He guessed the castle walls were ten paces taller than the city walls. The castle nestled in the middle of orderly rows of houses and businesses; streets radiated out from the fortress, connecting the pulse of the city at its heart.

Thero clucked to his horse to start down the small rise and enter the broad plain that stretched out between them and the city. The orchards were in full bloom and the air was sweet with the smell of flowers.

The hard packed road led straight to the city gate and their horses moved quickly along it. This time there were no lines waiting at the iron banded gates. Nathel noticed two score of watchmen pacing the walls around the gate. Most of these carried bows with full quivers at their sides. They passed quickly through the gatehouse; Nathel craned his neck around to look at the massive chains that held the inner gate from closing. Just inside the gate, a small gatehouse was carved into the wall on the right side and a pair of blue-coated soldiers stood silently watching all who entered. Nathel glanced at one of the men as they passed; his eyes briefly flickered to the youth's face before returning to their original forward stare.

Thero reached out and tapped Nathel on the shoulder. "Let's keep moving, who knows what information your uncle might have access too."

The street they entered was a wide stone paved affair. It had been split into two halves and a row of trees separated each part. It seemed to Nathel that the trees separated the people coming from the inner parts of the city from the people entering the city. Granite and stone houses dominated the landscape built so close together then in many places the rooflines touched. Despite the gray of the stone houses, they were surrounded by a myriad of flowers and shrub trees.

"Everything is so green," he commented. Nathel followed Thero along a wide avenue taking care not to bump their horses into the hundreds of people that walked along the same street.

"This city has been called the City of Life at times past. Sadly, that it is not so anymore. There was a time when all who visited here were left amazed at the amount of living plants and trees that thrive inside the walls."

Thero motioned to a smaller side street and followed Nathel as he entered the alley, "We shall stay this night at the Inn of the Night Owl. There we will be safe from prying eyes and any other things that might be lurking in the city."

Nathel was caught up in the moment and nodded absent-mindedly.

"Nathel!" Thero reached across and cuffed the youth alongside the head gaining his full attention for the first time since entering the city.

"Pull your head out of the clouds boy; we must keep our wits about us. Especially while we travel about the viper's lair," Thero hissed.

Nathel's face fell at the rebuke but he sat a little straighter in the saddle and gripped his staff a bit tighter.

"As for these staves they could pose us a problem. It is time for us to disguise them while we are in the royal city," Thero reached back into bag and brought out a pair of shiny iron spearheads.

The alley remained empty, the flow of people on the street ignoring the two men. Thero motioned for Nathel to slip the spear tip onto the end of the ironwood staff and twist it tightly into place. Nathel examined the disguised weapon in his hands, the balance of the weapon was wrong. What had felt perfect in his hands minutes before was now awkward and unbalanced.

Thero nodded, "It will feel odd in your hands for a while but you will have to learn to adapt and adjust to changing circumstances."

Nathel frowned, but held the weapon tightly promising he would learn to adapt to the changed weapon.

Thero led the way down the alley that in turn brought them to a smaller side street; once again the street was straight. Nathel squinted into the distance and found he could see the royal palace rising against the dark blue sky. Another side alley brought them to another street and by this time Nathel was thoroughly confused.

"Over here son," Thero motioned to a wooden gate on the far side of the street and they made a beeline for the latched gate. Thero leaned forward and tapped his staff twice on the wood door, leaning back in saddle he waited. Nathel heard movement on the far side of the door and he waited expectantly.

"Who goes there," a gruff voice demanded.

"One of the few," Thero spoke softly, just loud enough for the speaker to hear.

Immediately, Nathel heard the click of latches releasing on the far side of the door. Then the wooden gate swung wide allowing them to enter. Nathel rode his horse through the door entering a small courtyard. To the right was a barn crammed into the small space just large enough for six horses, whereas the courtyard seemed crowded with the two horses and three men. The speaker swung the door shut the moment they were inside. He wore a hard leather tunic and two heavy cudgels swung from leather straps around his wrists. It was his sheer size that left Nathel in awe. When Nathel dismounted he strained his neck looking up at the imposing mountain of a man, arms thick as iron bands sprouted from a body large enough to pick up a horse.

"Welcome back ancient one, it has been many years since you have graced our small home," he said. The mountainous man inclined his head, offered Thero a nod and a smile.

"You're looking well Sam, how are your wife and children," Thero dismounted and returned the nod.

"They are well. Merial brought me another son three years past and my oldest has married and brought me a strapping young grandson," a broad smile covered the gigantic face.

Moving with sure motions Sam latched the three heavy locks holding the door shut and then motioned them to follow him into the barn. The smell of hay and oats hung in the air as he led his gelding into the small barn, three stalls stood empty on the left side. The stalls on the right side held a stallion and two mares, so Thero and Nathel took two of the remaining stalls. It took a few minutes to bed down the geldings and by time they walked across the courtyard and entered the inn, darkness had fallen across the sky.

"Things are not safe after dark any more. The thieves' guild has run rampant through the town and the king in all his wisdom does nothing about it. Even the poor are found in the dark, beaten unconscious and rolled into the gutters," Sam shook his head in disgust. He led them down a small dark hallway along the back of the building. Three doors led off the hallway and Nathel glanced into each one as they past, the first offered a view of a small but well equipped kitchen, a fire glowed in the middle and a large bird roasted over a blazing fire, rotating slowly on a spit. The smell of the roasting bird brought a burst of saliva to Nathel's mouth and loud growl from his stomach.

"It sounds like your young friend is hungry Thero. Are you feeding him regularly?" Sam chuckled as he spoke.

Nathel blushed in the dimly lit hall. A thick oaken door blocked the end of the hall and Sam held it open as they passed and entered the glowing main room of the inn. A fire lit each side of the room and five wooden tables were scattered about the space. A number of customers were seated at each of the wooden tables eating. Two serving girls stood near another door that Nathel assumed also led to the kitchens, watching over their dining charges. An older woman stood near a long waist high bench on the far side of the room.

Thero glanced at Sam in question, "You added a bar?"

Sam grinned, "Only serving spiced ciders and a few other popular drinks, we have become somewhat of a trendy place for merchants to stop and relax."

Thero nodded, "Sounds like a good idea."

"Well I would like to take credit for it but it was all Merial's idea. Most of the good ideas are hers, I am afraid. If not for her business sense, I would be bankrupt," Sam flashed a wide smile across the room to Merial and she returned it ten fold. He led them up a narrow set of stairs to the second floor. Sam showed them to a small private dining room built into an overhang over the alley. A pair of small windows offered a narrow view of the surrounding city and Nathel stood staring out until their meals were delivered. The rising moon now illuminated the distant royal castle in a muted display of blues and whites. Pennants and banners flapped in the breeze that swept in from the south. Finally turning from the peaceful landscape, Nathel watched as the serving girl laid out a steaming platter of meats, breads, and fruits. Offering a smile she turned and exited the room.

"Come and eat, son. You have waited long enough," Thero motioned to the table and then took one of the chairs.

"Your rooms are next door down the hall," Sam motioned out the door.

"Thank you Sam may the elemental protectors watch over you for your kindness." Thero smiled as the innkeeper slipped out the door and left them in peace.

They ate in silence. Both men were tired from the long ride and the silence was a welcome change from the constant clopping of horse hooves on the stone streets. Nathel sighed in contentment as he ripped succulent pieces of moist turkey from the platter and folded them into warm slices of fresh bread. A thin wedge of cheese added to the flavor, along with a jug of spiced cider. Thero watched in amusement as he nibbled on slices of fresh fruit and sipped his own cup of cold water, "It never ceases to amaze me how much a growing boy can eat."

Nathel paused looking for the first time at the almost empty plate. Crumbs of bread and half a slice of cheese sat forlornly in the middle of the platter. Leaning back in his chair Nathel chuckled, "I think I am ready to go to sleep now. It's funny how a full stomach helps to put a person to sleep."

"Is the bell still safe lad?"

Nathel nodded, he patted the front of his shirt where the bell lay against his skin.

"Good. We will be in danger the entire time we are in the city. Tomorrow I will try and find a way to enter the Royal Library and search the records for any mention of the Chamber of Life. It will not be easy. Sam told me that the library is sealed. Only those with the permission of the king may enter its doors."

Nathel nodded as they left the dining room and walked the five paces of hallway that separated the door from their room. The room they entered was wide and deep running far along the small courtyard, a single window allowed a view of the back of the inn. Nathel crossed to the window and looked up, the moon was full in the night sky and it stared down at him. Nathel yawned loudly when a movement caught his eye. Out across the roofs of the city a shadow slipped from roof to roof.

"Grandfather, what is that," Nathel pointed. The shadow disappeared behind a tall stone chimney.

"Thieves guild, Son."

"Thieves? Why would they let them run around the city?"

"The guild is old and well connected. At one time it was considered a good way to control those that insist on stealing. It was better to control them then to let them run rampant across the city. But with the current king, he appears to not care about the activities of the guild or maybe he has struck a deal with them."

Thero turned from the window. After checking the iron latch, he swung the inside shutters closed, "It is better for us to get our sleep and worry about our current task."

Nathel looked one more time at the closed shutters and then nodded. The room held two beds. He was tired and the soft mattress and warm blankets beckoned to him invitingly. After stripping to his breaches, Nathel slipped under the covers and sighed in contentment. In no time his eyes slid shut and his breathing evened out.

Outside the inn, the shadowy figure on the roof slipped closer, leaving the shadow of the chimney. Further out on the rooftops, more black figures appeared, mirroring the movements of the first.

Chapter Fourteen
Thief!

he shadowy figure slipped over the clay tiles of the roof, running swiftly up the slanted roof and hurtling across the gap to the next. The soft leather boots gripped well. They were dyed black and coated in a substance that helped thieves run on the slippery tiles. A tight pair of pants and a form fitting black shirt with long sleeves revealed that the figure was a woman. Her hurried movements and the efforts of the shadows that were trailing her revealed that she was running.

Katirna glanced over her shoulder and saw that the four killers still pursued her stubbornly. Half a night of running and still they mirrored her every movement, tailing her across the city. She knew why they were there. The leaders of the thieves' guild did not take lightly to free lancers operating in the city. Katirna refused to pay tribute to the false king who lorded over the city.

Shaking her head, she brought her mind back to work and sprinted across the remaining tiles throwing her body into the air. An agile leap cleared the alley and landed her on the roof of the Inn of the Night Owl. A slight thumping sound accompanied her rolling form and she winced at the sound, which echoed loudly across the surrounding rooflines.

"Katirna you are going to wake every watchman and thief in a ten block radius if you are not more careful," she muttered to herself. She slipped over to the back side of the inn roof and dropped noiselessly to the balcony on the second floor. Reaching inside a wide belt that wrapped tightly around her waist, she slipped a thin knife out in one smooth motion and slid it between the windows. A flick of her delicate wrist and the locking bar slid out of place and she went head first through the window, sliding the shutters closed behind her. Waiting in the dark room, she listened for the movements of the four killers tracking her. At the count of ten she heard two of them drop quietly to the balcony and a moment later a slight tug pulled on the shutter. She gritted her teeth in the darkness and held the shutter closed as the killer tested it.

"It's locked. She must have gone to the next building," the whisper was so quiet she almost missed it, but her grin widened even more behind her mask.

"What are you doing in our room?"

Katirna jumped at the voice, and she lost her grip on the shutter. A part of her mind listened as the two killers on the balcony turned and pushed the shutter wide. She threw her body into a backwards roll, avoiding the wicked slice as the assassins piled through the open window. Four swords flashed in the darkness. Katirna came out of the roll between the two beds that dominated the room and reached down to her sides, a quick jerk of her hands removed two hardened round lengths of wood. Both parts of her weapon (commonly called a juntal by most thieves) were as long as her arms and she spun them clockwise, picking off the slicing attacks of the two killers.

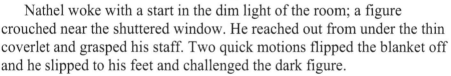

Nathel woke with a start in the dim light of the room; a figure crouched near the shuttered window. He reached out from under the thin coverlet and grasped his staff. Two quick motions flipped the blanket off and he slipped to his feet and challenged the dark figure.

"What are you doing in our room?"

The shadow whirled from the window losing the grip that held the window shutter closed. Nathel cried out in astonishment as the shutters burst open and in rolled a pair of black clad figures both wielding knife and sword. Across the room he saw Thero rolling out of bed and grasping his staff. A loud crash drew Nathel's gaze as two more figures crashed through the open window. Thero shouted a battle cry and launched himself forward, his staff spinning and lashing out.

"Help the girl, boy," Thero called over his shoulder. His staff snapped back and forth knocking the concerted attacks of the black clad assassins aside. A hard thrust of his staff forced the closer man to step back and then the swirling fight around Thero was forgotten.

Nathel leapt across the bed and landed on his feet facing the shorter of the two men facing the girl.

"Why don't you leave us alone," Nathel felt the anger rolling up inside him, "Ever since we left the village you idiots have been hounding us."

"What are you talking about boy!" the man said. A look of genuine confusion crossed the killers face for a moment. The black clad killers paused slightly as he spoke. The girl used the opportunity to snap both of her weapons forward slapping the knife from the hand of the startled killer.

Nathel whipped his staff forward intercepting the darting attack of the sword and then flipping it to the side to slap a second knife away. The fight dragged on and Nathel found himself hard pressed. The two killers facing them were veteran fighters, keeping their weapons under tight control. They fought a defensive battle not risking any attacks that left them open to Nathel's longer weapon. Nathel dared to glance at the girl beside him and he immediately regretted the action. The man facing him struck hard, the blows knocking the staff loose from his grip and sending it clattering to the floor.

"Ouch that hurt," Nathel muttered. As he spoke he realized how odd the words sounded as they echoed in the room over the ticks of weapons and grunts of the fighters. Nathel stepped back desperately reaching for his staff as it rolled under the nearby bed.

"Well that does not bode well for me does it," Nathel asked the question into the silence that descended with a matter of fact tone in his voice.

Amazingly, he heard the thief before him snicker and then the action exploded around him again, as Nathel mentally kicked himself.

The short man charged forward trying to bury Nathel against the bed; he leapt backwards turning a complete back flip as he rolled over the bed. Reaching out as he rolled, he threw the thin blanket into the air and scrambled under the bed searching desperately for his lost weapon. In the tight space under the mattress he reached out, the staff rolled to a halt just under the far side of the bed. He grunted as he stretched his arm out and grasped the end of the staff only to have the man kick the end of the staff and send it spinning.

"Oh bother," Nathel muttered. The spear tip came loose from the staff and rolled out into the middle of the floor. Yelping in surprise, he retracted his hand as the man leapt to the top of the bed and skewered his sword down into the mattress. The blade sunk into the floor almost as inch and Nathel could see it was stuck tight in a knot hole. Above the bed he heard the man mutter a curse as he tugged hard. Nathel grinned as the sword came out with the knot still stuck to the blade. Pulling his legs in under the bed, Nathel curled them under the bottom of the mattress. Then he pushed up as hard as he could. A startled cry sounded from above him as the mattress buckled hard and the man standing on top went flying across the room.

"Ah, there it is," Nathel grasped his staff and stood up completely throwing the remains of the bed to the side. Across the room he saw the killer he had thrown from the bed standing with a dazed look on his face.

Nathel chuckled as the girl spun in a complete circle again bringing both of her small staves around hard against his head in rapid succession. The blows sent him slumping to the floor, a thin line of blood trickled from the side of his mouth. To his amazement, the young woman whispered short blessings for the killer; he assumed that the killer's judgment would be harsh.

Nathel watched all this happenings in a split second. Turning, he stepped between the woman and the remaining man. He spun his staff in a circle once again knocking away the knife and sword as they lashed out against her unprotected side. As he fought, the symbols etched on his hands glowed brightly, the light drawing the man's attention from the spinning staff. Right, left, parry high block, low block; the battle went on for several long moments.

The opening that presented itself was slight, but Nathel seized the chance, lashing out with the end of his staff aggressively. The killer had left his arm extended too far, and he leapt back, dodging as he tried to avoid the end of the iron wood staff. The sound of the staff striking his arm was followed quickly by a loud cracking sound. The left arm went limp and the sword flew end over end, skittering to a halt against the far wall.

"Give up, you are defeated," Nathel said. He stepped back lowering his staff slightly but still keeping it ready to defend himself.

"The guild will never allow you to interfere in our business," the killer answered with a snarl that made Nathel's spine shudder. Turning, the man rushed out the window and threw his body from the balcony, "Never accept defeat." he cried. His body plummeted to the hard paving stones.

Nathel rushed to window and peeked out. On the ground far below the window lay the unmoving body. Near the door, Thero dispatched the second killer and knelt briefly, whispering over both of the fallen men.

"Their judgment will not be good, I fear. It never is for hired killers," the voice that spoke was melodious and it curled around Nathel's eardrums.

"Is the judgment better for thieves?" Thero asked the question of the black clad woman and calmly waited for her answer.

"There was a time when thieves were not as dishonorable as they have become," She spoke proudly and without shame or remorse.

"And you are one of those types?"

"There are many in this city who would take exception to the fact that I refuse to answer to the corrupt guild. They also do not like the fact that I target friends of the king," she answered wryly. A smile danced about her lips, at which Nathel stared shamelessly. Slowly, she reached up and pulled the tight fitting black cloth from her head. Nathel was shocked to find that she appeared little older than his own seventeen seasons. A long shock of strawberry blonde hair uncoiled from somewhere deep in the depths of the mask and fell across her neck. Her hair hung half way down her back, a stark contrast to the black clothing.

"Does your young friend have a name or does he simply stare awestruck at every girl he meets?" she glanced at Nathel as she spoke.

Nathel stammered his face turning a bright shade of red as he glanced away.

"Never mind," she said suddenly. "Someone should teach him to use his staff. He nearly killed me with his ineptitude."

"What!" he stammered. Nathel felt his blood begin to boil.

She turned away from him and strapped her weapons back to her legs and retrieved a small black bag from the corner.

Nathel went from fascination to irritation as she continued to berate him furiously for interrupting her. After all, she claimed, she had the fight well under control.

"Now wait a minute, there were four of them and only one of you! You should be thanking us for helping. What's more, you should apologize for sneaking into our rooms in the middle of the night and bringing in killers with you. The Elemental Protectors know we have had enough of people trying to kill us," he managed to control his voice as he fired back at her.

Nathel clenched his fist hard on his staff as his irritation with the blue eyed girl mounted. It even infuriated him more when she snorted and waved a hand dismissively. He watched as she went about picking up her dropped bag and checking the contents to see if any was missing. Thero chuckled and slipped into the hallway calling to Sam.

"Thanks for what? I could have finished those four idiots with ease. Next time boy, stay out of a professional's way," she retorted after slipping the black bag into her tunic. "Now I must be gone before the sun begins to rise. The rooftops are not as safe as they were in times past."

Nathel watched her step to the window and slip the shutters fully open. After a brief glance around her, she stepped out on the narrow balcony. Before scurrying up the side of the inn, she gave him a wide smile and a wink, and then she disappeared into the night sky leaping to the next roof. Nathel rushed to the window and watched as her figure disappeared from view over the clay-tiled rooftops of the city.

"What happened?" Sam's eyes popped wide open when he stepped into the carnage of the sleeping chamber. Unmoving bodies of assassins sprawled across the floor. The bed that Nathel had flipped over was rested against the far wall and the stuffing of the mattress was scattered across the floor. Here and there tiny white feathers still drifted in the air settling slowly to the floor.

"It seems that good people are not safe in their own rooms anymore," Thero leaned his staff against the wall. He motioned for Nathel to help him pick up one of the bodies. Nathel grabbed the feet and helped to hoist the man. Walking awkwardly, he and Thero carried the body down the narrow stairs and set it out in the front street. Sam disappeared into the night carrying a heavy cudgel, minutes later he returned with six members of the city watch. Dozens of questions followed and when it finally seemed the commander of the watch was satisfied, they were allowed to return to the main room of the inn.

When the watch was gone, Sam roused his two daughters and sent them to clean the room while Nathel and Thero sat talking with the inn keeper and his wife.

"What happened up there tonight? The city watch did not appear to believe your story of the four bursting and trying to rob you but they had little else to accuse you. Thero, you must be careful from now on. The city guards will have people watching you; they have little use for disturbers of the peace. Anyone that interrupts the false peace across the city is labeled and watched."

Thero lowered his voice and related the entire story to Sam telling him about the young woman and the full details of the fight.

"There have been rumors lately of a rogue thief, she has taken to hitting the homes of the friends of the king, but little is known of this thief. The soldiers have been watching for anyone traveling alone but they have focused on the men, discounting women as unable to carry on such an undertaking."

Merial snorted, "Typical men discount women for anything but bearing babies and cleaning houses," she stood and nodded to the three. With a last loud snort she stomped off to bed muttering about the ineptitude of the king and the city guards.

Sam chuckled after she left, "Don't get her get angry at you, things can go from good to ugly fast." Laughing, Sam rose and exited the room.

Several loud yawns later Nathel and Thero climbed the stairs, making their way back to their soft beds. The girls were exiting the room and they smiled despite their sleepy eyes and tired yawns.

"Thank you, to both of you," Thero offered a small hug and smile to each of the giggling girls.

The room was washed clean when they entered and Nathel found they had even sewed shut the mattress and changed out the sheets. It took Nathel a long time to fall asleep. He lay in the darkness and listened to Thero snoring across the room but his mind kept jumping to the face of the thief. An eerie quietness settled across the inn and each creak of the wooden walls and floor echoed loudly in his ears. Finally he dozed off dreaming of blond haired thieves and black clad killers.

The next day Nathel slept late. The sun had climbed well into the morning sky when he finally rolled out of bed. Thero's bunk was empty and so Nathel slipped down the hall to the washroom carrying a change of clothes and a thick towel. The inn boasted a heavy granite tub and Nathel found the water warm and clean in the gray stone tub. After a quick scrub with the thick bar of soap that sat on the edge of the tub he donned his clothes and retrieved his staff. It took him several long minutes to rummage through the pile of clothes in the corner and locate the loose spear tip from his staff. He struggled to fasten the tip back on the staff and wind a length of course twine around it. When at last he had tied off the twine the spearhead was securely fastened to the staff and he exited the room making his way down the narrow stairs to the kitchen.

Merial smiled at him when he entered the kitchen, she waved a loaf of bread at the young shepherd.

"Are you looking for some food?"

"If it is not too much trouble," he said politely. Nathel shrugged as his stomach growled loudly, protesting the late morning and the lack of food.

"Where is Thero?"

Merial motioned him over to a small table in the corner where she laid out two thick slices of fresh bread, a pat of butter, and two apples, "He said he had some things to take care of. Thero left you a small purse of coin and asked that you not wander too far from the inn until he returns."

Nathel frowned. It was unlike Thero to leave him to his own devices on his first day in a new city. Finally, he nodded and shrugged his shoulders; he wolfed down the apple in four big bites. The second apple disappeared just as fast, followed by both slices of bread and a cool mug of spring water. When he finished eating Merial handed him a small leather purse.

"The market is four blocks north. Stick to the main streets, if anyone still means you harm they will not do anything unless you are alone."

He nodded around a mouth full of bread and butter. His spear leaned in the corner near the table and he retrieved it. Placing his hand over his chest, he made sure the Bell of Creation was still securely fastened around his neck.

"Thank you Merial."

She waved to him from across the kitchen already preparing the food for midday.

He made his way through the quiet front room and exited the double doors into the street. Standing alone on the inn's wide porch, Nathel watched dozens of people move up and down the wide avenues. Most walked purposefully with busy looks on their faces. Finally, he stepped out of the shade and turned to the north joining the rush of people moving about the busy city.

"Out of the way fool!"

He jumped as a large cargo wagon rolled past, the driver cracking his whip above the team of heavy oxen. Four long city blocks later he found the market. The street widened and Nathel stopped to take in the scene. A double row of merchant's stalls ran down the center of the market and a third and fourth row bracketed the outsides. Right and left looked equally busy so he decided one direction was as good as the next and began to wander from stall to stall, examining weapons and goods.

"Leather armor!"

"Stout Blades!" the calls of merchants rang out on all sides.

Nathel stopped and looked closely at a stall where the merchant was selling pieces of soft leather armor; a set of intricately carved leather bracers caught his eye. The merchant sensed the longing and immediately started to bargain with the young shopper, Nathel ran his hand over the leather and even held the bracers when the merchant insisted he examin the stitching in the leather.

"These are imported by ship from the Southern Orkin Empire, my good lad. They are hand crafted of the highest quality leather," Nathel nodded. The greasy merchant continued to extol the quality and cheap price of the leather bracers.

Just as Nathel was about to agree to the set price a figure stepped up beside him,

"Hand crafted in the Southern Orkin Empire you say, more likely made locally of poor quality leather" the melodious voice immediately drew Nathel's attention. The sound took him back to the night before.

The merchant leveled a nasty stare at the girl who had caused the interruption. Sensing that the sale had been ruined, he set the bracers back on the table and stared venomously at Nathel. He smiled and shrugged his shoulders, offering an apologetic look at the skinny merchant.

"My apologies, good sir."

"Be gone," the merchant imperiously waved him off.

Nathel turned and walked to where she had stepped back to stand in the shade of a nearby tree.

"You look different this morning," Nathel offered. He was not sure what to think of the young woman standing in front of him. She was beautiful, blonde hair pulled back from her face to reveal a stunning pair of light blue eyes.

"So do you, when you're not stumbling around in your breeches," she smiled.

Nathel's face reddened and they both shared a nervous laugh.

"I am sorry for my comments last night. I am glad that you and the old man decided to help. Many people would not have chosen to get involved and risk the wrath of certain people," she took a look around at the market as she spoke. When she was satisfied that no one stood near enough to overhear, she motioned Nathel closer.

"After I left the inn last night I could not help but regret my harsh words to you. I am truly sorry," she linked her arm around his.

"Come, walk with me."

Nathel swallowed the lump in his throat and tried to calm his shaking hands.

She guided him through the market square walking casually like a woman out for an evening stroll. Nathel was dumbfounded and found himself hard pressed to answer any question with more than a nod or a simple yes or no.

"Let's have a bit to eat," she motioned to a small shaded vender. A number of round tables set out under the overhanging leaves of an olive tree. Each of the tables had a pair of chairs and they were far enough from each other to offer a small amount of privacy from the other diners. Nathel pulled out her chair for her and she seated herself daintily, pulling her ankle length skirt forward around her legs so it would not catch on the rough planks of seat. He walked around and seated himself opposite the young woman and fell silent. He was unsure of himself around women, and he did not know how to start the conversation.

"So, is this your first time in the big city? Or is your conversation always this dazzling?" she looked at him with unblinking blue eyes.

He gulped hard again and then grinned at the smile dancing around her lips.

"I am sorry," Nathel managed. He was painfully aware of how uncomfortable she was making him and it was starting to irritate him. "I grew up in a small herding village in the Highlands and there were few people around to talk to besides Thero." He shuddered as he let the name slip but then decided it made little difference.

When she nodded encouragingly he took heart and continued.

"We just arrived in the city last night, and our arrival was interesting to say the least," they both laughed. He nodded to the vendor as he delivered two orders. Each bowl held a thick pastry dipped in strawberry sauce and smothered in a brown substance that ran down the sides.

"What is this?" he asked as he took a big bite. Nathel immediately regretted it, the confection was rich and the mouthful was almost more than his stomach could handle.

"Small bites, and sip the drink in between the bites. The brown coating is called chocolate and it is imported from the Southern Orkin Empire, it's an acquired taste."

Nathel took a smaller bit and then a sip of the cold drink, the taste was much more palatable when taken slowly.

"And how long have you been in the city?" Nathel found his tongue somewhat loosened by the sugary treat. He looked over his plate at the mound of blond hair curled up on top of her head and realized that it actually held a bit of red, suddenly, it occurred to him that he still did not know her name.

"I have been here for most of the season, so far," she took a small nibble of her pastry, She closed her eyes and made a sighing sound in the back of her throat savoring the treat.

"Maybe, I should back up some. I want to at least find out what your name is before we are forced to part ways again," Nathel chuckled. The incident from the night before was becoming more comical for him. He could see himself squirming under the bed until he tipped it over.

"You may call me, Katirna, that is what my friends call me and it is a good name," She leaned closer and smiled. Her ruby red lips were still smeared with chocolate. She winked at him in a conspiratorial manner and whispered, "The local authorities have called me a few other things lately and none of them are very complimentary."

Nathel laughed. He leaned back in his chair and realized that he was enjoying her company immensely.

"And why are you and the old one in the city? Surely you have not come to be my knights in shining armor, whenever I bite off more than I can chew."

"We have come to study the ancient text in the king's library, if we can gain passes to do so,"

Nathel took another small nibble and swig of the drink.

Katirna's face grew serious, "I have heard that the library is sealed for all outsiders, only a select few of the royal court are allowed to enter the building. It is heavily guarded by the king's personal troops; I was almost caught the first time I tried to sneak inside."

"Why did you want to get into the library?"

"I am a thief after all. A guarded building is a challenge. I had to see if anything of interest was, you know, lying around." Katirna said. She leaned far over the table as she spoke quietly and Nathel was painfully aware of her beauty as her eyes fastened on him.

They sat talking for some time, enjoying the cool breeze blowing down from the north and bringing relief from the sun.

Nathel suddenly glanced up realizing how much time had passed, "I should return to the inn."

He blurted the statement stumbling to his feet, the rush of sugar in his system making him a bit unsteady.

"Let me help you. After eating chocolate for the first time it can take a bit to wear off."

He nodded as the street around him shuddered and his stomach complained loudly.

Katirna rose and looped her arm around his and together they walked south slowly, continuing their conversation until she dropped him at the front of the small inn.

Nathel watched her as she waved to him and walked away down the street to the south. Just before she turned the corner, she turned and looked over her shoulder offering him a wide smile that left his knees weak and his heart racing.

Chapter Fifteen
Rooftop Chase

athel walked back into the inn with his head in the clouds. Thero frowned at him from where he sat at a corner table, and motioned Nathel over.

"Where have you been all day?" Thero glanced at him as he slipped in the seat opposite the older man.

"Guess who I ran into this morning in the market?" Nathel leaned his staff up against the wall and sighed dreamily.

"Not our black clad friend from last night with the odd view of thievery," Thero said. He looked sharply at him.

"Yes," Nathel leaned back smiling.

"She is a thief son, you can't trust her."

"She's nice," Nathel retorted. His voice raised an octave as he defended Katirna's honor.

"I think someone has a crush on her is what I think. Don't worry, it will pass as soon as we leave the city," Thero stared hard at him over a half empty spiced cider.

He looked up and Nathel followed his gaze to Merial standing in the corner smiling widely.

Thero motioned the woman over, "What do you know of this morning."

"Why, I have no idea what you're speaking of. All I did was tell Nathel he should go shopping in the market. If he met some sweet girl in the market, it is none of my concern and it should be none of yours," she answered. Merial's face grew stern and Nathel huddled back as the inn keeper's wife gave Thero a challenging stare.

"Bah woman, what do you know of the boy, or what he needs to do yet. Go play matchmaker somewhere else."

"All I did was tell him to go shopping. If any match happened it is done by the elemental, protectors not me," Merial offered one more challenging stare and then stomped off muttering under her breath about know it-all-prophets and how little they know of life.

The moon had just peaked over the city wall when Thero arose from his seat, "I will be back in a while. There are a few things I need to check on."

"What am I supposed to do?" Nathel asked.

"Get some sleep; this may be the last time we have to rest."

Nathel frowned as Thero made his way to the door and slipped out into the night. He waited up for an hour more, sipping a cool drink in the main room of the inn. When it was obvious that Thero was not coming back soon, he climbed the narrow stairs to their sleeping chambers.

Tap tap

Nathel looked about the room, and then he turned back to his bed.

Tap tap tap

The knock on the window was light and Nathel almost missed it. At first he dismissed the sound as the night noises of the city but then it came again, and this time it was more insistent.

Unsure of what would greet him, he hefted his staff in one hand, then reached up and untied the twine that held the locking bar in place. Carefully, he slipped up the bar and stepped back as the shutters silently slipped open. Katrina's lithe black clad figure slipped through the window and closed the shutters; she slipped the tight mask from her head.

"Hello again." she offered Nathel a wry smile.

"Hi. Well...I didn't think I would see you again so soon,"

"Would you like to see the city from a different perspective?" her smile was playful.

Nathel laughed, but at the same time excitement welled up inside him, "I really shouldn't. Thero will be back soon, and he will worry if I am not here."

"Not to worry, we'll be back soon. Just a quick run along the rooftops to show you some real city excitement."

Katirna reached over her shoulder and tossed Nathel a bundle of black clothes that matched hers.

"I really shouldn't."

"Come on, it will be fun."

"At least turn around while I slip these on," Nathel pleaded.

Katirna turned back to the window. She pulled the shutter open and kept watch out across the city.

It took a bit of struggling to slip the pants on and then pull the long sleeve tunic down over his head. He was pleasantly surprised to find the gloves and boots fit like a second skin.

"Now the mask. It wouldn't do to have someone see you and be able to recognize you," she said. Katirna stepped back from the window and helped him pull the mask down across his face until he could see through the wide holes over his eyes. Nathel felt silly in the outfit but as soon as they were on the balcony he saw the use of the black material. The boots offered protection for his feet, but the bottoms were designed to let his feet feel and grip every dip and crack in the roofing tiles. Katirna showed him how to grasp the sides of the wall so that he could hold his balance and still move up the wall almost as fast as walking down the street. As he climbed, he was amazed at the strength that had developed in his arms and legs over the past weeks.

"This way," Katirna sprinted to the edge of the roof and launched herself out over the gap between the buildings.

Nathel waited until she landed lightly on the clay tiles of the second building. She turned and motioned to him to follow; crouching in the shadow of a stone chimney she waited for him to follow.

Nathel backed up nervously feeling the roof with his toes, "Well might as well take a chance," he muttered.

He sprinted forward throwing himself through the air; the jump more than cleared the gap between the rooflines. Arms waved frantically as he landed and tried to regain his footing. Katirna grabbed his hand as he stumbled past the chimney, keeping him from skidding off the far side.

"Less power, more aim next time," she whispered.

Nathel smiled behind his mask, he nodded and chuckled nervously. He followed her when she leapt to the next building. They ran north for almost ten long city blocks. He was getting tired when Katirna motioned for him to wait. The night was quiet and the moon full. They stood next to a thick clay chimney watching the night sky line. To the north, the walls of the royal castle sat dark and ominous, the dark shadows of sentries marching in ordered routes as they guarded the walls.

"There lives a false king," she hissed. Katrina's eyes narrowed as she stared at the castle.

Nathel looked at her, he wondered what cause she had for the hatred that was in her voice.

"Come on, let's make him pay." She slipped silently over the edge of the roof.

He clambered down to a wide balcony overlooking a verdant garden. "Keep watch for the city guard."

He nodded; crouching on the balcony he checked the streets below. The area below the balcony was quiet in each direction. "It looks clear."

"Good."

Nathel looked over his shoulder and watched as Katirna pulled a thin knife from her belt and slipped it through the crack in the door. A quick flick of her wrist and the door swung open. Reaching through the crack in the door, she caught the locking bar as it fell. He rose from the railing, took the bar from her, and set it on the floor.

"Thanks," she whispered. Katirna winked at him and motioned him to enter the luxurious mansion. Gold plated frames surrounded detailed paintings of the surrounding countryside, and wooden cabinets held silver and gold spoons and knives.

"The current residents are out of the city at the moment, only the servants are home and they sleep in the basement floors," she said. Katirna motioned Nathel and together they slipped into the hall. She walked casually down the hall passing by the first three doors. When they arrived at the forth door, she stopped and motioned him to stay against the wall. Taking out a long piece of bent wire, she knelt by the rough lock and slipped the wire inside. Seconds later the lock clicked open and they stepped out of the hall. The room they entered was even more opulent than the others. Gems and gold sparkled on every wall, with diamonds and rubies set into every item.

"This is how the king rewards those that choose to follow his path. Those that refuse are exiled, if they are lucky, and killed if they are not."

She moved to the wide desk in them middle of the room and pulled another knife from her belt. This time it was a thick bladed knife made for prying open, a quick twist of the heavy blade and the drawers of the desk were laid open. Small bags of diamonds, rubies, and other rare gems were laid out in even rows in the first drawer. The second one held sacks of gold coins, Nathel picked up one of the bags and pulled out a coin.

"For god and country," he read aloud.

"Humph," Katirna grunted.

Katirna removed four bags of gems and passed them to Nathel, "Put these in your belt."

He fumbled with the narrow pockets around his waist, finally managing to secure all the gems.

Katirna slipped four bags of coins into her own belt leaving the empty drawers lying on top of the desk, "Come let's make our exit."

Nathel followed her as they moved out of the office and back down the hall. Silent as wraiths, they slipped back out of the open door and up onto the roof. He grinned widely as they stood looking at the few lights on the castle.

"That was amazing," he started. Suddenly, he was interrupted by a harsh voice.

"We warned you once girl, stay out of our city. Now you will both die." A dark figure detached itself from the shadows around the chimney.

Nathel back away, as the figure brandished a rapier in his hand.

"No one controls these roof tops. Not you or the guild, Rathier. You cannot stop me, you have tried before."

"But this time girl, I don't have too. I brought some friends," the ear splitting howl of a wolf broke the silence of the night and the shouts of soldiers filled the streets below.

"Good luck girl. Those that I tipped off will not be as kind as I might have. I would have offered a position in one of my establishments, if you have not killed four of my men."

Katirna grunted and threw her hand forward in a whipping motion. The thick knife that she had used to pry open the desk flew straight and hard, but the thief was already moving. The knife only dug a deep hole in the side of the clay-tiled chimney.

"Let's move, Nathel," she whispered.

He followed her as she sprinted hard for the edge of the roof. Below them, Nathel heard the shouts of soldiers and the howls of hunting wolves. The surrounding streets were alive with sound and then the chase was on.

Over an hour later Nathel slumped to the roof panting, Katirna leaned back against a stone chimney nearby.

"Did we lose them?" he asked. They were resting against the side of a tall building near the southern wall of the city. In the distance the howls of the wolves and the shouts of the city guard had faded, but they could still be heard. Watch fires burned across the city as the city guard swept every corner of the streets, atop the buildings more lanterns waved. Scores of men shouted as they swept south in a long line searching each rooftop.

"We can't stay ahead of them much longer, and we are running out of rooftops to hide on," Katirna shook her head.

Nathel risked a glance around the corner of the building, then jerked his head back as an armed patrol rounded the corner. A pair of burly mountain wolves stalked towards the building where they were hiding and soon the howling started again.

"Wolves and soldiers coming this way," he hissed.

"We have one last chance," Katirna whispered as she climbed up the rough wall. When they rolled over the edge of the roof, she led the way back north. Off they went, leaping across the rooftops. Nathel noticed that this time Katirna picked a straight path at the line of torches that were coming at them.

"What are you doing," Nathel grabbed her hand. He pulled her to a halt two buildings before they crashed into the searching guards. Nathel could hear the shouted voices and warnings as the armed guards cleared each roof.

"We have one chance to escape. If we can break through the line and get near the castle, we can hide in the library until the night passes," she whispered. Katirna yelled at him as she made the next jump.

"Go hard. Don't stop running until you reach the castle wall. Wait for me at the last building. I will find you if we get separated," she cried.

She pushed him forward, then she shouted a challenge at the nearby guards. Cries of alarm filled the night sky. She pulled out her twin staves and charged a young guard wielding a short sword and a torch.

Nathel growled in frustration but did as he was told. Sprinting hard, he made his way north. With the sounds of fighting to the east he had little trouble breaking through the splintering line of sentries. Three buildings later he slipped behind a nearby chimney and he watched as Katirna beat a double tap off the guards helm, then she scooped up his torch and a nearby lantern. Making a leap to the east, she landed on a wooden roof and Nathel gasped as she slammed the lantern down scattering oil and sparks everywhere.

"Sam said the weather was dry so far," he whispered. He watched as the flames roared into the air.

The wood roof caught fire immediately. Katirna was off and running again, racing ahead of the two guards that had managed to slip past the flames before they spread across the entire roof.

Nathel rose from his hiding place and ran hard, always moving north, leaping from roof to roof. The howls of the wolves echoed across the city, but now they came from two locations. The wolves had not been fooled, they hunted by scent and fire and smoke had done little to stop the stalking animals. As the moon began to fade in the early morning sky, Nathel found himself huddled at the base of a clay chimney waiting for Katirna. He nearly jumped out of his skin when an unlit touch tapped him on the shoulder, spinning around he started to lash out with a closed fist. He stopped when Katirna collapsed into his arms; a long cut dripped blood from her forehead and wide blood stain soaked across her hips.

"Katirna," he whispered. Nathel held her close as she drew a painful breath.

"I will be ok, but we need to get under cover. The wolves have left the city but the guards are still searching house to house."

He helped her to her feet; she limped over to the edge of the roof and pointed across a wide gap. Twenty paces to the north near the castle wall was a gray granite building. Narrow stained glass windows were inset into the granite and soaring peaks ranged into the sky.

"How do we get across the street," Nathel whispered. "It's too far for us to jump."

"Here," Katirna slipped a length of thin rope from her waist and handed it to him, "You have to loop this over the edge of the small peak on the library," she pointed.

Nathel could see a hook shaped stone sticking up into the air. Quickly he looped the tripled headed hook around the end of the rope and tied it securely in place.

"You must be quick," she muttered. Nathel glanced to the east, already the sun was beginning to peak over the horizon.

"I will do my best."

He played out a length of rope and stood up next to the edge of the roof.

His first throw went wide to the right and he had to coil the rope back in and try again. Finally, on his forth try he snagged the granite hook and with Katirna's help he fastened the thin gray rope to the edge of the roof. Hand over hand, they both went across the gap.

"Look out," Katirna cried. She grabbed Nathel by the arm and pulled him back against the wall behind the outcropping.

They huddled in the corner and watched as almost a dozen men swarmed onto the roof. One of the men pulled a knife from his belt and slashed the rope loose; Nathel's heart fell as the end of the rope fell towards the ground.

"We should not be here. This place has an evil feeling about it," he said.

"There are rumors in the city that a creature of immense evil has taken up residence inside. We must be careful and watch our backs. Above all, we have to be out of the library by night fall," Katirna said. She pushed hard on the side of the nearby window, the glass turned sideways on cleverly hidden hinges. Together, they slipped inside and slid the window closed behind them.

"Here comes the sun over the wall."

Nathel watched as scores of soldiers flooded out from nearby alleys.

"They were watching us," Nathel said. He reached out and grabbed Katirna's arm, gently he turned her back to the window. They watched as the guards set up a wide perimeter around the building dozens of men armed with bows watching the silent walls, waiting for them to try and escape.

"They herded us here on purpose." Katirna's voice cracked in fear.

The interior of the library was dark and even the rising sun did little to alleviate the impending doom. The window ledge was connected to a stone walkway that circled the top of the library walls. Nathel looked out over the edge of the balcony and stared at the long rows of shelves and the piles of scrolls and books scattered about the tables and floors.

"It's like they left in a hurry," Nathel whispered. He turned and leapt back just in time to catch Katirna as she collapsed to the ground. Carefully, he lowered her to the cool stones and pulled the mask from his face. With trembling fingers he gently pulled her mask loose over her coiled hair. The gash on her head was superficial and had stopped bleeding and Nathel dismissed it. Slowly, he rolled up the side of her tunic and gasped in shock. The broken end of an arrow was stuck deep in the side of her stomach, gently; he rolled her to the side and noted that the tip of the arrow was sticking out the far side.

"I am sorry Katirna but this will hurt some," Nathel whispered. He remembered what Thero had told him after the battle with the Fallen in the mountain kingdom.

"I have to push it through and bandage it tightly," he said. Nathel was unsure if she could hear him so he worked quickly; he hoped she had passed out.

Nathel grimaced, he used one hand to hold her steady, and then he grasped the end of the arrow and pushed gently. Katirna gasped in pain and then thankfully she passed out completely. Two hard pushes and he had the rest of the bolt out; blood covered his hand as he held steady pressure on the wound. Using his mask as a bandage, he packed it tightly against the wound on her back under her shirt. A moment later he had her mask rolled and used hers to compress the wound on her stomach.

"Now, I need something to hold these in place," Nathel muttered. Already the flow of blood was slowing and so he grabbed her thick belt and felt for a release. It took a long minute to free the belt, but he finally did and then wrapped it tightly around the makeshift bandages.

"Water," Katirna gasped as her eyes fluttered open.

"I don't have any," he said. Nathel's heart raced as he watched her eyes flutter again.

"Help me Anatari; I don't know what to do." He whispered, it was a desperate prayer but he said it with all his heart. He reached his arms under Katirna and lifting her easily, he walked towards the far end of the library. When he arrived at the far door he slid it open, an empty room greeted him and he made his way across it. The next door opened into a wide staircase, this led him down to the main floor and he made his way down the stairs feeling his way with his toes. The main course of the library was wide and tall, shelves of books and scrolls cut off his view of the far side. Katirna cried out in pain as he walked along the wide rows of books. After passing dozens of tall shelves filled with books, he entered the center study area of the library.

"A fountain!" he cried out. He broke into a careful jog towards the marble structure.

The tall fountain dominated the middle of the room and it was completely dry.

Nathel felt tears of frustration well up in his eyes, "Please, someone help me."

Crash

"Who is there," he called. He turned in a complete circle searching for the source of the noises echoing in the main room of the library.

"Please, elemental protectors, help me. Tymothel, I need water and a weapon. You said that if the Pillars gave you leave you would help me, I need help," the prayer was desperate and heartfelt. Nathel stood by the edge of the pool wondering what to do next when a small stream of water trickled down from the top of the fountain.

"Thank you Tymothel."

Slowly, the small stream widened until it had filled the lower part of the pool. After a moment he scooped up some of the cool water in his hand and splashed it on Katirna's face. She sputtered and slowly her eyes cracked open.

"We have water," Nathel grinned at her. She drank greedily, as he scooped up some more; the change on her face was evident. Relief flooded his mind as her eyes brightened and some of the color returned to her face, Nathel knelt down and sipped some of the water. As he drank he watched the empty hall, searching for any signs of movement.

Again he heard sounds echoing in the corners of the library but there was no sign of movement. Sitting down next to the fountain, he held Katirna close and waited. She slept in his arms as he watched the sun track across the sky slowly through the dim windows.

The sun was high overhead when Katirna woke again asking for more water. Once again he helped her drink her fill.

"In my pouch there was a small vial of liquid. Help me drink it."

Nathel nodded and searched the pouches of her belt; the small vial was almost brown in color. When he pulled the stopper from the top, a pungent smell wafted up making his eyes water.

He tipped her head back and helped her drain the entire vial in one long gulp; to his relief she sighed and leaned back in his arms. Moments later she fell asleep again. She wormed closer to him in her sleep, wrapping an arm around his waist as she slept.

The rest of the day pased slowly and Katirna slept soundly. Nathel watched the stained glass windows, keeping a watch on the movements of the sun as best he could.

It must have been getting late, Nathel thought, for the sun filtering through the windows began to fade, and a rainbow of colors filled the library as the last rays of light finally lit the stained glass windows. Katirna woke with a start and lifted her head staring at Nathel.

"What happened?" her eyes were awake and alert but Nathel noticed she did not remove her arm from around him.

"You caught an arrow in the stomach. I pushed it through and then helped you drink from a vial in your belt," he said. Nathel nodded to the empty vial on the edge of the fountain. The water had stopped flowing but the bottom of the fountain still held over a foot of sparkling pure liquid.

"We need to move, something is in here with us. I have been hearing sounds echoing from the corners," he said. Nathel helped her stand to her feet. "Are you feeling better?"

"Yes, much better," she said. She lifted her shirt to examine the arrow wound, her deeply tanned stomach tight with muscle. All that remained where the arrow had passed through her abdomen was an ugly pink scar.

Nathel reached up and gently brushed her hair to the side. He ran his fingers across her forehead, wiping away the dried blood that had caked across the wound; nothing remained of the long gash.

"I can explain later," Katirna said. She motioned for him to follow her, they moved quickly down the long rows of books heading for the front door of the library.

"Maybe the soldiers have gone," Nathel said. He felt powerless without his staff so he stuck close to Katirna. She held her staves ready and walked cautiously, from the back of the room another crashing echoed loudly. Before them a long ramp of stairs led up to the double doors blocking their escape.

A grating sound from directly overhead made Katirna and Nathel leap back. Before them a gray object fell to the ground. The impact, scattered dust and rock fragments in a wide radius.

"What is that?" Katirna asked. She backed up two more steps as the gray creature slowly stood, flexing its long arms.

"It looks like the stone gargoyle that was carved into the walls outside the library," Nathel said. He joined her backing away, his hands searching for a weapon of any kind.

"Can we make a run for the doors?"

"Don't, you would never make it," Nathel said. He placed a calming hand on her arm and pulled her towards the bottom of the stairs.

The stone gargoyle stretched its arms wide and began to flap the creaking stone wings in long slow sweeping arcs. Two horns curled around its head and glowing red eyes swept the main floor of the building.

"Who disturbs my home?"

Nathel's spine shuttered as they creature's voice echoed across the main floor, he pulled Katirna along, until they stood hidden in a dark corner of the library floor.

Nathel stopped and watched from where he stood, partially hidden by a tall shelf of books.

"Someone is opening the door," he whispered.

Atop the marble stairs, the doors of the library swung in enough for a tall gaunt man to slip through the crack.

"That is the king. Some day I will find a way to kill him for what he did," she said.

"You will have to explain what happened to me sometime."

"I told you that no one was allowed in the library, it is my home now, King Grend," the gargoyle addressed the thin man, spitting out the words as it spoke.

"They are a pair of thieves, you may do to them as you wish my lord," he said. Grend's voice was raspy and harsh; Nathel found himself taking an immediate dislike to his uncle.

"I do not like being disturbed during my slumber. If I am to continue to aid you in your goals, I require undisturbed rest during the daylight hours."

"I will make sure you are not disturbed again," the king replied. Grend bowed his head and slipped back out the wooden doors, leaving the stone monster to his own devices.

Nathel pulled his head back behind the shelf, as the creature turned from the door and began to slowly stalk down the wide staircase. Through a gap in one of the scroll racks he watched as the elemental flapped its wings. Gusts of air threw up papers and sent loose scrolls rolling across the smooth granite floors.

"Time for us to find a way out of here," he said. Nathel grabbed Katirna's hand and together they sprinted for the far end of the room, behind them the stone gargoyle let loose with a tremendous cry. He glanced backwards as they fled; a flash of gray near the ceiling told him the gargoyle was airborne. The shadows covering the stone arches made locating the flying creature nearly impossible.

Katirna screamed and skidded to a halt. She pulled back hard on his hand as the gargoyle swooped low, swinging its long arms. The blows missed them but connected with a tall bookshelf.

The blows sent pieces of the shelf spraying in a great arc and the shelf itself teetered, papers and books filled the air scattering in every direction.

Nathel slammed his shoulder into a nearby door sending it flying open and the two of them tumbled hard across the stone floor.

"Come on, lets go," Nathel shouted. He pulled Katirna to her feet and they dashed across the room making for the second door. Behind them the gargoyle crashed to the floor and tore the door behind them from its hinges. Dust and rocks flew everywhere as the beast smashed a wide hole in the wall. It stepped into the smaller room, each step of the beast's clawed feet left deep marks in the floor.

"You cannot escape me little humans," the elemental called.

The voice reminded Nathel of two rocks beating against each other. Swinging open the next door, he pulled Katirna through. Together they descended down the stairs leading them into the underbelly of the library.

Stone stairs flew by and Nathel crashed shoulder first into the door at the end of the stairs sending it flying open. A dank, musty corridor opened up before them. Behind them, they heard the gargoyle smashing its way down the stairs taking out large chunks of the wall and ceiling as it battered its way along. Nothing seemed to slow the creature. Open and closed doors flashed past as they ran down the long hallway. Nathel glanced over his shoulder again and immediately wished he had not. The gargoyle was closing fast on them. Chunks of granite and debris swirled in the hall as the creature broke into a loping run.

"How can we stop it?" Katirna screamed. She slammed shut a door at the end of the hall, and started up a long flight of stairs.

Nathel shrugged and he gasped for air as he struggled up the stairs after her. They burst out of the stairs, back into the main floor of the library. Behind them, the stone beast smashed through the door and then leapt into the air.

"It's flying again!" Katirna screamed.

The elemental dove low, its wings spread out, smashing the remaining shelves into kindling.

Nathel dove to the side rolling to avoid the falling shelves.

Oomph, the breath left Nathel's body as he came to a halt against the granite fountain in the middle of the room. Stars danceed before his eyes for a few moments while he shook his head. The gargoyle slammed down to the ground a dozen paces away and started towards him. Katirna leapt forward, taking two hard swings with her staves. Nathel heard two loud cracks, as the staves shattered into a thousand pieces. He cried out in fear as the gargoyle swung a stone fist and landed a grazing blow that sent her rolling head over heels.

"Katirna!" Nathel screamed. Her limp body rolled away, hurled like a rag doll against a nearby shelf. He struggled back to his feet looking about for some type of weapon that would help him to battle the gargoyle. Nathel circled the fountain as the gargoyle stalked him, then he spotted the end of a staff sticking up from the crack in the middle of the fountain. The smooth wood of the staff felt cool under his fingers and he yanked with all his might. It slid free of the crack easily. As Nathel turned to face the creature, brilliant runes etched into the staff glowed brightly. Symbols for spirit, water, air, ground, and fire blazed like the sun as he held the staff defensively in front of him.

The gargoyle swung hard at him and Nathel struck out with the staff throwing his weight into the blow and whispering a prayer.

"This is it," Nathel muttered. Time seemed to slow down as he watched the blazing staff intercept the first of the fists. The wooden weapon struck the stone fist and sparks of power flew far and wide. To Nathel's surprise, the fist stopped and flew back. He swung the staff in the opposite direction into the other fist. Again the fist flew backwards, and Nathel stepped back with his staff held ready. The gargoyle stared at him and took in the weapon.

"You think you can defeat me, boy? Bedbezdal has empowered me on this world. Elutha and his protectors have left this world to its own devices and no longer care about puny humans. You are ours to do with as we please."

"Well, that answers that question. He is definitely an elemental," Nathel muttered. He searched over the gargoyle for the binding gem that held the fallen elemental in the mortal world.

"Go back behind the barrier where you belong, foul creature of the dark lord," Nathel shouted.

"Come boy, let's see how long your staff lasts against the might of the ruler of this world."

Nathel dodged and blocked desperately as the blows began to rain down from the stone creature. Fist after fist bounced off the staff, driving him back until he was standing with his back against a high book shelf.

"Time to die boy. Then I am going to kill your little friend slowly and painfully, her tortured cries will haunt this city for months," it snarled. It pulled back its lips in a grotesque mockery of a smile.

"There it is," Nathel said. He spotted the gem set into the top of the gargoyle's mouth. Knowing that he could not block the next blow, he stepped forward and lashed out hard. His staff struck the gem and shattered it to pieces, the hideous laugh turned into a wail of anger.

The gargoyle stumbled backwards. Screaming in rage it took flight, careening about the library, smashing into pillars, and striking the stone supports. Huge holes opened up in the walls, and pieces of the wall and roof went flying in all directions.

Nathel shook his head as he tried to clear the spinning lights from his vision, and then ran to where Katirna was still struggling to get to her feet. He scooped her into his arms and ran for the steps leading out of the collapsing building. Great chucks of the roof rained down as the weakened walls of the structure started to sway.

Crack

One by one Nathel heard the stained glass windows break under the pressure and sheets of glass shards fell, showering him and Katirna with pieces of colored glass. The stairs to the front doors loomed wide and Nathel took them two at a time despite the shuddering floor. He slammed into the double doors throwing them open as the roof of the royal library began to cave in. The falling chucks of stone smashed great holes in the floor further weakening it. Nathel could hear the shouts of alarm as soldiers rushed towards the building tumbling down around him.

Rough hands grabbed Nathel, holding him upright and pulling him away from the building. Suddenly, they let loose as the stone gargoyle screamed in rage and rose into the sky above the collapsing building. The soldiers froze, all eyes turned skyward and stared as the gargoyle screamed one last time and then imploded with a thunderclap explosion. Brilliant flashes of light lit the night sky and roar of the falling library buried the books and scrolls deep under thousands of tons of rock and debris.

Nathel stood memorized as the walls collapsed sending a billowing cloud of dust and dirt that obscured his vision, Katirna clung tightly to him. Turning away from the shouts of the soldiers he walked away through the shouts and screams, disappearing into the darkened streets of the city, and heading for the inn as fast as he could move.

A low fire burned in the stone fireplace when he stumbled through the front door of the inn. His face and body covered in dust, glass, and dirt. Rough coughing wracked his body as he tried to expel the dust. The common room of the inn was quiet; Thero leaned against wall stroking his beard. Sam and Merial sat at a small table sipping steaming drinks. They all stared at him as he collapsed to his knees, in his arms Katirna groaned loudly.

"Where have you been, boy?" Thero started in and then stopped. He stroked his chin one more when he saw the battered condition of the pair.

"What happened?" he asked. Thero rushed over and helped Katirna as Nathel lay her down on the floor.

"Stand back. Let me look at her," Merial said. She knelt for a moment, Nathel stepped back and watched as she brushed back Katirna's hair. When she seemed satisfied that both would live she rose and ran out the door calling over her shoulder that she would return with medical supplies.

"We made a slight detour to the royal library and found out what has been haunting it," Nathel said. He wearily pulled an empty chair over to Katirna's side and collapsed into it. Despite the dirt on his sleeve he wiped his arm across his face and began to tell the story to Thero and Sam. He glossed over the part of stealing from the house as best he could and then told of the chase and the wolves inside the walls.

"They pushed us into the library on purpose and my uncle told the gargoyle to kill us. The elemental was here to give him orders and he listened to everything the stone beast said."

"We must get you out of the city," Sam said. He rushed for the door. "I will prepare supplies. We must get you over the city walls. If the fallen are searching for you they may already know you are here. Tthey have spies everywhere."

"What possessed you to go out onto the roof tops? Didn't you realize how dangerous it was?" Thero asked. He shook his head. He seemed more disappointed than angry.

"I have to take credit for talking him into going, sir." Katirna gasped. She coughed hard again, expelling a burst of dust from her lungs.

"I know I shouldn't have gone grandpa, I am sorry. It just sounded like innocent fun when we left. You have been so busy and mysterious, that I was a little bored."

Thero stared at the both incredulously and then broke out into a loud chuckle. The chuckle quickly became a laugh as he stumbled backwards and sat down on wooden bench.

"Well, I certainly hope you both learned your lessons. No good will come of thieving and sneaking around on rooftops. As for my being mysterious I was doing a bit of sneaking myself. Each day I went into the library to study the records, I could sense the evil but as long as I was gone by nightfall it was safe. I guess that is done, now we are faced with the problem of finding another place of knowledge that will help us."

Sam walked in as Thero was talking, he was holding a pair of heavy packs stuffed with food and supplies, "You should try the Monastery of One near the Northern Orkin Empire it is said by traveling traders that their collection of books and scrolls is even greater than the royal library."

"I was hoping to avoid the long trip their but I guess our two thieves have left us little choice. We will have to make our way there and restart our search."

"I am coming with you," Katirna said. She pushed herself up slowly, she swayed slightly but fended off the helping hands offered to her.

"There is no need for that girl," Thero replied. His voice was gruff but there was still some softness in it.

"I have lived seeking revenge for long enough," she said. That simple statement was all she said as she slipped into a thick cloak offered by Sam. "Besides, this city has become a death trap for me now, and Nathel did save my life. I feel I owe it to him to help you."

"We are happy to have you along Katirna," Nathel piped in before Thero could say anything else. He was delighted that she had decided to come with them.

It took several minutes to complete the hurried preparation, Thero gasped in anger when he saw Nathel passing Katirna the stolen bags of gems and gold. The four bags had remained safely stowed in his belt for the entire chase and fight at the library.

"What have I told you of stealing, Nathel?" Thero frowned. His face was flushed as he jabbed a finger into Nathel's chest.

"We took this from one of the king's houses outside the castle," Katirna said. She spoke quietly pushing herself between Thero and Nathel.

"My father was captain of the guard for many seasons. Four seasons ago he was falsely accused of being part of the Fallen, the king had him put to death and then exiled the rest of my family. I know the elemental protectors say vengeance belongs to the creator but my poor mother has seven other mouths to feed and my nightly activities will keep them with food and clothing for many months, or even years to come."

Thero stared at her, a slight smile curling around the corners of his lips. It seemed to Nathel he was struggling to remain angry but failing, "Well in that case, I still don't like it, but as long as you are giving it to a worthy cause. I have heard many tales of your father Miss Katirna Divuria. It is said that he was a good and honorable man."

Nathel was glad Thero let the subject drop as they hurried back to packing up their traveling gear. Sam scurried upstairs and sent his daughters down with arms loaded with food and extra clothing.

The moon had almost finished its circuit through the night sky when Thero led then down a shadowy alley. Across the city Nathel still heard the shouts of the night watch and the patrols of soldiers sweeping the streets. Thankfully, the howls of the wolf pack were absent from the night sky, but he strained his ears as they fled down one dark alley and then entered another.

"Move quickly boy, now is not the time to sight see," Thero hissed. His hushed whisper brought Nathel back to the present and he pulled his cloak even tighter around his shoulders. It took them the next two hours to reach the edge of the city wall. Nathel could see the shadows of the sentries walking along the top of the tall stone edifice. He almost let out a strangled scream when Thero boldly strode up the wide stone stairs and approached one of the plate-armored sentries. A crossbow hung from the man's belt and a wide broadsword and shield were strapped to his waist.

"Bless Elutha and his servants," The sentry offered a salute with his left hand while his right hand gripped his sword.

"Bless the guardian elementals that do his will and hold back the evil one until the Day of Judgment," Thero answered. It was long winded but it seemed to satisfy the stern soldier and he offered Thero a second greeting.

"How are you ancient one?"

"Good, son, but we must leave the city quickly and quietly. There are packs of the Fallen about the city and the kings men are searching even as we speak," Thero explained.

Nathel's spine shuddered as a lone wolf howled inside the city, almost as if on cue. All along the wall lanterns flashed to life as the sentries pulled weapons from their scabbards.

"Quickly then, this way. The commander of the watch will start his round soon. He always checks the walls when there are wolves about."

The tall, wide soldier led then across the top of the wall to a spot where the wall met a wide tower. He deftly looped a rope around a wide stone and lowered it the fifty paces to the ground.

Thero went down first. Going hand over hand, he descended so quickly that it left Nathel shaking his head. Katirna followed, moving almost as fast as Thero despite her heavy load and recent wounds. Nathel nodded to the sentry and threw his leg over the wall while grasping the rope tightly. Again the howl sounded in the city, and this time it was answered by a second howl much closer then the first.

"Go, son! I will take care of any wolves or fallen that try to pursue." The sentry nodded and pulled his sword completely free.

Nathel nodded and started down the wall.

"And, son, when you come to your throne, remember the few faithful that still hold out hope in this forsaken city," the sentry said. His face was sad as he spoke.

Nathel clung to the rope speechless, his feet dangling over the edge and his face just above the wall.

"I will," he replied. Then he nodded and lowered himself, hand over hand down the rope. At the bottom, he followed Thero away from the wall to the east, behind them a third and forth wolf howled mournfully. Moments later, Nathel heard a battle cry ring out from the top of the wall, and the clash of weapons echoed in the night sky. All along the wall alarm bells pealed and soldiers rushed about searching for the source of the howls.

Chapter Sixteen
Long Roads Ahead

 even days later, Nathel and Katirna followed Thero as he strode down the narrow dirt track wandering through the dark forests and lush meadows of river country. Small creeks and rushing torrents of water crisscrossed the meadows and cut wide swathes of forest in half. It had sprinkled for almost two days straight and every gully and low track of land was soaked with water.

"Another creek," Nathel groaned. "I just got my boots dried out from the last one."

"You should learn to watch your step on those rocks."

"Easier said than done, especially when you have someone throwing things at you."

Nathel glared at Katirna as he unlaced his boots once again. The young thief laughed and skipped nimbly across five rocks that stuck out of the water. He had been half way across the last stream when she had thrown a heavy stone into the water next to him. The resulting splash had destroyed his concentration and therefore his balance. It had taken him many long minutes to wring the water from his clothes.

"No more games from you," Nathel said. He sat on a moss-covered log and rolled his pants legs up above his knees. Thero waited patiently while his grandson ventured into the water.

"The water is actually kind of warm," he smiled. He was half way through the sentence when a pair of rocks struck home on either side of him sending fountains of water into the air. Nathel let out a strangled yelp and reached out with his staff in a desperate attempt to regain his precarious balance.

"Nice try," Nathel grunted as he righted himself and then hurriedly waded to the far shore joining the laughing pair.

The next day they approached a small cabin on a tiny dirt road. In the distance a village straddled the junction of two roads. Just beyond the village Nathel heard the rushing sound of a fast moving river. Timber and clay houses lined a flowered avenue; the street itself pierced the center of the village leading to an arching footbridge. Stacks of timber piled up against the walls of the houses told the tale of cold winters that swept across the low lands.

"This way," Katirna said. She abruptly took the lead from Thero after entering the village. As they walked, young mutts ran barking alongside until Thero shooed them away. A narrow street led them north to a tiny cottage on the outskirts of the village. Three young children played quietly in a patch of grass and Katirna held her arms wide when they rushed to greet her.

"Kat," The youngest cried. The young child wrapped the thief in a tight bear hug.

"Mum will be happy to see you," another said.

Nathel guessed that the child was about eight seasons old. He glanced nervously at Thero.

"It's alright, they are my friends." Katirna reassured them.

Nathel smiled broadly, holding out his hand in greeting. Cautiously, the eldest child took the proffered hand and shook it slowly.

"Welcome good sir, my name is Ralth, and these are my two sisters, Ana and Mortha," Nathel shook each of their hands in turn.

"Come inside, you must meet my mother," Katirna beckoned them to the green tinted door at the front of the cottage.

"KAT!"

Nathel looked up and saw an elderly woman with blond hair and blue eyes that matched Katirna's perfectly.

"Welcome home, girl." Tears streamed down her eyes as she enfolded her daughter in a warm embrace.

"It is good to be home, mom."

"Who are these two men? You are not trouble are you?"

"No, mother. In fact, were it not for Nathel and Thero, I probably would be in trouble." Turning around she said "Nathel, Thero, this is my mother Junia.

Nathel suddenly found himself buried under a warm hug, "Oh thank you." He stepped back as she hugged Thero and his grandfather patted her gently on the back.

"Now all of you come in and drink some tea," Junia said. She bustled back to the door and held it open for them.

The cottage was small but neat and even with the five of them seated around the small table the room seemed comfortable.

"I brought you something mother," Katirna said. She pulled her pack forward and dug out a heavy bag. She set it on the table and pushed it towards her mother.

"I told you child, I won't take money that was thieved. No matter who it came from," Junia said. Her face was set in stone as she stared at the bag on the table.

"Mother, please consider it back wages for what happened to father. Take the money for the children if nothing else."

Junia turned her head to stare at the children outside the single window of the tiny room, "It goes against everything we raised you to become child. Your father would not approve of your choice of professions."

"No he wouldn't. But that didn't stop that strutting peacock in Juthel from having him killed, did it? It is time that someone made the crown pay for crimes they have committed against all of us."

"The elemental protectors will not forget their children."

"They have forgotten us," Katrina exploded. She slammed her fist down on the table.

Junia's face went pale she rose and grabbed Katirna's arm, "Don't you ever say that again. Hope is all we have left, and I will not give that up."

Katirna bowed her head as she spoke, "I am trying to help this family do more than scratch out a bare living from the dust of this village. With the money I have collected from the false king, you can buy a larger house. You can buy food for a year, and new clothes for everyone." Katirna's voice faded off as she could see her mother was not listening.

Nathel could almost see the wall between mother and daughter.

Thero took his cue as the awkward silence descended around the table. Skillfully, he moved the conversation to new topics and soon Junia and Katirna were smiling and laughing.

As darkness fell, Nathel, Thero, and Katirna took their leave of the small home and made their way to the single boarding house in the small village.

Nathel stood in the hallway watching as Katirna walked slowly to her room, her head hung low and her feet dragged across the wooden planks of the solid floor.

"Kat," Nathel started. He stopped as he watched her shoulders slump even more. He walked down the hall and gently put his hand on her shoulder, "Is there anything I can do? I can sit and listen if you want someone to talk too."

"Thanks for trying, Nathel. I just need some time to myself." She spoke without turning her head then disappeared into her room and closed the door quickly behind her.

Nathel stood staring at the door for some time in the darkness of the hallway wishing he could help her in some way.

The moon was full in the sky when Nathel finally slipped into his bed. The cotton sheets were clean and the bed was soft, but despite the comforts around him he could not fall asleep. Thero's snores were filling the room when Nathel finally drifted off. As he slept, he dreamed he was fleeing across the rooftops of Juthel, legions of soldiers hunted him and packs of wolves roamed the streets.

The next morning dawned with a brilliant burst of sunshine. At the open window an annoying songbird perched on the sill and warbled it's greeting to the sleeping shepherd. Nathel grumbled as he stomped over and slammed the window, chasing the startled bird away and then stumbling back to his bed and falling back into it.

"This easy living is making you soft, boy." Thero grinned from where he stood near the door.

"Stupid bird." He flipped back the cotton coverlet as he swung his legs over the edge of the bed and reached for his clothes.

Katirna was eating breakfast when Nathel finally stomped down the stairs and entered the eating room of the inn.

"Hey there, sleepy."

"I am starting to hate mornings," he said. Nathel slipped into the seat opposite her and helped himself to the tray of bread, fruit, and cheese.

"Are you better this morning," Nathel asked. He removed a shiny red apple from the tray and bit deeply into it, using his hand to catch the streams of juice that ran down his chin.

"Yes, a good night's sleep always puts me in a better mood." Katirna offered him a halfhearted smile.

It was mid morning when they left the small village and entered the outskirts of the Black Forest. The forest stretched out for fifty leagues before them. The Isies River and the Mistel River cradled the giant swath of trees. Filled with towering black oak and dozens of other ancient hardwood trees, it was a place of mystery and legend. Most lowlanders cut a wide path around the thickly forested countryside.

"Are you planning on going through the forest?" Katirna asked. She stood in the middle of the path staring at the dark shadows filling the floor of the forest.

"It would take us an extra two weeks to travel around it and we must make haste to the Monastery of the One. If we are careful, the creatures that guard the forest will not even know that we have passed," Thero replied. He stopped and faced both of the younger travelers.

"There are a few precautions we must take in order to make our passing remain unnoticed. First, no fires of any kind while we travel through the forest. The protectors of the trees do not take kindly to fires; also we will gather nothing from the forest floor. Above all, stay on the narrow path, other paths may open and offer an easier route but you must not stray from the narrow path. Is that clear to both of you?"

Thero's voice was stern as he spoke and Nathel could hear that he would accept no conditions to the rules he had laid out.

"We understand grandpa," Nathel said. He nodded assuring the Ancient one that they would follow his rules to the letter.

"You better because your life depends on it," Thero grunted. With one last glare at both of them he turned and led them to the edge of the trees.

"Where is the trail grandpa?"

Thero did not reply but walked straight up to the edge of the forest, and stood staring at the wall of trees. Nathel shrugged and he reached out and took Katirna's hand. "Come on, when he gets something into his head, you can't change his mind."

Katirna snickered but she clung tightly to his hand as they followed the gray haired Thero towards the wall of trees.

"Ah, here it is," Thero pointed.

Katirna looked closely and noticed a small trail leading between two massive oak trees. It was no larger than the game trails she used to see wandering through the fields and meadows.

It was only wide enough for one to go at a time and Nathel motioned for Katirna to precede him. She almost refused but when she finally entered the trail she reached back with her arm so that she could still cling tightly to him. Nathel followed her quickly using his staff to hold his balance on the narrow trail.

"It's so quiet," Katirna whispered to Thero. The forest was silent around them except for the occasional rustle of leaves as unseen creatures passed.

They walked down the trail together. The path had widened some and Nathel was able to walk along beside her. She wore her hair bound back behind her head in a ponytail and more than once Nathel almost tripped over exposed roots on the trail. He soon learned to watch where he was walking rather than watch her. Her hand was soft and even in the dim light of the forest the bits of sunshine found her hair and sparkled.

"The forest is full of life but many of the creatures are watching us and remaining quiet until they decide whether we are a threat or not," Thero said. He motioned to a nearby tree where three birds perched on one of the top branches. All three watched the intruders with their heads cocked to the side, it almost seemed to Nathel that they were asking why their solitude was being interrupted.

"Look there, I told you not all wolves have fallen under the sway of the Fallen," Thero said. He pointed out to the west. Sitting quietly in front of an swaying willow tree was a lean wolf. Brown in color, the wolf nodded at Thero then it turned and disappeared into the forest.

"Well that was interesting." Thero turned and eyed the two young people.

"What is interesting?"

"Did you not hear what the wolf told us?"

Thero's back was turned but Nathel could hear the smile in his voice, "Come on grandpa, you know we have no idea what just happened."

"The brown lady that just left us said that a pack of the Fallen is approaching the edge of the forest. She is going to gather the faithful but it will take time to match the power of the pack. We must move quickly. I would rather avoid a confrontation in the darkness of the forests."

Nathel nodded and they followed Thero along the narrow trail. It was not too much later that far in the distance the haunting cry of the hunting pack echoed along the tops of the trees and added a sense of urgency to their flight.

For two days the narrow trial led them along its winding path through the forests with little sense of direction. At times it seemed to double back on itself and Nathel was positive he could see the next part of it through the edge of the trees.

"Thero its right there we can skip through the trees and gain time instead of walking in circles," Nathel said. He pointed out between the thick tree trunks. He was so positive that he even took a step towards the edge of the trees. He pulled on Katirna's hand wanting to bring her along.

"BOY!" Thero's sharp voice cut through the haze in Nathel's mind bringing him to a sudden halt, his foot rested lightly on the edge of the trail waiting to take the final step out into the shadowy forests.

"Remember what I told you, do not leave the path for any reason. One step and you would be lost hopelessly in the darkness of the forests. A second step and I would never be able to find you, even with my knowledge of the forest."

Nathel stepped back. His eyes cleared some but he still stared longingly at the tantalizing trail visible between the oaks.

Katirna pulled hard on his hand, "Come, let's follow your grandfather, Nathel."

Nathel turned and they hurried down the trail, behind them the howls of the fallen took on a more sinister tone.

The race through the trunks took on almost a dream-like quality for Nathel as they ran through the trees, he could see what was happening around him but his mind seemed to be a thousand paces away. Katirna kept a tight grip on his hand and pulled him along, making sure he stayed with Thero as they fled along the narrow trail, behind them wolves began to filter through the tree trunks mirroring their path. Snarling fights could be heard breaking out behind them as the faithful creatures of the forest emerged to battle the Fallen.

Late in the third day they reached the heart of the forest and the trail widened. Thero slowed to a walk allowing them to catch their breath, deep behind them in the forests they could hear the pack searching for them.

"We are safe for the moment. I do not think even the pack will enter the heart of the forest. It was planted by the stone elementals," Thero said. He motioned them forward and they made their way to a clear pool of water sitting serenely in the middle of the glade. The water was cool and it did much to clear the fog that had been cast across Nathel's head. All around them the thick trunks of ancient trees reached up to the sky, the branches shifting under a refreshing breeze.

"What do we do now?" Nathel asked. He sat at the edge of the stream looking around as if he was seeing the forest for the first time.

"We must reach the far side of the forest in front of the pack. We can cross the Isies River into the Duchy of Alast. It will take the pack time to find a way across the river; by the time they cross over we will have found a ship bound for the Northern Orkin Empire."

Katirna nodded, "I have crossed the river a few times, and there are several ferries that cross from the southern part of the duchy to the city of Alast. The trip to the two port city of Albalter is less than two days with fast horses."

Suddenly, Thero leapt to his feet facing south, "Something is approaching, something powerful."

Nathel leapt to his feet with his staff held ready in his hands. Katirna stepped two paces to the side and drew out two daggers from her belt.

"South and west."

Around them the ground shook and Nathel heard the snapping of branches. At the edge of the glade, the tops of the trees swayed under the violent blows, and he struggled to keep his balance with each step of the approaching creature.

"What is it, grandpa?" Nathel asked. He stared at the hideous creature that pushed its way through the trees.

"Swamp troll, and the biggest one I have ever seen," Thero watched as the lumbering creature stepped forward, its long arms dragging on the ground. A massive ax dragged along behind the troll scarring the thick carpet of grass. Nathel stared in amazement at the ugly creature. Long fangs stuck up from his bottom lip. Yellowed and stained with blood, they added to the fearsome image of the creature.

"What do we do, Thero?" Nathel cried. He clutched his staff tightly watching as the troll approached across the shaded glade.

Thero turned his head motioning for them to be quiet, "Its vision is poor but its hearing is exceptional." Thero back up slowly, he motioned for them to step back.

"Help is close by but we must reach the inner heart of the forest,"

Thero led them away slowly. Behind them, Nathel could hear the troll moving about smashing into trees and swinging its ax wildly.

"Grandpa, I don't see a gem of binding. Where it is?" Nathel tried to ask the question quietly but Thero still offered him a silencing glare.

Behind them the troll's head whipped around and it lumbered after them, landing a big foot in the clear pool. Instantly, the water was filled with mud and a foul looking alge formed on the surface.

"Quickly, this way! It's not an elemental, boy, it's just a violent beast left over from long ago." Thero turned and led them at a run away from the glade.

Nathel dared to glance back, behind them small trees were crushed, and the troll's clawed feet left slashing imprints in the soft ground.

Thero led them to the deepest part of the clearing; despite the crashing of the troll the dim light of the forest seemed peaceful. A single tree grew from the center of the clearing, massive and old it soared into the air dominating the sky, its trunk was so thick that Nathel was sure his arms would not even go a third of the way around it.

"Why have you brought that creature into my home?" a deep rumbling voice asked. All around them the ground erupted. Nathel stumbled backwards as roots of the massive oak pulled free of the ground, thick branches reached down trapping them on all sides.

Thero strode forward walking right up to the massive oak, "Heart of the Forest, you know me. Search your memory. I would not bring this evil creature into your home lightly. We must reach the far side of the forest quickly. The world is changing. Even now, a pack of the Fallen does battle with the faithful in the forest, and the troll hunts us. Bedbezdal is moving his pawns across the face of the realms. The final battle is approaching and the elemental protectors are all but trapped in prisons of their own making. I beseech and beg you to help us stop this evil creature so that we can reach the Monastery of One before the Fallen can move against it."

The ancient oak fell silent as it weighed the words carefully, "What you say rings true. The power of the forest is being drained away. I cannot feel the trees beyond the river any more. It appears I have slept for too long. The Fallen are driving back the Faithful in the forest. Go now, I have opened a passage for you to the river Isies. Somehow, I will stop the trolls that pursue you."

"There is more than one?" Nathel shuddered. He turned to see three of the massive brutes step from the forest and into the clearing. The trolls roared as they lumbered across the intervening space with their rusty axes held high. The tree groaned as it tore the last of its roots free of the ground. Taking slow steps, it moved forward to meet the trolls. Thick branches swung like clubs as it attacked the trolls, knocking the creatures back but accepting horrible blows from the axes in return.

"Quickly, we cannot help with this fight." Thero grabbed Nathel and Katirna by the arms and dragged them across the clearing stepping onto a narrow path that opened up before them. This time the narrow path was straight and level cutting through the rest of the forest.

"How...?" Nathel stuttered. It took them less than two hundred paces to escape the dim reaches of the forest and look out over the shining blue waters of the Isies River. Thero stumbled, suddenly grabbing out to the young people for balance. His face went pale as behind them the forest shuddered.

"What happened?" Nathel asked. He knelt down and put his arm around Thero's shoulders.

"The Heart of the Forest has died. The great trees will no longer protect the forests from intruders." Tears formed in Thero's eyes as he spoke.

"Come, we have to keep moving," Nathel urged this time. In the distance Nathel heard the howls of the fallen echo into the evening sky; the sound brought the urgency back to their steps.

"Yes, you're right." Thero pulled himself up to his feet. His face was still pale and his breath came in shallow gasps. Motioning Nathel and Katirna on, they entered the Duchy of Alast. They ran down the road towards the river, breaking into open farm land. Soon a small farm village came into view, along with a wide bottomed ferry boat floating calmly along the shining ribbon of water.

The sun set slowly in the western sky as they approached the village perched on a bend in the river. A rocky bluff to the east looked down over the town like a watchman.

Thero's face was returning to its normal color but he refused to speak any more of what he had felt.

Nathel glanced over and saw the pain on his grandfather's face so he held his peace.

Thero led the way down the main street, flickering lanterns hung from metal posts along the wide street lighting the way with dancing lights.

Once again in the distance a chorus of howls broke out as the pack broke from the forest and raced across the fields. The sound was chilling, and Nathel shuddered as they hurried towards the ferry. He could see six men standing on the flat bottom wooden boat looking towards the sound of the wolves.

"Come we must make it to the ferry!" Thero cried. He sprinted along the road ignoring the shouts of the townsfolk as they stepped from their well lit homes to stare at the evening sky.

Most went back inside and locked the thick wooden doors. Many even began fastening their thick shutters closed, cutting off all view into or out of the houses and cottages. Nathel could see the men working the ferry beginning to cast off the mooring lines holding the boat to the near shore.

"Wait for us!" Thero yelled. They hurtled down the bank to the wooden pier reaching out into the rushing river.

"Stay back!" A burly man waving a cudgel screamed at the trio as they raced ahead of the darting shadows of the pack. Nathel glanced back, catching sight of the gaunt pack leader staring down at the fleeing humans from the cliff overlooking the village. Behind them cries of fear echoed across the village as scores of tall mountain wolves flooded into the village streets.

"Jump for the ferry!" Thero cried. He launched himself into the air, throwing his staff at the cudgel wielding human as he jumped. The thrown staff knocked the man back and Thero landed lightly on his feet sweeping up his staff and charging forward towards the men working the windlass that would pull the ferry into the deep water.

"Hold for the boy and girl," Thero's voice offered no other choice and the ferrymen stopped, watching fearfully as Nathel made the leaping jump and landed on the ferry. Katirna made the jump look easy and landed on her feet two daggers out and eyes flashing at the scared men.

"Now put your backs into it!" Thero said. He turned and watched a dozen wolves broil out onto the pier, racing for the slow moving ferry. The thick ropes creaked loudly as the men working the windlass threw their bodies into the machine, the ferry jerked as once again it started across the river.

"Defend the ferry!" Thero yelled.

Nathel nodded as he watched as the first wolf soar over the water with a tremendous leap that cleared both his and Kat's heads.

"Take the first Kat. I will take the next one," Nathel said. As he spoke a second tall lean wolf landed on the deck planks of the ferry. The wolf gathered itself and leapt forward, teeth slashing as Nathel brought up the rune staff. The hardened wood intercepted the flashing teeth and knocked several from their sockets. The wolf yelped and scrambled to put a bit of space between itself and the dangerous staff.

Thump Thump, Nathel spun his staff hand over hand as two more wolves landed on the deck. In quick succession three more landed and then the ferry was swept into the rushing river out of jumping distance of the remaining members of the pack.

Katirna whipped her daggers back and forth in wide arcs keeping the mountain wolf facing her back as she searched for an opening, Thero rushed forward to engage the wolf that had leapt over their heads but was forced to skitter backwards when the beast lunged for the petrified ferry hands. One of the ferrymen broke and flung himself into the water screaming in fear. It only took a moment for the swift moving river to pull him away and dash him against hidden rocks.

Thero dodged back and forth keeping as the wolves at bay as they split into pairs and lunged for position on the bucking and tossing wooden deck. The ferry master was at the tiller. Wide eyed, he clung to the wooden tiller as the ferry strained at the guide ropes.

"Thero, the wolves are trying to chew through the guide rope," Nathel pointed. He kept the staff spinning, the rune hardened wood blocking any attempt by the pair facing him to attack. On shore Nathel watched the pack leader leap for the guide rope, its razor sharp teeth hacking through the thick ropes. Another jolt hit the ferry as the ropes fell free and the low bottom boat swung free of the guides. One of the deck hands instinctively grabbed the rope as it slithered past on the rough deck and before anyone could shout a warning he disappeared over the side of the boat.

"Blast it," Nathel growled. He stopped his staff in mid-spin, Both wolves lunged forward-one went low, and the second went high. Forearms flexed as he sent the bottom of his staff forward catching the bottom wolf as it lunged and sending the tawny animal rolling across the deck. He ducked his head and spun the top of the staff back around, catching the leaping wolf in the middle of the chest. Whispering the blessing of the Elements, Nathel watched his blow send the wolf spinning over the edge of the ferry and into the raging water. All around them rocks rose high out of the water turning the swift flowing water into raging white rapids. The ferry lurched as it entered the rapids; crushing blows hit the wooden hull repeatedly, tearing away great sections of the bow. Nathel watched as Katirna stabbed a dagger home into the wolf she was battling. Suddenly a heavy strike brought the ferry to a halt, the wooden hull beaching itself high on the boulders.

Katirna tumbled backwards losing her grip on both knives as she grabbed hold of the heavy oaken railing; the wolf's body tumbled away into the river disappearing into the frothing water.

Then a loud tearing sound started from the stern echoing across the water. Nathel watched in horror as the entire stern of the ferry broke loose.

Half of the flat bottomed boat swung away, spinning in circles down the darkened river carrying Thero, the two remaining ferry hands, and two mountains wolves off into the night.

"Thero," Nathel screamed into the darkness but only the sound of rushing water answered his cry.

"Nathel help!" Kat screamed.

He spun around from where he had watched the stern of the ferry disappear; Kat was clinging to railing as it began to collapse. Nathel lunged from where he stood and caught Kat's hand just as the railing gave way.

"Hold on!" The spraying river water was making Katirna's hand wet and slippery. Nathel pulled back with all his might. Then with a rush, she tumbled back over the edge of the ferry. Nathel stood and watched as the ferry rocked, the rushing water continuing to tear away large pieces of the ferry.

"Here, untie the rope on those barrels." Nathel pointed to the row of barrels tied to the remaining deck planks.

Katirna scrambled to the far side of the row of barrels and pulled a third dagger from her belt, two quick cuts and the ropes fell free.

Nathel pulled one of the ropes and looped it around two of the barrels. Working quickly he tied off the end securing just the pair together. Around them the remaining half of the ferry groaned loudly as the river continued to tear at it. Nathel motioned Katirna to grab the other side and together they pushed the makeshift raft to the far side of the ferry.

"Hold on!" Nathel yelled above the roar of the river.

Kat nodded and grasped the rope tightly, as he pushed hard sliding the barrel into the river. Then clutching his staff tightly Nathel leapt off the disintegrating ferry and grasped hold of the end of the rope.

The current whisked them quickly downriver spinning them in circles around rocks and logs. Nathel's body was battered and bruised as the rocks tore at him, trying to break his death grip on the roped barrels.

Finally, the river ran into a calm stretch and Nathel pushed wearily until the raft ran aground on a sand bar.

"Are you alright?" Katirna asked. She pulled herself free of the ropes and helped Nathel to his feet.

"At least I didn't drop my staff." He smiled. Leaning wearily, he used the weapon to brace his body and stumbled towards the sandy shallows. Free of the added weight, the barrels floated off down the river running back into the next stretch of rapids and disappearing into the darkness.

Around Nathel the sounds of the river filled the night and the chirping of a hundred crickets filled the night sky. Behind them in the darkness Nathel could hear fish jumping as he dragged his weary legs out of the water and collapsed on the sandy beach. Katirna fell to the ground beside him gasping for breath and coughing to clear inhaled river water from her lungs.

"I hope Thero made it out of the river."

"I am sure he did," Katirna said. "He has not survived for as long as he has without learning a few things."

"I suppose you're right." Nathel doubled over as a spasm of coughing wracked his body, and then he leaned back against the cool sand.

"Where do we go from here?" Katirna turned her head to the side; pale light lit her face perfectly as the patchy clouds cleared. Overhead the moon broke free from their grasp, its light filtering into the clearing through the willow branches.

Nathel was lost for words as she looked at him, stammering he tried desperately to remember the question that had been asked.

"Where do we go from here?" Katirna said again. She smiled at him, reaching up she brushed a stray strand of hair away from her face.

"Well, I think we should try and find the nearest city. From there we work our way to the Monastery of One, and with any luck Thero will meet us there. If not, we can begin searching for the answers to where the Chamber of Life lies."

Katirna nodded, she turned her head back to stare up at the moon as clouds danced by the glowing orb, making its light flicker and prance across the nearby water.

Nathel continued staring at Katirna until sleep took them both where they lay; overhead the rustling branches of the willow trees guarded their sleep.

Matthew John Krengel

Chapter Seventeen
Different Paths

hero watched with dismay as the raging river swept him further and further south, until Nathel and Katirna disappeared in the distance. It was a miracle that his small section of raft stayed together at all. Thankfully, the mountain wolves had been swept from the deck as had the remaining ferry hands.

"Please protect those poor souls," Thero prayed. Why the Elemental Protectors felt it necessary to split the small group up was beyond his understanding. All that he could do was trust that the creator's guiding hand would keep the Nathel and Katirna safe despite the dangers.

Amazingly, the small section of deck planks that he found himself floating on remained fastened together. The ropes binding the planks were strong, and despite the pull and tug of the water they held firm. The river was wide and fast and few rocks reared their heads. The speed of the water kept him clinging to the raft as it stuck like a blood hound to the center of the river.

"Well boy, I trained you to use your head and to defend yourself. Trust your heart to get you to your destination," he muttered, wishing he could talk to Nathel just one last time.

As the river slowed, he took a seat on the raft with his staff in his hands and watched the countryside slip past. The Duchy of Alast was filled with lush green countryside but the few towns he would pass were small. His only chance of rescue would be as he entered the port city of Alast. Even there the current was swift, and if he went past the city at dusk or after the sun went down, he would float out into deeper waters and could drift for days.

Thero watched the distant shore line hoping to see a fishing craft or cargo ferry on the widening river. Despite his vigilance, the water remained silent and quiet, as the sun sank lower in the western sky Thero began to worry. Far to the east he saw columns of smoke drifting up into the evening sky, staining the colorful sunset with ugly patches of black. The closer he drifted to the port, the worse the smoke became.

"What is happening?" Thero mused to himself. Thankfully, the current swung the raft closer to the shore than it had in hours. Just as he was about to strike out swimming for the closer shore, he rounded the last bend that hid Alast from his vision.

"Oh, Emperor Orlin, what have you done?" Thero gasped. He stared at the blockade of heavy, low slung warships across the wide river. Green banners snapped and whipped in the breeze drifting off the oceans. Thero leaned on his staff as the tears rose to his gray eyes, rolling down his cheek and losing their way in his beard. In the distance, he watched long lines of armored figures march down boarding planks and trot off towards the scarred and blackened walls of Alast. The Duchy was under attack by the Emperor's elite Ironback Divisions and Thero suddenly knew why the protectors had broken the small group up.

"Hello the raft."

The gravelly voice of an Orkin sentry echoed across the dark water of the river as Thero drifted within shouting range of the middle warship. Brilliant green sails hung limp where they had been lowered and tied to the cross pieces and in the distance Thero heard the war horns calling the troops away from their assault on the once beautiful white washed walls of Alast. Known around the world as *the alabaster city,* it was a sight to see in the setting sun. Thin towers and onion shaped minarets rose into the air, built more for decoration than defense. Thero knew that if he was unable to talk sense into the short-sighted emperor, things would go from bad to worse for the fragmented kingdoms of the low lands.

"Hail the warship," Thero stood and leaned on his staff as the raft drifted closer to the looming ship. He noted the two archers watching from the aft of the ship, short bows held ready.

"Stand by to be taken aboard his majestie's ship of the line."

The sentry motioned to a second figure hidden from view on the broad deck. Thero looked over the ship as he drifted closer. The Orkin warships were broad with shallow drafts which allowed them to sail up the rivers of the lowlands. Blocky square sails were reefed against the three masts, and a pair of ballista was mounted to the stern of the ship.

Scores of archer's posts scattered about the ship made it a formidable fighting machine in the shallow rivers and coastal waters. The wide holds held plenty of room for hundreds of troops, their weapons, and supplies.

"Please convey my thanks to his Majesty for a timely rescue from my current predicament," Thero said politely. He scurried up the rope ladder that was tossed over the side for him.

As he threw his leg over the railing he was grasped in rough hands and his staff was pulled from his hands.

"Orkin hospitality has faded some if this is how you treat rescued guests, even during time of war." Thero's face was stern; his ire was beginning to rise as the Orkin warriors pulled him along towards the stern of the ship. The armored soldiers were a head shorter then he and most wore tightly woven chain mail.

"Quiet you, the Emperor wishes to speak with you." The bottom half of the sentry's face was hidden by a green mask that left only his eyes glaring out of the cloth and leather mask. Thero held his peace the soldiers hustled him across the deck to a ornate door set into the stern of the ship.

"The Emperor himself is along for the ride this time? Good, I would have hated to travel across thousands of leagues to talk some sense into the senile old fool."

"Hush you!"

Thero's eyes flashed as the young sentry hushed him.

The frightened young warrior opened his mouth once again, then thought better of it and hurried to open the ornate door.

"Your majesty, here is the castaway that we told you was drifting towards the blockade."

Thero counted ten armed warriors placed about the wide cabin making the expansive room still seem small. As the door closed, he turned and swiftly removed his staff from the grasp of the sentry. Drawing himself up to his full height, Thero's eyes flashed and he slammed the tip of staff against the deck. A sudden rush of power pushed over everyone present, and more than a few of the soldiers blinked in confusion as if realizing for the first time where they were.

"Where is the old fool Orlin, and why does he lay siege to Alast? He should be mustering his armies to defeat the armies of Bedbezdal."

"Thero?" A wavering voice spoke.

Thero peered at the ornate bed bolted to the floor in the corner and his voice drifted off as he looked at the fragile orkin. Emperor Orlin of the

193

Southern Orkin Empire lay reclined on a soft bed of cushions. He was a mere shell of the robust figure he had been in years past. As the moment of confusion passed by, his sentries raced forward placing their armored bodies between the anger of the Ancient One and the frail emperor.

"Stop, no fighting," Orlin struggled to raise his hand.

"Why are you attacking Alast? The duchess has always been a friend of the Orkin empires. The Alabaster City has always been open to all peoples." Thero demanded. He settled back on his heels as his anger faded, only to be replaced by curiosity.

Before he took Nathel to the Highlands, he had spoken extensively with Emperor Orlin and the aging orkin had assured him that the two empires would not fight one another. After years of raids and invasions Thero had gotten the two leaders to sign a treaty and peace had settled across the divided land.

"The duchy has supported the Fallen and must be punished," Orlin muttered. The aging monarch's voice cracked as he spoke and his eyes grew distant.

"What? Who told you these things?"

"All who support the Fallen must be punished, don't you agree, Thero? Perhaps you too have fallen under the sway of Bedbezdal in your long absence from the world." Orlin turned his head to stare at the white bearded prophet.

"Are you daft, Orlin?" Thero growled. He was now beyond irritated with the aging orkin, he was downright filled with wrath at the emperor. "I have spent a thousand years thwarting the will of the Dark One."

Orlin ignored him and Thero fell silent as he listened, "Five years ago a man came to the Southern Empire and began to preach about the Pillars of the world. His words rang true to all who heard them and we knew he was sent by Anatari to take your place. Emperor Ratchuth and I signed a treaty and we have answered the call of the Elemental Protectors to punish the lowlanders for bringing the Fallen onto the world. It is only by punishing the ones who harbor the Fallen that we will be assured our proper place in eternity. The combined armies of the orkin peoples will cleanse the Fallen from the low lands and then we will take our true place. It is good that we have found you Thero. In your absence from the world, it has been decided that you are a member of the Fallen, and orders were issued for your arrest. You will be punished for your crimes after a proper trial."

Thero stood staring at Orlin as the old dieing emperor finished his speech and sagged back into the stacked cushions.

"Who is this new teacher that has so clouded your vision that you have forgotten all the things I taught you? You have abandoned order for chaos, and ignored the truths taught in the Lost Books to embrace madness," Thero thundered. His voice rose until his words filled the room. The power in his voice, made the armored guards take a step back and made Orlin cringe in his bed.

"Ahh Thero, I am glad I made it here in time to enjoy your execution."

The voice that spoke was raspy and rough and Thero closed his eyes knowing what he would see when he turned.

"Always good to the see you Grenth, son of a false king. I see you are still moving about the world causing problems. How is your father enjoying the redecoration of the royal library?" Thero asked. He turned to face the thin man. Thero gripped his staff tightly knowing that father and son were both skilled swordsmen and that the son shared his father's explosive temper.

"Everyone out!" ordered the thin human.

The orkin guards trooped out of the room. Thero watched as the door slipped shut closing out the cool night air and locking in the oppressive heat of the cabin. With the guards gone, the space was once again roomy and Thero leaned casually on his staff.

"I have no idea what you speak of, heretic Thero," Grenth said. He spoke slowly as he gritted his teeth and painted a smile across his face.

"It is you that spreads your father's lies? What can you hope to gain? Bedbezdal is still imprisoned."

"For now, but that will change soon. You have been absent too long old one. Even now the Elemental Pillars that have guarded my master's prison for a thousand years are crumbling."

"The end of the age is not yet upon us," Thero countered firmly.

Grenth laughed, "You and your foolish beliefs in the Lost Books. How long has it been since you have even seen that dusty collection of scrolls?"

Thero narrowed his eyes but held silent.

"Those scrolls are not the only writings to speak of future events. I have read prophetic writings that say Anatari will be banished to the same prison that has held my master for the last millennium."

"Is that what this is about? A prophecy written by an insane human drunk on grog? You think creating chaos throughout the lowlands and

Kashguth will give you the strength to overthrow the order brought by the Elemental Pillars?"

"That is something that you will have to wait and see." Grenth slipped his sword from its sheath and stepped towards Thero. "In the mean time I have one last task: to slow you enough that you will never reach the lowlanders in time to help."

"Orlin!" Thero cried. "Anatari, hear my cry. Free his mind from this web of deception." Thero traced the symbol of the Elemental Pillars into the air one at a time. They glowed brilliantly and hung in the air before Orlin's face. The lights played off the Orkin features and slowly the light returned to his aged eyes.

"What is that vile creature doing on my ship?" Orlin's steady hand reached out and struck a golden bell bolted to the floor of the ship deck.

Thero whirled as Orlin's eyes flared wide and his senses screamed warnings at him. He raised his staff as he turned to face Grenth, snapping his staff out at chest height as Grenth lunged forward with his sword extended. A score of guards rushed into the room and chaos broke out as Grenth screamed for them to restrain Thero and then ran for the door.

Thero struggled to reach the door but was quickly dragged to the floor by dozens of rough hands.

"The emperor is dead." The cry came from the back of the room where a ring of iron surrounded Orlin.

Thero was yanked to his feet and the ship captain turned to face him.

"Why have you killed the Emperor?" The words came slowly as though the man was struggling physically against something compelling him to move and speak.

"I carry no blade, good captain, I tried to stop the killer," Thero said. He pointed down at the floor where Grenth's thin sword lay on the deck, a small rivulet of blood rolled lazily across the planks.

"While you waste precious time, the killer has made his escape." Thero's words broke across the room and angry muttering broke out around the cabin.

"Brave warriors! Orkin of the legendary Ironback Division! You have been led astray by an evil man. I am the prophet of the true creator and you must listen. We must right the wrongs that have been committed this night."

Silence descended across the room and the orkin warriors stood rubbing their eyes like those awakening from a long slumber. Cries of horror and gasps of surprise rang out around the room and more than one warrior dropped to his knees and began crying.

"Is the Emperor's son with the army?" Thero asked. He addressed the captain of the ship who was struggling to hold his tears back.

"He was thrown in the ship's hold for daring to defy the Apostle and the Emperor's commands."

"Send some soldiers to get him quickly, and send word to the troops around the city to call off all attacks. I think enough blood has been shed for one night," Thero ordered. He walked over to where Orlin lay and gently closed his eyes.

The ship's captain nodded and motioned to some of the warriors standing near the door to carry out the orders.

Matthew John Krengel

CHAPTER EIGHTEEN
KIDNAPPED!

athel awoke with a start. A light breeze was drifting in from the north carrying with it the sounds of birdsong filtering through the nearby trees. Katirna was rubbing her eyes as he sat up. Picking up his staff from where it lay, he said "I am going to rinse my face off, I feel like I bathed in dirt last night while we were swimming to shore."

"You look like you bathed in dirt too," Kat laughed and dodged the chunk of dirt that Nathel flipped from the end of his staff at her.

Nathel leaned over a calm pool of clear water on the edge of the river and slipped slowly into the water, "Come on, it's not to cold." The chattering of his teeth betrayed the true temperature of the water and Kat laughed as she slowly dipped her arms into the water, and then rubbed some across her face.

"I think I will pass on the full bath for now." Rising to her feet Katirna looked to the north. The hilly forests of the northern part of the duchy of Alast stretched out before them.

"Hills and forests between here and the mountains that guard the northern orkin empire," Katirna stopped talking for a moment and cocked her head to the side listening to something that was lost on Nathel.

"Do you hear that?" Katirna looked at him questioningly.

"Hear what?" Nathel asked as he brushed the water from his hair. Pausing, he listened but the only sound he could hear was the rumble of the river.

Sand and grime fouled the formerly clean pool of water as Nathel dipped his head one more time in the cold water, holding his eyes closed tightly to avoid getting it in his eyes.

"Nathel," The horrified scream brought him to his feet.

"Kat," Nathel cried back as he grabbed his staff and rushed towards the river bank, Katirna was hovered on the upper bank of the river. A dark shadow rocketed down out of the sky dropping on Katirna and covering her completely. Through the shadow Nathel could see the stone gargoyle that had been haunting the royal library grinning hideously at him.

"Come to the Fortress of Winds, boy, if you want to see your little friend alive ever again." The voice sent shivers through his spine and made his limbs freeze in terror. Katirna was limp in the clawed talons as the stone wings beat slowly. With a rush of air, the gargoyle lifted off the ground, the winds once again blowing Nathel head over heels into the deep pools of the river.

Nathel scrambled up, fighting against the current that threatened to rip him from the bank and take him swirling down the river again. Finally he scrambled up the bank and raced up to the top of the sandy crest. The gargoyle was a distant speck in the morning sky, moving on stone wings it flew faster than a horse could run.

He glanced to the northeast, in that direction laid the Monastery and his grandfather. It took but a moment for him to make his decision; he turned and began walking northwest after the diminishing gargoyle. Thero had told him once that if you walk north until you see a towering cliff of stone you would be close to the Fortress of Winds, he would not leave Katirna in the hands of the fallen elemental.

The Fortress of Winds was dark despite the early hour; little light reached the brooding fortress. The walls straddled the wide pass leading into the northern mountains. The land beyond the fortress was completely veiled in misty darkness and only whispers of sound could be heard from the blackness.

Inside the fortress, the frozen form of Miceali stood facing the open door. The fortress on the far side of the Chamber of Light was in shambles. Most of the walls had been torn down to make room for the flooding hordes of soldiers that now moved at a shuffling pace through the chamber. Tens of thousands of tawny mountain wolves moved through, padding on silent feet coming at the call of the chosen master. Slow moving and clumsy giants ducked low, at times dropping down on all fours to crawl through the passages. Minotaurs' ducked their heads to make sure the spiked horns on their bulls heads cleared the lower parts of the roofline. The slow moving horde parted as it passed the frozen warriors, moving only at the command of their master. Bedbezdal himself was still bound in his prison, but the bounds holding him there were weakening, and soon he would be loosed on the world again. With the weakening of the elemental pillars he sent forth his most powerful servant to take the Fortress of Winds. Now with the castle in his possession, his troops were massing. Like a flight of locust, he would send them south, spreading war and pestilence on all fronts. He would destroy the low land kingdoms and then surround the mountain kingdom of the faithful.

Standing silently in the Chamber of Light was the creature charged with taking the fortress. Standing no taller than an average human, it was cloaked in blackness and evil radiated from it. A high cowl surrounded his face and a long black sword hung unmoving from his waist. Every so often the creatures head shifted from side to side as it watched the hordes of creatures part and then come back together on the far side of the frozen warriors.

"My lord, the outer gate is falling. It has taken weeks but we are almost free of the Fortress." A particularly large minotaur soldier stepped forward to address the black cloaked creature. All he received in answer was a nod and it turned to go.

"As soon as the gate falls, send the scouts out. In three days we will march south." The soft voice stopped the big soldier in its tracks. The minotaur shifted its five hundred pounds of weight from foot to foot nervously.

When no more orders came the massive warrior saluted and wheeled about disappearing back into the recesses of the fortress. Tens of thousands of lesser creatures moved silently past the silent statues; Uncounted hordes of Goblins, Medusas, wraiths, and slow moving Basilisks. A myriad of creatures all dedicated to evil answered the call of their master and marched south to the coming war.

The sound of stone wings brought the black creature from its silent contemplations, "Did you succeed in your mission?"

The stone gargoyle dropped Katirna to the ground and settled to the floor in front of the black clad creature, "The boy is coming, master; he is the last of the royal house of Juthel. He carries the bell and will follow the girl no matter where she goes."

Katirna groaned and then fell silent as she glanced up; fear froze her where she lay.

"Once the bell is in our hands we will kill the boy. After the bell is carried to the chamber, our task is complete. My father will be loosed from the pillars and Anatari will be bound. Then it is our turn to have rule over this world."

The gargoyle nodded then he pushed Katirna forward and flapped its wings. The elemental moved off to watch over the armies moving towards the falling outer gate.

"You, my dear can join this pathetic guardian of the fortress in eternal slumber." He reached down and grasped Katirna by the wrist.

Katirna screamed as the cold fingers closed around her wrist, the sound echoed through the chamber and then she fell silent. Her flesh, changed to stone in the blink of an eye.

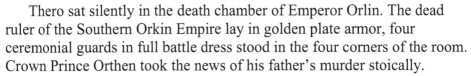

Thero sat silently in the death chamber of Emperor Orlin. The dead ruler of the Southern Orkin Empire lay in golden plate armor, four ceremonial guards in full battle dress stood in the four corners of the room. Crown Prince Orthen took the news of his father's murder stoically.

He walked into the room slowly and knelt by the bedside. He bowed his head for a moment and then stood and wiped a single tear from his eye.

Thero saw the pain in his eyes but he held peace knowing that more important things were at stake. "Orthen, we must move quickly. People are still dying."

Orthen nodded, he gave his father one last look and then turned and motioned to a nearby messenger. "Call back the troops immediately and we will begin cleaning up this mess."

"You have grown much since the last time I was present in the royal palace." Thero offered a small bow and then grasped the rough mail clad hand that was extended to him in greeting.

"Prophet, I am glad someone was able to make my father see the light before things went out of control." Orthen led Thero up onto the wide deck of the warship. All across the city walls the soldiers of the Ironback legions were pulling back, more than a few armored bodies remained unmoving close to the walls.

"Thank the elementals you arrived before the serious assault started on the walls." Orthen leaned on the wooden railing looking down at the reflections of the light across the water.

"How did you come to be floating down the Isies River into the middle of the invasion fleet?" Orthen glanced at the silent prophet standing beside him.

"That, my good prince, is a story that is too long for this night. Come, we should go parley with the Duchess and beg her forgiveness for marring the white walls of Alast. There is much going on in the world right now and we must prepare the low lands for the inevitable. There is war looming on the horizon that will take all four of your fathers famed Ironback Divisions to hold the tide in check."

The orkin warships were roped together and wide planks were placed from railing to railing to allow the passage of troops from ship to ship. Together they made their way across the boarding planks, walking in silence. It took crossing seven wide battle ships to reach the far shore and Thero shook his head sadly as they entered the wide beaches that surrounded the southern half of Alast. Heavy catapults in various stages of completion sat in a long row just out of range of the city, Thero counted a score of the siege engines.

"Tear the engines down and ready them for travel." Orthen had donned the gleaming crown of the Southern Orkin Empire and his face booked no room for argument from the surprised soldiers.

"My prince, what has happened to the Emperor?" The captain in charge of the siege engines dared to ask as he sent his men scurrying to dismantle their heavy weapons.

"He was murdered by the false prophet that led him astray. Now move quickly. I believe the protectors have brought us to the low lands for a reason, and making war on the peaceful duchy is not that reason."

The armored warrior nodded and then stomped away with his helmet tucked under his thickly muscled arm. Thero nodded in approval as Orthen moved up the beach giving orders to each commander.

"Ready your men to march, and move away from the city."

The fields before the city were empty as Thero and Orthen walked slowly up the wide road leading to the ornate gates. The white wash on the walls was scorched where boiling oil had been dumped by the defenders. Scores of orkin warriors lay unmoving near the gate, but overall the oil had missed many of its intended targets. Orthen stopped fifty paces from the gate and waited. He shook his head as he took in the thin walls and poorly designed gate defenses.

"How this city has ever survived with such weak defenses is amazing," he commented. They waited until a small postern gate slipped open and woman approached. She was escorted by a score of soldiers in white tunics.

"Why have you attacked my city?" She demanded. The raven haired woman's face was flushed with anger and more than a few smudges of soot.

Thero had always considered the Duchess one of the classic beauties of the mortal world. She was radiant even with her ivory skin smudged and dirty. Her white cloak hung open in front revealing the finally crafted armor flashing in the flickering light of the fires that still clung to the ground around the gate. A thin sword hung at her side and her hand rested comfortably on the silver bound hilt.

"Duchess Athelia, I must offer my sincere apologizes for the poor decisions of my father. He was led astray and I was briefly imprisoned when the purpose for our trip was revealed to me." Orthel spoke slowly. With the crown on his head he held his helm tucked under his arm, his small snout trembled as he spoke.

Thero knew this was an outward sign of the pain the young prince was feeling on the inside.

"The traitor that misled my father has fled after murdering him, and I am now the emperor of the Southern Orkin Empire,"

The duchess stood open mouthed and staring at him. Thero could see her active mind picking up on the cues written on the new emperor's face.

"I offer my sympathy to you at the loss of your father, Orthen. Sadly there are many who are fatherless after this night's misunderstanding." She nodded her head and stepped back indicating that they should accompany her to the city.

"Shall we discuss this in the warmth of the gate house rather than here in the lights of a misguided war?"

Orthen nodded and Duchess Athelia motioned the stern faced warrior standing beside her to silence. "General Marack, tell the city guard and the army to stand down from the walls. Tell them to help the water brigades put out the last of the fires."

The stern faced general nodded and wheeled about disappearing back into the postern gate of the city. Shouts could be heard as the soldiers rushed from the walls to douse the fires still burning across the city.

Orthen followed the duchess through the small gate and paused as she motioned away the circle of soldiers with drawn weapons facing Orthen and Thero, "Clear the gatehouse, captain."

The sputtered protests died on the soldiers lips as he glanced at the face of the Duchess.

When they were at last alone, Thero stood before the two rulers and motioned them closer, "We have little time. I believe the fortress of Winds has fallen. Bedbezdal is moving his armies south and soon the low lands will be engulfed in war."

Two shocked faces nodded but listened quietly as Thero hurriedly sketched the events of the past days.

"Things are changing in the world to the point that it that may never be the same again. We must try and find Nathel. He alone is the key to stopping the Dark One."

"How will this affect my lands?" she pondered.

"My lady, your standing army is not large enough to help at this time." Thero shrugged apologetically at her, but she nodded. "We ask your permission to offload the Orkin troops to the north of the city. They will need to pass through the northern reaches of your kingdom in order to link with Emperor Ratchuth."

Orthen nodded his agreement, "If Thero thinks that the fortress has fallen, then I will march my army there to battle. The creator protect us if we are unable to contain the hordes of the Dark One."

The Duchess stood silently pondering the request for many long moments and Thero hoped she would see the wisdom in the request, "I hope you understand why I am so hesitant. The word went out from Alast when the orkin battle standard was spotted. Much of the surrounding countryside is in turmoil; people are fleeing inland and flooding into the cities. We have reports of chaos gripping most of my lands. The addition of eighty thousand troops marching across the countryside might well send my people into rebellion."

"If you wish to send escorts along, my men and I will travel with our weapon straps holding our weapons in place. Nothing will be touched or taken without proper payment. Also, when I return, proper compensation for the damage inflicted on your city can be discussed," Orthen added. He hoped that the fiery duchess would allow his soldiers passage, if he was forced to sail north to find a landing, it would add at least a week to the travel time.

"Very well, I will send two thousand cavalry to escort you across the northern reaches of my lands."

Thero sighed in relief. It helped to know that he would be backed by eighty thousand soldiers of the Ironback Divisions when he approached the fortress.

Thero motioned for the two rulers to listen for a moment. "There is something else that I need you to do for me, Duchess. You must spread the word to all the kingdoms of the low lands. You must begin mustering your armies. If the fortress has been completely destroyed, it will mean a war unlike the world has seen in two thousand years. If the evil one has been released from his prison and is marching his armies south, it will not take them long to cover the wilderness of Endeg with his minions."

"I will send the messengers and I will begin gathering my army." She nodded her agreement.

"Even as we speak the armies of the Mountain kingdom are moving. They should be marching from Jechiro already. It is the plan of General Timoth to move the army to the east of Juthel. He was going to skirt the edge of the Black Forest in order to avoid confrontation with King Grend of Juthel. This leaves a potential hostile force to the rear of our armies but it cannot be helped. The only other choice was to march straight into Juthel and fight our way through. Grend has not been idle, packs of fallen roam the countryside at night and the army of Juthel is already mustered. Most are not in league with the fallen, but he has placed his servants in key positions."

"I cannot fight against Juthel and sadly I will be of little help. My army is small and ill prepared for a long conflict. I am afraid that outside of my personal guard and the five thousand knights of the Order of Dunthent we are a peaceful land. I might be able to muster ten or twelve thousand soldiers given enough time and some weeks." Duchess Athelia said. She sat down wearily in a nearby chair and rested her head in her hands.

Orthen waved his hand, "The Ironbacks will bear the brunt of any attack for now. My soldiers or the mountain army can hold for some time until Emperor Ratchuth can swing his army west. He should be somewhere along the edge of the wilderness of Endeg right now. His forces marched out from the Northern Empire at the same time we left our lands to the south."

Thero nodded, "Prepare your people, Duchess. If we fail, the low lands will be inundated with the Fallen."

Nathel looked about, scanning the horizon as he walked west. He kept his pace quick, but not fast enough to leave him exhausted. At first he had struck out across the landscape in a straight line north by northwest. When he took time to reflect, he altered his course and mirrored the winding path of the Isies river.

"Why walk the entire way when I can acquire a horse in village close to the river and then ride north. The time made up riding will easily make up for the longer route," He muttered to himself. In the distance he caught sight of the shining ribbon of water again.

Three days later and six meals of berries, wild potatoes, and water from river, Nathel was beginning to get very hungry. It was late in the afternoon when he spotted the bridge spanning the Isies River and the flapping flag with the insignia of Juthel waving in the breeze. The design was the same as the one he and Thero had passed through weeks ago on the southern border. The same number of soldiers guarded the crossing.

"State your business." Once again the soldiers were all business, not cracking even the slightest of smiles as they went about their routines.

"I am looking to buy a horse in the village ahead."

"How did you come to be on foot on the wilderness side of the river?"

"I was on a ferry near Alast when the ferry tipped. I managed to swing to shore," Nathel said. He answered honestly knowing that the vague information was true but would not bring suspicion. He leaned on his staff until the soldier nodded and indicated for him to sign the worn log book. Sure that he was safe, Nathel stepped up to the wooden stand holding the battered log book. A quill pen and a small glass bottle of ink set on a small ledge above the book, Nathel bent over the thick parchment when a blow to the back of his head sent him spinning head over heals. Stars exploded before his eyes, followed by a looming darkness wrapping its arms around him. He felt hands grab him and pull away his staff.

"Tie his hands and feet,"

He felt the rough ropes being wrapped around his wrists as the last bit of consciousness left his stunned mind.

"Ahhh," a voice groaned. Nathel thought that it sounded like his own but a pounding in his head made it impossible for him to concentrate.

"I told you that blow to the head was too hard. King Grend wants him alive not a vegetable."

"Next time you can hit him and see if you manage any better."

Nathel heard the voice but then his dark world jarred and darkness closed in on his mind again.

The next time he awoke his head was pounding and his throat was parched. He strained with his hands to touch his face and he found he could not. His eyes snapped open and Nathel started violently struggling against the bonds holding him. A wave of dizziness passed over him and he paused for a deep breath. Carefully he opened his eyes and looked about. His arms were chained to a wall in the middle of a stone room. A closed door and two barred windows were the only features in the cell walls.

His arms and legs were held tightly with iron bands, thick chains that made moving nearly impossible with the weight of the chains holding him down.

"LET ME OUT!" he screamed. Pain exploded in his head, his whole body ached and throbbed and the sound of his voice nearly sent him back into unconsciousness. Outside the door he heard a shuffle and he held still hoping someone would come for him.

"Keep it down in there, someone will be along to see you shortly!" Someone yelled through the cell door at him.

Nathel found that if he was still, his body hurt less so he sagged to the floor and waited. From his seat on the floor he examined his cell. The door was built of wooden planks thick and banded together with iron strips; a large lock dominated one side of the door while heavy iron hinges held the opposite side tightly to the frame. The back wall where he was chained was heavy stone blocks held together with gray mortar. Moisture clung to the stone blocks and the mortar was green with slime. The side walls were both constructed of smaller bricks and the mortar seemed fresher, Nathel strained hard to reach the side walls but was brought up just short by the heavy chains. A small window offered a small bit of light from outside and brought a slight breeze and some fresh air. The smell in the air told Nathel it was morning and he waited hopefully for a few rays of sunshine to stream in the window.

A sound at the door brought his attention back to the front of the cell. He watched as the door swung in and his thin uncle strode in.

"How do you like your new accommodations, boy?"

"Let me go. I did nothing wrong." Nathel lunged to his feet and stepped forward. He moved as far as the chains would allow.

"I think not, boy. Do you realize the troubles I have gone through over the past years to find you? I started something years ago and it remained incomplete because of the meddling of that old man. That Thero is a trouble-maker." Grend said. He stopped and pulled his black cloak forward obscuring his gray pants and tunic, a pair of leather riding gloves hung at his waist.

"The elemental protectors will stop you," Nathel spoke quietly watching the slicked back hair and darting eyes of his uncle. "It is never too late to stop, uncle." Nathel said, desperate for any sign of weakness from the man.

Grend barked out a shrill laugh, "Nice try boy, but their time is past and my life belongs to Bedbezdal now. When I finish my job, he will rule the world and a time of darkness will come upon the world such as has never been seen. Anatari will be cast into the same prison that he locked my master into so many years ago."

"Now then there is the matter of the bell. I must thank you for bringing it out of the Mountains for me." Grend laughed. He grabbed Nathel's hair and pulled his head back, then he tore the golden chain from Nathel's neck.

"Amazing isn't it, all these troubles over a small bell. How can such a small item bind an elemental for thousands of years?"

"Give it back! Only one of the king's bloodline can carry the bell." Nathel lunged forward crashing to the end of his chain hands straining to reach the small bell.

"Ha, Boy, you're not the only one who can carry this bell, I may not be the true king but I am still of his bloodline. I can carry it and I can ring it in the seat of creation. I can do all for my master that you can do for Anatari. This little bell is all we need to cloak the world in darkness."

"You will never win," spat Nathel.

"I don't need to win, boy" Grend laughed. "All I need to do is make sure no one in the world ever remembers the Creator or the Elemental Protectors. The world will be ours."

Grend back-handed Nathel hard across the face and then turned to go. He walked to the door, and paused as he stepped out of the cell. Smiling, he glanced back at Nathel.

"Don't worry, Boy. I will take good care of your lady friend and the bell. You on the other hand, are going to the headsman where you belong. It is high time to take care of the business that you skipped out on years ago. And this time no one will be there to stop it. There have been too many rumors flying about the city since the collapse of the library. It is time to finish this once and for all. When Bedbezdal's army marches into Juthel, they will find a kingdom ripe for the picking. In two weeks, the entire low lands will be awash with the fallen. War will reach every corner of the mortal world."

Grend exited the door laughing, Nathel heard him tell the jailor, "Take him to the headsman in the morning. I want the little brat dead by time the sun sets tomorrow."

"Yes, your grace." The clipped tones of the jailor answered and were followed by another door slamming shut.

Nathel slumped dejectedly. The chains on his wrists held him tightly and removed any chance of escape from his mind. The night passed slowly for Nathel and he sat silently staring into the darkness, "Why?" He muttered to himself over and over, "Why?"

Nathel stared up at the brick ceiling mouthing the words, "I thought the Protectors would watch out for their own. I thought that the creator would send someone to help. I have done what was asked of me. Why am I bound while he walks free?" There was no answer from the ceiling so Nathel slumped even lower.

He waited for an answer and silence surrounded him in the darkness of the cell, but somehow the peaceful silence seemed comforting, "Odd," Nathel muttered to himself. Maybe the elements were watching him after all, maybe the impossible would happen and Tymothel or one of creator's servants would find a way to help him. Until then he could do nothing, so he worked his body into a comfortable position and lay down.

He smiled as he laid his head down on the hard stones and soon he was fast asleep.

Chapter Nineteen
A Day of Surprises

orning came and the first rays of sun briefly shone through the small window waking Nathel. He yawned and stretched as best he could with the painful metal still digging into his flesh.

A short soldier entered the cell seeming surprised to find that he had been sleeping.

"Not every man can sleep the night before he is to be executed."

"I seem to have found my peace," Nathel said. His voice was calm and caught the soldier by surprise. "Have you?"

He stared hard at Nathel chained to the wall, "How can you find peace chained to the wall of a dungeon?"

"The Elemental Protectors have watched over me every step of the way over these last few weeks. I think that they will find a way for me to finish what has begun. If not, then I think the world will not be worth being around to see."

The jailor shrugged, going about his business. He unchained Nathel's legs, and then he helped Nathel to his feet. Calling in a burly soldier from the next room, they carefully removed the hand chains. Nathel struggled to regain the feeling in his fingers and toes, stumbling towards the door when the burly soldier pushed him in the back.

"Easy, Bruth." The smaller man issued a sharp rebuke to the burly soldier.

"What difference does it make? He will be dead before the sun peaks," Bruth laughed. He kicked Nathel, hard sending him tumbling against the far wall.

Nathel lay dazed as a small trickle of blood ran down his forehead. After a moment he struggled to regain his feet and move towards the door when a second blow sent him flying again. This time he heard the short soldier say "I said stop hitting him."

"Or what, Captain Haust? You have spent to long down here in the dungeon coddling the trash. King Grend wants them broken before they die. Why do you think you were sent down here instead of a field command? It's because you're weak."

Nathel struggled to focus as the burly soldier wheeled and stood toe to toe with the first soldier.

Nathel watched quietly as Captain Haust stood looking at the mountain of a man in front of him, chain mail covered both men but Bruth also had a heavy war hammer and a thick shield hanging from his waist.

"Have you not heard what happened years ago? I was in the king's service then, not this false king but with King Tero. Grend is not the real king, he is a usurper to the throne," Haust spoke softly.

"Baseless rumors,"

"I served in King Tero's court as a young man, Bruth. Do you think I would not recognize the son of Tero? Up until now I have done my duty because Grend was crowned king, but now it is time for things to change."

As Captain Haust stopped speaking both men exploded into action each one sensing what the other was thinking.

Bruth slipped his hammer and shield from his belt and gave a hard thrust at the dodging Haust.

Captain Haust threw himself backward turning a complete back flip in order to avoid the thrusting hammer and wrenched his short sword from its sheath.

"I have been looking forward to this day, traitor." Bruth stalked forward, his shield held in front of his body and hammer held loosely to the side.

Captain Haust crouched and moved lightly on the balls of his feet eyeing the big soldier as he stepped forward. The hammer whistled through the air impacting the stones where Haust had been standing but the agile soldier was rolling and dodging almost before the blow started. Haust rolled to the right throwing himself past Bruth and coming out of his roll behind the big man, a slashing blow with the short sword glanced off the chain mail drawing a deep line in the metal but not penetrating.

Moving more slowly this time Bruth advanced, swinging his hammer in wide strokes in front of his body. He worked the weapon, using his massive bulk to push Haust towards the door.

Haust backed up slowly, staying out of range of the heavy hammer and watching for a chance to end the fight quickly. The veteran soldier knew he was outclassed by the younger fighter but he had years of experience to draw on. Darting forward, he slashed at Bruth's weapon hand. Again he was forced to dive to the side as the young man swung the heavy hammer in a long stroke. Rolling to the side, Haust dodged the hammer and then jumped up. He rushed in behind the stroke.

Bruth struggled to stop the hammer and pushed his shield forward to block the slashing strike he felt sure was coming. When nothing hit his shield he stopped and pulled back bringing his hammer back to its ready position. Only then did he realize that the smaller Haust had vanished while his vision was blocked by the shield, "What...where?" He sputtered, spinning his body to the left.

"I have never been a traitor... " Haust's voice whispered close to Bruth's ear. The burly soldier turned, desperately swinging his hammer in a wide arc, trying to drive the smaller man back, while Captain Haust drove his sword hard into the chain mail protecting Bruth's back. The steel of the armor parted before the driving force of the weapon, and the younger soldier gasped in pain. Bruth's hammer struck Haust on the shoulder, sending the older man reeling, but the force of the blow had faded. Bruth slumped to the floor, his eyes staring vacantly into the air. "...but you have been one from the moment you unquestioningly followed Grend's orders."

"Come on, son. Let's get you out of those shackles." Captain Haust moved quickly to Nathel's side and helped him to his feet. A small iron key pulled from Haust's belt opened the iron shackles.

"Thank you, Captain Haust. What will we do now?"

"Never fear, son. There are many soldiers among the castle guards and in the army that served under your father. Many are tired of the evil that Grend has done and they are ready for a change. If the true son of King Tero were to enter the throne room most of the army and castle guards would pledge allegiance to him without question."

Haust led Nathel out of the cell and into a long corridor lined with cells. Dozens of torches burned brightly lighting the corridor and adding an overwhelming wave of heat to the area.

Nathel stumbled along guided by Captain Haust until they were safely hidden in a small guest room in the stone fortress.

"Now then, son. We need to find you some new clothes and get you to the throne room. After the collapse of the royal library and the emergence of the gargoyle, certain of the city's more powerful citizens sought me out. Over the past weeks, I have been quietly gathering what information I could about Grend. Many people were killed the night that he ascended to the throne."

Nathel was in a daze and his face must have showed it for Captain Haust stopped and stared hard at him.

"Nathel, we need to move fast while the fallen are off balance in the city. The loss of the gargoyle and the sudden departure of King Grend will further confuse them. If we move now, we can sweep the city and remove the insidious evil that has festered in this fair city for much too long."

"What must I do, captain?"

Haust smiled from ear to ear, "I am going go find a change of clothes - something in royal purple I think. We will call an emergency meeting of the city council and the royal court. Stay here. Use the water basin to clean yourself up and comb your hair. I will knock twice when I return. Allow no one but myself in that door. There are still many servants of the fallen walking about the castle."

Nathel nodded and watched as Captain Haust slipped out the door. After he closed the door Nathel dropped the locking bar in place. Walking back to the basin he splashed the cool water across his face and arms.

It took him many long minutes of scrubbing to clean his face and hair. When he was done, he stood staring out the small window. The courtyard bustled with activity. Scores of silk lined carriages entered the castle gates. Robed and bejeweled men and women climbed from the luxurious carriages as they rolled to a halt. Most of them walked stately up the long marble stairs that led into the main portion of the castle. Soon scores of carriages were packed into the courtyard and young liveried pages rushed about carrying packages and holding horses. The soldiers Nathel could see were watching all sides, some paced. Others stood watching the growing crowds of people entering the castle. Still more stood silently watching the rooftops of the nearby city for any signs of trouble.

Sometime later Nathel was beginning to worry when two soft knocks sounded on the wooden door.

"Nathel, open the door." He rushed to remove the locking bar.

Nathel breathed a sigh of relief when Captain Haust entered carrying a thick package under his arm. He was smiling from ear to ear.

"Things are falling into place. Hurry! Get out of those old clothes and put these on."

Nathel stripped off his traveling clothes, reaching for the fine silks that were held out to him by Haust.

"First, the breeches. I hope they fit, I had to steal them from a visiting duke's closet."

Nathel had to pull hard but the tight pants fit over his legs fairly well. He grabbed the billowing shirt and pulled it over his head being careful not to lose the bell.

"THE BELL!" Nathel screamed the words as the events of the night before flooded back to his mind.

"What bell?" Captain Haust looked at him in confusion, motioning for him to hold his voice down.

"Grend, he took the Bell of Creation from me when I was in the cell." Nathel was frantic, he darted about the door wringing his hands together. His eyes flashed about for a way to pursue the false king.

"Focus, Nathel. First, we will put you on the throne. Then we will deal with the fallen in the city, and then we call out the army and march north. It is a long trip across the northern wilderness. With the trackers and bloodhounds we can lead a light cavalry force north ahead of the army and intercept Grend."

Nathel stopped where he was standing eyeing the calm captain, "Alright let's do this, for my parent's sake. And we must hope that the elemental protectors hold for a bit longer. If we are not able to retrieve the bell before he enters the Chamber of Creation, the world will fall under the shadow."

Captain Haust nodded; his eyes were completely serious as he helped Nathel shrug into the purple flowing cloak. Over the cloak a second long flowing gray cloak shrouded the elaborate designs sewn into the purple cloth. Haust then turned and removed a thin gold circlet from a box on the table. With steady hands he placed the gold circlet around the top of Nathel's head.

"Now then pull the hood down low so that no one can see your face."

"Follow me closely; we are going to enter the Chamber of Arms. There is a towering portrait of you father and mother in the chamber. When I tell you I want to pull back the hood."

Nathel nodded and followed the soldier out the door and into the corridor. With the hood pulled over his face he was all but blinded as he followed the flashing polished boots of the soldier. Lush carpets flashed past his shrouded vision, broken at regular intervals by polished granite floors and the bases of plant holders.

Then Nathel heard a door swing open and a low rumble of voices filled his ears. He shook his head slightly trying to ward off the cold chill that rippled up and down his spine.

"Captain Haust, how dare you call a meeting of the council? You have severely over stepped your authority." A harsh high pitched whining voice spoke close at hand.

Nathel missed the sharp retort but the gasp that followed told him the Captain was in little mood for any arguments.

"What's this all about, Haust?" This time the voice that spoke was low and deep and Nathel almost raised his head out of curiosity.

"One moment, General, and I think you will understand," Captain Haust replied. His voice remained calm despite the heated arguments going on around them.

"Ladies and Gentlemen!" Captain Haust voice echoed across the room cutting through the murmurings and bringing an uneasy silence to the room.

Nathel was standing shrouded in the shadow of a tall statue at the edge of the room. Haust had led him to the spot and then told him to stand still and wait for his signal.

"A great injustice has been ignored in this fair city for far too long. Many years ago we had a good and just king who was taken from us. Although many of the cut throats were tracked down and hung, the guiding force behind the attack was never found."

Murmurs of agreement echoed through room along with more than a few scoffing laughs, Nathel listened to the jeers. His blood began to boil at the laughs.

"After this accident the King's own brother took the throne and began removing all traces of the dead king. No attempt was made to honor the memory of King Tero or his lovely wife. Their images were removed from every room but this one, and then King Grend began to show his true spirit. Hatred and greed became commonplace and none of the kindness showed to all by King Tero remained. Many loyal servants disappeared who spoke out against Grend and many more were sent to the gallows."

Once again the agreements echoed through the room and still more than a few scoffs were sprinkled through the room.

"What's the point, Haust? It does not make a difference how Grend came to the throne. He is our king. Are you suggesting treason against the king?" The high pitched voice whined loudly. The speaker was close to Nathel.

"Councilman Standly, you have long been one of King Grend's biggest defenders. Despite his despotic rule, why don't you shut up and sit down. We all know where you stand." The calm voice of the general spoke quietly but it silenced the room almost instantly.

"Thank you General Fritts." Captain Haust continued, "Recently, I was assigned to watch over the dungeons. Yesterday, a young man was brought into the dungeon and placed in my care. Our king went to visit him and what I heard him say made me realize that this king we now followed is nothing but a worthless dog."

Gasps echoed across the room and more then one cry of traitor echoed into the lofty recesses of the chamber.

"Is it treachery to fight against The Fallen?" Captain Haust's voice grew more commanding once again silencing the crowd.

"Then I will plead guilty as charged. But hear me out; yesterday I realized that the true heir of the throne was not dead. Not all of the royal family died on that horrible night so many years ago as we were led to believe."

Haust's voice grew louder as Nathel heard him approaching, the hard soled boots pounding on the granite floors.

"He is alive, ladies and gentlemen! I give you crown prince Nathel!"

With a trembling hand, Nathel reached up and drew the hood back from his face. Dozens of surprised nobles stared at him in amazement and the murmur of voices rose to a thunderous crescendo. Nathel realized that some stared at his face and some stared at the towering tapestry hanging on the wall behind him. He closed his eyes and turned, then slowly opened them and looked up. A hundred bright colors were woven into a vast country scene, riding a pair of brown horses were the images of a man and a woman. Golden crowns sat on their heads and the king's face was almost an exact match to his own.

"Amazing." An older man in a dark blue uniform approached him staring hard at his face. Silver bars were attached to the flowing dark blue cloak thrown across his shoulders.

Silence descended on the room as all eyes were riveted on the old general. Then Captain Haust stepped forward, he knelt on one knee and bowed his head before Nathel.

"King Nathel, I pledge my sword to you. To serve you with all my life until I die."

Once again loud gasps echoed through the room as the assembled court and city leaders stared at the young king and the kneeling soldier. Slowly and silently General Fritts knelt on the stone floor and bowed his head to the young king. Across the chamber members of the court stepped forward and dropped to their knees on the hard granite.

"I won't be party to this foolishness." Councilman Standly stomped from the room followed by a score of his allies.

Captain Haust rose to his feet and motioned to a nearby castle guard, "Have them followed and watched."

"King Nathel, it appears that most everyone agrees with me." Captain Haust smiled.

"You have been planning this for some time, haven't you, Captain?"

"I must plead guilty. Thero told me to always be ready for the return of the crown prince. It has not always been easy but we did what we could. General Fritts, are we prepared?" Captain Haust asked. He led Nathel to the side of the room walking next to the older general's side.

"I have ten battalions of soldiers north of the city, and five more south of the city. We will move into the city and check every building for the fallen."

"Good. Prepare four companies of cavalry; we have a matter that is more pressing then the clearing of the city." Captain Haust spoke quickly knowing the importance of tracking down Grend and the bell.

General Fritts eyed the pair with astonishment in his eyes, "Leaving before the city is secure? I do not approve, but if what you say is true, it is necessary. I will have the cavalry ready by noon and waiting at the north gate."

"Thank you, Sir. That gives us enough time to get Nathel some traveling gear and armor before we meet them at the gate." Captain Haust offered a smart salute to General Fritts. Then he turned and guided Nathel out of the room and away from the kneeling men and women of the royal court.

Nathel tried hard not to stare as the court couriers bowed and cried out: "Long live the King"

At first he tried to nod and offer a smile to each one but after the tenth time he gave up. Instead he concentrated on following Captain Haust as they hurried along the corridor.

"The throne room is ahead down the wide hall, the armory and storage are below this floor. That can wait for now. We can get you a full tour of your new home another day. I had your butler set out a set of travel gear and supplies. We will get you ready and then go find a horse that suits your personality from the stables."

Nathel nodded as he entered a door that the soldier held open for him. Inside stood an elderly man, he wore a gray hose and a billowing shirt. He leaned over a table arranging a finely crafted set of supple leather armor and sturdy cotton pants and shirt.

"Your majesty, I think you will find everything to your liking. We had to guess on the exact sizes since we had no time to get a proper measurement. Here your majesty, let me help you with that." The butler reached out only to have his hands slapped away.

"I think I can handle dressing myself." Nathel glared hard at the retreating butler and offered the same glare to the chuckling soldier.

"Are you coming along for the trip, Captain?" Nathel slipped the pants and shirt on liking the feel of the new material. He grabbed the stiff leather greaves and fumbled for a moment before finally relenting to allow the butler to help him fasten the buckles. The engraved and lacquered chest piece fit perfectly across his chest, twin wyrms were entwined in battle across the chest adding a fierce look to the armor.

"Yes, your majesty. I did not spend years preparing and waiting to have you killed inside the first week." The captain smiled but there was little humor on his face.

Nathel found that the armor moved and bent with his body once the straps had been tightened and placed at the right points.

"You should keep wearing the crown and we have a purple cloak." The butler fastened the cloak around his neck. Nathel sat down and pulled the polished black boots on over his feet, the supple leather was lined with cloth and fit his foot perfectly.

"We also found your staff, it was hidden in Grend's personal quarters." Captain Haust handed the ironwood staff back to Nathel.

He took the weapon and brushed his fingers across the ironwood, inside he felt whole again for the first time since the ambush at the river crossing.

"Come, your majesty. We must move quickly." Captain Haust led him down the wide hallway.

He walked quickly and the pace left Nathel little time to examine the wondrous sights and sounds of the castle. The murmur of servants silenced to hushed whispers as he passed. The excited banter doubled in volume as they approached the doors leading down to the courtyard. The stables were a sea of activity as Nathel stepped into the dim rows of stalls. The nickering of horses filled the air and the poignant smells of manure reminded him of the stables in the mountain kingdom.

"Your majesty we have several mounts for you to choose from." A grizzled man with a barrel chest and arms that could have bent iron bars grinned at them from behind a thick beard.

"Finally found your missing king, didn't you Haust? It's about time."

"Thank you, brother."

The grizzled man roared with laughter as he led them to a wide area devoid of stalls. The ceiling vaulted high in the stables and Nathel watched five warhorses being held tightly by grooms. Nathel glanced at Haust but he simply motioned the young king forward.

"Choose your mount, sire."

Two black stallions rolled their eyes at him and Nathel dismissed them in his mind immediately. He did not wish to battle the strong willed horses for the entire trip. On the other hand the brown gelding was too calm and docile. He needed a horse with spirit but not more then he could handle. Nathel walked up and down the line looking at each horse in turn but not liking any of what he was seeing.

"Are there any others we can look at?"

The grizzled man walked over from where he was talking to Captain Haust.

"Captain, your kingship. If you would follow me I can show you some of our other warhorses."

'Do you have any horses that are not trained simply for war? I need stamina, endurance, and speed."

Nathel knew that the warhorse was good in battle but he wanted stamina and endurance not a heavy warhorse.

"I need a horse that can run for days and still have stamina for another day if I ask that of it."

"I think I have what you need, your majesty." The stable master motioned for him to follow and led him to the farthest corner of the long stable. In a corner stable by itself was a long limbed tall dun stallion.

"We found him wandering out of edges the Wilderness of Endeg. He must have run all the way from the Plains of Slith beyond Loch Isies. Took three of our fastest horses to run it down, the old boy was wearing a saddle and bridle but the rider was nowhere to be seen. Poor beast had wolf bites and claw marks covering its legs and flanks. Also had more than a little wolf blood and hair embedded in his hooves and teeth. The beast has been completely calm since it was brought into the stable, as long as he is left alone. The first rider spent days healing."

Nathel felt an immediate connection to the long limbed horse, there was a sad look in its eyes. It was a stare that longed for home, but there was also a calmness that one rarely sees in wild or domestic animals.

"Find me a saddle for him. Wwe need to leave immediately." Nathel lifted the latch on the stable door and entered holding his staff in the crook of his arm.

"Easy boy," Nathel whispered. He approached the stallion slowly and the horse stared at him with deep brown eyes. His ears were forward and he huffed twice.

"I need your help," Nathel said. He ran his hand down the dun's neck as he spoke. "That creature took Kat and I want her back. I need your help to get her. Will you help me?"

The stallion reached out with his nose and nudged the staff once. Then he stepped forward and waited patiently while the grooms rushed in with saddle and bridle.

When the dun was saddled and ready Nathel led him from the stable. All around him was a flurry of activity as soldiers rushed about the castle. Captain Haust followed him leading his own mount as a groom put the finishing touches on Nathel's tack.

"We placed a spear holder next to the stirrup, your majesty. That should make it easier to carry your staff."

"Many thanks to you, and give my thanks to the stable master." Nathel swung up in to the saddle feeling the stallion tense under his legs and hoping the creature would not bolt and throw him. Instead the tensed muscles relaxed and Nathel nudged the horse forward joining Captain Haust who was riding a heavy war horse.

"Let's go find my uncle, captain."

"Yes, your majesty." This time it was Haust who was forced to move quickly to keep up with the determined young king.

Nathel set his eyes northward and the dun seemed to sense his urgency. They exited the castle gate at a trot startling the soldiers on guard.

"Make way for the king!" The cry echoed through the streets and Nathel raced the cry all way to the north gate. Thousands of city dwellers flooded into the streets wanting to catch a glimpse of their new king. It amazed Nathel but it seemed that word spread fast in the city, but even amongst the groundswell of support many hostile faces could be seen.

True to General Fritt's word, four hundred cavalry were massed at the north gate. Nathel burst through the north gate sending the sentries scrambling. He pulled up on the dun and skidded to a halt, almost losing his grip on his staff. The soldiers of the cavalry held their chargers in long, even ranks,. Lances held upright, the sun glinted off their polished chain armor. Royal blue pennants snapped and fluttered in the breeze adding a flash of color to the silvery armor.

Captain Haust reined his charge to a halt beside him, grinning as his horse pranced, "I think you have chosen the right mount for a chase my king."

Nathel laughed, leaning forward to pat the dun's long neck, "We will find my uncle and return what he has stolen. And then we will track down Katirna and finish this business with the gargoyle once and for all."

"Sir?"

"The thief I was with when the royal library came down. She was kidnapped by the same gargoyle that rose from the building. I thought we had finished it but obviously it found a way to return to the mortal world. It kidnapped her three days after we were separated from Thero."

"Why didn't you tell me earlier your majesty!" Captain Haust actually seemed angry when Nathel turned to regard him.

"Captain, as much as I miss Katirna, we must recover the Bell of Creation, without it the world is lost. What will it gain me if I rescue Katirna, only to have the Fallen sweep through the entire world?"

Captain Haust nodded; he turned in his saddle and motioned for a small group of men to approach. The riders all wore buckskin clothes and carried an odd assortment of weapons.

"King Nathel, these are the best trackers in the lowlands. Until recently, your uncle used them to track down people he thought had slighted him. I believe that it is time we returned the favor."

Nathel nodded, "We must find my uncle Grend before he reaches the Northern Mountains and the Fortress of Winds."

The leader of the trackers was a short man barely reaching to Nathel's shoulder. Of the trackers present two were elves and three were orkin. A quick nod was all he received and an even quicker bow as they turned and scattered to their mounts.

"Go north, your majesty. When we gain his trail I will send a runner each morning and evening to correct your course. He was seen this morning riding hard north, straight towards the Fortress of Winds."

"Captain Haust, how long would it take to put the entire army of Juthel on the road to the Fortress of Winds?"

"A week at least your majesty, but the fortress has never been breached." The captain's face was doubtful as he spoke. "I highly doubt that the Dark One's forces could take those walls."

"Captain, I think you should have General Fritts muster every available man. Tell him that a week is too long, I want them marching to the fortress in four days." There was little room for argument in Nathel's voice and Captain Haust nodded.

He motioned a runner forward. Moments later the white faced messenger leapt to his horse and bolted into the city.

Nathel turned trotting his dun to the road north and waving forward the even ranks of cavalry.

Matthew John Krengel

Chapter Twenty
The Chase

louds of dust rolled out across the land north of Juthel, Nathel led his small force at a fast pace. They followed the daily directions of the trackers and it took their force almost three days to reach the Isies River.

The border guards watched in amazement as Nathel pulled his dun to a halt in front of their small watch tower, red faced and scared, the soldiers rushed to kneel before him.

"We did not know your majesty." The sergeant that was responsible for small outpost held his iron helm in his hands as tears rolled down his face.

"Are you loyal to the crown or will you cast your lot with the Fallen?" Nathel dismounted and advanced towards the cluster of frightened men. Behind him the cavalry fanned out forming a barrier of iron.

"Die, you pathetic fool!" a tall lean man near the river cried out. He drew his sword and charged Nathel. Before he covered half the distance the rest of the border guards grabbed him and hauled him to the ground.

"We are loyal to the crown of Juthel, my lord."

"Good, have that one placed in irons and sent back to Juthel."

Nathel stopped as he turned to mount the dun. "Has my uncle passed by recently?"

"Almost one day ago your majesty, he rode like the Fallen themselves were chasing him." He replied. He waved his hand to the north where a wide wagon trail cut through the forests and over the hills.

"He raced across the bridge and galloped north; at that pace he will kill his horse in a day."

"Well then, we will catch him quickly." Nathel turned and remounted the dun.

"Forward." Captain Haust's voice echoed above the rumble of the river and the cavalry began to cross the sturdy bridge four abreast. The thick planks rattled and shook under the weight of the warhorses.

"How far is it to the Fortress of Winds?" Nathel called. He shouted to be heard above the rattle of the hooves.

"At least twelve days," Captain Haust replied. The noise subsided as they left the bridge behind and rode into the wilderness side of the Isies River.

"Look, here comes one of the trackers." Nathel pointed out to the distance where a lone horseman plunged down a long sloping hill.

The wilderness side of the river was a stark contrast to the Juthel side. They had spent the last three days riding through rolling hills, rich green pastures, and fertile farmland nestled between stretches of thick forests. A network of roads crossed the countryside connecting the farmers and their markets in the larger cities. People in the small villages had watched with interest as the large force moved quickly down the wide road. The country on the wilderness side was thickly forested but broken by wide stretches of rocky ground. The soil was bad for crops and it seemed the only thing that took root was patches of grass and weeds.

"Long ago a single road was cut through the forests north at heavy cost, thousands died of disease and accident." Captain Haust explained when he asked about the road. "The only travelers are the supply wagons that move to the fortress of winds and they move only in large numbers. It is said that the woods are haunted and some even claim to have spotted tribes of Goblins."

Nathel listened intently as they rode up the wide road. He noted that the trees had been cut back fifty paces on all sides, leaving clear views of the approaches to the road.

Thero chaffed at the delay but still they had moved further than he thought possible in the last four days. As they crossed out of her lands, the soldiers of the Duchess turned back and began the journey back to Alast to continue with the clean up. The general population knew of the attack on the alabaster city, and angry mutterings followed the Ironback divisions at every turn.

Soon after leaving the duchy they turned straight north moving to meet up the soldiers of the Emperor Ratchuth and the Northern Orkin Empire. Dozens of messengers were dispatched running north east and west in an effort to find the armies of Emperor Ratchuth but still no word was received. For two days the Ironbacks moved lazily north and sometimes a bit east marking their course by the distant peaks of the Elabridg Mountains; each day waiting and hoping for word of the second army.

"We found them!" A scout raced up to Emperor Orthen. The young orkin stood with Thero, pouring over a detailed map of the low lands.

"Where are they?" Thero blurted the question before the young emperor could even respond.

"My apologizes, Emperor Orthen," Thero said immediately. He dipped into a small bow despite his impatience, realizing that his questioning of the scout was out of place. Despite the respect offered him by the young orkin ruler, he was still a guest.

Orthen wrinkled his nose once and then waved off the interruption, "Think nothing of it Prophet Thero, if it weren't for you I would still be locked in the hold of my own ship. Most likely Alast would be a slag heap of rubble."

"Well then, where are they?" Orthen turned his attention back to the hesitant scout.

"They are near the southern spur of the Elabridg Mountains, your majesty. Emperor Ratchuth said he would await your arrival there."

"Good, it's time to show the prophet how soldiers in the Ironback divisions can march. Send out the word. I want all of the divisions at the southern spur by tomorrow afternoon."

Thero sighed inside. He knew it was still a ten day march to the Fortress of Winds. Elements willing they could cut a few days off that time.

It was early afternoon when they arrived at the sprawling camp of Emperor Ratchuth. Green banners and flags waved around the campsite, but the emperor of the Northern Orkin Empire was a soldier first and a ruler second. When going into battle, the orkin carried only what was needed. The camp was Spartan. Soldiers scurried everywhere preparing the camp to march as soon as the Ironbacks crossed the final stretch of forest separating them from the mountains.

"Eight days, Thero! We will reach the Fortress of Winds in eight days." Emperor Ratchuth assured the prophet when they arrived at his tent. Orkin soldiers scrambled everywhere packing and cleaning. By time the Ironbacks were into the camp, the Turtle Legions of Ratchuth were ready to move.

"Brave soldiers of the Orkin Empires, we must arrive at the Fortress of Winds in less than eight days. We will march until the moon is high in the sky, and we will resume long before the sun has risen. Travel light. Leave any extra burden here. We will not slow for any that fall behind!" Emperor Ratchuth words rang across the low mountain, and the cheer that rose to answer him echoed back and forth swelling in power until it was deafening.

"Eight days Thero. I think my soldiers have wanted a challenge, and this will motivate them."

"Remember my good Ratchuth the soldiers must arrive with the strength to fight if needed," Thero was worried that perhaps had stressed the need for speed too much.

"Orkin are always ready to fight prophet. It's why there are two Orkin Empires - so that we can fight each other when the lowlanders are tired of fighting."

Orthen and Ratchuth laughed heartily snorting in glee at the joke and even Thero found himself chuckling.

"Last night one of the scouts of the Mountain Army visited me. They have made it to the Isies River and are ferrying the soldiers across now. Timoth will be only a day or two ahead of us at most."

"Excellent. Maybe we should take this opportunity to clean out the Wilderness of Endeg and the Dakretua Mountains once and for all." Orthen nudged Ratchuth and both of them laughed again.

Thero grew serious, "I am afraid that there are not enough soldiers in the lowlands, the empires, and the mountains to clean out the Dakretua Mountains. Those that live there have long denied Anatari and given themselves fully to the Dark One."

An uncomfortable silence descended on the three until Thero continued, "We must make all speed to the Fortress of Winds. If it has fallen we must give battle to the hordes of the Dark One in the wilderness areas. If the hordes of Bedbezdal have breached the defenses, the best we can hope for is to fight a delaying action. We must hold out until Nathel is able to complete his task. That is the only path to victory."

Orthen nodded and motioned to Thero, "Let us march then, and let our enemies quake as the ground shakes under our feet."

Close by a low drum began to thrum in a long slow cadence and around them the gathered armies took up a war chant that grew in power. Across the camp more and more drums took up the beat.

"Come, prophet. We must run now. Run because our world needs us," he cried. He waved his ax in the air and led his men west. Behind him the drummers took up a running beat matching the impact of their boots to the rhythm of the drums.

The Fortress of Winds sat in darkness; no more soldiers marched through its devastated interior. Still, a lone figure stood in the Chamber of Light waiting. He felt the Bell of Creation moving closer and he had a final job to do. The numbers of soldiers that had passed through the fortress was beyond count.

After breaching the doors they had sent forces in all directions but the most powerful force had marched south. Over one hundred thousand of the massive minotaurs anchored the center of the army. Thousands of tall mountain wolves ranged the flanks ready to counter any cavalry charge, hundreds of medusa slithered their snake bodies across the ground. Each had six arms and each hand held a long sword, from their mouths fangs dripped poison.

Scores of ghostly wraiths moved silently blending from shadow to shadow. Nearly two hundred massive Basilisks stepped ponderously, taking care not to crush the smaller soldiers under their clawed feet. Finally, the most numerous of Bedbezdal's soldiers - the wiry Goblins rounded out the army of evil. Hundreds of thousands moved in disorganized masses listening to the orders of the lesser elementals that directed the force.

Other creatures had joined the forces as they moved south, but many disappeared into the night as darkness fell. The score of towering mountain giants wandered off into the Wilderness of Endeg, their small minds not comprehending what was happening around them.

Now the chamber where the dark figure waited was dark and silent. The bright lights that had shone with the light of the sun were darkened. The frozen forms of Katirna and Miceali sat in the darkness waiting. Over time, a tear formed in Katirna's stone eye. It worked its way from her eye and down her cheek. There the stone tear stopped waiting for the right moment to drop to the ground.

Six days had passed and still Nathel led his small force north at a brutal pace. He pushed until late in the evening, and was back in the saddle early, the dun never complaining once. The trackers still reported that they were less then half a day behind the fleeing Grend. But despite their haste, they seemed unable to close the gap. Each time they caught a glimpse of his fleeing form disappearing over a hill, he was gone when they arrived. Nathel was frustrated, but he held his anger in check and whispered desperate prayers to the elemental protectors each time they thought they were going to catch Grend. The morning of the seventh day found Nathel and the four hundred weary soldiers racing north along the rough road.

"Do you hear drums?" Nathel asked. He turned around in his saddle and looked to the east. In the distance the low thrumming of drums could be heard faintly.

"One of the scouts said the drumming started last night but they were unable to send anyone to investigate. He reported that they have spotted Grend again and are trying to slip past him. If they can drive him back towards us we may catch him today. We must end this chase soon or the horses will be of little use." Captain Haust's war horse was weary as were many of the big beasts.

Nathel nodded as he watched the cavalry saddle their mounts, many of the chargers looked spent.

"This fog should burn off soon and then we can pick up the pace a bit." Nathel motioned to the fiery orb that was rising slowly through the dense fog.

"Your Majesty, there on the road ahead." Captain Haust pointed through the fog that still held onto the wilderness with a tenacious grip.

Nathel peered ahead into the distance his heart leaping in his chest when he spotted the tall thin form of Grend leaning over the unmoving body of his horse.

"Let's get him boy." Nathel leaned forward whispering into the dun's laid back ears. The horse responded with a burst of speed that nearly sent Nathel tumbling from his saddle.

Shouts of alarm sounded behind him as Captain Haust motioned his men forward.

"Protect the King!" Haust dug his spurs into the heavy warhorse's flanks trying to keep pace with the tall dun.

Nathel's vision narrowed until all he saw was the startled form of Grend crouching beside the unmoving body of his horse. At twenty strides Grend bolted towards the woods less then fifty paces from the road. Nathel nudged the dun to the right with his legs holding his staff ready as he closed on the fleeing figure.

Thud

A hard strike with the butt of his staff sent Grend flying head over heels. The thin man came to a sudden halt against the trunk of a particularly big oak tree. Nathel took his time dismounting and asking the dun to wait for him. When the horse nodded, he approached the dazed Grend who was struggling to climb to his feet.

"Return the bell to me Grend, and I will spare your life." Nathel spoke calmly, despite the anger he felt knowing that he was looking at the man responsible for his parents death.

"Ha! You think you can win boy? Do you think your pathetic force is any match for my friends?"

"I don't see any friends, Grend. What I do see, is you alone and without a horse." Nathel stepped in closer as Grend pulled his sword from its scabbard.

"Come on, boy. Let's see who the better fighter is." Grend smiled at Nathel and it seemed to Nathel that he was regaining some of his bravery.

Nathel crouched back keeping his legs bent and ready to move, his staff held protectively in front of his body. Grend moved forward one step stabbing his sword straight ahead in an attempt to skewer him. Nathel stepped to the side and quickly snapped his staff out to knock the sword wide. Stepping back Nathel rotated the staff and lashed out with a lightening attack at the unprotected head of his uncle. He was not surprised when Grend threw himself backwards avoiding the attack.

"Nice try, boy. You will not find me that easy to defeat."

Nodding Nathel stepped forward going on the offensive, snapping his staff back and forth. He launched a lightening string of attacks only to have each one picked off by the fast moving sword.

"Is that all that you can do, boy? That idiot Thero should have taught you better. He probably spent more time spouting lies about his precious Elemental Pillars then he did making you learn to use that weak staff. You

231

cannot stop me boy. I am sure Thero told you that once I ring the bell in the Chamber of Creation at the top of Devil's Peak the world will be mine. Bedbezdal has promised to make me ruler of all the lowlands and nothing will stop me." Spittle rolled down Grend's chin as he ranted, his eyes unfocused and waving his sword about erratically.

Nathel held his peace, he circled slowly to the left until his back was against the woods and Grend was facing north.

"Actually, he taught me to fight. What's more, he also taught me to watch my surroundings and always pay attention to where I was standing." Nathel nodded looking past Grend's shoulder.

"Anytime you're ready Captain Haust." Nathel smiled as Grend spun in a circle. The thin man turned just in time to catch Captain Haust's armored fist as it smashed into his face.

"Your majesty, you can't simply take off like that. How are we supposed to protect you?" Haust commented. He grinned as he looked down at his handiwork. Grend lay groaning on the rough ground with a steady trickle of blood coming from his broken nose.

"Relieve him of his weapons," Haust motioned two men forward.

Before they approached, Nathel leaned over the unconscious man and removed the Bell from around his neck.

"Is that it your majesty?"

Nathel nodded and he slipped the golden chain around his neck. After the chain was securely in place he let the small bell slip down inside his shirt.

"Sir, I think you should come see this." Sergeant Canfel called. He was second in command of the force and he reined his horse to where they stood.

Haust and Nathel leapt back into their saddles and followed the sergeant up to where the road passed over the peak of a small hill. Far to the north they saw clouds of dust rising into the air.

"What is it?"

"An army, sire. Nothing else would raise so much dust."

As he spoke, the approaching army crested the far hill, masses of unorganized creatures marched along the road.

"I don't think they have seen us yet."

"Perhaps we may yet slip away." Captain Haust sounded doubtful.

"I think the Fortress has fallen. I would assume those are Goblins from what my grandfather told me." Nathel said. He moved the dun back off the hill, and they rode back to their waiting forces. They rejoined the cavalry where they waited, the road widened as it came off the hill and there was room for fifty chargers to stand abreast.

Quickly the soldiers of Juthel took up their places just out of sight of the top of the long hill. Despite the noises of the moving horses and weapons, the mass of Goblins continued down to the bottom of the far hill unaware of the approaching storm.

"Sound the attack, front rank only," Captain Haust motioned. With measured steps, fifty warhorses started over the hill. They were half way down the slope when the Goblins had finally noticed the long line of horsed warriors. They came to an uncertain halt where they stood, nervously fingering their rough spears.

"Charge!" The advancing force broke into a gallop aided by the slope of the hill.

Caught in the open, the Goblins scattered as the humans brought down their long lances and crashed into their milling mass. Iron hooves ground hundreds of the wiry fighters into the hard ground as the fifty chargers rolled to the bottom of the hill. Captain Haust and Nathel watched as the force reached the bottom of the hill and slowed to a halt.

"Captain, there are more coming over the hill." One of the elf scouts slipped from the woods and ran towards them waving his arms.

"Signal the men down there to return." Captain Haust frantically motioned for the man holding a brass bugle.

Three quick blasts rang out from the hill top and Nathel watched as the fifty men wheeled their horses and charged back towards them.

"What are those?"

"They look like humans crossed with bulls," Nathel commented. A score of the massive minotaurs stopped on the distant hill and pulled heavy battle axes from their shoulder harnesses.

"Sir, the forests are alive with Goblins and wolves. We must fall back." The second elf scout burst from the trees with a black arrow stuck in his shoulder. He shouted the warning as he whipped his horse. Then a second arrow flew from the trees and toppled him from his mount.

"Move everyone back; make for the Valley of Kirden." Nathel remembered what he had seen of the wide valley, it had taken them hours to pass through the valley floor. A dry river bed was all that remained of the once green valley. Not more than a score of small watering holes existed now in the parched valley.

Turning as one, the soldiers turned and urged their horses onward fleeing faster than they had driven them north.

"Captain, go with the men. I must find a way around this horde, my path lies north still," Nathel cried. He offered the surprised Haust a quick wave and then turned the dun to the west where the trees were thinnest.

"You must run now for me, boy. Like you have never run before," he whispered in the dun's ear. The tall horse responded with a burst of speed that left the open mouthed Haust sputtering.

"Nathel, no!" Haust yelled back. It was far too late already Nathel had disappeared into the trees, his horse moving with the speed of an eagle.

"Stay safe." Haust gave a last frustrated look after the racing young king and then he sent his charger down the trail to the south.

Nathel raced into the thin stands of trees moving like a bolt from a crossbow. A pair of Goblins spotted him and hooted as they threw crude spears at his flashing form but missed completely. The dun was sure-of-foot and swifter than any animal he had ever ridden before. Nathel clung tightly, trying to dodge the branches that threatened to tear him from the saddle. He was slipping dangerously to the left when the dun slowed allowing him to regain his balance. Then they were off yet again. Bursting free of the thin trees, Nathel stared in amazement as they raced west, thick columns of troops covered the hills to the north. Fleet mountain wolves took up the chase but the dun snorted and put on a burst of speed that left them panting in a cloud of dust behind him.

Nathel had left the main bodies of black armored troops well behind him when he turned the dun north. The land became flat with thin scatterings of trees and the dun stretched its legs. Nathel relished in the power of his steed as the horse ran full out. He felt the dun's joy at being able to work his long legs again. Two more times the dun carried him past the marching battalions of the dark lord's troops. Several times lean wolves raced out to intercept the fleet horse, and each time the dun left them panting in the distance.

Darkness was falling when Nathel spotted the towering cliffs guarding the Dakretua Mountains.

"There it is, Boy. Not a friendly looking place is it?"

The dun tossed his head snorting his disdain at the towering cliff.

Nathel stared as they approached sheer rocks, he craned his neck in both directions but he saw no handholds. The sheer cliff had been thrown up out ground cleanly, creating a barricade that was impossible to penetrate. He turned the dun to the east and rode until darkness forced him to stop. Night passed slowly for Nathel and the dun. Together they huddled in the rocks near the bottom of the cliff. Looking out into the distance, Nathel shook his head in amazement. The night sky glowed with the light of hundreds of camp fires as the army of Bedbezdal marched south. The fires spread as far as he could see, reaching out to cover the land. Morning came and went with a cover of clouds hiding the sun; a soft sprinkling of rain came and went dropping just enough water to dampen the ground. The moisture kept the dun's hooves from raising the small puffs of dust that had marked their trails the day before.

When Nathel rode into view of the Fortress of Winds he was hard pressed to tell how much time had passed. The cloud cover was thickening and even more storm clouds piled high in the sky. Black and dark green clouds filled with lightning roared in a constant barrage of thunder.

The walls of the Fortress were dark and Nathel approached slowly, wondering if the invading army had left any sentries. Silence greeted him as he paused before the massive gates. Sundered from the gate houses, the gates lay in ruins, torn to pieces by the some powerful force. Darkness and silence greeted him as he entered the courtyard of the fortress. One hundred paces wide, the courtyard was designed for defense. Towers filled with arrow slits covered every part of the castle entrance.

Nathel approached the inner fortress cautiously and noted that the gate was closed. As he drew close to the silent castle, the inner gates opened slowly, swinging wide on silent hinges. Nathel stared into the gloomy darkness for a moment, then urged the dun forward while gripping his staff tightly in his hands.

Matthew John Krengel

Chapter Twenty-One
Battle is Joined

aptain Haust knew fleeing any further was pointless, "The horses are too tired from the ride north." He muttered to the men riding around him.

"Form the line on me!"

The well-trained cavalry brought the horses to a halt and swung about to face the advancing hordes. Even now, hundreds of the big minotaur creatures were visible as they moved ponderously in pursuit. The woods on the north side of the Kirden Valley were alive with the smaller goblin creatures.

"Wolves, sir. On both flanks."

Haust nodded. He had noted the shadowy wolves flickering along through the distant trees, and even an odd snake-like creature. It was as though the nightmares of every generation were pursuing his small force. They faced an army vaster then anything he had ever seen and despair flitted through his mind.

"Hold the line!"

The cavalry waited and rested their chargers on a small rise on the floor of the Valley of Kirden. Captain Haust had driven them until they reached the middle of the wide valley before the horses began to give out. Now his soldiers sat waiting as the northern walls of the valley flooded with hooting and jeering creatures.

"Unfurl the battle standard! No quarter will be given and none will be asked!" Captain Haust squinted at the blue sky watching as the blue and black battle standard of Juthel was unfurled and the warm breezes swept it open.

"Anatari, welcome us to your arms as we fight to defend your people." Haust whispered the simple prayer. Around him he heard hundreds of men whisper the same words. Captain Haust breathed a happy sigh of relief knowing that General Fritts had carefully picked his force of faithful men.

"Die well my friends and pray that the Elemental Protectors guide Nathel through the darkness ahead." Captain Haust said. His voice was so quiet that the last words were for him only. Then he lowered the visor on this helm. The cavalry formed a single line across the bottom of the valley and on a silent command they hoisted their lances. Even now thousands of enemy soldiers were starting down the shallow sloping sides of the Kirden valley.

Captain Haust watched with wide eyes as the valley came alive with enemies. Towering minotaurs, surrounded by wolves and Goblins too numerous to count, and pockets of snake-like Medusas that slithered forward, hissing as they moved. Then the ground shook as a score of ponderous Basilisks arrived on the ridge and then started slowly down the ramp towards the waiting humans.

"Anatari save us. Sound the attack!" Haust voice echoed loudly inside his helm.

As one, the four hundred men urged their charges forward expending their hoarded energy in one last charge. At twenty paces distance from the skirmish line the lances came down. The cavalry swept across the valley floor like a giant silver scythe. Just as Captain Haust slammed his lance deep into the broad chest of a minotaur, a shadow passed over head. Before him a groan went up from the monstrous horde.

He dropped his broken lance and pulled his long sword from its scabbard and split wide the helm of the nearest goblin with a heavy swing. Then, as the creatures before him turned and fled, he urged his horse forward. Looking through his visor from side to side, he sought out more enemies.

"What is this?"

Haust pulled his charger to a halt. All around him he could see confused soldiers looking about, wondering why their foes were abandoning the skirmish. Glancing up, Captain Haust opened his visor and felt relief flood through him.

"The Mountain Army has come!" The cry went up quickly as scores of cavalry soldiers pulled up and pointed high above them.

Circling above the valley floor were scores of wyrm soldiers of the mountain army. Mounted atop each of them was an eagle eyed bowmen raining death from the skies on the advancing creatures of the Dark One. Arrow after arrow fell from the sky striking death across the valley.

"Pull back." Captain Haust turned his horse and urged the weary chargers out of the battle. A score of Goblins and wolves lay dead around him, each one with a single arrow through its body. Leading most of the four hundred mounted force, Captain Haust wearily worked his way up the southern side of the valley wall. He leapt from his horse when he arrived at the vally rim and grabbed the reserved Timoth in a bear hug.

"Thank you. I feared we were done for."

Timoth smiled as he helped Haust regain his balance.

"I fear we are not out of danger. The rest of the army of Juthel is still two days behind us and we have yet to hear anything from the Orkin. My scouts reported that both were moving this way."

Captain Haust wiped the tears from his eyes and looked about the valley wall. Ten thousand broad dwarf warriors wielded spade and shovel as they threw up a hasty ramp along the valley wall.

Thousands of archers and swordsmen stood in ordered ranks with weapons held ready. Overhead Haust watched as dozens of wyrm riders swept in from the north. Their riders snatching the offered quivers and urged their mounts back into the air to loose the missiles against the seeming unending masses of the enemy.

It was evening when the weary wyrm soldiers landed and stayed on the ground; Some of them falling asleep where they landed with their wings tucked tightly against their bodies.

"Can we hold the ridgeline until the army of Juthel arrives?" Captain Haust asked. He sat in a small tent with Timoth looking at a rough map of the Kirden Valley drawn with charcoal.

"The enemy has sent his forces in all directions, Captain. This is just the largest of the forces. If any of the other forces turn and attack our flanks, we will be hard pressed to hold our current position. Many of the smaller forces by themselves are an equal to us. My scouts counted fifty thousand moving north from Juthel under the banner of Anatari. I sent three more scouts searching for the Orkin to the east. Once all our forces have arrived, we might stand a chance of defeating this army. Then and only then could we worry about the others." Timoth made a small row of marks with a thin piece of charcoal tallying the numbers as he marked them down.

"Timoth, we must hold here. Nathel has the item and is headed to the Fortress of Winds. It will take him a day to reach the fortress. From the fortress he needs time to ride to the Devil's Peak. We must give him the time he needs."

Timoth nodded, he understood the price of failing, "In that case, we will hold here and give him his time."

Timoth nodded to Haust and exited the tent; the great dwarf gave his orders in a quiet unassuming voice. They stood watching as darkness spread across the sky. Hundreds of cooking fires could be seen on both sides of the valley as the encamped armies waited for daylight to batter each other to pieces.

Nathel held the reigns tight in his hands as he peered into the looming darkness, the interior of the castle was a wreck. Nearly every wall had been torn down, and gaping holes broken through the ceiling stared back at him. Hewas glad for the small amount of moonlight that shone into the darkness.

Nathel held his staff tightly as he edged the dun forward.

"Easy boy," He whispered. Immediately, he regretted the words as even the light whisper echoed in to the absolute silence. Time stretched out for the sweating young monarch. The path left by the rampaging army was wide, and the floor was ground smooth by their passage. After an eternity of feeling his way into the darkness, Nathel found himself in a dimly lit room. A stone statue stood and dominated the center of the room.

"Elemental warrior," Nathel stared in awe at the being. The sense of power in the room was palpable, but the power holding the warrior bound in the stone was stronger and so the warrior stood unmoving. Overhead, the roof was completely gone and the moonlight illuminated the frozen warrior.

Nathel's eyes swept the room and came to rest on a second figure crouched on the floor near the first. Tears leapt to his eyes as he dropped the reins and threw himself to Katirna's side.

"I am so sorry, Kat." His tears fell freely to the floor, some landing on the upraised face of the young woman.

A voice spoke. 'I can give her back to you, boy." A voice spoke. It came from all sides at once and Nathel leapt to his feet. Whirling about, his staff clenched in his trembling hands, he scanned what he had thought to be an empty room. The motionless figure stood ten paces away, hidden by a single patch of shadows.

"Who are you and why have you done this?"

"Do you want her back?"

The figure did not move and Nathel strained his eyes in the gloom. It wore a dark cloak; all that was visible was a pair of glowing red eyes and a small amount of pale skin around the face.

"The Elementals have failed you, Boy. My master has given me power here in this realm. I can restore this loved one to you-for a price."

"What price." Nathel asked the question slowly wondering what evil the creature of Bedbezdal would demand. "What price does your foul master demand for an innocent life?"

"Haha."

Nathel shuddered. The dry and shrill laughter rang in his ears.

"None are innocent, boy. If you have not figured that out yet, there is little hope for you."

"What price."

"The bell, boy. I will trade you the girl's life for the bell."

"You ask the world for Katirna's life. That is a heavy price."

"Not so heavy, boy. When will you realize that Anatari has lost? My master has broken the fortress and his armies are loosed on the world. There is none with the strength to withstand the armies assembled against the low lands. Even if every human, orkin, elf, wyrm, and dwarf was outfitted for battle you would still be outnumbered twenty to one. The world will burn; it will be made ready for the arrival of my master."

"The Elemental Protectors will stop you."

"Haven't you been listening, boy? They are scattered and most are bound; soon now, even the Elemental Pillars will fail. And my master will be loosed upon the world." The figure stepped forward.

Nathel noticed the black bladed sword held loosely in his shrouded hand.

"Give me the bell, Nathel. It was never your burden to carry." He reached out towards Nathel, his hand opened to receive the bell.

Nathel ran his hand gently across the stone image of Katirna. He almost felt the warmth of her skin through the stone, and then he stood facing the black creature.

"I cannot agree to your terms. The price you demand is too much. I will never let you hold this Bell. Though I may lose, I will fight you with every breath in my body. Even if you loosed every goblin and minotaur in the north there will always be some that will resist you no matter what the odds."

Nathel held his staff out defensively crouching slightly and flexing the muscles in his legs to hold his body perfectly in balance. He was calm despite the power of the creature he faced. He watched as the black clad being stepped forward, moving slowly to stand in front of him.

"Then I will kill you and take what I want from your corpse. Time to die, boy."

Nathel crouched even lower as the black hand pointed at him and darkness flowed over his body. He felt the cool stone hardening over his legs, as his torso fell cold he held his staff high over head.

"Please, hear my plea. I cannot do this in myself, I need your help. Please."

Nathel whispered the words and his spirit was calm. The stone had reached his neck and he could no longer feel his body when his staff began to glow brilliantly. As the darkness approached his eyes felt the power of Anatari flowing through him, his staff fairly hummed with power.

"What is happening? No it cannot be! I have the power here on this world."

The light from the staff flowed down his body and the stone that threatened to engulf him fell away.

The strike from the black sword moved with the swiftness of a diving eagle, it came in the blink of an eye and the force would have felled any warrior. The surprise on the pale face was complete when the rune encrusted staff intercepted the blade and turned it aside with a shower of sparks.

Again and again he struck out with lightening speed and each time the glowing staff turned the black blade away. With lightening speed he changed attacks and lunged hard at Nathel.

Nathel spun away. He turned his staff slightly and angled his body away from the blow. Once again the blade passed harmlessly through the air where he had stood a moment before.

"Light the darkness," Nathel whispered. He held his staff high and the light from the runes filled the darkness.

The response of the creature was swift and powerful, waves of darkness flowed out in an overwhelming flood. For a time they strove against the light flowing from the staff.

The blade swept forward again in a dazzling display of strikes, this time trailing darkness. Each blow threatened to darken the entire area. Showers of sparks fell as the staff slapped the blade away again and again.

"You will die, boy." The black creature stepped back but now Nathel saw the uncertain flickers in his red eyes backed by more then a bit of panic.

Nathel waited until the sword swept from left to right and he lashed out knocking the sword back. This time, Nathel stepped in, knowing he was giving away his advantage of reach to the shorter weapon. He pulled his staff in tight to his body and then thrust out hard feeling the sudden jerk as he struck the black clad body. In the corner of his eye Nathel saw the sword rise up into the air and start its descent. He heard the sudden gasp of pain and then bowed his head waiting for the blow that would kill him, there was no defense against the falling blade. Determined to make his death worthy he thrust even harder until he felt the creature's body begin to fall back under the strike. For him, time slowed down as the glow of the staff intensified. A moment later the sword clattered to the ground behind Nathel, falling harmlessly to the stones.

"No, this cannot be!"

The hissing voice whispered just loud enough for Nathel to hear.

"Anatari take this one to judgment, and send him screaming to the depths of hell." Nathel growled the words fiercely into the pale face, the red eyes widened as he spoke and an eerie wail echoed through the room. The explosive blast that accompanied the black creature's departure knocked Nathel from his feet and sent his staff flying across the paving stones.

"Ooo"

Nathel rolled from his back and struggled to regain feeling in all four limbs. A trickle of blood traced down his face and dripped into his eyes, making him struggle to see.

A hand reached out and grasped his shoulder and fear raced through him. He looked up, catching a glimmer of his fallen staff through the trickle of blood that blinded him. Then he was enfolded in a warm embrace.

"Nathel, you came for me. I knew you would." Katirna's voice was soft and she reached out and wiped the blood from his face.

"You're alive," Nathel stammered. His joy at hearing her voice bound his tongue and made his breath come in short gasps.

"Yes, the creature turned me to stone. I could still see and hear what was happening. When you struck the final blow you broke its power over me."

Nathel reached out and grabbed her by the shoulders pulling her close. They clung to each other for a long time laughing and crying at the same time.

"Mortals. You must flee this place."

A thundering voice surprised Nathel and he spun around drawing Katirna to the side so that she was shielded by his body.

The stone warrior that stood in front of Katirna had also been freed. The elemental warrior walked towards them with his long sword rested on his shoulder.

"Much evil has been done and it will not be easy to undo. I must find my brethren and go to the aid of the mortal armies. You have a quest you must complete son."

Nathel nodded as he struggled to form his thoughts into words.

"Go, quickly! You must reach the seat of the world." The elemental took a step before Nathel was able to stop him.

"Wait!"

"What is it, boy. Quickly now, every moment lost means more death and destruction."

"I was told that the seat of creation is at the top of Devil's Peak, but I do not know where that is found."

"It was not always known as Devil's Peak but after Bedbezdal was banished to the north, that is what it was called. Go north up the pass to where the lava enters the valley, and then make for the tallest volcano. At the peak of the volcano is the seat of creation surrounded by circle of stones, at the center is a stone altar to Elutha."

"Elutha?"

"The creator of the world, Nathel. He who stood outside of time and spoke the world into existence. He who removed his cloak called time and spread it over creation."

Turning, the elemental warrior strode from the room, as he walked, light once again filled the crushed rooms of the Fortress of Winds.

Nathel watched him leave, "You should follow him south its probably safer then what I must do." Nathel turned and offered a grim if somewhat uncertain look to Katirna.

"I will not be separated from you again! Ever!" The fierce conviction in Katirna's voice matched the determination in her eyes.

Nathel smiled and offered her his arm. He retrieved his staff, and together they walked north.

"I hope my horse did not go too far."

Katirna shook her head, "Any horse would have fled that thing."

"This is no ordinary horse," Nathel said.

Within ten paces Nathel saw the dun standing quietly and waiting for them. If the horse was bothered by the battle that had taken place or the destruction of the surroundings, he showed none of it. He turned his head to stare at them and flickered his tail at an imaginary fly.

"Can you carry two, boy?" Nathel asked as they approached. He squinted as he pondered how much the intelligent horse actually understood.

The dun turned sideways and huffed twice.

"What a magnificent beast," Katirna gushed. She ran her fingers around the duns ears and scratched the pale nose. The dun huffed again and shook his mane as he reveled in the attention.

Moments later the dun burst from the ruined north gate of the Fortress of Winds. Moving at a canter, the dun's powerful legs propelled them along the smooth valley floor.

Matthew John Krengel

Chapter Twenty-Two
Bull Men in the Center

imoth stood staring at the advancing wall of iron. His calm and patient manner was a steadying influence on the soldiers standing close to the great general.

Haust had been shaking his head ever since the mountain army had arrived. The soldiers worked in shifts as they threw up a ten foot high rampart of dirt along the entire front. Hundreds of trees dragged from the nearby forests were driven into the ground and then sharpened with sure strokes of double bladed axes.

"One of the scouts returned this morning. He found nothing but another army marching east. If the Orkin are out there, they are hidden in the wilderness somewhere." Haust nodded from where he stood beside the wide general.

"While we wait, their numbers swell beyond count." Haust spoke quietly, not wanting to state the obvious, but he worried just the same. Trickles of Goblins and minotaurs still marched in from the north.

"Trust in Anatari and his protectors," Timoth said. He reached out and engulfed Haust's elbow with his grizzled hand. Years of swinging a sword had left Captain Haust's hands calloused but they were baby soft compared to the dwarf warrior.

"We will position the chargers above the narrow ramp in the middle. If things play out they way they did in the Drought Wars, the evil one's tactics are not subtle. He prefers to attack straight against any target. I am certain he will try and bury us under weight of numbers. If that fails, he will send forward the Basilisks. But we have a surprise for them when they show their scaled faces."

"Are they are big as the tales say they are?" Haust pondered. He muttered the question to himself as much as to Timoth.

"Bigger. Wingless monsters. The evil one stole the strength of the Wyrms and made them bigger. He sacrificed the ability to fly for the size and weight of a mountain."

Captain Haust's face paled as he glanced towards the still sleeping wyrm, only two of the wyrm soldiers were aloft and they were riderless, acting as scouts to watch the enemy movement.

"Come let us take our places, the enemy will move soon." Timoth said. They began walking down the battle line, thousands of red cloaked warriors stood shoulder to shoulder. Longbows were in hand and each had a bundle of arrows strapped to their sides. The archers stood in a thin line behind the infantry spread out to offer a bit of protection to the entire front.

"Sir, there is movement from the enemy army!"

Timoth hurried forward and the ranks parted enough to let Haust and Timoth slip to the front.

Haust scanned across the far side of the valley noting that the minotaurs were forming to the center of the battle line. The tall heavy bull men carried weapons that would have stood to Haust's waist. Many were painted with bright colors and bits of bone and feathers hung from their long horns.

"Just what we expected," Timoth said. "The bull men are forming to the center, and they are moving the Goblins to the edges. What worries me is that there is no sign of the Medusas. They can be a vicious enemy. A single bite of the snake women will send a warrior into convulsions. If any of the wraiths have answered the Dark One's call they will probably come riding the Basilisks."

"There to the west!" He pointed a thick hand, then turned and bellowed in a loud voice, "Medusas to the west!"

A scurry of movement erupted at the rear of the battle line and Haust could make out the darting forms of agile elf warriors scurrying to the west.

The noise from the minotaur battle line was growing as the bull men stamped their hoofed feet on the ground. Many beat the flat sides of their weapons against their broad muscled chests.

"Come, it's time for us to take our places." Timoth turned and stepped into a wide opening in the dwarf battle line filling the entire space with his bulk.

"You're fighting in the front rank?" Haust was aghast.

"This is the war to end all wars, man. We have the chance to exterminate most of the Dark One's forces forever. Ha! We should be thanking the Elements for this day. Isn't that right men?"

A chorus of hearty cheers erupted around Timoth as the thick bodied dwarf warriors erupted in cheering. Hundreds and then thousands of shining weapons were hoisted into the air and a thunderous cheer erupted from the mountain army.

Haust shook his head as he turned to where the cavalry were taking up their positions just beyond the ramp.

As he glanced back he saw Timoth remove his helmet from his massive head. Haust watched as the mailed armored hand pulled the horned helmet free and he stared with mouth open wide as Timoth knelt to the ground.

The words of the prayer that Timoth led the dwarf warriors in would ring in his mind for the rest of his life.

"Anatari hear us. Strengthen the Elemental Pillars that bind the Dark One. Make our blades keen and our arms strong. Bring us victory or welcome us into your arms."

The prayer echoed up and down the dwarf battle line as the red cloaked warriors repeated the prayer. The main forces of dwarf warriors held the center of the line. It was up to the humans and elf warriors with their long reaching bows to turn back the swarms of Goblins that were even now beginning their descent to the valley floor. The night before, five archers had slipped into the valley and marked out with stones the firing range of the long bows wielded by the red cloaked archers.

Haust turned and ran to his waiting charger. The heavy war horse sensed the coming battle and pranced about until Captain Haust pulled down on the reigns.

"This is it men! If we die, die well and take many enemies with you. Rest assured we are fighting for the greatest army ever assembled."

Captain Haust waited on the small rise, watching as the the minotaurs started forward. The thunder of their combined footsteps shook the ground.

"The waiting is worse then the battle," Captain Haust whispered under his breath. He watched wave after wave of bull men crest on the far side of the valley and begin the long descent. Seven long ranks crested and started down before they stopped coming. Uncounted hordes of Goblins advanced in unorganized masses, and Haust noticed the smaller creatures stayed clear of the towering minotaurs. The Goblins engaged the flanks of the Mountain army long before the bull men closed with the dwarf warriors. Haust watched waves of arrows leap from the flanking archers and scythe down thousands of Goblins. Despite the horrendous losses, the beady eyed creatures still ran forward. They leapt over the dead and dying to close on the smaller battalions of swordsmen that protected the archers.

Captain Haust's horse shook its head in unease as a long line of shadows passed over head. The wyrm soldiers each carried two archers and they swept in low, firing long barbed arrows with weighted heads at the minotaurs. Many of the shafts found their targets and as the enraged bull men pulled the arrows loose the heads of the arrows broke off under their skin. The iron tip stuck tight and left painful wounds to hamper their movements. Haust noticed the heavy arrows the night before when Timoth had taken him on a tour of the wyrm soldier's weapons.

The meeting of the dwarf warriors and the charging bull men shook the ground; the dwarf soldiers were lighter but much more heavily armored. Thick shields held strong to turn aside the powerful strokes of the Bull men's heavy weapons.

"Sir, the Medusas are in range."

Captain Haust watched as the small group of snake women slipped past the flights of arrows without taking a single loss. Just as they engaged the battalion of swordsmen defending the west flank, two score black clad figures raced out. Amazingly fast, the elf warriors ducked and dodged, wielding twin blades they struck and retreated leaving the Medusas dazed. Just as the snake women started forward they raced out again striking but this time the Medusas played a surprise of their own. Five of the snake women spun about lashing out with long tails. Five of the elf warriors fell writhing on the ground and the rest fell, back letting the archers launch a volley of arrows point blank at the slithering forms. The ballet of death went on for many long minutes on the west flank with the black clad warriors dashing forward, spinning and ducking to avoid the lashing tails and biting heads of the snake women. Finally, the snake women broke off the battle by slithering backwards through the charging Goblins back to the safety of the far ridge. Sadly, over half of the swordsmen lay dead and nearly that many of the elven swordsmen would never fight again.

"Sir, its time! The battle line on the ramp is giving way." The trooper beside Captain Haust pointed at the intense battle raging about the narrow ramp. True to what Timoth had guessed the minotaur warriors were drawn to the easy path up the ramp. As they charged the lines compacted and made them easy targets for the battalions of archers launching arrows as fast as they could draw their bowstrings.

Haust nodded, he lowered the visor on his helmet and eased his lance forward. "For the King!" The long wooden lance was twice the height of a man and as thick around as his wrist at the handle and tapered to a sharp point.

Urging his war horse forward, he dropped his lance to chest level. It took a light touch of his spurs in the chargers flanks to send the heavy animal forward. The few remaining dwarf warriors still blocking the ramp fell back. Already hundreds of the armored warriors lay dead from the hacking blades of the minotaurs, more then a few were gored with long thick horns as they fell. Haust dropped his lance and slammed it into the chest of a particularly tall bull man, snapping off the lance with a twist of his arm and then turning his horse to the side and sweeping along between the ranks of dwarf warriors. The cavalry behind him formed into a rank four wide and charged down the narrow ramp. Each drove his lance deep into the bull men and then snapping off the lances and sweeping around to the back of the line to grab another lance.

The dead minotaurs blocked the ramp completely after two passes and Haust fell back with his cavalry without losing a single rider.

"Captain Haust, the east flank is buckling!" A breathless archer screamed above the din of the battle. His red cloak was torn and blood dripped from a gash across his cheek.

Captain Haust motioned his second in command forward, "Attack when needed. I am taking two companies to reinforce the east flank."

The dusty barrel chested man nodded behind the thin eye slit on his visor.

"First and third companies forward." Touching the spurs to his charger Haust led two hundred of the cavalry across the distance separating the main battle line from the buckling flank. The red cloaked archers had been forced to drop their bows and defend themselves with short swords as the three battalions of swordsmen were completely engulfed by screaming hordes of Goblins. Haust saw the square formation fighting to hold together, but the numbers were just too much. He dropped his lance tip low to the ground and urged his big war horse on at a gallop. The surprised Goblins turned to stare at the charging cavalry and melted away.

Goblins would fight men on the ground with little fear of their own lives but the massive horses were too much for their simple minds. Captain Haust struck out repeatedly with the lance until it lodged completely in the rusted armor of a particularly large goblin. Again he snapped off the lance with a quick twist of his wrist, spotting another target he threw the lance hard breaking the Goblins neck. Ripping his long sword from its sheath, Haust let loose with a war cry and charged forward. Scattered groups of cavalry answered his cry and pushed their horses forward crushing dozens of the fleeing Goblins until they had reformed their battle line. Forward Haust led his cavalry, sweeping between two of the reformed battalions of foot soldiers. Once again the waves of arrows streaked from the archers as they broke from the melee and put their longbows to work again.

"Pull back!" Captain Haust pulled his charger up at the bottom of the valley and motioned his men back.

"Sir, we can push them all the way back to the far side if we attack now!" A young trooper gasped breathlessly, the battle lust bright in his eyes.

"Son, they outnumber us two hundred to one, if they figure that out when we are hundreds of paces from the covering fire of the longbows we will be dead to a man. Now I said, pull back!" Haust turned his charger and urged the tired mount back up the sloping valley wall. To his right, the minotaurs were breaking off the attack and pulling away from the dwarf battle line, hundreds of bull men lay dead at the foot of the rampart. Haust counted as he crouched low over his horse's neck, more then a few armored figures lay peacefully amid the carnage, the dwarves had paid a heavy price for the defense.

Timoth was covered in blood and dirt when they arrived back at the dirt and stone ramp. He turned and saluted Haust.

"What happened?"

"The east flank was overrun but we turned them back!" Haust stepped down from the saddle and retrieved a fresh lance. He always enjoyed the smell of a fresh lance; it focused his mind away from the smell of battles ragging around them.

"You're good man in a fight, Captain. I wish I had ten thousand more like you." Timoth smiled and smacked Haust on the shoulder hard enough to rattle his armor.

Captain Haust smiled, biting back the involuntary cry that had been close to slipping from his mouth. "Will they hit us again today?"

"Well from the ancient text the bull men believe that they only fight once a day. If they still hold to that belief we might have a break for the rest of today. Of course, the Dark One may have worked that superstition out of them over the past two hundred years."

As soon as Timoth stopped speaking the cry went up from the front again. "Looks like no rest for the faithful." Timoth winked and hurried back to the front of the battle line.

Haust could not help but notice the blood stains spread across the broad head of the massive battle ax the veteran warrior carried. Then he turned and remounted his charger.

"Sir, no bull men this time." The man beside him pointed out over the heavy helms of the dwarves to the advancing enemy lines. Captain Haust watched as wave upon wave of Goblins moving tentatively forward

"Something is driving them forward sir. They look to have no stomach for the battle."

"Yes, but what?" Haust scanned up and down the line but he was unable to see anything. At places in the line there were simply empty spaces with ten or twenty paces where no goblin dared enter.

"Wraiths on the battle field!" The cry went up as the Goblins hordes decided the physical weapons facing them from the mountain army were less of a threat then the invisible weapons wielded by the wraiths.

"How do you fight them?" Captain Haust wondered. He grabbed a nearby elf and asked the question above the shrill battle cry of the attacking Goblins.

"They wield no physical weapons, fear is their weapon and they use it well. They can touch the soul of any mortal and bring their worst fears to life in the mind. The only way to fight a wraith is fire. If the Dark One is pushing Goblins forward he is simply trying to tire us and use up our arrows."

The archer drew back his bow after knocking a long shaft, he continued aiming as he spoke to Captain Haust. The elf had long blond hair that was pulled back from a square face that seemed chiseled from granite. The muscles in his bare arms were corded as they held the quivering bow steady.

"And it might work. We used up tens of thousands of arrows already, and it seems they have Goblins to spare." The elf smiled grimly and released his arrow, swiftly he drew a second from the quiver on his belt and sighted a bit lower and released again.

I can guarantee that I kill one with each shot but I fear it may not be enough." The elf pulled a third arrow and dropped his aim just over the helmets of the engaged dwarf warriors. This time Captain Haust watched in amazement as the arrow tore through a goblin's head that was charging up the ramp and slammed into the chest of the goblin behind it.

"Actually, I think their plan is much simpler. I think they are just trying to fill in the bottom of the rampart." Captain Haust pointed to where a slight dip in the valley wall allowed them to see the bottom of the rampart. Already the Goblins were taking terrible losses as they threw themselves against the armored mountain warriors. However, the waves still coming up the hill no longer scrambled to climb the sharp rampart dug by the mountain warriors. Now they charged over the bodies of their fallen partners.

The attacks continued until the sun began to dip behind the distant mountains. Then as suddenly as began, the waves of Goblins faded off fleeing for the safety of the far valley wall.

Timoth was breathing heavily when Captain Haust found him seated near his tent. The dwarf was covered in grime and gore, his ax was dented so badly Haust wondered if it would ever hold an edge again.

"What a battle!" He exclaimed. "I haven't seen that many bull men or Goblins in one place ever. We gave as well as we got today, but with the loss of the ramparts it will be harder to push back the bull men tomorrow."

"One of the scouts returned today. He said that there are two more armies converging on the north side of the valley Mostly Goblins but he said there is more than enough to erase the Dark One's losses today."

"Just full of good news aren't you," Timoth chuckled. His smile seemed genuine to Captain Haust and the cavalry man shook his head in amazement.

"How can you stay in such a good mood when your soldiers are dying to an enemy that can't be beat? There are too many of them, Timoth. I thought we could hold them for three days but now I don't know. Where are the Orkin armies? Where is the army of Juthel?" Captain Haust's face was weary and he had given up hope.

"Son, the Creator would not allow us the chance to destroy his enemy's mortal strength without providing us with the skill and courage to do it. Anatari will not turn his back us. But we must not lose our hope."

Timoth retrieved his battle axe and pulled a wet stone from the ground beside his wooden chair, offering the captain a smile he began to remove the dents and burrs from the broad axe blade.

"I wish I had your faith," Haust said quietly.

Timoth looked up sadly from his ax, "But you freed the rightful king of Juthel from certain death captain. You have held strong through years under the rule of an evil man, are you so certain that your faith is lacking?"

Matthew John Krengel

Chapter Twenty-Three
Devil's Peak

vening came and went and still the dun carried Nathel and Katirna north. Before them stretched the wide road that led up the valley, a flowing trickle of lava took shape adding a red glow to the surrounding cliff walls. The clopping of the dun's hooves on the flat rocks was the only sound that broke the stillness of the night, even the stars seemed to avoid shining down on the valley floor.

"Look up ahead." Nathel pointed with his staff, morning was approaching. Katirna dozed fitfully from where she sat in front of Nathel on the dun's back.

She peered through the approaching grayness of dawn. A thick river of lava cut to the east passing through a wide gap between two towering mountains.

It was noon when they finished climbing through the mountain gap and the dun was showing some signs of weariness. Nathel pulled him back to a walk letting the horse catch his breath and rest his weary legs.

"You ok, boy?" He whispered past Katirna's slim form. The dun flicked his ears reassuring him that he was ready for whatever was asked.

"I don't think there has ever been another horse like this one and I don't think there ever will be again," Katirna said. She spoke softly but the dun turned his head to glance at her and whinnied.

She reached forward to rub his ears and stroke his neck.

"I think we found the Devils Peak." Nathel reined in the dun and pointed ahead. They topped out on a small stone strewn rise and looked down on a wide expanse. Smoking behemoths dotted the landscape, small rivers of lava worked their way down the sides of the mountains and joined together to form a slow moving river of lava that emptied into the valley that they had just ridden through. In the center of the obsidian fields was a volcano that dwarfed the others, a gray cloud sat unmoving atop the mountain shrouding its peak from sight.

"Well, sitting here isn't getting us any closer." Nathel urged the dun forward. He breathed deeply and gave Katirna a small squeeze around her waist wanting to reassure her.

In return she leaned back against his chest and sighed. Enjoying the quiet, they moved down into the maze of lava and steam vents.

Evening was falling when Nathel finally reined in the dun. They were half way across the black fields and the devils peak loomed high above them.

"It is taking us longer to get there then I thought it would." Nathel sat down gingerly on the side of a smooth shiny obsidian stone. He found out the hard way that the stones were razor sharp on the sides and the cut he received on the palm of his hand was painful.

"It's been two days I think, since I entered the Fortress of Winds. That means the armies of the Dark One have been driving south for two full days. I wonder if the army of Juthel has engaged the enemy yet, I sent word for the army to march north as fast as they could."

Nathel related the events of the past few days to Katirna as they rode, starting from where she had been taken by the stone gargoyle and ending with his entrance to the Fortress.

"I wish I had been there to see Grend suffer." Her face clouded with irritation despite the enjoyment of hearing how Nathel had beaten the false king.

"Vengeance is not worth living for. Thero always told me that. I think his fate in the hands of the Dark One is worse then any pain you could inflict on him. His future is sealed. If we succeed, he will be imprisoned with Bedbezdal."

"I know that but I still wish I had been there. I have lived my whole life with one thing on my mind. I am not sure what to do now that I don't have my revenge anymore." Katirna slumped on the rock beside him. The ground was covered with a fine dust that puffed up whenever they moved.

"Katirna, why not stay by my side and rule as the queen of Juthel." Nathel took her by the hand and stared into her wide eyes.

"Katirna Divuria, will you marry me. I have never loved anyone up till now and even though we have not known each other for long, I love you more than anything in the world." Nathel found himself kneeling in the gray dust holding her hand amid the reddish glow from the lava.

Katirna sat staring at him like he had lost his mind, but Nathel watched the tears forming in her eyes as his words took hold.

"From the moment I saw you in the upper room of the Night Owl, I knew you would be part of my life somehow. Although, I never dreamed we would rule a country together. Yes, Nathel! I will marry you gladly."

Nathel jumped his feet and whooped for joy drawing her to her feet and picking her off the ground. He swung her in a circle that brought them perilously close to the edge of the lava stream. Laughing and crying all at once Nathel collapsed to the ground not caring that the dust billowed around them, Katirna collapsed beside him and they lay staring at the dark sky catching their breath. High above them a single rain cloud spread across the sky and a warm breeze blew in from the south carrying with it the scent of rain. A few moments later a warm rain began falling to the ground, hissing as it struck the lava and darkening the landscape around them. High above, Nathel heard the same cry as he had heard when the stone gargoyle had taken Katirna near the river.

"I think the Elemental Protectors have saved us again. It sounds like our stone friend is searching for us once more."

Katirna nodded and together they spread a cloak over their heads and leaned against the dun's damp flank. Thankfully, the rain was warm and they were cozy despite the storm clouds.

The next morning dawned with a brilliant burst of sunshine and found Nathel brushing the flanks of the dun. He found a small stiff brush in his pack and the dun sighed in pleasure as he worked out the dirt and dust.

Katirna leaned over a nearby rock slicing cheese and bread for a cold breakfast. The dun for his part stood patiently munching on a handful of oats.

"I wish there was more, boy. Hopefully, we will be gone from this place soon."

The dun shook his head, being careful not to drop any of the precious grain. Seeking more food, the horse leaned over and nuzzled Katirna almost knocking her over.

"Stop that you!"

Nathel laughed as she shook her finger at the dun.

The sun had just begun its ascent into the sky when they started up the sides of the volcano. The eerie cloud above them was deathly quiet, and even the dun seemed weary. The heat was intense this close to the mammoth volcano, and the rivers of lava grew in size until they surrounded the single trail that led up the mountain side.

"Come on, boy. You can make it."

Nathel and Katirna dismounted and walked for a while, letting the dun collect his strength for the long climb ahead.

Hours passed with much of it spent riding up the trail through the gray fog. The cloud closed in around them and gray mist swirled past them as they rode. Nathel reined in and they dismounted again, not wanting to ride off the edge of a cliff. Speed would do them little good if they fell off a thousand pace precipice.

"Look ahead through the mist, something is moving." Nathel whispered lightly in Katirna's ear, he pointed ahead with his staff. The runes started glowing slightly as they entered the thickening cloud, and it gave them a bit of light to pierce the fog.

"What is it?"

Nathel squinted again, but he lost sight of the movement and so he led the dun forward again. Then the fog broke and they found themselves squinting against the bright sun shining down on the lip of the volcano. Before them a sea of lava boiled and hissed a hundred paces down the mouth of the volcano. In the distance, suspended above the sea of red, a round stone fifty paces wide floated peacefully above the chaotic lake.

"How do we make it out there?" Katirna came around the side of the dun and stared out across the boiling lake.

"There must be a way..." Nathel peered to the north along the rim searching for a path. Nathel pointed to the far rim. "What's that over there?"

Pulling on the dun's reins, he led them north, skirting around the edge of the precipice. They picked their way carefully to avoid the razor sharp rocks protruding from the ground. Below them in the boiling lake a towering geyser erupted, throwing lava high in to the air.

When Nathel finally stopped he stood next to a narrow strip of stone that arched into the air. The end of the thin ribbon of stone rested lightly on the floating stone.

"Well, you asked how we were going to get out there. I think this is our last test." Nathel turned and untied the straps holding the saddle to the dun's broad back.

"If we don't survive, boy, get out of here and go back to your wide plains." Nathel patted the horse affectionately. A tear formed in his eye as he struggled with the feelings he had developed for the spirited stallion in the short time he had been around the animal. It seemed the dun knew what he was thinking even before he knew sometimes.

Katirna reached up one last time and scratched the tall pointed ears. She whispered her goodbye to the dun and then turned and walked to the narrow bridge.

"Place one foot ahead of the next. Use your staff for balance." Katirna placed one foot on the rock to test the surface.

"At least it's not slippery." She walked confidently out across the glowing lake, moving with the surefootedness of a mountain goat.

Nathel set his first foot on the rock, holding the ironwood staff out sideways with both hands. He shifted the weight using it to offset the small movements that threatened to make him loose his balance. Going was slow at first and it seemed to take Nathel forever to reach the center of the bridge.

At the center, he glanced down at the boiling lava and immediately regretted the action. The waves of heat and the bubbling surface rolled and shifted before his eyes, making him feel like he was rolling with it.

"Don't look down, silly." Katirna reached out from where she stood steadying Nathel and looking deep into his eyes.

"Look at me, and walk with me." She kept a hand on his face as she backed up towards the floating stone.

Nathel stared at the woman, losing himself in her deep blue eyes.

"See how easy that was." Katirna laughed at him. Then her voice faded when he failed to respond still staring deeply into her eyes.

Nathel blinked suddenly looking around and realizing that he was standing in the middle of the floating stone. "It does work well." He laughed and took her by the hand as he turned in a slow circle. The walls of the volcano rose around them and the stone arch began to rise into the air.

"Are we supposed to be falling?" Katirna asked the question lightly.

Nathel snapped his eyes back to the stone bridge. They watched in dismay as the arching bridge of stone rose into the air passing quickly out of reach. Below them he saw the lava reaching up, trying to wrap is glowing arms around them. Nathel walked slowly to the center of the stone and stood looking about. "What do we do?"

Katirna raised her hands helplessly as geysers of lava erupted close by but missed the falling platform.

Finally, he put his arm around Katirna and they stood in the middle of the stone. He pulled the bell from inside his shirt. The gold of the small bell glowed fiercely in the reddish light of the lava, reflecting its pure light back tenfold.

"Ring it and see what happens." Katirna motioned for him to try, under their feet the stone lurched as it settled in the lake of lava then it began to sink slowly into the red lake. The burning rock rolled over the edge of the stone and crept slowly towards where they stood.

The warriors of the mountain army stood quietly waiting. This was the third attack of the morning and the archers frantically searched for arrows amid the carnage of the battle lines. The Goblins struck time after time, driven forward by the wraiths. They came unwillingly, but they fought like caged devils when they contacted the battle line. At one point hundreds broke the line and flooded up the ramp only to be turned back by repeated attacks by the massed cavalry.

Captain Haust wearily pulled his mail gauntlet from his hand and wiped the sweat from his eyes. The Goblins were taking a heavy toll across the battle line. Haust had lost more then one hundred of his cavalry and double that number of horses.

Timoth still anchored the center of the battle line as more warriors died. The lines contracted and gaps began to open between the flanking forces and the dwarven lines.

Red cloaked archers called for more arrows up and down the lines. The replies from the supply wagons were not good; the bundles of arrows were gone from the supply train. Broken swords were replaced but in places the battalions who defended the flanks were forced to fight with long knives or clubs.

"Here they come again, sir!" A bloodied and dirty human wearing a smudged and torn red cloak raced up from the front line.

"Goblins? Or are the bull men showing their faces?"

"Bull men, Sir. They mean to break us today."

Suddenly, an excited shout went up behind the weary men. A chorus of trumpets echoed across the southern ridge of the valley and from the wide road to the south a silver snake of men and cavalry came into view.

Captain Haust whooped for joy and leapt to his weary charger, racing down the road. He held the standard of Juthel high in the air waving it at the approaching army.

"Greetings, General Fritts. It is good to see you." Captain Haust cried. He pulled his charger to a halt, the poor animal heaving as its weary lungs struggled to draw the air it needed.

"By the Elements, man. You're going to kill that poor beast." Fritts looked disapprovingly at Haust. "Report!"

"The minotaurs are massing and our lines will not hold. Cavalry follows me, send five division up the center after us and three on each flank! And tell the reserves to haul up arrows and spare swords!" Captain Haust saluted General Fritts and spun his weary charger back up the road to the north, behind him he heard the white haired general replaying his orders. Two lines of fresh cavalry urged their heavy war horses forward following Haust back to the embattled ridge line.

Captain Haust arrived back at the top of the ramp leading almost two thousand fresh cavalry. Behind him, thousands of footmen wearing the blue tabards and silver chain armor of Juthel broke into a run. The minotaurs were already half way up the sloping valley wall when the fresh forces arrived.

They rushed into gaping holes that opened in the mountain army's battle line. Many of the soldiers of Juthel carried long pikes and they immediately dug the end of their thick handles into the churned up ground. Behind the line Haust watched lines of men carrying armloads of arrows to the red cloaked archers who raised their longbows, cheering the new arrivals.

"By the Elements, your countrymen know how to time things close." Timoth grunted. Despite his gruff tone, a wide smile split his lips as he watched the reinforcements flood across the ridge line.

"Basilisks to the north." The cry erupted from the gravely voices of a dozen dwarven warriors.

"This is it, Captain. The moment of truth." Timoth turned and jogged towards a dozen covered wagons sitting just behind the battle line.

"Prepare the wagons! Move them up fast to the head of the ramp."

Dozens of solders near the wagons dropped their weapons and surrounded the wagons. They dug in their heels and pushed them across the uneven ground to the top of the sloping ramp that led down to the valley floor. Haust watched the wagons slip over the edge and roll down

under their own power. He turned to the right where six more wagons were rolling down the east flank.

As they came to a halt, Captain Haust was aghast to see two figures leap from each of the wagons. They flipped the canvas covers back and began rolling large barrels to the ground. When scores of barrels covered the valley, the sun glinted off axes and hammers as the tiny figures broke open the barrels letting the contents flow across the valley floor. Already the slow moving Basilisks had entered the bottom of the valley, two hundred more paces and they would be on the frantic figures working over the barrels. Across the bottom of the valley a black slick flowed across the ground as dozens of barrels were broken open and dumped across the landscape.

"Timoth, those men will never get back in time." Captain Haust grabbed a nearby trooper and pulled him out of his saddle. He vaulting onto the fresh horse and motioned a score of troopers forward.

"Get those soldiers back to the lines!" He cried. He dug his spurs into the flanks of his charger and dashed down the ramp. Almost two score riders followed him, riding hard as they bent over their horses necks.

Captain Haust raced to the furthest figures as he finished breaking open the last barrel and reached out to catch the offered hand. Haust grabbed the extended hand from the burly human solder wearing a red cloak and bloodied armor.

"Hold on tight this is going to get bumpy!" He cried. Wheeling the horse about, he glanced back to see thousands of Goblins flooding around the slower moving Basilisks, racing to cut off the retreating soldiers.

Captain Haust pounded back up the dirt and stone ramp reining to a halt and letting the burly human slide off the side of the horse.

"Prepare to fire." The scores of mountain archers stood mingled into the front rank of dwarf warriors with blazing fire arrows held high.

Behind Captain Haust the last of his cavalry charged up the ramp and further down the valley the first of the massive green scaled Basilisks ignored the sticky black oil and ponderously moved forward. A quick count told Haust that more then a score of the huge beasts lumbered towards them. Behind them massed hordes of minotaurs and Goblins.

"By the stars, their numbers have actually grown during the last two days. The bodies of the Dark One's servants were spread across the battlefield by the thousands and still they outnumber the faithful ten to one."

"Fire."

A wave of fire arrows launched skyward hanging steady for a moment and then dropping to the oily slick. The arrows fell all around the Basilisks who ignored them as they skipped off the thick armored hides. High above the combined armies of the mountain kingdoms and Juthel the wyrms soldiers took flight again. They soared up, each one carrying a thick timber with a metal cap on the end in each claw. Haust scratched his head as he watched.

"Can you burn them?" he asked Timoth

"It's not enough to burn them, their hides are too thick." The grizzled veteran dwarf called as he jogged back to the gathered cavalry. "We need to break open their armor enough for the burning oil to seep inside and drive them crazy.

"Watch now; let us see if our plan works."

"Are you telling me you don't know if this will work?"

"It's been hundreds of years since anyone has seen a balisk south of the divide." Timoth grinned at him. "We did the best we could with the information we had."

The first wave of wyrms passed low, releasing the timbers. Immediately they pulled up hard to avoid hundreds of short darts and arrows that rose from the Goblins to defend the mired Basilisks. Some of the falling timbers missed completely, burying themselves in the packed dirt of the valley floor. Others struck their targets solid blows and the heavy metal heads tore gaping holes in the heavy armor protecting the Basilisks.

The effect was immediate. Wherever the fire touched the sensitive flesh under the thick armor, the Basilisks went wild, attacking the nearest thing. Minotaurs were thrown high in the air as the enraged Basilisks fought with each other across the blazing inferno that raged along the valley floor.

A cheer went up from the troops manning the southern valley wall but it was quickly silenced, then a second cry went up, "Enemies to the south."

Timoth groaned and for the first time Captain Haust saw a frown break across the dwarf general's face. Racing to the south, they found General Fritts shouting orders and bringing the remaining divisions of the army of Juthel into a defensive front facing the distant line of trees.

All across the forest, a sea of activity erupted, bull men emerged from the trees. They were surrounded by tens of thousands of Goblins and several bands of Medusas.

"More to the west!"

Small figures appeared and flooded along the valley wall and filled the open spaces between the pine trees.

"They let us kill Goblins for two days just to trap us here," Timoth fumed. "Trapped by the very enemies I wanted to destroy."

"Sir there is more movement to the east." A gasping runner came to a halt in front of the pair of commanders.

Timoth turned, expecting to see more of the Dark One's servants, but what he spotted brought a glimmer of hope to his eyes.

Captain Haust urged his charger to the east standing high in the saddle to find a clear view. Then over the archers and swordsmen protecting the east flank, he saw the blue standards of the Ironback Division of the Southern Orkin Empire flutter in the breeze. The blue banners filtered through the trees to the south of the valley as the orkin cleared a path for the embattled armies to escape.

"Sound the retreat! Get everyone moving east!" Timoth bellowed. He grabbed a nearby messenger and urged him to hurry to the west to reach the vastly outnumbered archers on the west flank.

Matthew John Krengel

Chapter Twenty-Four
The Dark One

 o not," a melodic voice said. The figure of a man walked across the boiling surface of the lava towards them. "Who are you?" Nathel asked. He held the bell tightly ready to ring at a moments notice. The figure strode through the shimmering waves of heat that rose from the boiling lake. Tall and well built he came to a halt ten paces from them. Clothed in a white ankle length robe his hair matched the obsidian stones around the lake edge. Two piercing eyes stared at them and Nathel found he could not look at them. They reminded him of the sorrow of reading his parents names and knowing he would truly never know them.

Next to him Katirna's eyes grew misty and he wrapped his free arm around her offering her some support.

The mysterious man stepped from the lava to the stone and Nathel gaped as his feet left marks in the surface of the stone.

"Don't come any closer or I will ring the bell, Dark One," Nathel's voice was fierce and he took a step back pulling Katirna with him.

"Foolish boy, I am not the enemy you seem to think I am. I must apologize for the zeal of some of my servants. They take things out of context sometimes; I never meant you any harm. Yes, I freely admit, I am Bedbezdal. But I have been called many things Dark One, Servant of Light, Son of Elutha. So many names over the time I have existed in this world. Is it so bad for me to want the best for this world?

My brother has given up on this world, However, I have not. I still find hope for the people in the lowlands, they can be saved. Son, with your help as the most powerful king in the lowlands we can save them."

Nathel eyes were slipped shut as the silky words drifted in and out of his consciousness. He leaned heavily on Katirna as he shook his head violently, trying to clear the images of him ruling the entire lowlands. Above them the blackness of night closed in and the only light left was the reddish glow that emanated off the lake of lava.

"No!" he cried. Nathel gripped his staff tightly and on the back of his hands the runes glowed fiercely. He shook his head again and looked up at where the Dark One had stood. In the glow of the rune he saw past the white robe, towering above the human puppet rose the Dark One. He took the form of an elemental of immense size and power. Glowing red eyes stared down at him and the figure he saw was hideous to behold. Two bat-like wings flapped slowly on each side and long curled horns pierced the sky above the bulbous head.

"You will never have this world creature of darkness," Nathel screamed.

Bedbezdal sensed his grip on Nathel was slipping and he reached out with a clawed hand. He howled when the silver and blue runes on Nathel's hands combined with the runes on the staff and formed a shield that stopped his hand.

Nathel crouched next to Katirna as the Dark One screamed in rage. He looked up as the shield of light flared against the impact of a tremendous blow.

"This will not stop me!"

Fire raced across a long black sword as the Dark One raised it into the air and brought it crashing down against the shield.

"Anatari, please help and protect us," Nathel whispered. Above his head the shield bent down under the force of the blow but it held.

"Ring it, Nathel!"

He dropped the bell that he clenched tightly in his hand with the chain wrapped around his fingers. They watched the small golden bell hit the end of the chain and bounced back. The tiny ringer in the bell swung violently impacting the side of the bell.

Time seemed to slow for Nathel, he stood holding Katirna and listened as the single note rang across the lake of lava. The sound was pure, almost golden and it circled crisply around the lake bed wrapping around the Dark One.

Nathel watched the horned figure began to expand, darkness flowed from his mouth trying to smother the golden note. For a time the golden note seemed to fade but then Nathel saw the tiny remnants of light break into a thousand pieces and flash out in a hundred different directions.

"How odd, I can actually see the sound," Nathel whispered. The chain and bell dissolved into the air and disappeared but the sound rolled on without any interruption. All around them, the Devil's Peak volcano erupted spewing ash and lava high into the sky. Then, as it seemed the landscape could not take any more, the ground shook as earthquakes tore across the Dakretua Mountains. Mountain peaks across the north began to collapse under the shaking, peaks fell into valleys and all along the separating cliffs began to tumble down. Gigantic rocks cracked out of the cliff face, crashing hard to the ground and adding even more shaking to the strain on the ground.

Nathel and Katirna dropped to their knees when the shaking got so intense that they could not keep their balance. As if they had completed some great task, the bits of golden light returned to the Chamber of Creation and coalesced once again around the Dark One. Bedbezdal struggled against the rays of light that lanced down, wrapped themselves around Bedbezdal, and pulled him down into the lake of lava.

"Next time, boy. There will be a next time. This is just the beginning of the Time of Testing!"

"What Time of Testing?"

"You will know soon enough. I am still the master of this world."

Nathel continued to stare as Bedbezdal's face disappeared below the boiling lava.

"Time to go, little ones."

Nathel struggled to his feet turning towards the voice that spoke behind them. Four elementals stood behind them, two of them Nathel had seen before. Tymothel offered him a smile. "I think you found good use for the staff."

Miceali nodded at the two humans and then turned to his companions, "Let us take these two and go rescue the armies fighting to the south. With the Dark One loosed, this prison is no longer needed. It will be erased, returned to the oceans from where it was raised."

Nathel gaped at them, "What do you mean he is loosed? I thought ringing the bell would bind him?"

"That is up for debate. We do know that before he can be forced back to his prison, he must be loosed for a time."

Nathel sputtered but words escaped him.

"Come. We must be gone from this place."

Miceali and Tymothel each reached out a hand to Nathel and Katirna and drew them up into the air as the last remnants of the stone platform sank below the surface of the lava.

Nathel looked down as they flew over the destruction below them. Briefly he thought he could see the face of Bedbezdal staring up at him etched into the lava then it was lost from sight.

"The whole mountain range is sinking below the ocean!" Nathel shouted over the rush of the wind. He watched as massive mountain peaks slid free of their roots. The view from the air was astounding and it took their breath away. All along the Dakretua Mountains, massive peaks were crashing to the ground and the subsequent earthquakes were opening cracks in the surface of the ground. The cold waters of the Northern oceans rushed into the gaps. As they reached the wilderness, the last of the mountain peaks slipped under the dark blue waters.

"It is finished, the monstrosity is gone." Tymothel smiled grimly. "Now it begins."

"What begins?" Nathel asked.

"We are not allowed to say. Have faith, Nathel. It is all that will see you through."

Wind rushed past the flying figures, it roared in their ears and drowned out the rest of the words. Katirna turned to Nathel and pointed in the distance.

Nathel turned his head squinting into the wind and following her gaze into the distance, there on the horizon flew the familiar figure of Venthern.

Nathel was speechless as Timoth and Miceali slowed to a halt before the mighty wyrm. It seemed to Nathel that the wyrm soldier's wing span had doubled and instead of his red lacquered armor he now wore a breastplate of beaten gold.

"Well met, Nathel. It is good to see you once again." Venthern turned and dipped a wing so that they speechless pair could scramble on board his broad back.

"Take them to the battle, Venthern. They are yet many that need to be rescued. Without Nathel the battle may yet be lost."

"Fear not, Tymothel. They will arrive in time." The wyrm soldier dipped his head to the elemental and then turned and winged to the south and east.

"But I saw you die." Nathel blurted the words as he clung to the ridges on the wyrm's armored back.

"Anatari agreed to give me this last honor. After this battle, I will find my peace in the paths of the Endless Gardens. Until then, I have been given leave to lead the armies of heaven into battle. Nathel, I will take you to where the Ancient Evil One has drawn up his forces for the great battle of this age."

Nathel smiled and clung tight as once again the wind whipped past them. Behind him Katirna held tight to his waist leaning out in fascination to watch the distant ground sweep past.

It was late evening when the combined armies of the four nations stopped to rest. The Dark One's servants had fallen back, pursuing just enough to keep them running for most of the afternoon. As night fell, it was easy to see why they fell back. Timoth, Thero, and Captain Haust stood on a small rise and looked out to see the cooking fires of the Dark One's minions spring up all around them.

"Bedbezdal must have emptied the entire north land and sent them south," Thero whispered in awe.

"Not even during the First War of the Lowlands before the Fortress of Winds was built did he send this many of his servants south."

"We are surrounded. Is there any place around that is defensible?" Timoth was unable to see far in the gloom despite the prolific fires that lit the night on all sides.

"Skull Mountain to the north. It is the only place." Thero motioned to the north were the cooking fires were somewhat thinner.

"We will loose many soldiers moving in the dark." Captain Haust spoke quietly even though the Dark One's were far from where they stood.

Timoth sighed and turned to Thero, "What say you Ancient One."

"We must move, if we are surrounded in the open we will be cut to shreds." Thero turned and walked down the hill motioning the nearby commanders to join him. Timoth stared one last time at the distant fires and then followed Thero leaving Captain Haust gazing in the darkness by himself.

The forced march through the darkness went smoother than Thero had expected, and morning found the combined armies under the command of Timoth and Thero marshaled around Skull Mountain. Calling the bald hill a mountain was a stretch of the imagination. It was thick and wide and surrounded by baked ground and rocks. No trees grew through the rocky ground making it impossible for anyone to sneak up on the massed armies. Rank after rank of grim faced humans, dwarves, elves, and orkin faced out on all sides, waiting as the armies of the Dark One gathered in the distance. Tens of thousands of archers took their final quivers of arrows and strung their longbows. All they could do was wait to launch the first strike against the massive enemy forces.

Thero, Timoth, Captain Haust, and the Orkin Emperors stood silently on the highest point on the hill. They watched the morning mist slowly burn off as the sun rose.

"Something has happened." Thero commented as he looked to the north. Far away a rumbling sound erupted and every living being on and around the mountain stopped to stare. Across the north every volcano across the Dakretua Mountains erupted at once.

"The Dark One has succeeded?" Captain Haust commented as clouds of smoke and ash roared into the air. No one answered for a long time.

In the distance, the shrill horns called the Goblins hordes from their holes, and rank upon rank of minotaur warriors gathered in the distance. They beat their chests and roared in defiance as they strapped weapons across their broad shoulders. As the volcanoes spewed forth their molten rivers, the servants of the Dark One cheered, shaking their weapons in the air and calling down curses on the lowlanders.

"I do not think so." Thero countered the dark view, "I think that Nathel has shaken the roots of the world. I think Anatari has turned his face back to us in our time of need."

A broad smile broke across the Ancient Ones face, in the distance his vision caught the sight that made his heart leap for joy. Nathel and Katirna swept in from the north riding on the back of a venerable old wyrm, golden armor blinded those that tried to look at the creature and it wasn't until Venthern had retreated that Nathel and Katirna were seen by all.

"Hear me servants of Anatari," Thero's voice echoed across the mountain, drawing every eye in the assembled forces to him. In the distance the bull men and Goblins started forward. Gathered in hordes beyond number, they came to extinguish life from the lowlanders forever.

"The Dark One is free from his prison, but he has fled. Even now, his prison sinks into the depths of the sea. Now is the time to fight as you never have before. Help is coming. The creator is sending his elementals to fight for us. Be strong, hold to your faith, and send the minions of the Dark One to their judgment." Thero stopped as around him a tremendous shout rose from the gathered soldiers.

Across the field of rock, the advancing minotaurs and Goblins paused when they heard the shout. Then they surged forward once again, eager to taste blood.

Matthew John Krengel

Chapter Twenty-Five
Warrior of Anatari

athel leapt from Venthern's back and then reached back helping Katirna to leap down.

"We will hold them until you return."

Venthern nodded his armored head then tossed a wrapped bundle to the ground at Nathel's feet.

"Wear this into battle and none will be able to stand before you." With a nod of his head, he swept back into the air and disappeared to the east faster than he had appeared.

Nathel grabbed the bundle and tore the cloth that bound it together. As he opened it, four items spilled out onto the ground. A thin golden breastplate lay at his feet and he reached down and picked it up reverently. As the battle was joined around the hill, he strapped the breastplate on. To his left lay a silver and gold helm. The helm fit over his head like it was crafted for him and the runes etched into the surface of the metal captured the light and returned it tenfold. Katirna handed him a pair of greaves that had fallen to the ground to his right. With her help, he strapped the gem studded armor into place. Turning in a circle, Nathel spotted the last item where it lay amongst the tall weeds. The royal blue cloak settled around his shoulders and Katirna's soft hands worked the golden chain that fastened it into place.

Nathel walked to the top of the mountain where Thero watched. "Fight well, grandfather."

He looked back to Katirna; he was not surprised to see her standing quietly. She held both her long daggers in her hands.

"Are you ready, my love?" Nathel smiled at her his staff held steady in his hands. The runes etched in the ironwood glowed fiercely making the staff look like it was made of pure light.

Katirna nodded, wrapping her arms around him and placing a warm kiss on his lips. "Fight well."

"I think someone else has come to join the battle." Katirna motioned past Nathel.

He turned to see the dun racing through a small gap in the enemy lines. Crude arrows flew from goblin bows arcing out at the racing horse but none came close. A hundred wolves gave chase but they fell behind the flashing hooves as the dun put on a burst of speed.

The magnificent steed raced up the hill and skidded to a halt beside Nathel.

"Good to see you again," Nathel said. He smiled and rubbed the horses flank, noting that he was fully saddled again.

He grabbed the reins and swung himself up onto the broad back. Nathel swung the prancing plains horse towards the massed enemies to the south. He settled his helm firmly on this head and he watched the Dark One's armies approach.

"Let's show them what happens to those that serve the Dark One," Nathel whispered into the dun upright ears. Without any urging the dun leapt forward, the morning sun glinting off his coat. The brilliant light played off Nathel's golden armor casting blinding rays of light across the battlefield. With a mighty shout, the blue-bannered army of Juthel that was massed behind Nathel surged forward crying: "Long live, king Nathel!"

The brilliance of Nathel's armor left the minotaurs and the Goblins rubbing their eyes, many cast their weapons down and tried to flee. Nathel found himself in the center of a group of towering bull men who had managed to shield their eyes from the light. They stood strong holding the middle of the line. Nathel saw the long handled ax swing in a wide arc as the towering bull man aimed a strike for his head. Ironwood staff intercepted the ax above his head. Brilliant bursts of power released from the staff as it impacted the ax. The blow shattered the iron head of the axe into a thousand pieces and sent the shattered body of the bull man flying through the air.

Nathel became the hand of the protectors as he tore through the remaining battle line that still held together to face the men of Juthel. All around him he could hear the screams of the men as they smashed into the ragged formations. All along the swirling battle line, the army of Juthel struggled as they thrust with their spears and trusted in their thick shields to stop the blows from the dark weapons.

Nathel struck time and time again with his staff, each time sending the smashed body of the horned warriors flying away. The dun carried him like an avenging elemental through the battle lines until he broke free far south of Skull Mountain. Reining in the plains horse, Nathel swung to face the rear of the Dark One's hordes. Looking up and down the engaged armies, he watched as the army of Juthel pushed the Dark One's back, inflicting heavy losses.

For every two servants of the Dark One that slipped to the ground screaming in rage cursing, one of the blue clad soldiers slipped peacefully into the arms of Anatari.

Nathel urged the dun forward racing the horse west around the edge of the battlefield. The Ironback legions were being pushed back towards the bottom of Skull Mountain and he knew he must bolster their defenses.

The sun rode high in the sky as Nathel reentered the battle. He plunged into the rear of the Dark One's servants and cried with a great voice, "Hold strong, hold fast!"

With his staff held high Nathel saw the surprise in the eyes of the dark creatures as he crashed into the battle line.

Nathel swung his staff at a tall bull man and sent his battered body flying away. Out of the corner of his eye he saw a long spear flying at him and he closed his eyes.

"Thank you for letting me serve your master, Anatari."

When the blow failed to fall he opened his eyes. A shining sword flashed past his staff and took the bull man in the chest sending him crashing to the ground. Nathel reined in the dun as Miceali flashed past him, swinging his long two handed sword in great arcs that sent dozens of Goblins flying in all directions. Miceali and Tymothel led a group of elemental warriors tearing into Bedbezdal's great army, and the battle on the northern front quickly became a rout. Then he saw something that made his blood run cold.

"Tymothel!" he cried. Nathel pointed to the east. "The Dark One's are not out of surprises yet!"

Miceali and Tymothel stopped almost as one turning to the east.

Nathel counted hundreds of fell creatures advancing in a long front towards the legions of the northern Orkin Empire. The Orkin were again forced backwards until they were backing up the hill. Thrusting with their short spears and hurtling throwing axes, they fought bravely but still thousands had fallen.

A group of Medusas spearheaded the attack. Their wicked blades danced in all directions, killing hundreds of Orkin who struggled to throw them back. Behind the Goblins came hundreds of fallen elementals. Cruathila the winter wolf led a pack of mountain wolves that covered the hills to the east. Overhead, the gray stone gargoyle swooped low in the sky, followed be a score of his kin. Four towering giants strode forward, led by a group of stone looking elementals. They grasped at boulders and rocks, hurtling them at the embattled Orkin.

"The Orkin are breaking. Come on, boy. Let's go meet our fate!"

Nathel urged the dun forward and they dashed across the northern front. The light from his armor left thousands of Goblins rubbing their eyes. He glanced back, behind him followed thousands of cavalry broken from the remains of the army from Juthel. They crashed into the Goblins, trampling them into the ground, and then he lost that part of the battle from view.

He arrived just as the legions of the Northern Orkin Empire turned to flee.

"Stand fast! Help is coming" His voice echoed across the low hills. Cruathila led the attack, his long legs covering the distance in leaps and bounds.

"This time you will die, boy!" The great wolf growled as its flashing teeth tore at the charging human. The teeth came so close that Nathel smelled the fetid breath.

"Time to go back to your master, foul beast!" Nathel cried. He pulled the dun around, charging after the dodging wolf. Swinging his staff high in the air, Nathel aimed a lightning strike at the twisting winter wolf. The impact of the staff against the gaping maw of the winter wolf nearly tore the weapon from Nathel's grasp. The effect on the winter wolf left Nathel watching in stunned silence as the battle swirled around him.

More elementals continued to arrive and Tymothel led them into battle against the Dark One's servants.

Nathel squinted as the golden light from his staff exploded into the winter wolf tearing into his skin and fur. The bands of light wrapped around the creature and pulled it howling in fear into the ground.

"The Pillars will judge you for your deeds." Nathel sat on the dun panting and feeling suddenly very small as the elemental warriors tore at each other. The big stone gargoyle snatched a wide body elemental that looked almost dwarven from the ground. He swept high into the air to try and drop the dwarf to his death. The short elemental wrapped its strong arms around the gargoyles wings trapping them against his back. Together they plunged to the ground where the impact shook the eastern side of the battlefield.

"Nathel! Go help the Orkin. This fight is beyond your strength," Miceali cried as he swung his sword at a towering giant.

Wheeling the dun back to the struggling Orkin troops, Nathel rode along the battlefront singling out and striking at the biggest of the Dark One's soldiers. Crying out his challenge, Nathel rallied the faltering legions. They drove forward once more sending the Goblins scattering like leaves and killing hundreds of minotaur soldiers. Behind him the Orkin warriors surged forward, strengthened by the appearance of the elementals and Nathel's brave charge.

The battle raged on for hours as the sun finished its long descent into the sky. Despite their bravery Miceali and his breathern were driven back. All around Skull Mountain, the forces of the gathered armies retreated until they ringed the mountain.

"Anatari, we cannot do this in ourselves. Please help us." Nathel whispered the prayer from where he waited.

As he finished his prayer he looked up at the sky and saw a brilliant light descending slowly towards the top of Skull Mountain. As one, the Goblins and Minotaurs turned and fled, dropping their weapons in fear and seeking places to hide in the surrounding wilderness. The Medusas went berserk, many impaling themselves on their own swords as the light touched them. The only of the Dark One's soldiers that seemed unaffected were the scores of massive Basilisks that trundled forward.

As if they sensed their coming demise, the fallen elementals attacked with a fury that drove the faithful back almost to the edge of Skull Mountain.

Then with an explosion that threw everyone to the ground, the ball of light erupted. Overhead, the full armies of the heavens rode out of a rift in the sky on horses that shone like stars. Wielding blades of living flame, they drove the fallen elementals from the battlefield and sendt them sinking into the ground, pulled down by the binding bands of golden light. The swarms of mountain wolves turned and fled, many running until they threw themselves into the grinding ice surging across the newly formed northern ocean.

Nathel clung to the dun with all his strength as the armies swept past him. They split, sweeping around the edges of Skull Mountain. Around the low land armies, they drove away the Dark One's servants like chaff in the wind.

After circling the battlefield twice they turned and silently rode back to the mountain where a clear trumpet call echoed over the field. The blinding light of the army swept by the mortals and flashed back up into the sky where they faded from view trailed by a single figure in a flaming chariot.

No sound reached the ground as Nathel watched the glowing army ride back into the glowing rift in the sky.

"Thero, No!"

Nathel urged the dun back to Skull Mountain. He watched in dismay as a familiar figure on the top of Skull Mountain rose into the sky. Urging the dun on faster, he raced past the soldiers of the low lands and charged up to the peak of the mountain.

"Grandfather, don't leave me." Nathel leapt from the dun and tore his helm off and threw it to the ground. He fell to his knees as Thero was drawn up into the sky.

"I don't know how to rule a kingdom. I don't know what Anatari wants of us."

"Things will work out, son. Seek the Lost Books. When you find them, they will guide you on the right path. Until then, follow your heart. I have lived on this mortal world for far too long. It is time for me to rest until I am needed again," Thero said. He offered Nathel a sad smile and then he rose quickly into the closing rift of light. As he disappeared into the light, something shiny dropped from his hand landing at Nathel's feet. Then the rift imploded as it disappeared from sight.

Nathel leaned over searching in the late evening sun until his hand struck something hard and smooth.

"The healing drops from Tymothel." Grasping the vial in hand he blinked back the tears that threatened to slide down his face.

Around him, the ragged armies of the lowland nations and the mountain kingdom stood blinking in the sudden darkness. The afternoon had passed during the battles around Skull Mountain and the evening fell quickly. With a brilliant burst of red the sun faded in to the distant sky.

Here and there, a scattered few pockets of Minotaur and Goblins survived. They fought to the bitter end as they were crushed by charges of the blue-bannered cavalry and the rolling attacks of the Ironback legions. Finally, when darkness of night began to thicken, the soldiers wearily gathered back at the base of Skull Mountain. Of all the armies that began the battle that morning, less than a third survived. Thousands lay silent, among the unnumbered legions of Bedbezdal's servants. Far to the east and north, the few remaining faithful elementals that remained on the mortal world pursued the remaining fallen elementals. They followed them across the wilderness, driving them until they either escaped or were sent to the Dark One's prison.

Nathel walked wearily down the sloping side of Skull Mountain. Before him, Orthen, the young emperor of the Southern Orkin Empire led his exhausted troops back to the few fires burning near the mountain.

"Nathel, we grieve for the loss of the Ancient One." Orthen intoned the words slowly. He reached out his hand and offered his sympathy.

Of all the commanders and rulers to enter the battle only Timoth, Nathel, and Orthen had survived the battle. Emperor Ratchuth fell as he led his personal guard into a gap in the eastern battle line; a score of wolves had swarmed him after he had killed half their number. Captain Haust fell mortally wounded leading the charge to break the last group of Minotaur. The bull men had held their ground, until they were crushed into it. General Fritts was killed battling the Basilisks as they threatened to overrun Skull Mountain,

"Where is Katirna?" Nathel asked. He looked about, stricken with panic as he searched the mountainside for her.

Timoth turned slowly and motioned forward a pair of slim elf warriors. They carried a litter forward strung across two spears, carefully laying it down before Nathel. Tears formed in his eyes, blurring his vision, and he collapsed to his knees. Katirna lay on the litter, her eyes closed, with a great wound torn into her side. From the gash a steady stream of blood pooled, dripping over the cloak and soaking into the scorched ground.

"She will not live long," Timoth said slowly and quietly. He pulled his iron helm from his head, his bushy beard hid the tears that fell from his eyes.

Nathel collapsed to the ground beside the litter gently taking her hand in his and feeling the warmth begin to fade from her skin. He lay the vial on the ground beside her, and he grasped both her hands. Then he stopped, grabbed the small crystal vial and shouted for joy.

"She will not die!"

With trembling hands, he pulled the crystal stopper from the vial. Gently, he tilted Katirna's head back and let a single drop fall into her mouth. Almost immediately, Katirna's breathing steadied. Orthen and Timoth stared wide-eyed as the gaping wound in her side began to knit itself together.

"Bring me the wounded as fast as you can. There are many we can save!" Nathel shouted.

The clusters of soldiers scattered to spread the word. Soon thousands who were hovering near death were laid about Skull Mountain. Nathel spent the night moving from litter to litter stopping just long enough to let one drop of the healing liquid to roll into each mouth. Dawn broke as he finished with the wounded and he walked wearily back to the crest of Skull Mountain. Katirna's side was fully healed and she woke from the healing sleep and looked up at him.

"Nathel you found me!" She leapt to her feet and rushed into Nathel's waiting arms.

"Don't you ever leave me again, shepherd. Even Death will not be able to protect you if you do that again."

Nathel did not reply, he just hugged her tightly and fought back the tears that threatened to bring him to his knees.

Epilogue

hree weeks had passed since the routing of the Dark One's armies. Nathel led his remaining forces in small skirmishes for almost two full weeks. Many Goblins and dark creatures had gone into hiding in the wide expanses of the wilderness. When no more enemies could be found, Nathel called a halt to the fighting and the armies marched south.

The arrival of the combined armies was greeted with some apprehension in the city of Juthel.

Sometime later, Nathel stood quietly in the reopened Temple of Elements in the city of Juthel. He wore his royal purple cape and a richly embroidered vest. Matching pants and white shirt with billowing sleeves stuck out around the arms of his vest. The crown of Juthel sat on his brow.

A small crowd of well-wishers gathered in the vast chapel as the last rays of sunlight lit the soaring stained glass windows high overhead. At the double doors that led into the temple, Katirna entered followed by her mother. She wore a flowing white gown of purest satin. A silver crown interlaced with her strawberry blond hair, and a brilliant smile lit her face when she saw Nathel standing silently at the front of the temple. Slowly, she walked to the front of the stone temple, treading softly on a long red silk rug that reached from the waiting groom to the entrance of the temple. When she arrived at the front of the temple, Nathel offered her his arm and together they climbed the stairs. Together they stood before the priest from the Monastery of One, ready to begin the new chapter in their lives.

Matthew John Krengel

About the Author

Matthew John Krengel graduated from Pensacola Christian College with a Bachelor's Degree is Criminal Justice and a double minor in History and English. He is an avid reader of fantasy and science fiction and is also very passionate about writing. He currently lives in Minnesota with his wife and children.

Forthcoming Titles from Odyssey Illustrated Press